This Simon Spotlight edition September 2022
Copyright © 2022 by Simon & Schuster, Inc. All rights reserved, including the right
of reproduction in whole or in part in any form.
SIMON SPOTLIGHT and colophon are registered trademarks of Simon & Schuster, Inc.
YOU'RE INVITED TO A CREEPOVER is a registered trademark of Simon & Schuster,
Inc. For information about special discounts for bulk purchases, please contact Simon
& Schuster Special Sales at 1-866-506-1949 or business@simonandschuster.com.
Designed by Nicholas Sciacca. Text by Matthew J. Gilbert. Based on the text by Michael
Teitelbaum. Art Services by Glass House Graphics. Pencils, Inks & Colors by Giusi
Lo Piccolo. Color assistants: Nataliya Torretta, Antonino Ulizzi, Santino Triolo and Gabriele
Cracolici. Lettering by Giuseppe Naselli/Grafimated Cartoon. Supervision by Salvatore
Di Marco/Grafimated Cartoon. The illustrations for this book were rendered digitally.
Manufactured in China 0522 SCP
10 9 8 7 6 5 4 3 2 1
ISBN 978-1-6659-1567-0 (hc)
ISBN 978-1-6659-1566-3 (pbk)
ISBN 978-1-6659-1568-7 (ebook)
Library of Congress Catalog Card Number 2022934415

YOU'RE INVITED TO A

# CREEPOVER®

THE GRAPHIC NOVEL

# YOU CAN'T COME IN HERE!

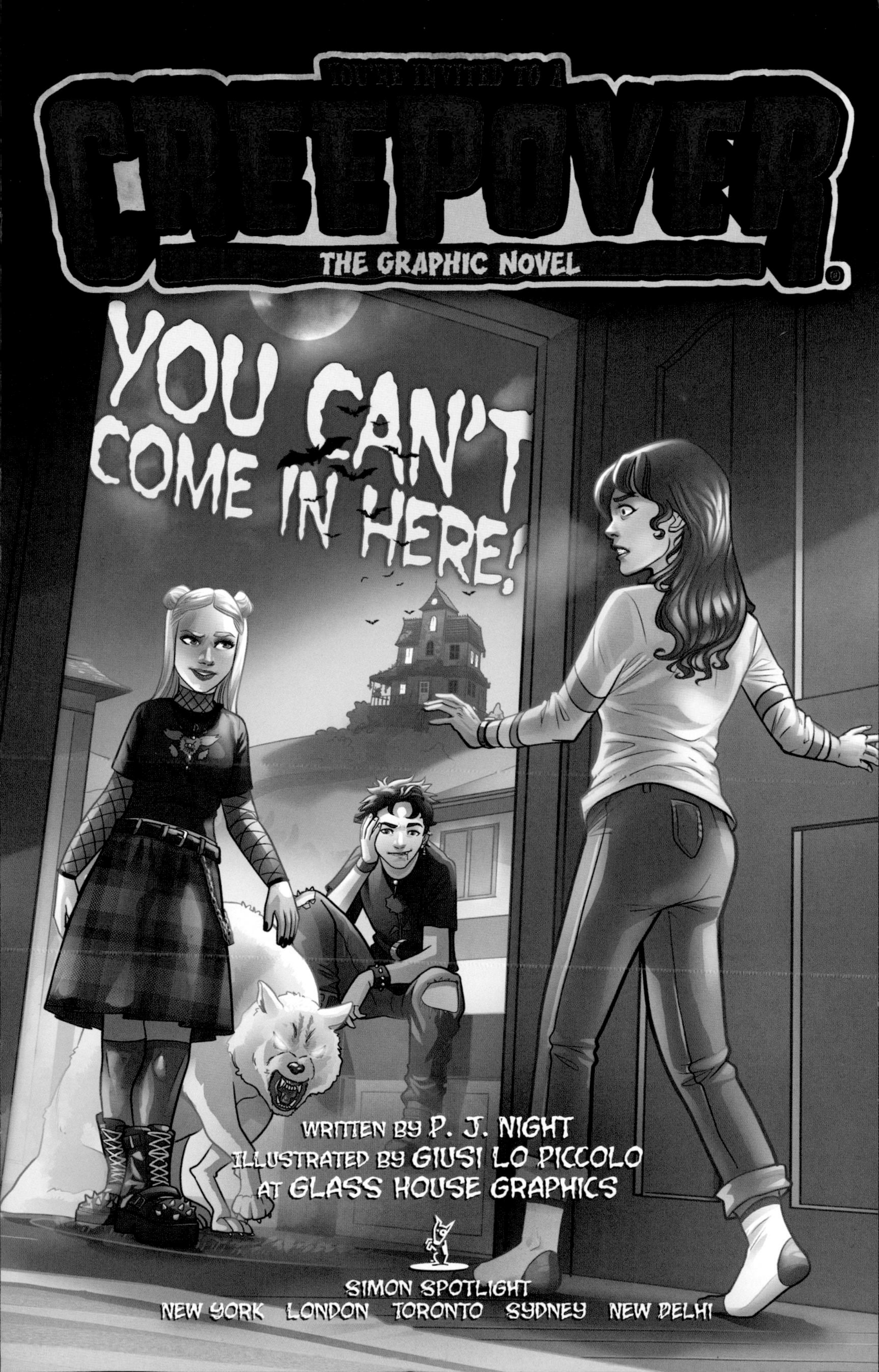

WRITTEN BY P. J. NIGHT

ILLUSTRATED BY GIUSI LO PICCOLO

AT GLASS HOUSE GRAPHICS

SIMON SPOTLIGHT

NEW YORK LONDON TORONTO SYDNEY NEW DELHI

CHAPTER 1

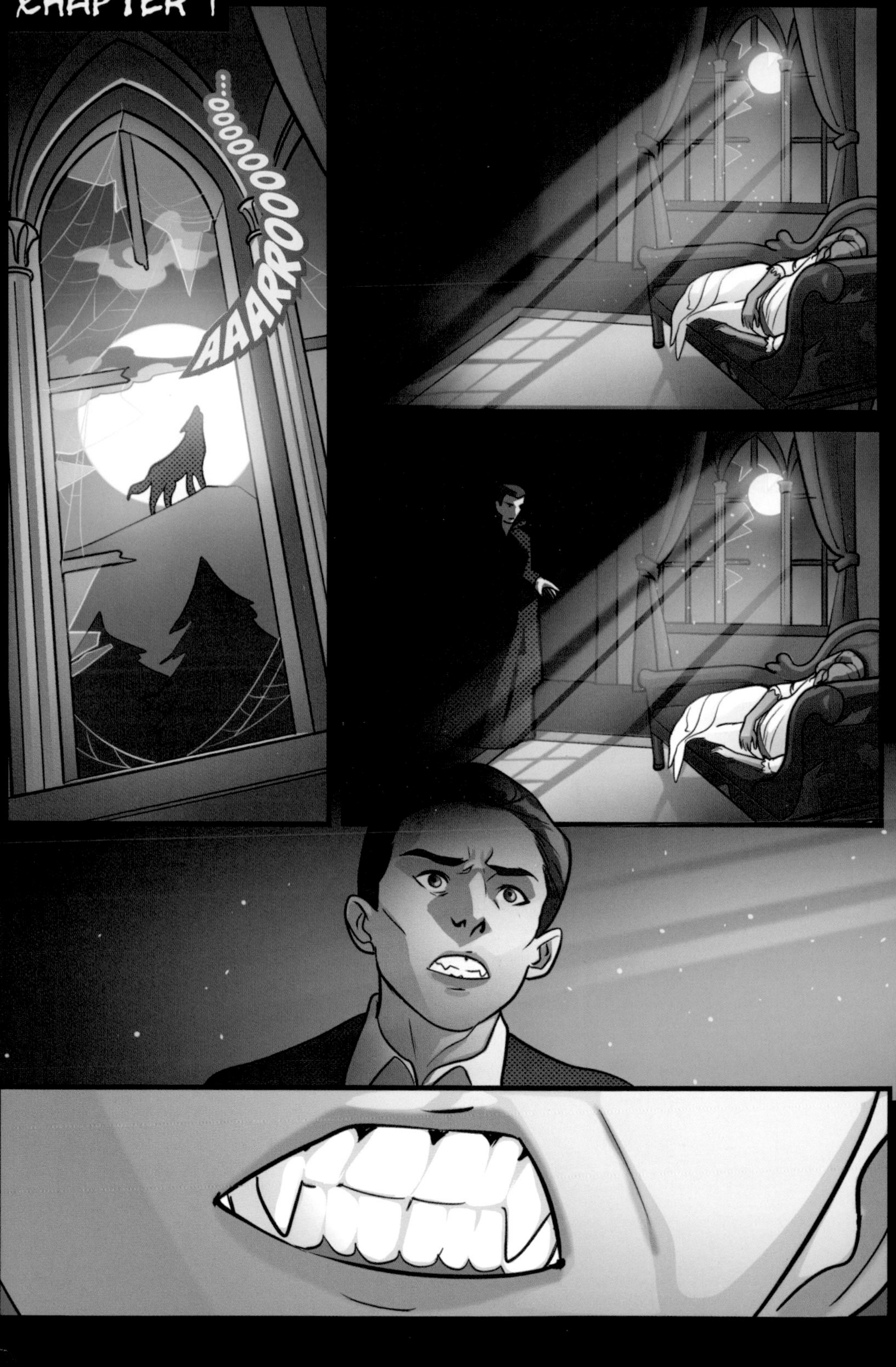
AAARROOOOOOOOOO...

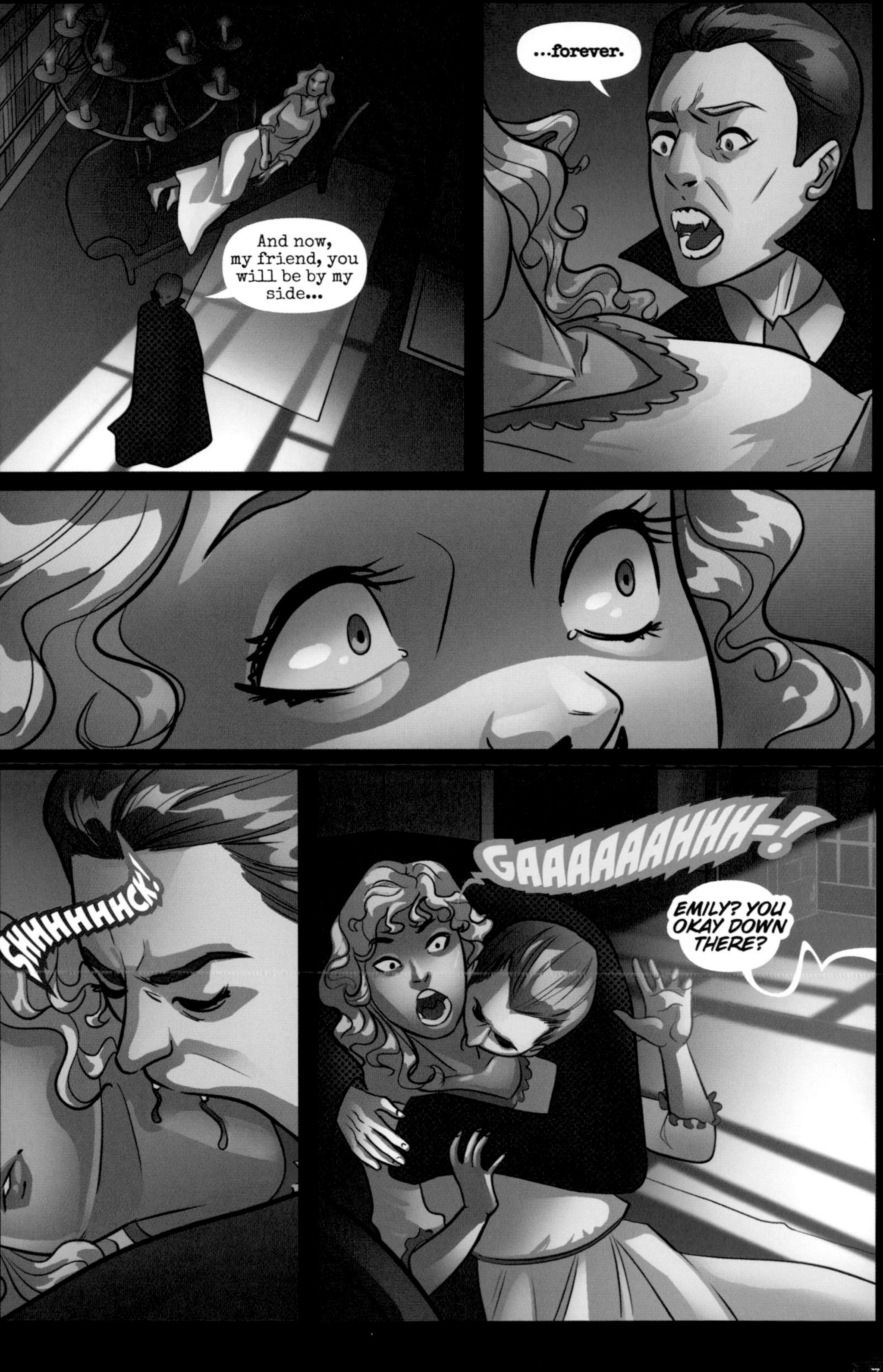
And now, my friend, you will be by my side...
...forever.
SHHHHHHCK!
GAAAAAAHHH-!
EMILY? YOU OKAY DOWN THERE?

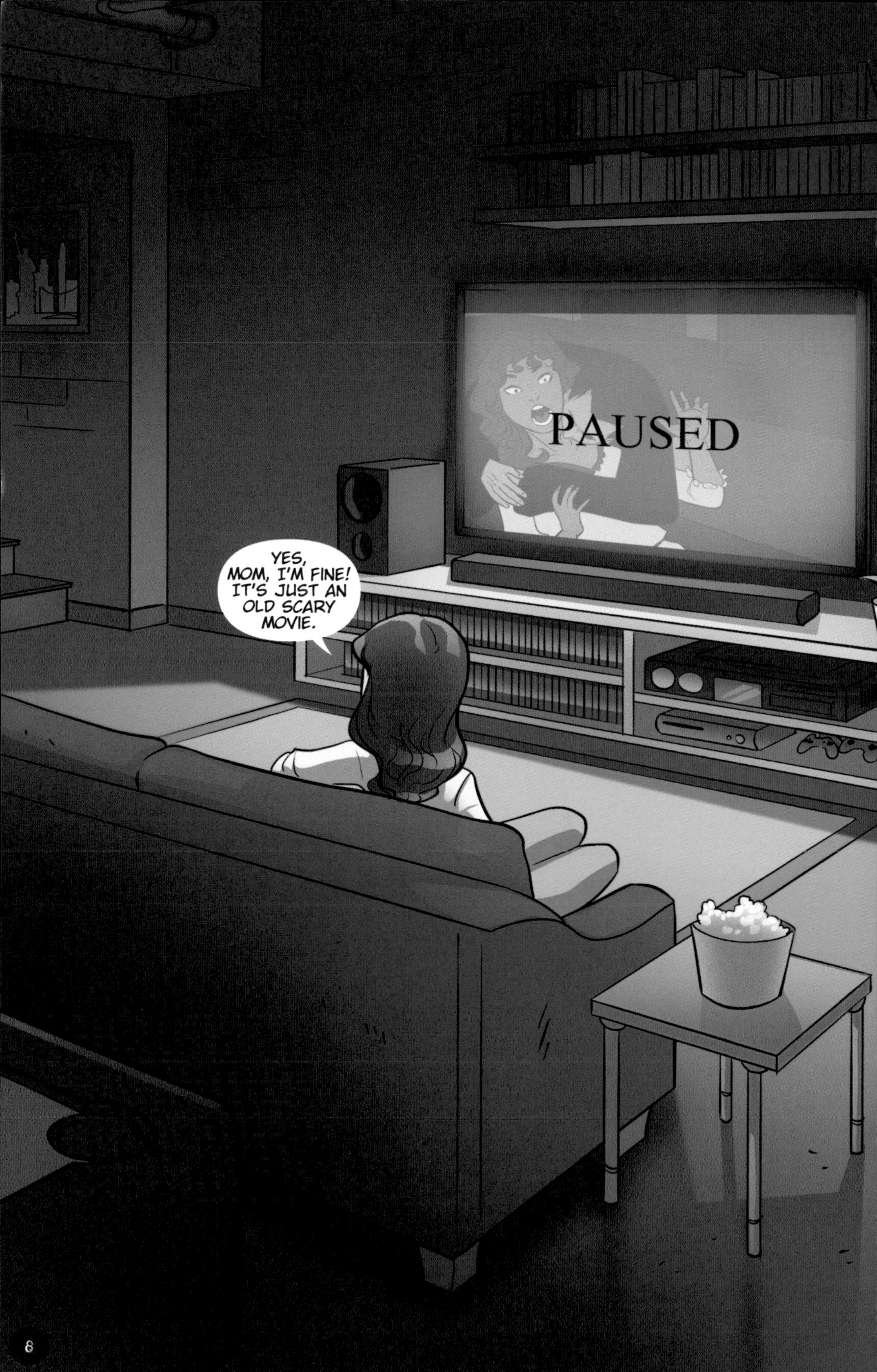
PAUSED
YES, MOM, I'M FINE! IT'S JUST AN OLD SCARY MOVIE.

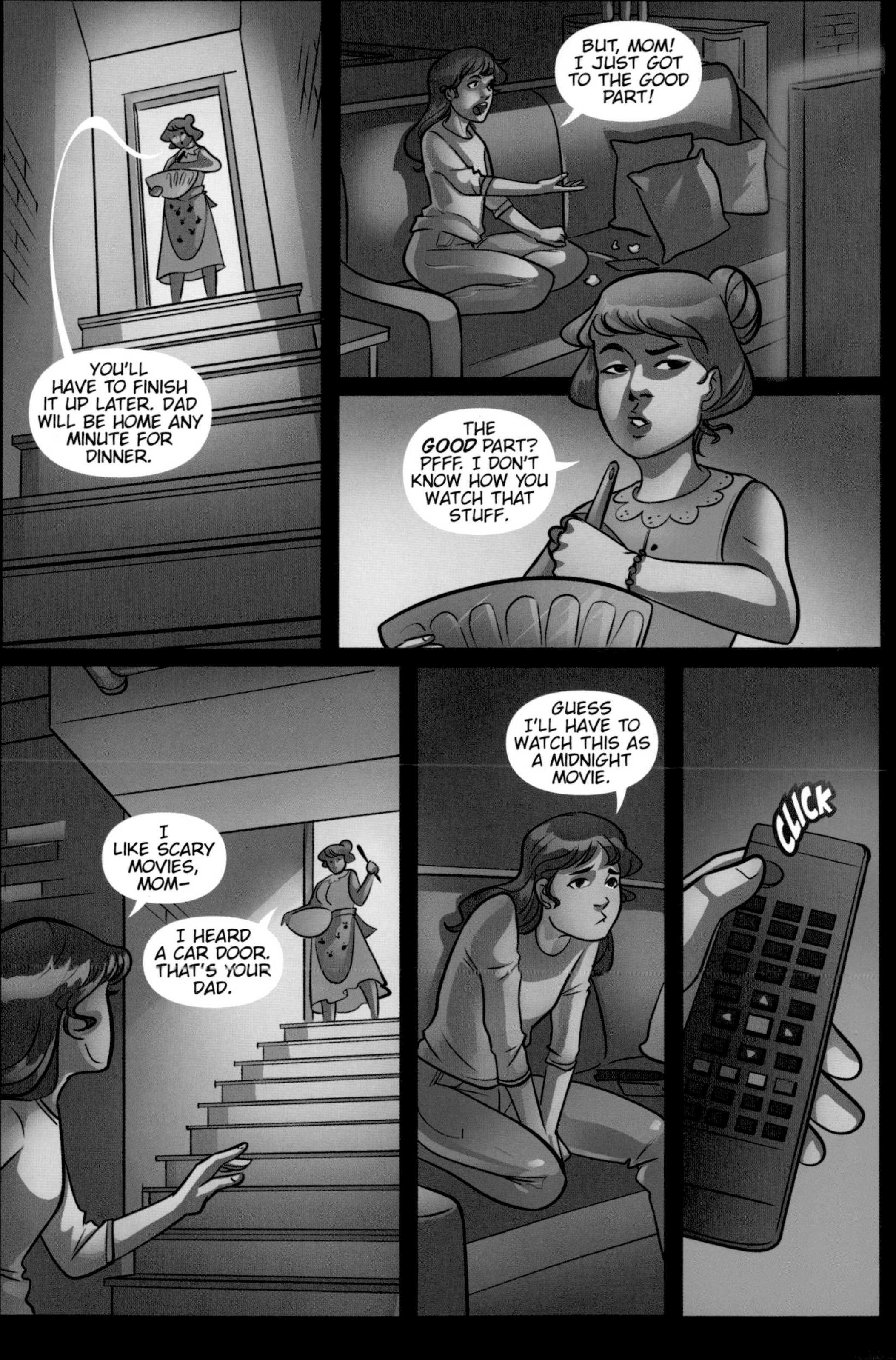
YOU'LL HAVE TO FINISH IT UP LATER. DAD WILL BE HOME ANY MINUTE FOR DINNER.
BUT, MOM! I JUST GOT TO THE GOOD PART!
THE *GOOD* PART? PFFF. I DON'T KNOW HOW YOU WATCH THAT STUFF.
I LIKE SCARY MOVIES, MOM–
I HEARD A CAR DOOR. THAT'S YOUR DAD.
GUESS I'LL HAVE TO WATCH THIS AS A MIDNIGHT MOVIE.
CLICK

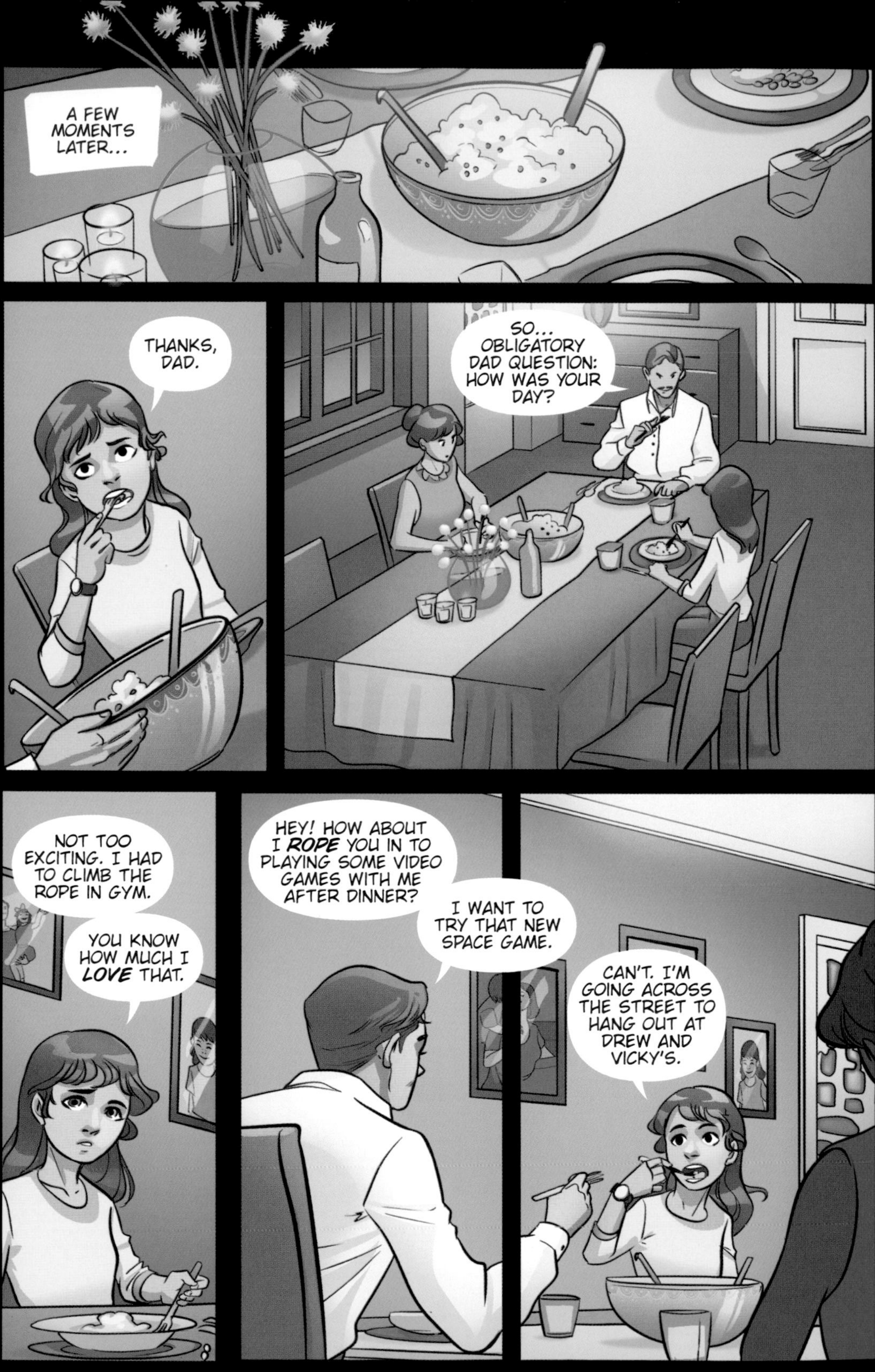
A FEW MOMENTS LATER...
THANKS, DAD.
SO... OBLIGATORY DAD QUESTION: HOW WAS YOUR DAY?
NOT TOO EXCITING. I HAD TO CLIMB THE ROPE IN GYM.
YOU KNOW HOW MUCH I *LOVE* THAT.
HEY! HOW ABOUT I ***ROPE*** YOU IN TO PLAYING SOME VIDEO GAMES WITH ME AFTER DINNER?
I WANT TO TRY THAT NEW SPACE GAME.
CAN'T. I'M GOING ACROSS THE STREET TO HANG OUT AT DREW AND VICKY'S.

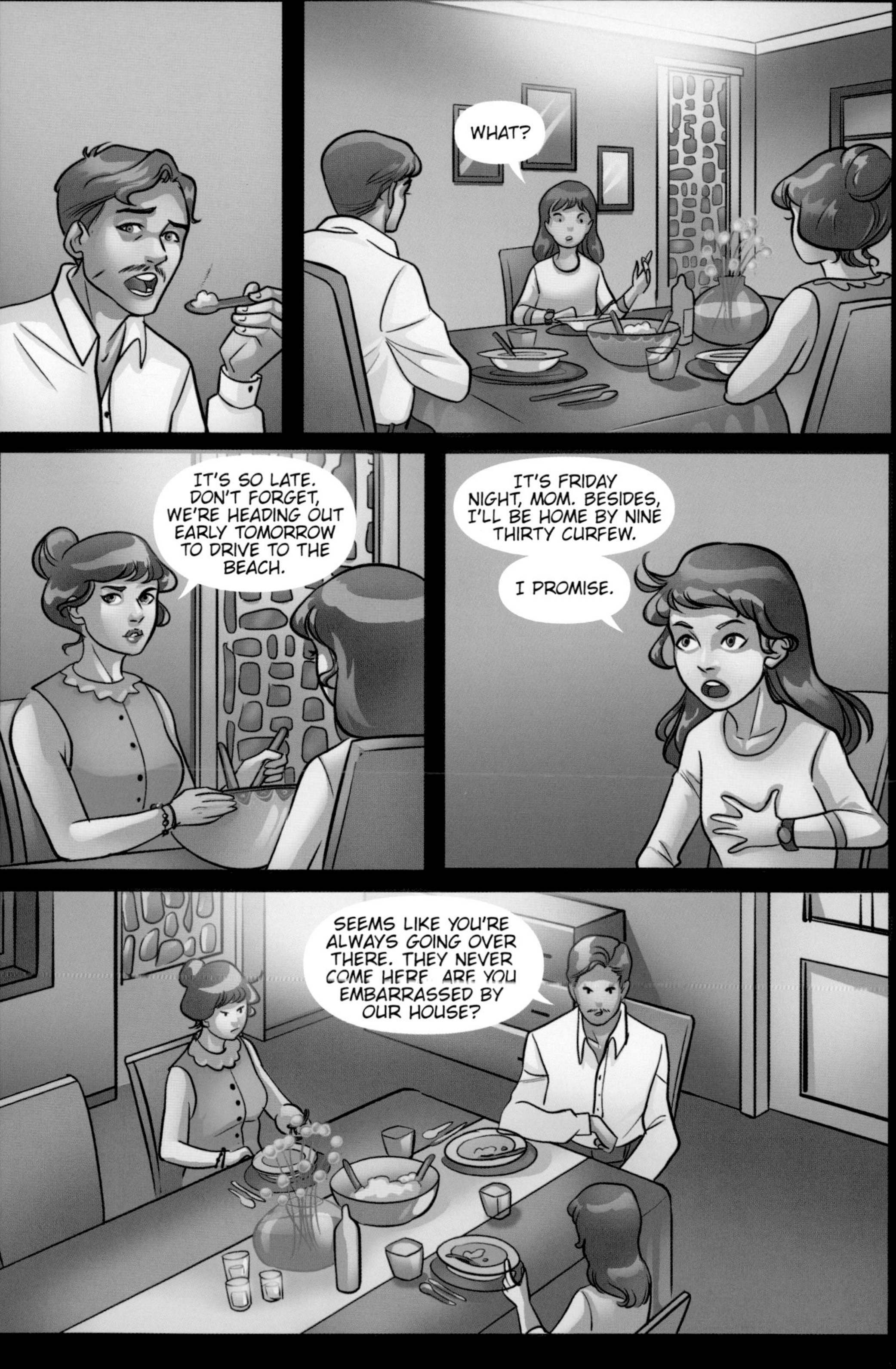
WHAT?
IT'S SO LATE. DON'T FORGET, WE'RE HEADING OUT EARLY TOMORROW TO DRIVE TO THE BEACH.
IT'S FRIDAY NIGHT, MOM. BESIDES, I'LL BE HOME BY NINE THIRTY CURFEW.
I PROMISE.
SEEMS LIKE YOU'RE ALWAYS GOING OVER THERE. THEY NEVER COME HERE. ARE YOU EMBARRASSED BY OUR HOUSE?

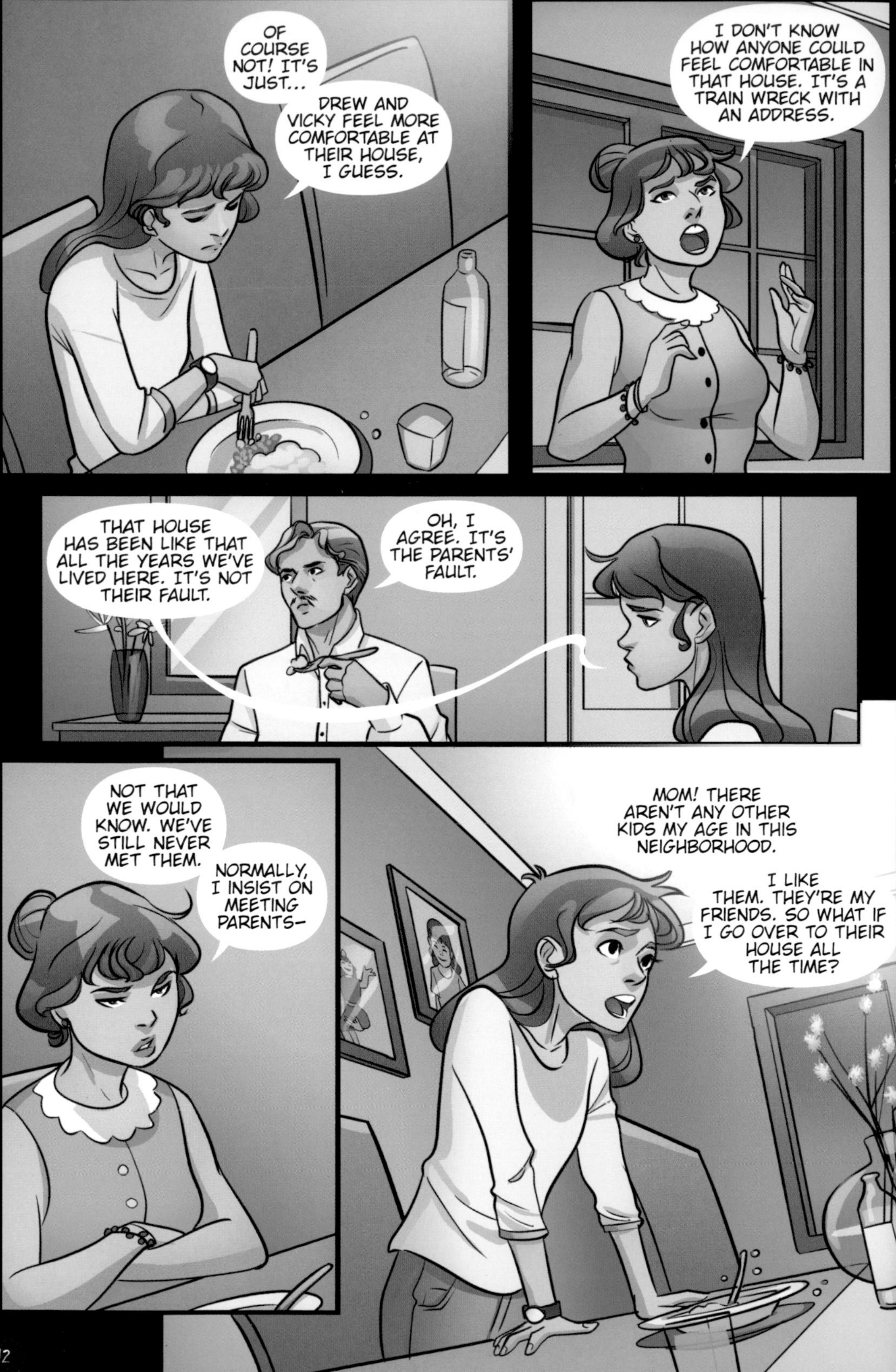
OF COURSE NOT! IT'S JUST...
DREW AND VICKY FEEL MORE COMFORTABLE AT THEIR HOUSE, I GUESS.
I DON'T KNOW HOW ANYONE COULD FEEL COMFORTABLE IN THAT HOUSE. IT'S A TRAIN WRECK WITH AN ADDRESS.
THAT HOUSE HAS BEEN LIKE THAT ALL THE YEARS WE'VE LIVED HERE. IT'S NOT THEIR FAULT.
OH, I AGREE. IT'S THE PARENTS' FAULT.
NOT THAT WE WOULD KNOW. WE'VE STILL NEVER MET THEM.
NORMALLY, I INSIST ON MEETING PARENTS–
MOM! THERE AREN'T ANY OTHER KIDS MY AGE IN THIS NEIGHBORHOOD.
I LIKE THEM. THEY'RE MY FRIENDS. SO WHAT IF I GO OVER TO THEIR HOUSE ALL THE TIME?

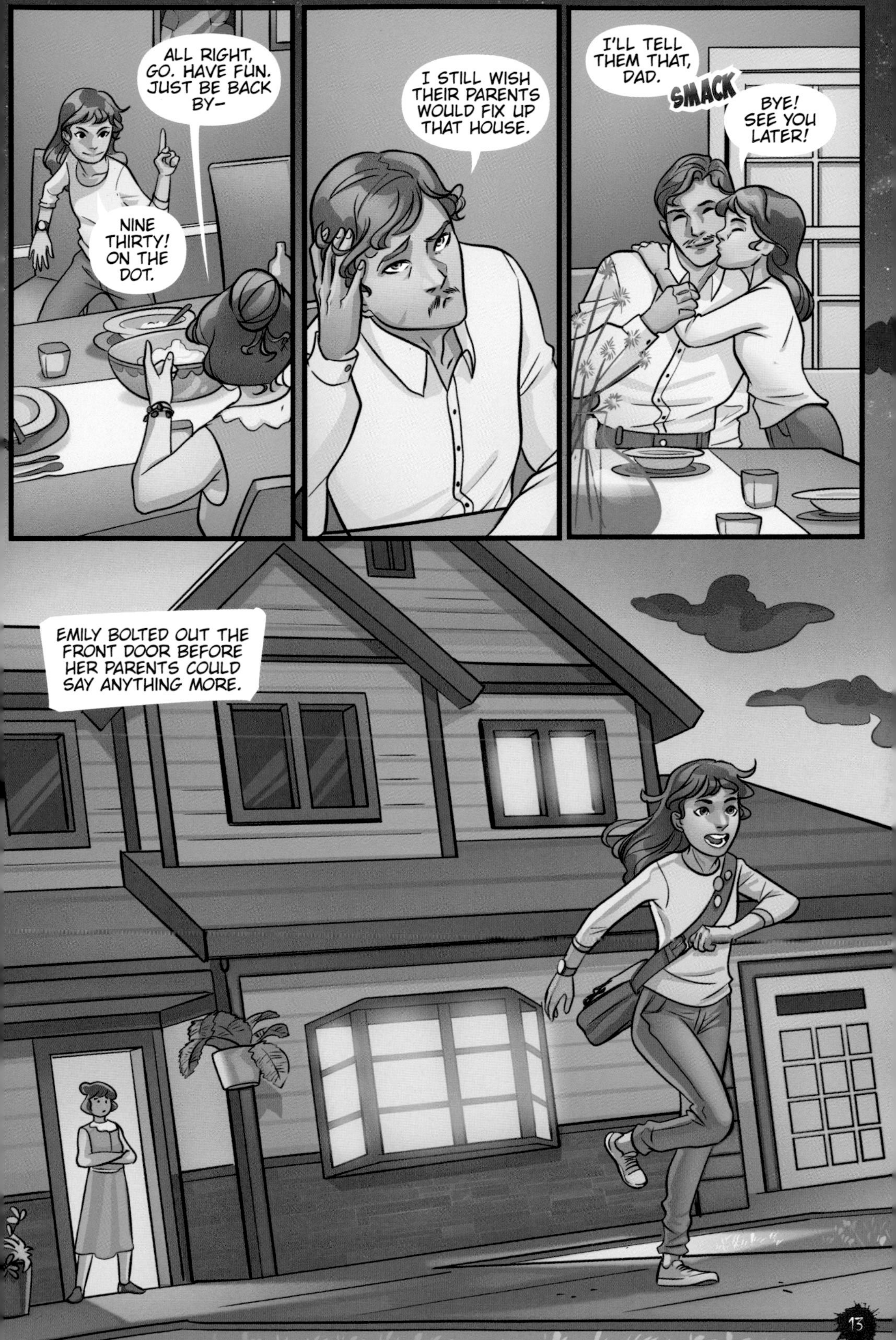
ALL RIGHT, GO. HAVE FUN. JUST BE BACK BY–
NINE THIRTY! ON THE DOT.
I STILL WISH THEIR PARENTS WOULD FIX UP THAT HOUSE.
I'LL TELL THEM THAT, DAD.
SMACK
BYE! SEE YOU LATER!
EMILY BOLTED OUT THE FRONT DOOR BEFORE HER PARENTS COULD SAY ANYTHING MORE.

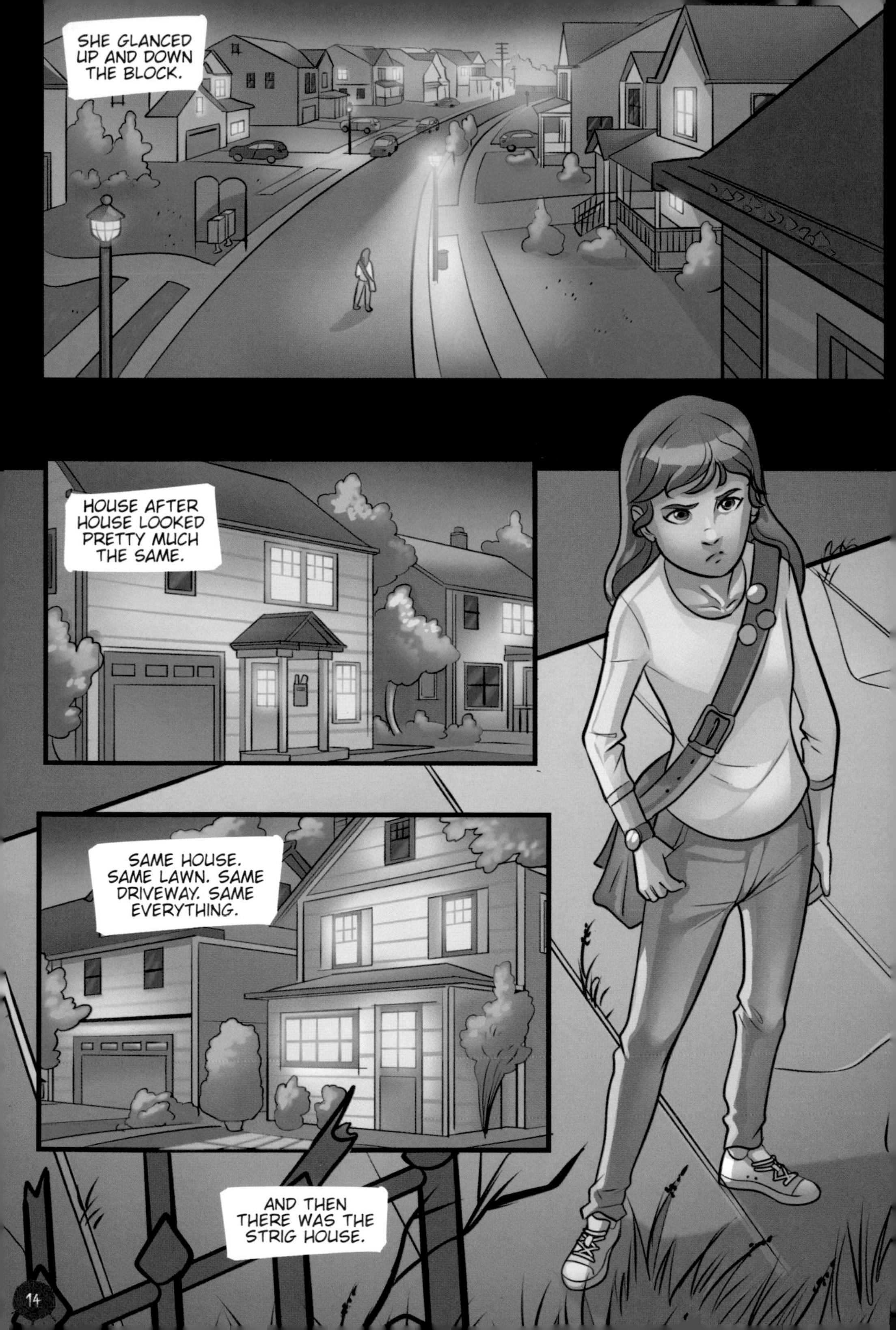
SHE GLANCED UP AND DOWN THE BLOCK.
HOUSE AFTER HOUSE LOOKED PRETTY MUCH THE SAME.
SAME HOUSE. SAME LAWN. SAME DRIVEWAY. SAME EVERYTHING.
AND THEN THERE WAS THE STRIG HOUSE.

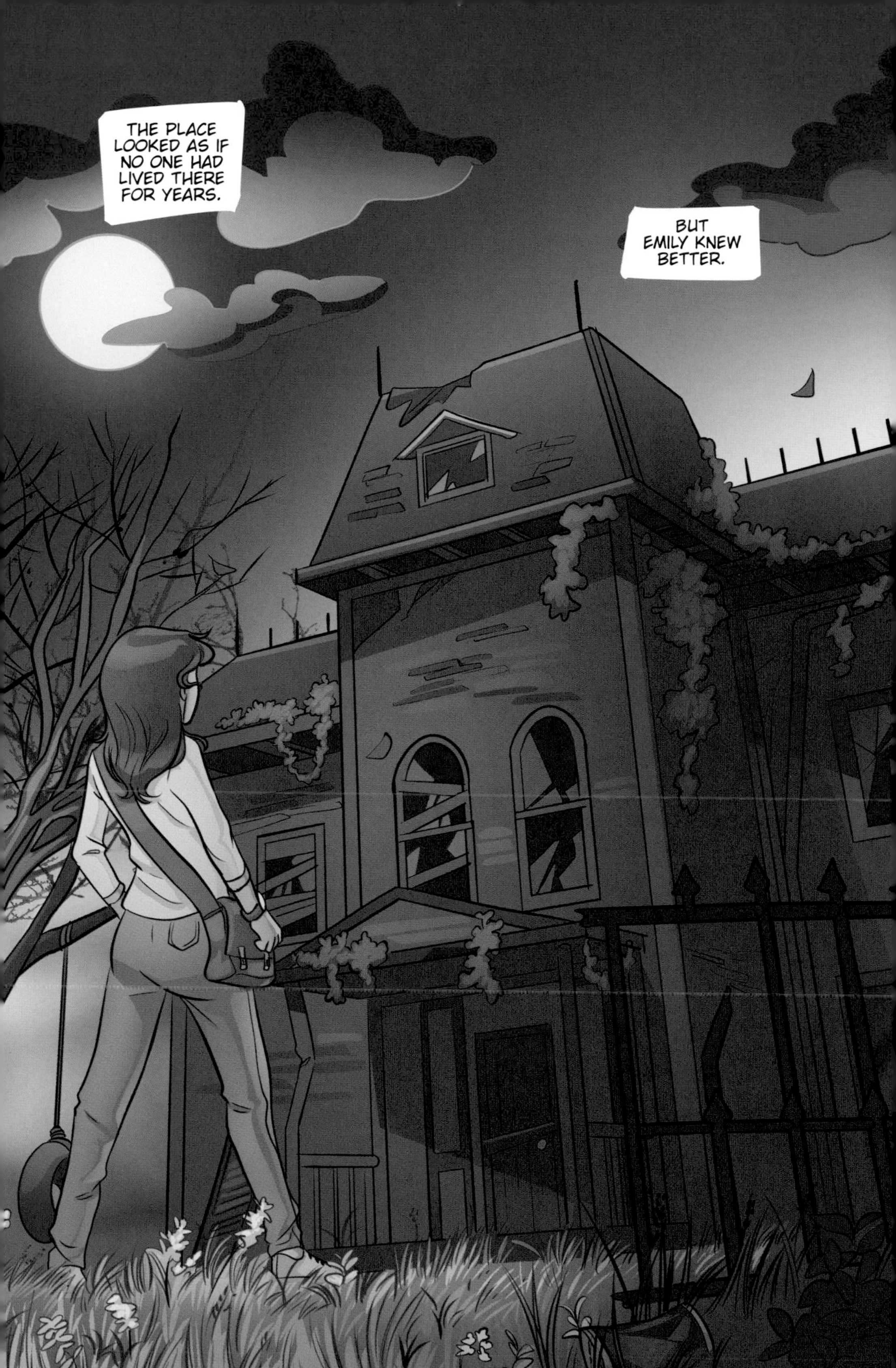
THE PLACE LOOKED AS IF NO ONE HAD LIVED THERE FOR YEARS.
BUT EMILY KNEW BETTER.

CHAPTER 2

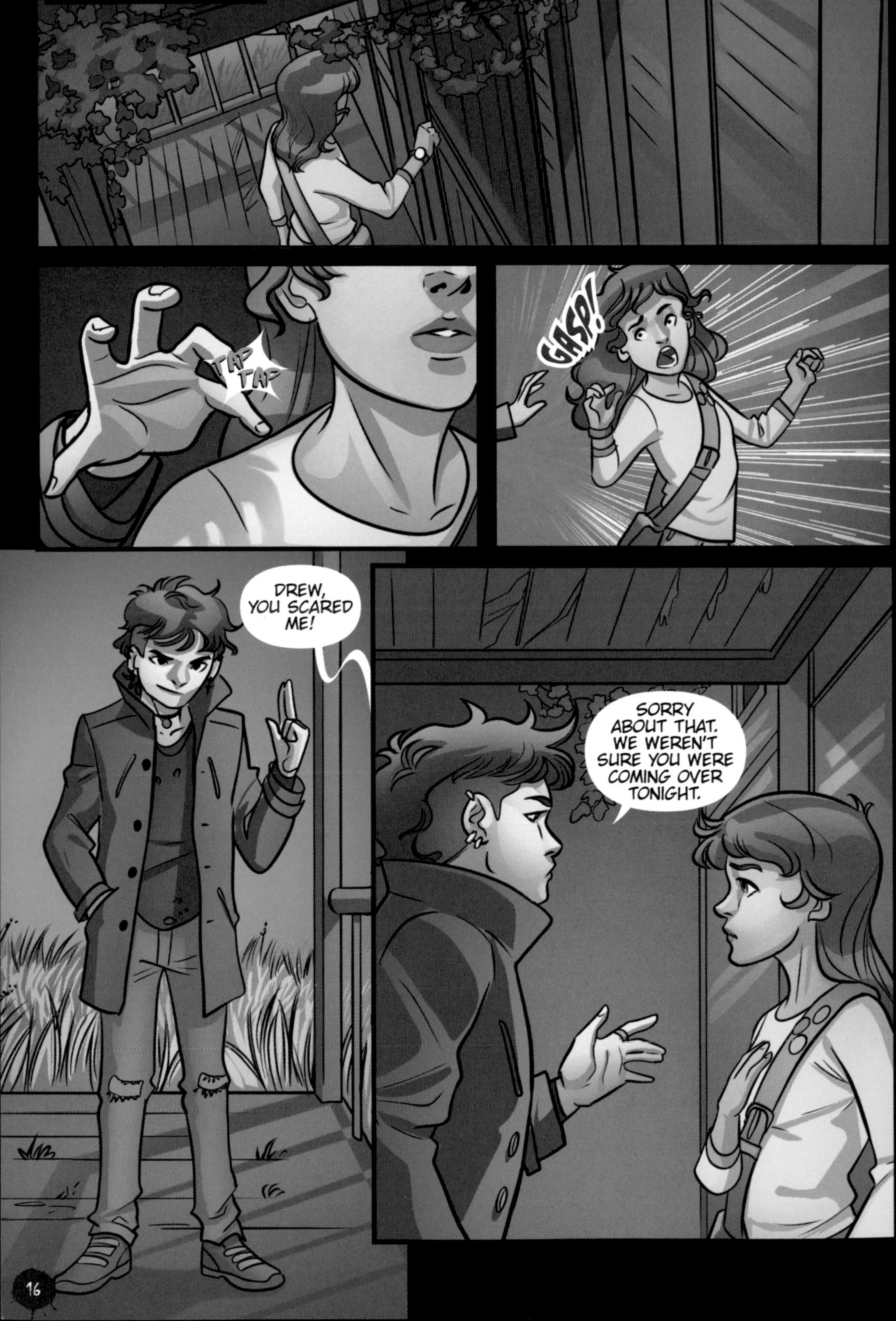
TAP TAP
GASP!
DREW, YOU SCARED ME!
SORRY ABOUT THAT. WE WEREN'T SURE YOU WERE COMING OVER TONIGHT.

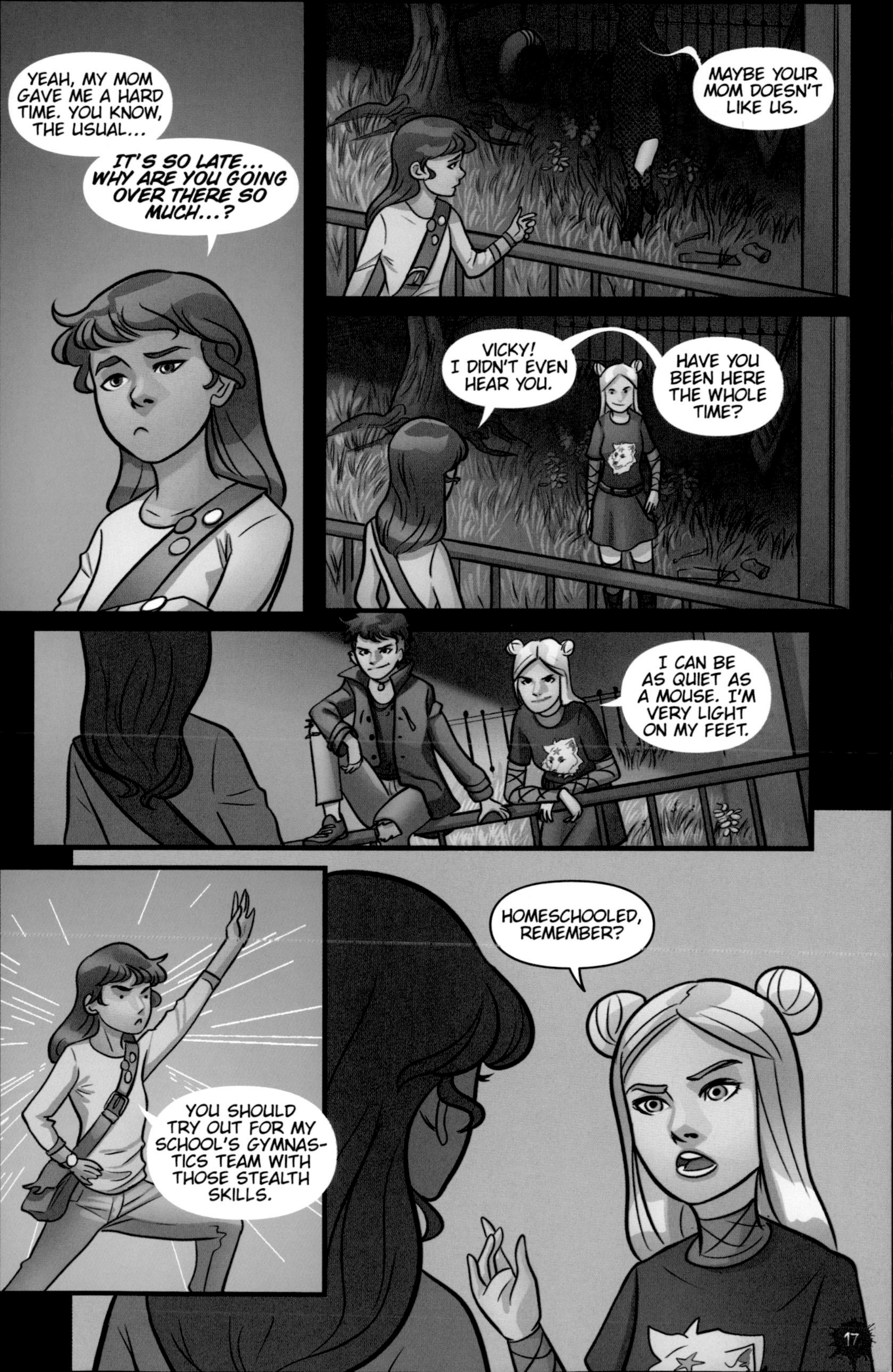
YEAH, MY MOM GAVE ME A HARD TIME. YOU KNOW, THE USUAL...
IT'S SO LATE... WHY ARE YOU GOING OVER THERE SO MUCH...?
MAYBE YOUR MOM DOESN'T LIKE US.
VICKY! I DIDN'T EVEN HEAR YOU.
HAVE YOU BEEN HERE THE WHOLE TIME?
I CAN BE AS QUIET AS A MOUSE. I'M VERY LIGHT ON MY FEET.
YOU SHOULD TRY OUT FOR MY SCHOOL'S GYMNASTICS TEAM WITH THOSE STEALTH SKILLS.
HOMESCHOOLED, REMEMBER?

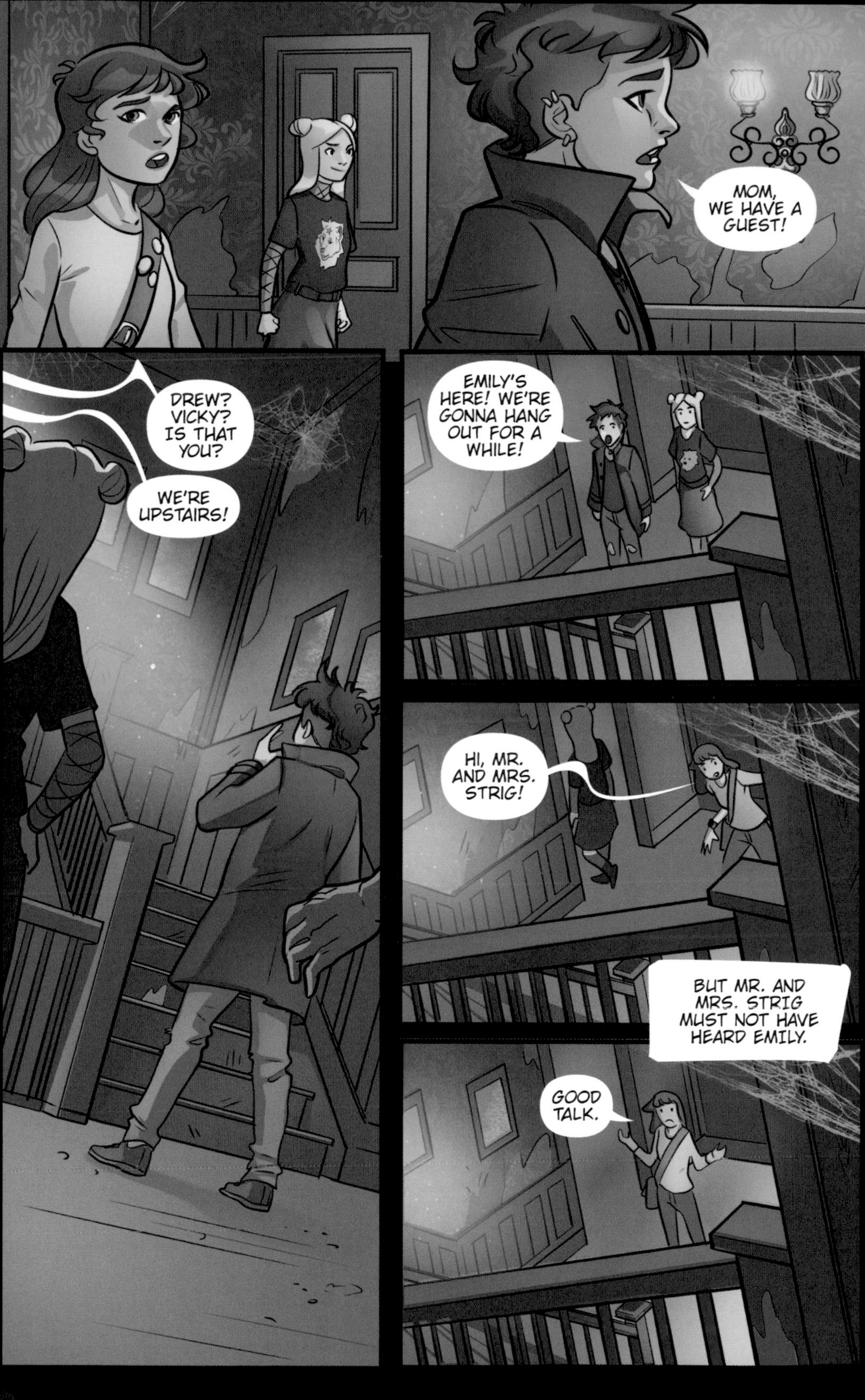
MOM, WE HAVE A GUEST!
DREW? VICKY? IS THAT YOU?
WE'RE UPSTAIRS!
EMILY'S HERE! WE'RE GONNA HANG OUT FOR A WHILE!
HI, MR. AND MRS. STRIG!
BUT MR. AND MRS. STRIG MUST NOT HAVE HEARD EMILY.
GOOD TALK.

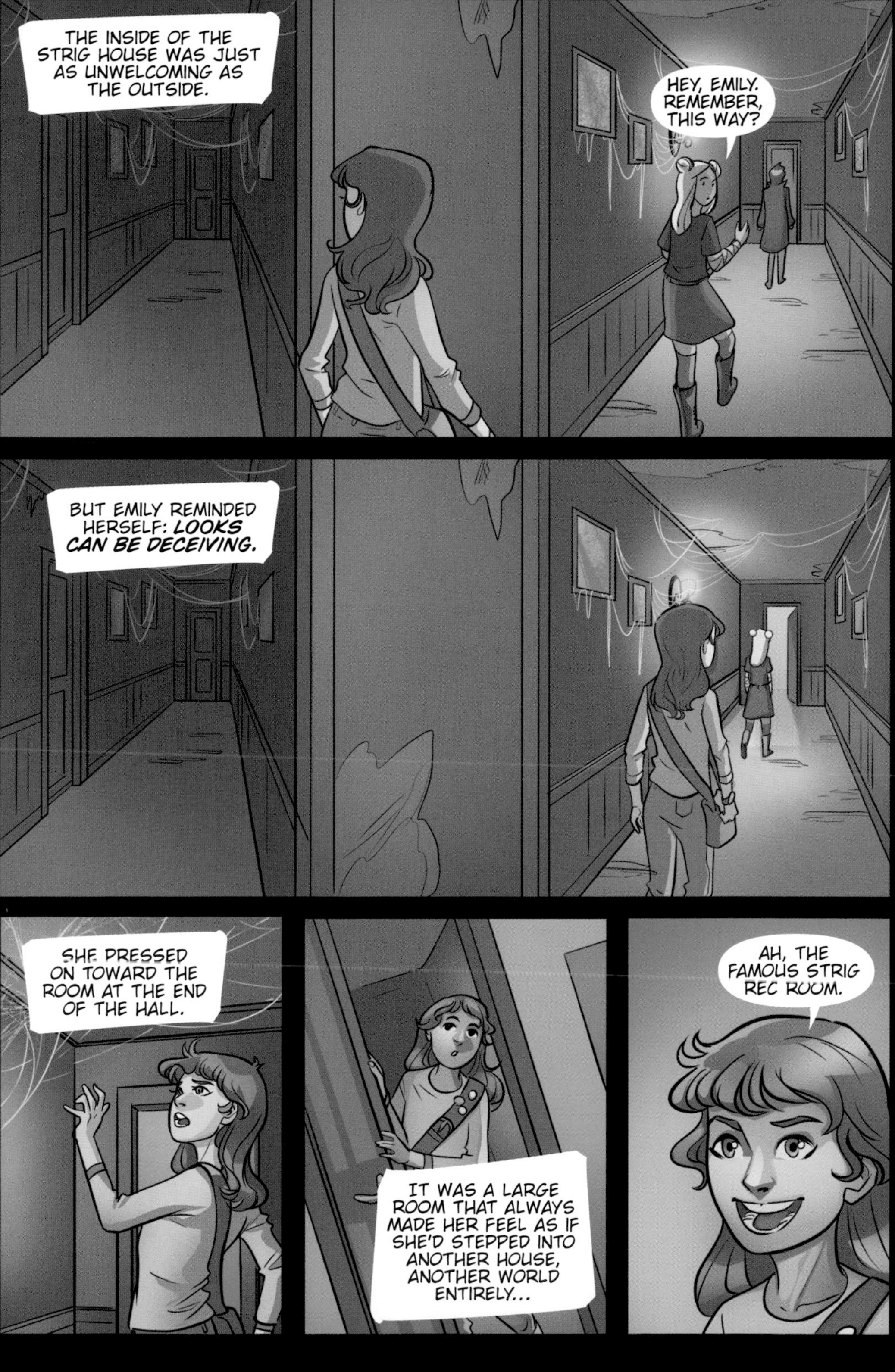
THE INSIDE OF THE STRIG HOUSE WAS JUST AS UNWELCOMING AS THE OUTSIDE.
HEY, EMILY. REMEMBER, THIS WAY?
BUT EMILY REMINDED HERSELF: *LOOKS CAN BE DECEIVING.*
SHE PRESSED ON TOWARD THE ROOM AT THE END OF THE HALL.
IT WAS A LARGE ROOM THAT ALWAYS MADE HER FEEL AS IF SHE'D STEPPED INTO ANOTHER HOUSE, ANOTHER WORLD ENTIRELY...
AH, THE FAMOUS STRIG REC ROOM.

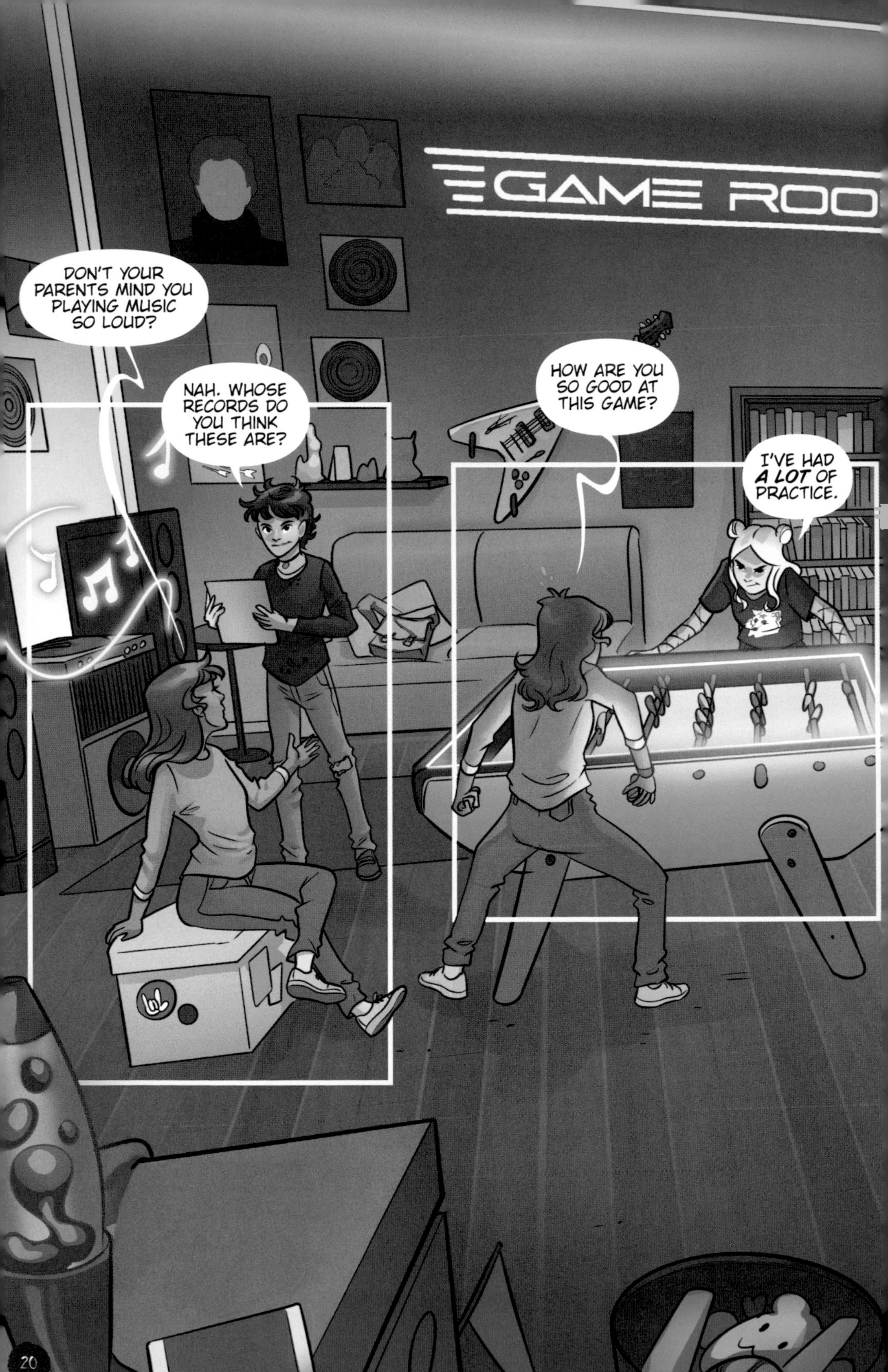
GAME ROO
DON'T YOUR PARENTS MIND YOU PLAYING MUSIC SO LOUD?
NAH. WHOSE RECORDS DO YOU THINK THESE ARE?
HOW ARE YOU SO GOOD AT THIS GAME?
I'VE HAD A LOT OF PRACTICE.

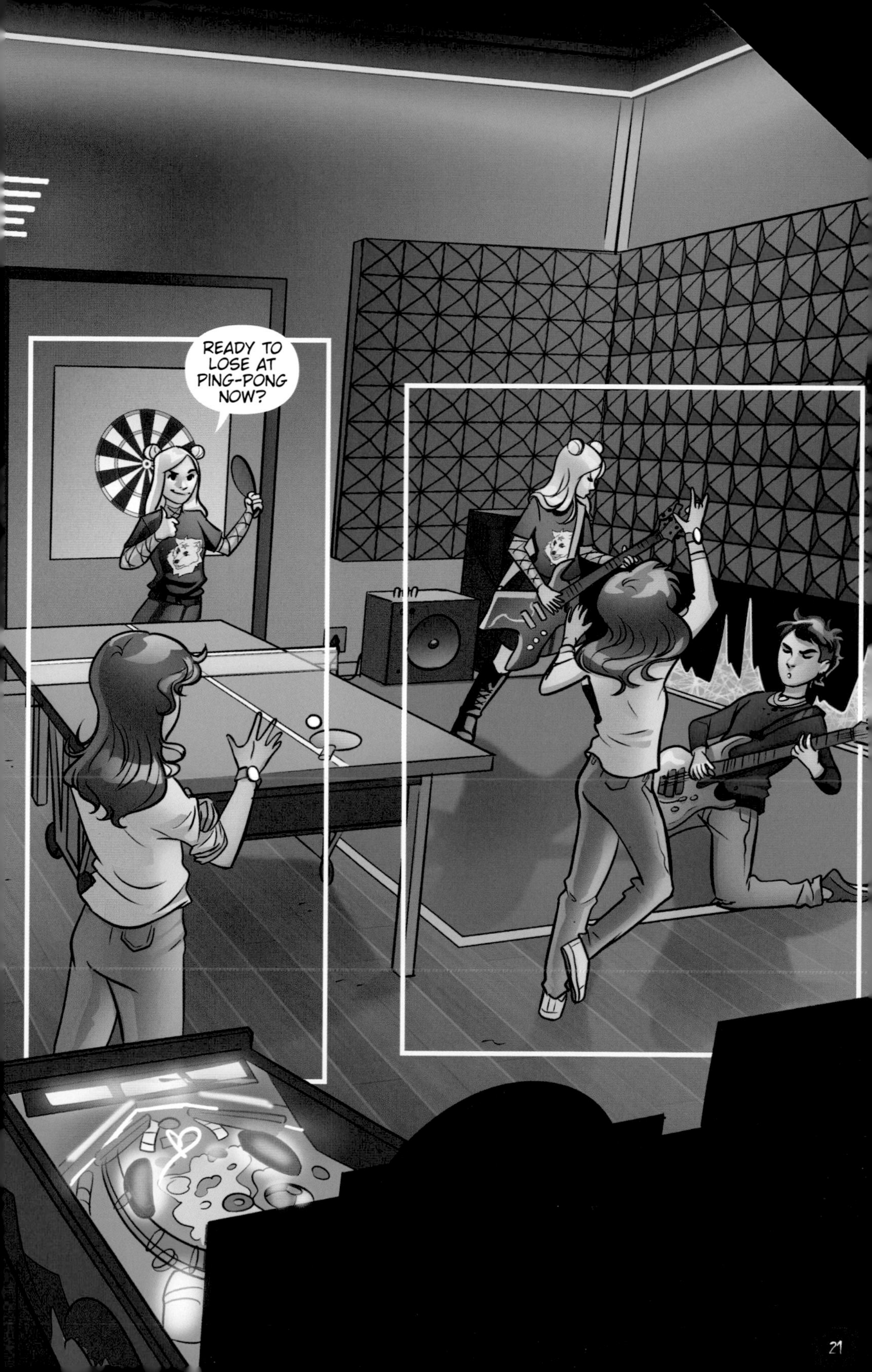
READY TO LOSE AT PING-PONG NOW?

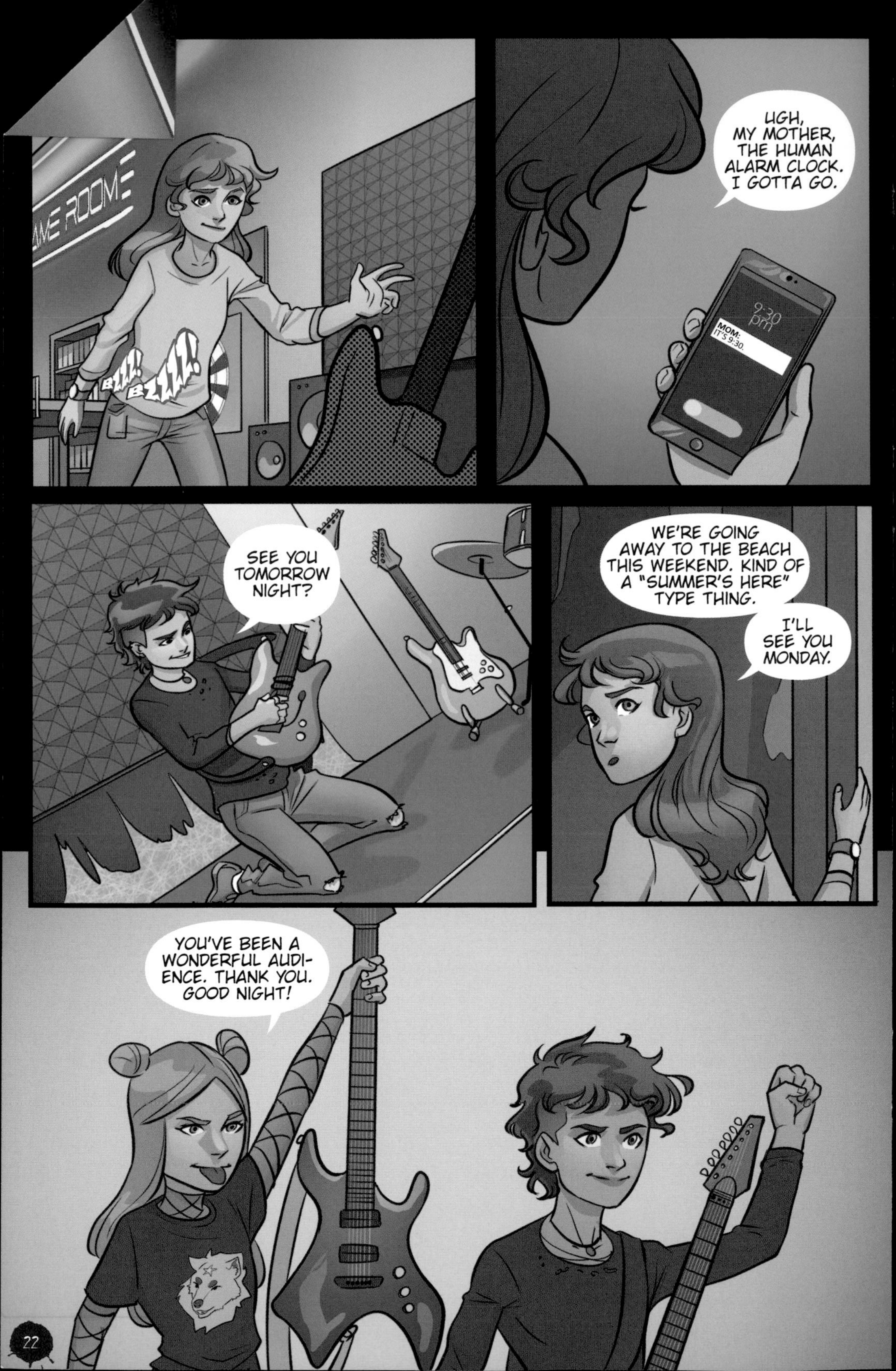

GAME ROOM
BZZZZ! BZZZZ!
UGH, MY MOTHER, THE HUMAN ALARM CLOCK. I GOTTA GO.
9:30 pm
MOM: IT'S 9:30.
SEE YOU TOMORROW NIGHT?
WE'RE GOING AWAY TO THE BEACH THIS WEEKEND. KIND OF A "SUMMER'S HERE" TYPE THING.
I'LL SEE YOU MONDAY.
YOU'VE BEEN A WONDERFUL AUDI-ENCE. THANK YOU. GOOD NIGHT!

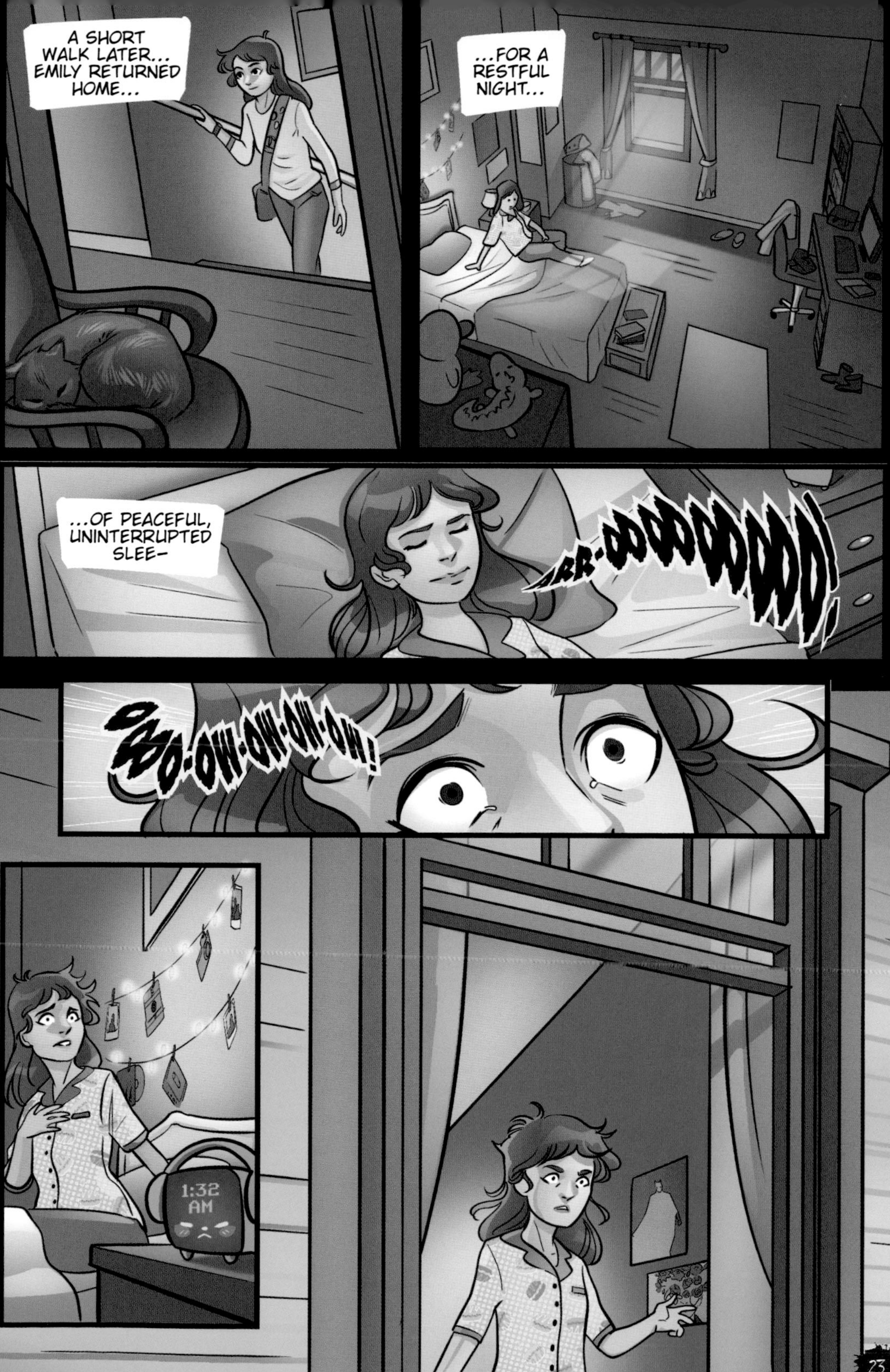
A SHORT WALK LATER... EMILY RETURNED HOME...
...FOR A RESTFUL NIGHT...
...OF PEACEFUL, UNINTERRUPTED SLEE–
ARR-OOOOOOOOO!
OWO-OW-OW-OW-OW!
1:32 AM

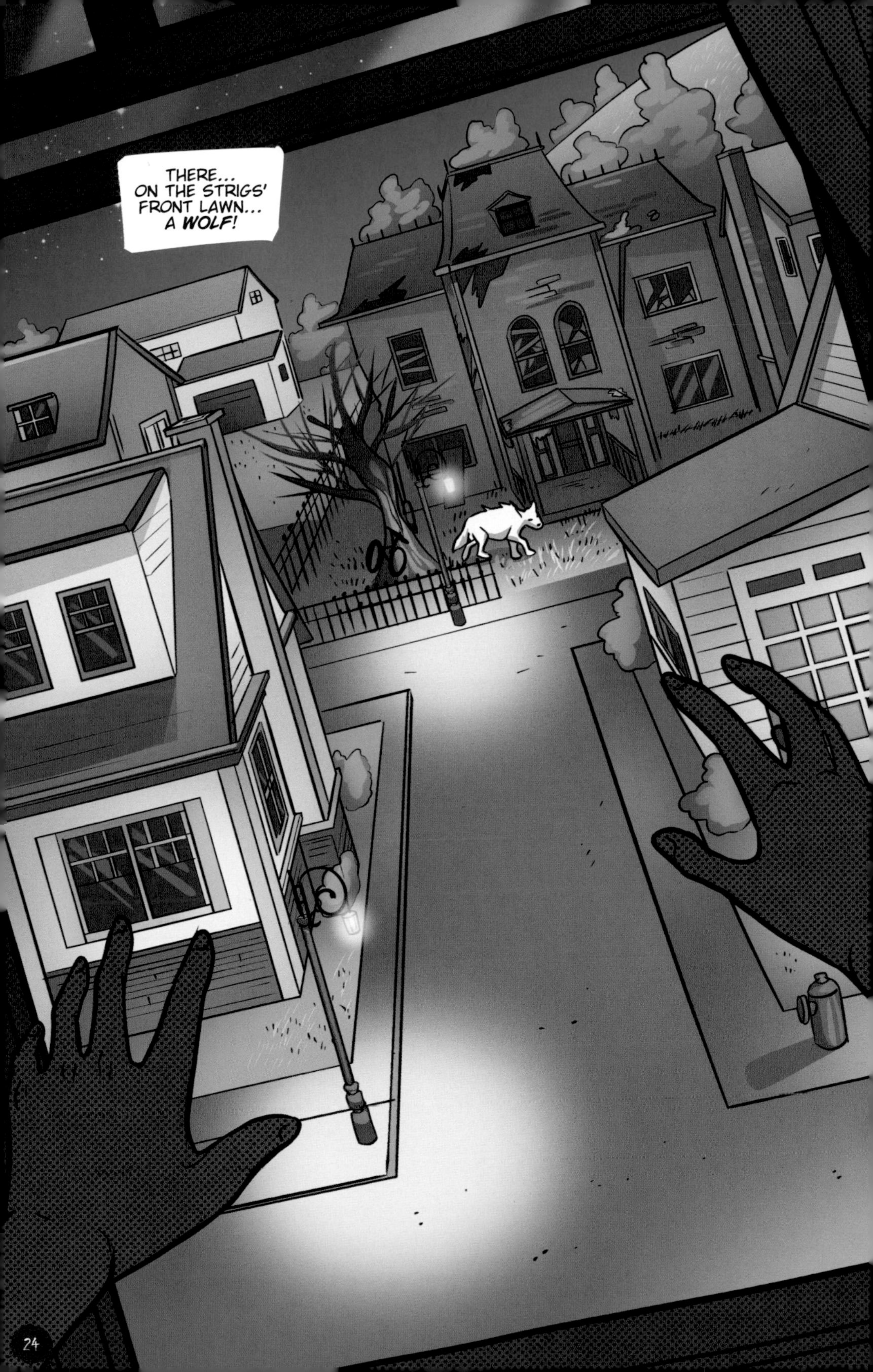
THERE... ON THE STRIGS' FRONT LAWN... A WOLF!

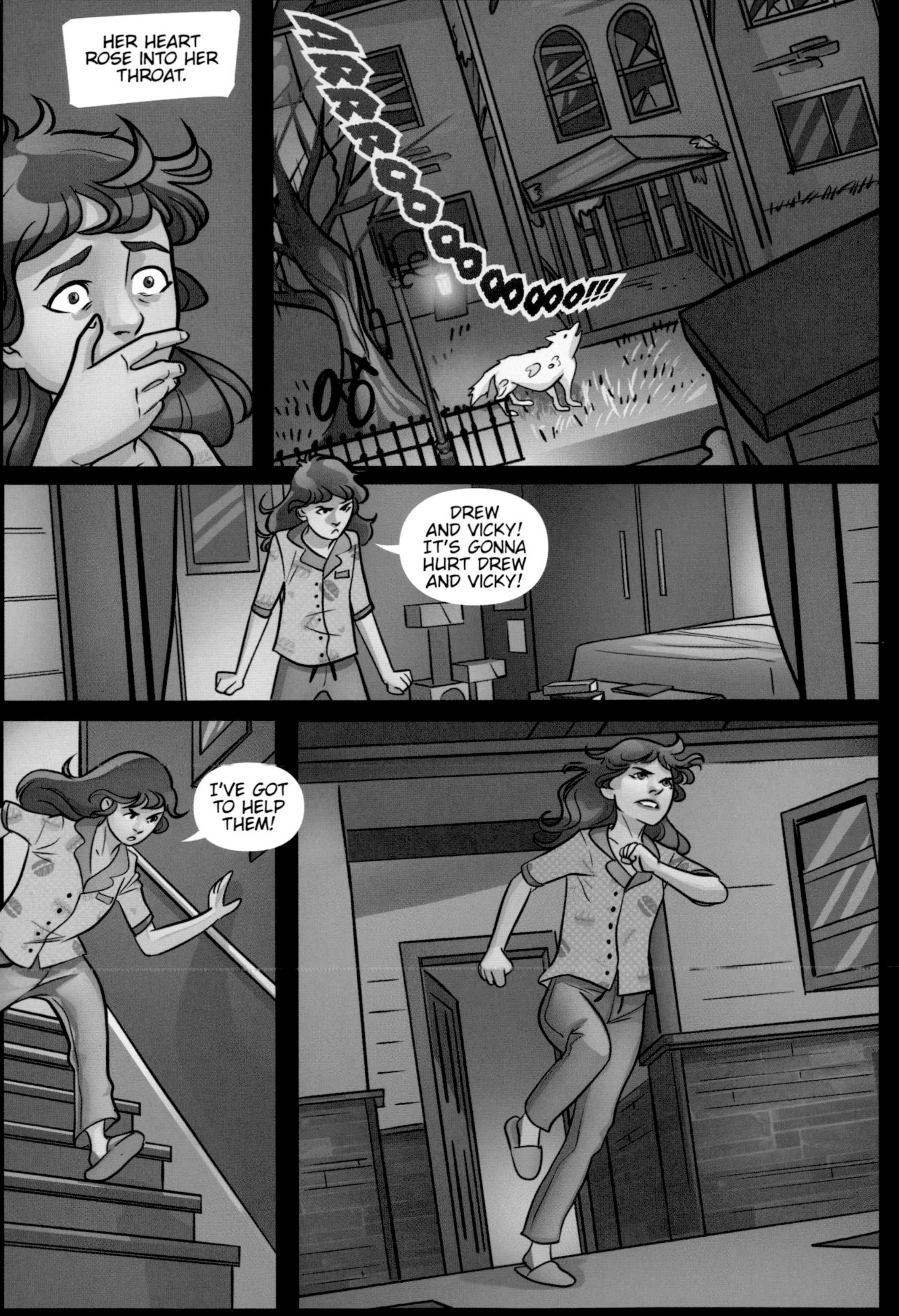
HER HEART ROSE INTO HER THROAT.
ARRROOOOOOOOOOOO!!!
DREW AND VICKY! IT'S GONNA HURT DREW AND VICKY!
I'VE GOT TO HELP THEM!

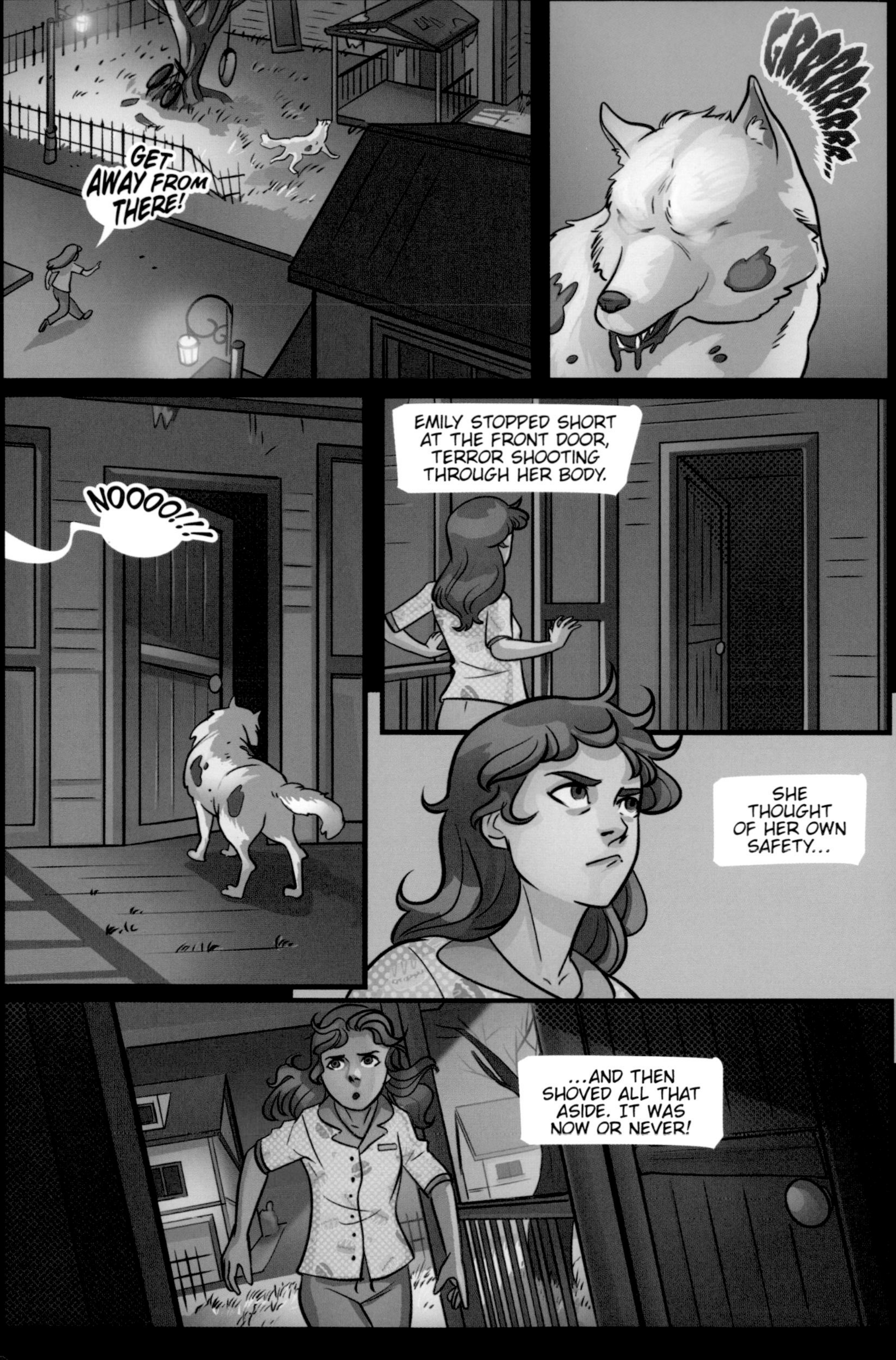
GET AWAY FROM THERE!
GRRRRRRR...
NOOOO!!!
EMILY STOPPED SHORT AT THE FRONT DOOR, TERROR SHOOTING THROUGH HER BODY.
SHE THOUGHT OF HER OWN SAFETY...
...AND THEN SHOVED ALL THAT ASIDE. IT WAS NOW OR NEVER!

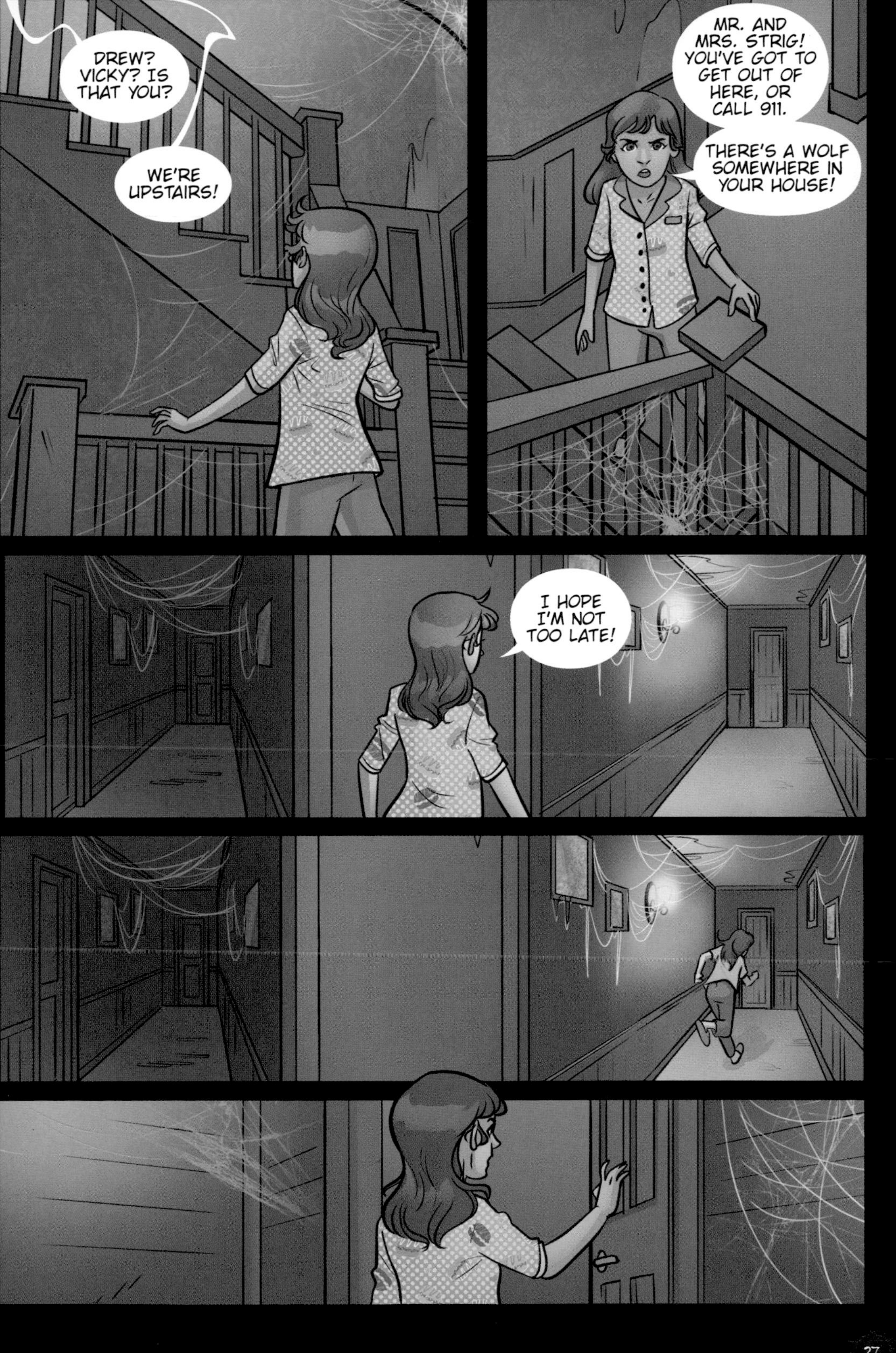
DREW? VICKY? IS THAT YOU?
WE'RE UPSTAIRS!
MR. AND MRS. STRIG! YOU'VE GOT TO GET OUT OF HERE, OR CALL 911.
THERE'S A WOLF SOMEWHERE IN YOUR HOUSE!
I HOPE I'M NOT TOO LATE!

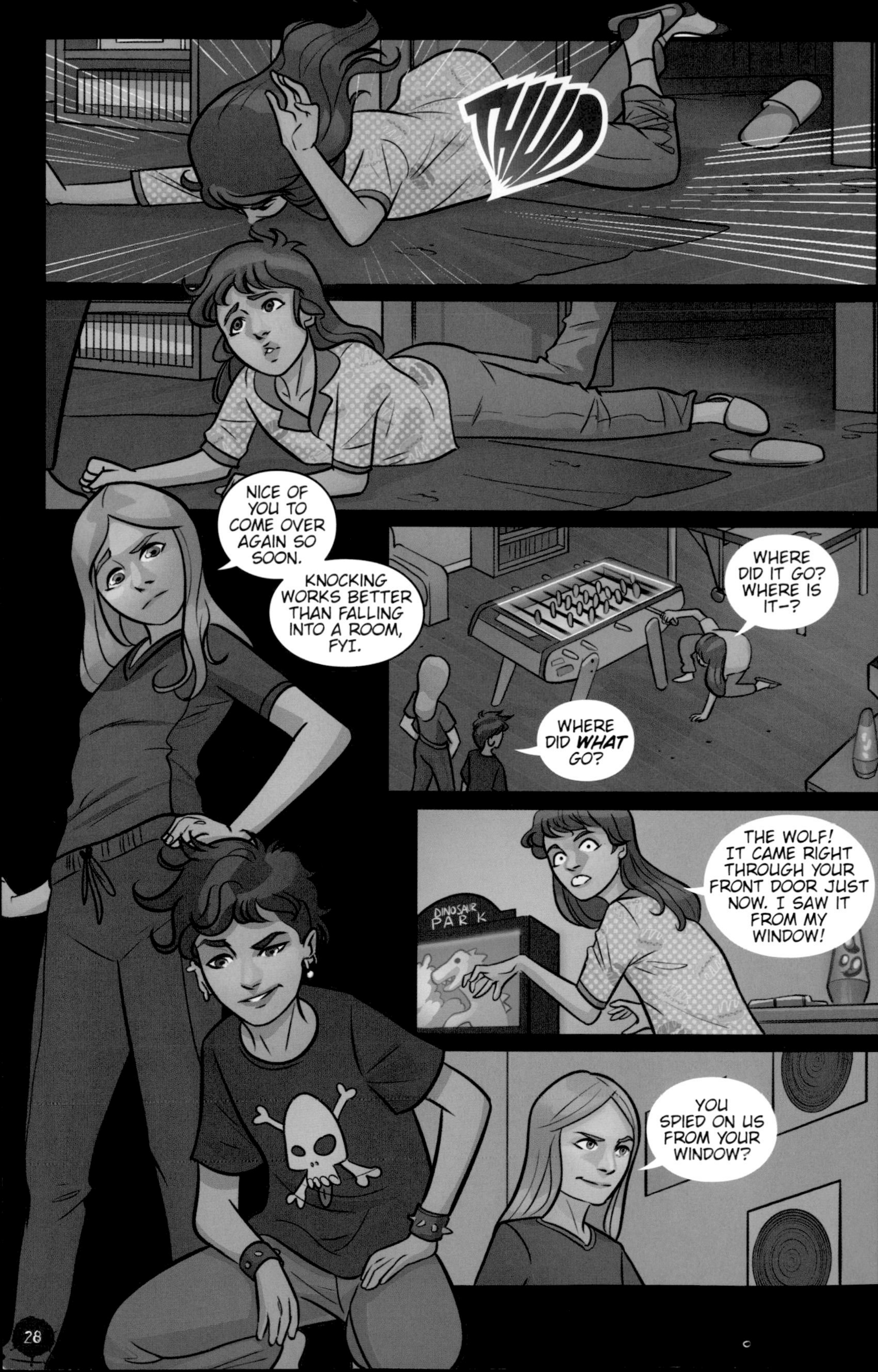
THUD
NICE OF YOU TO COME OVER AGAIN SO SOON.
KNOCKING WORKS BETTER THAN FALLING INTO A ROOM, FYI.
WHERE DID IT GO? WHERE IS IT–?
WHERE DID **WHAT** GO?
DINOSAUR PARK
THE WOLF! IT CAME RIGHT THROUGH YOUR FRONT DOOR JUST NOW. I SAW IT FROM MY WINDOW!
YOU SPIED ON US FROM YOUR WINDOW?

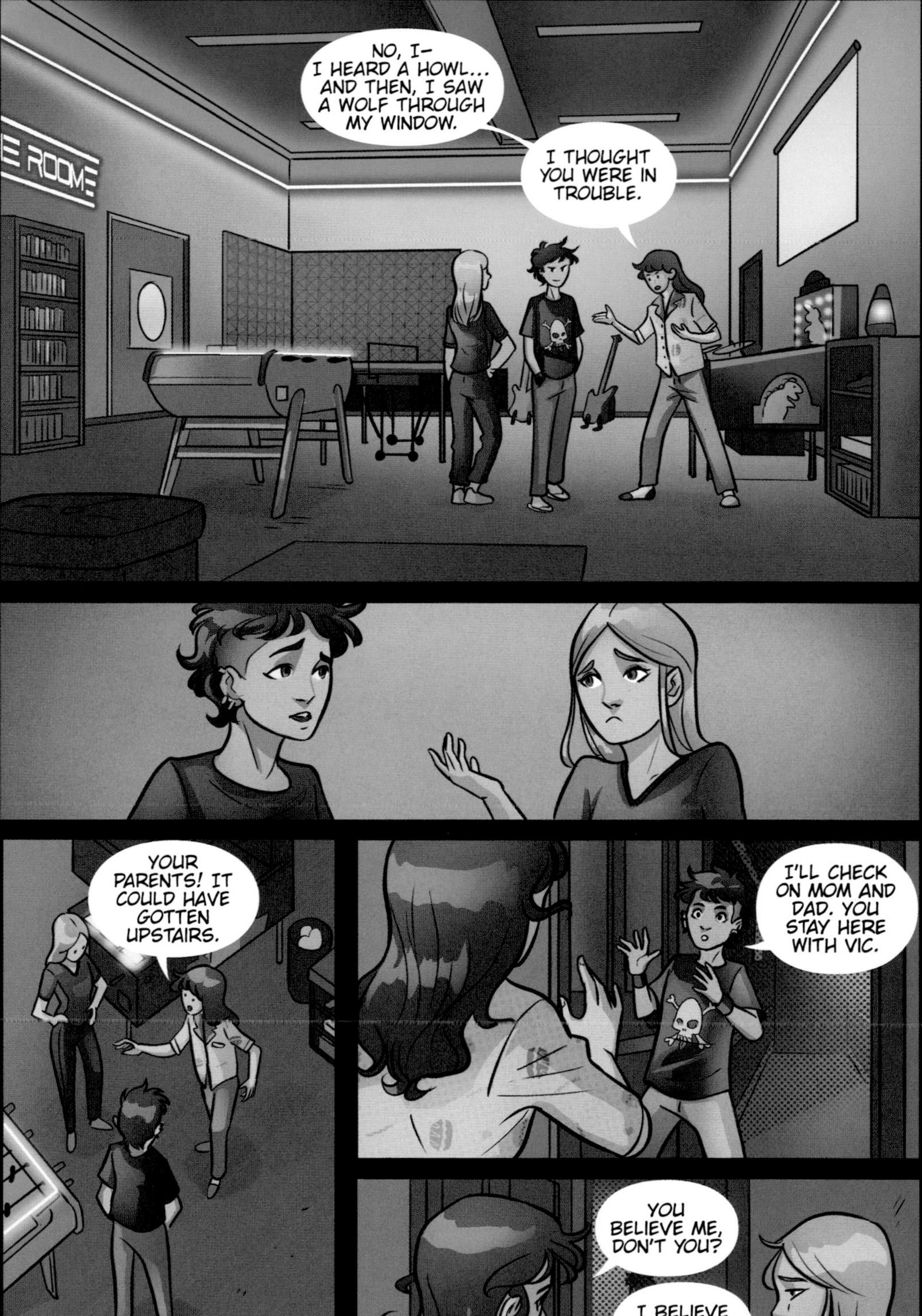

E ROOM
NO, I– I HEARD A HOWL... AND THEN, I SAW A WOLF THROUGH MY WINDOW.
I THOUGHT YOU WERE IN TROUBLE.
YOUR PARENTS! IT COULD HAVE GOTTEN UPSTAIRS.
I'LL CHECK ON MOM AND DAD. YOU STAY HERE WITH VIC.
YOU BELIEVE ME, DON'T YOU?
I BELIEVE YOU HAD A NIGHTMARE.

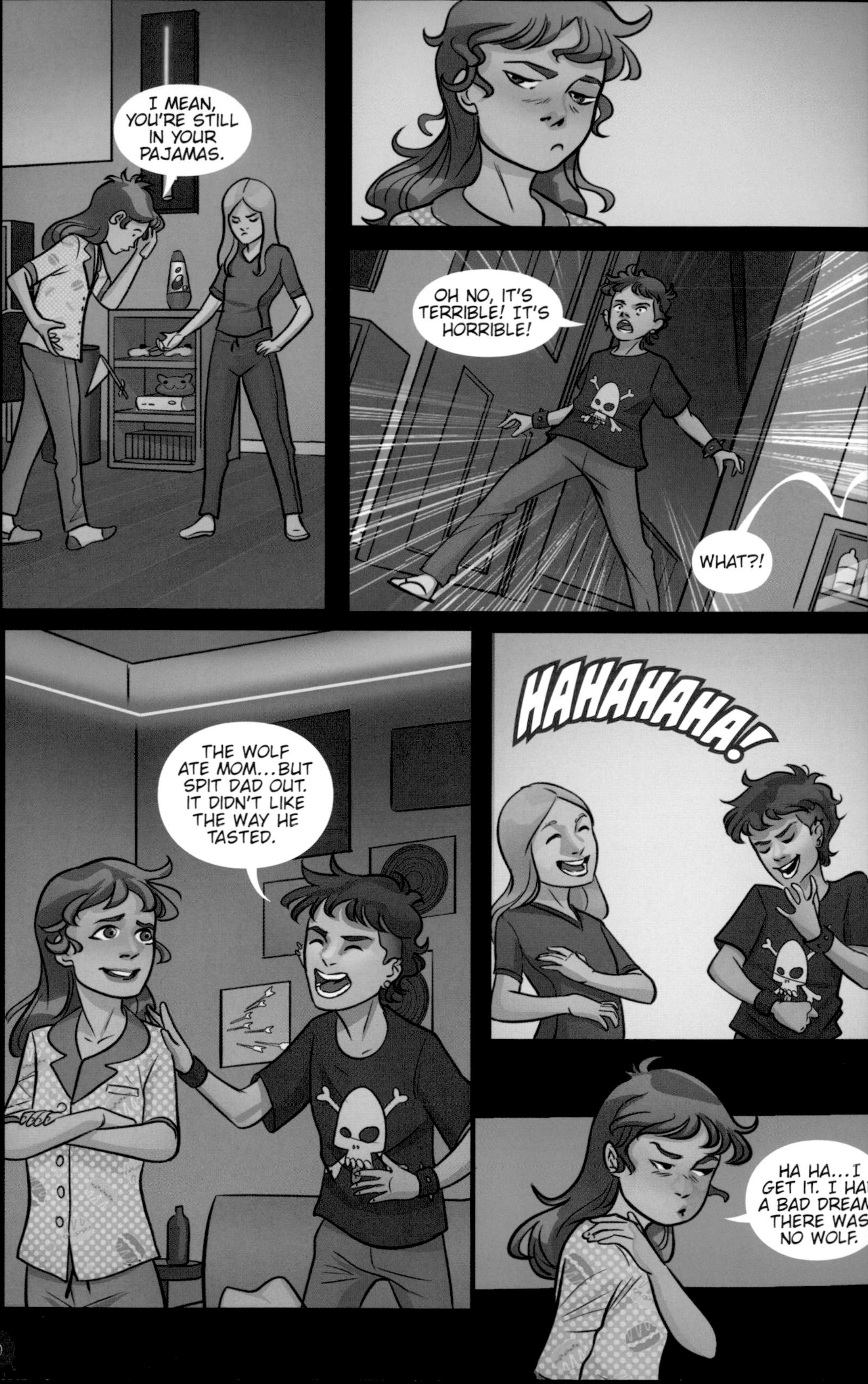
I MEAN, YOU'RE STILL IN YOUR PAJAMAS.
OH NO, IT'S TERRIBLE! IT'S HORRIBLE!
WHAT?!
THE WOLF ATE MOM...BUT SPIT DAD OUT. IT DIDN'T LIKE THE WAY HE TASTED.
HAHAHAHA!
HA HA...I GET IT. I HA A BAD DREAM THERE WAS NO WOLF.

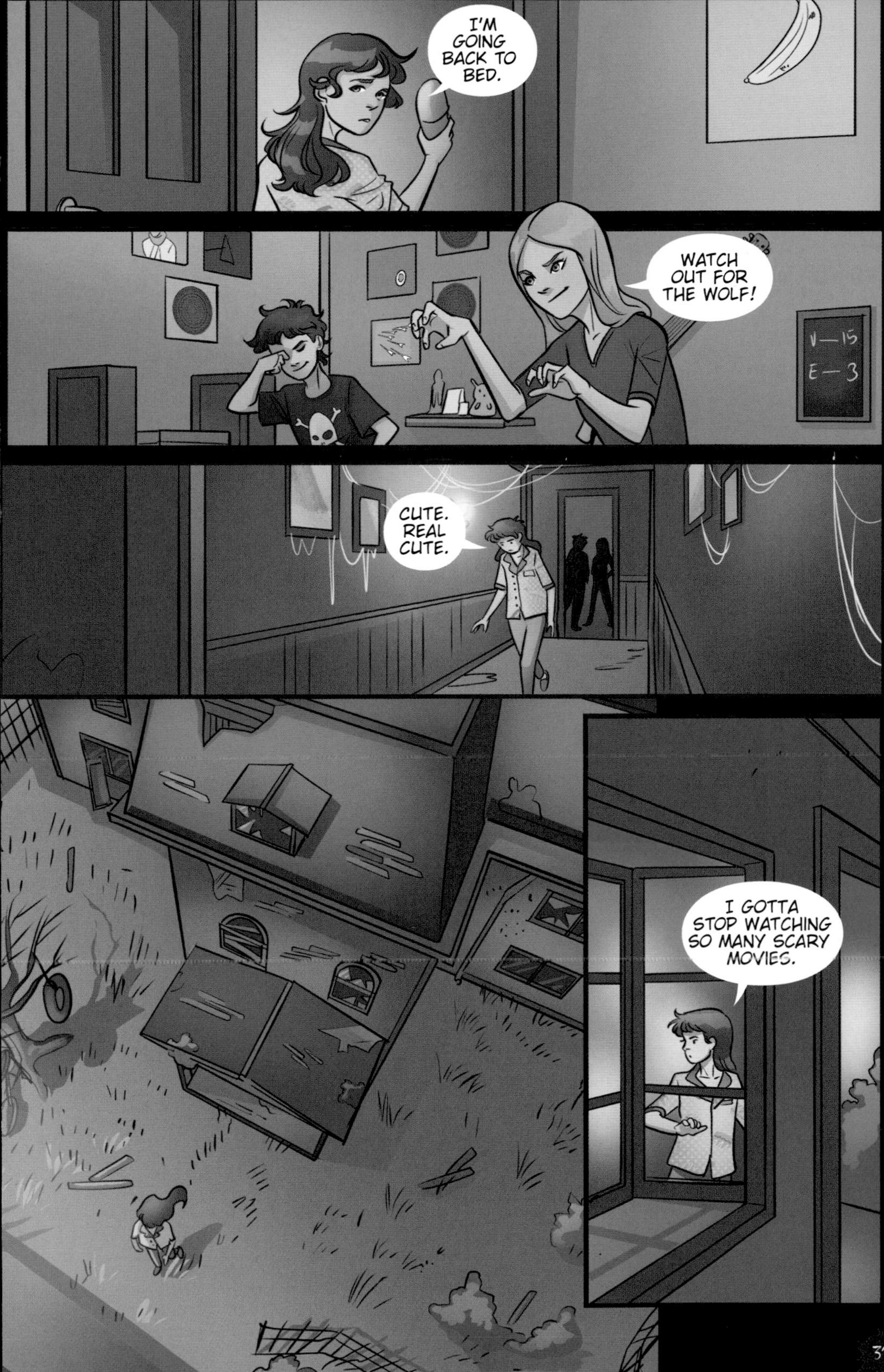
I'M GOING BACK TO BED.
WATCH OUT FOR THE WOLF!
V—15
E—3
CUTE. REAL CUTE.
I GOTTA STOP WATCHING SO MANY SCARY MOVIES.

# CHAPTER 3

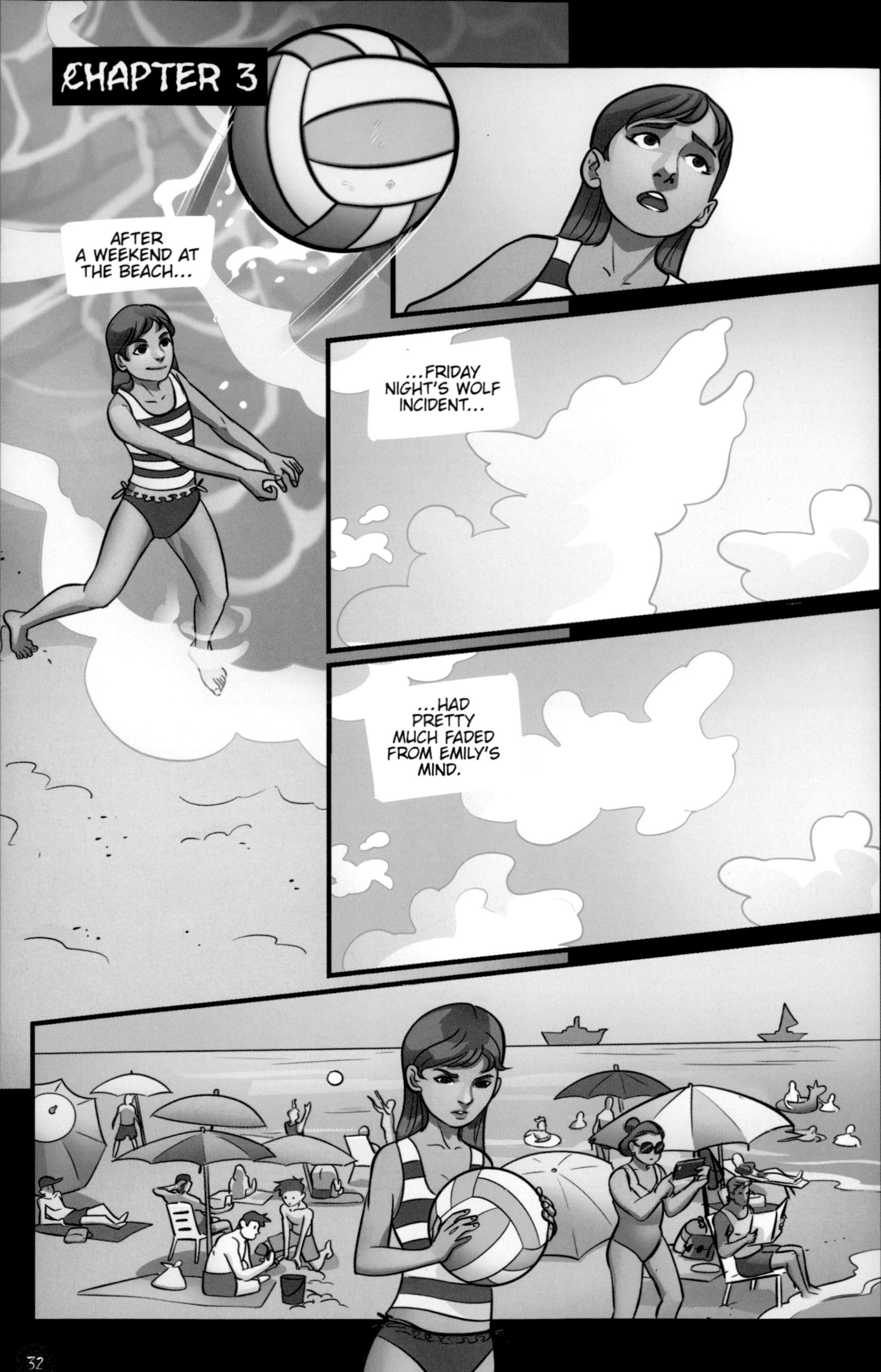

AFTER A WEEKEND AT THE BEACH...
...FRIDAY NIGHT'S WOLF INCIDENT...
...HAD PRETTY MUCH FADED FROM EMILY'S MIND.

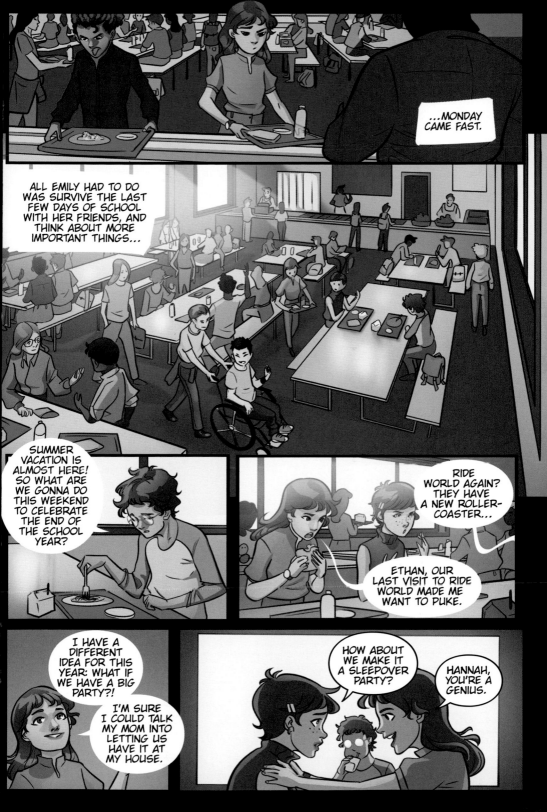

...MONDAY CAME FAST.

ALL EMILY HAD TO DO WAS SURVIVE THE LAST FEW DAYS OF SCHOOL WITH HER FRIENDS, AND THINK ABOUT MORE IMPORTANT THINGS...

SUMMER VACATION IS ALMOST HERE! SO WHAT ARE WE GONNA DO THIS WEEKEND TO CELEBRATE THE END OF THE SCHOOL YEAR?

RIDE WORLD AGAIN? THEY HAVE A NEW ROLLER-COASTER...

ETHAN, OUR LAST VISIT TO RIDE WORLD MADE ME WANT TO PUKE.

I HAVE A DIFFERENT IDEA FOR THIS YEAR: WHAT IF WE HAVE A BIG PARTY?!

I'M SURE I COULD TALK MY MOM INTO LETTING US HAVE IT AT MY HOUSE.

HOW ABOUT WE MAKE IT A SLEEPOVER PARTY?

HANNAH, YOU'RE A GENIUS.

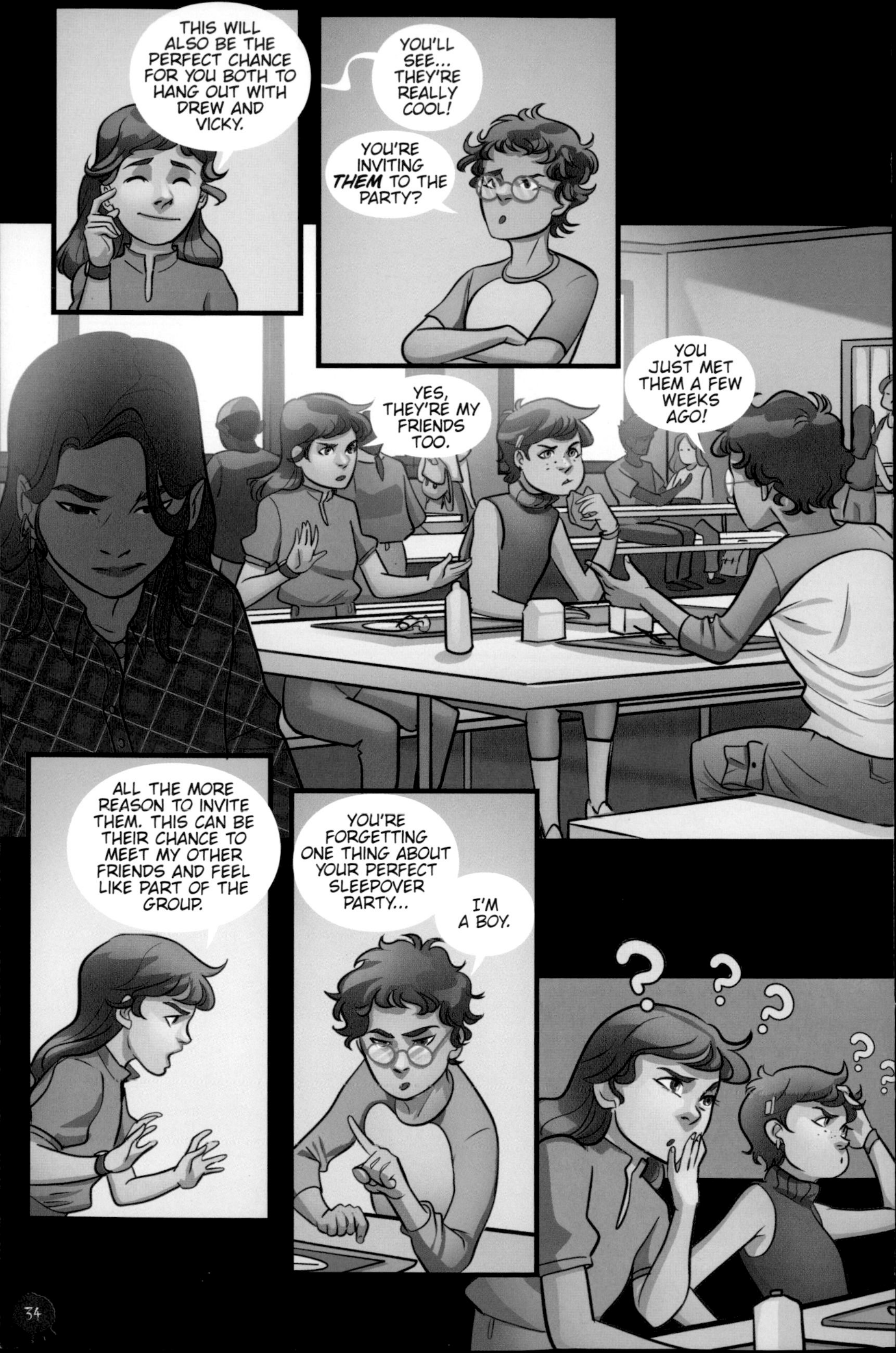
THIS WILL ALSO BE THE PERFECT CHANCE FOR YOU BOTH TO HANG OUT WITH DREW AND VICKY.
YOU'LL SEE... THEY'RE REALLY COOL!
YOU'RE INVITING *THEM* TO THE PARTY?
YES, THEY'RE MY FRIENDS TOO.
YOU JUST MET THEM A FEW WEEKS AGO!
ALL THE MORE REASON TO INVITE THEM. THIS CAN BE THEIR CHANCE TO MEET MY OTHER FRIENDS AND FEEL LIKE PART OF THE GROUP.
YOU'RE FORGETTING ONE THING ABOUT YOUR PERFECT SLEEPOVER PARTY...
I'M A BOY.
? ? ? ?

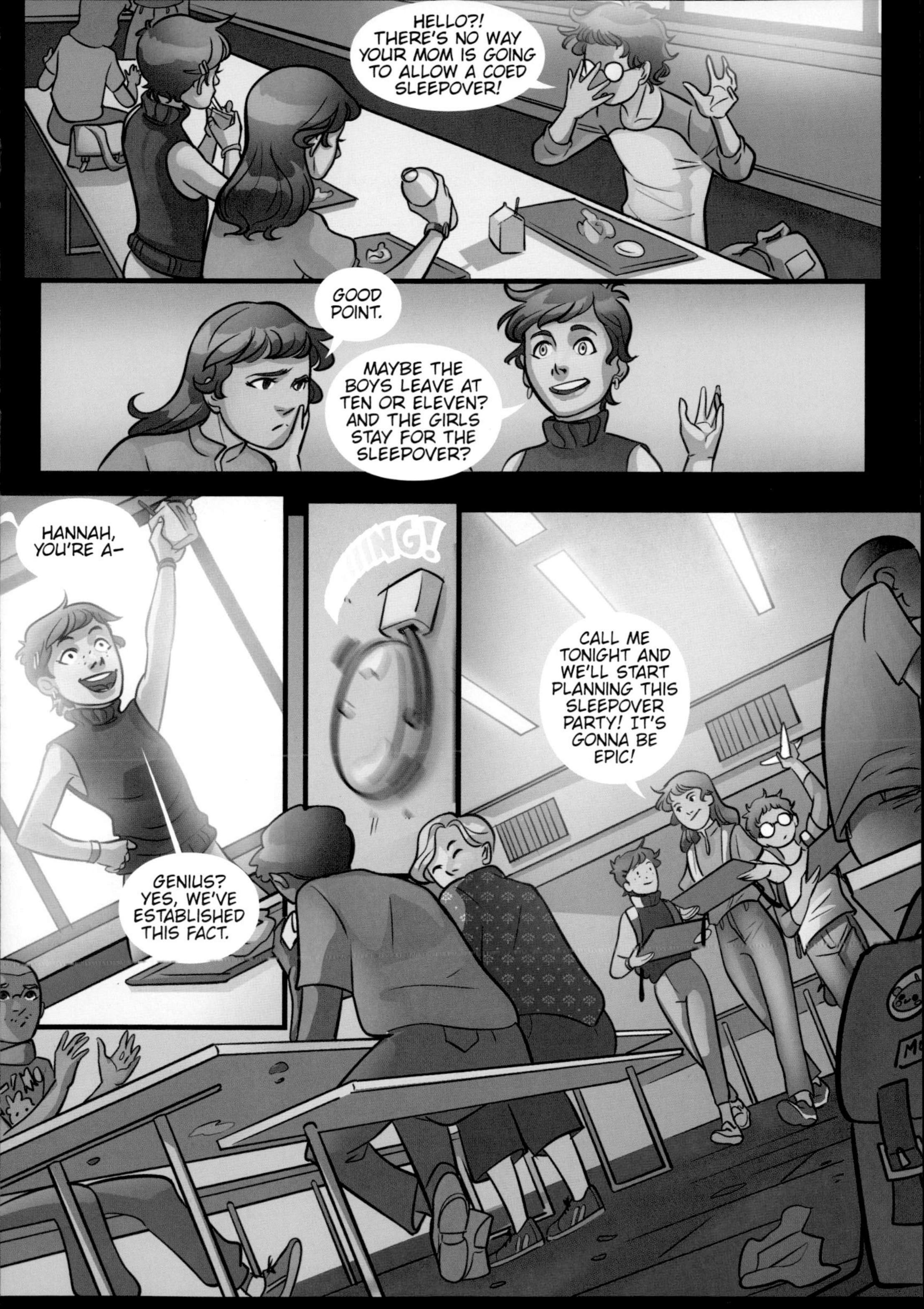
HELLO?! THERE'S NO WAY YOUR MOM IS GOING TO ALLOW A COED SLEEPOVER!
GOOD POINT.
MAYBE THE BOYS LEAVE AT TEN OR ELEVEN? AND THE GIRLS STAY FOR THE SLEEPOVER?
HANNAH, YOU'RE A–
GENIUS? YES, WE'VE ESTABLISHED THIS FACT.
CALL ME TONIGHT AND WE'LL START PLANNING THIS SLEEPOVER PARTY! IT'S GONNA BE EPIC!

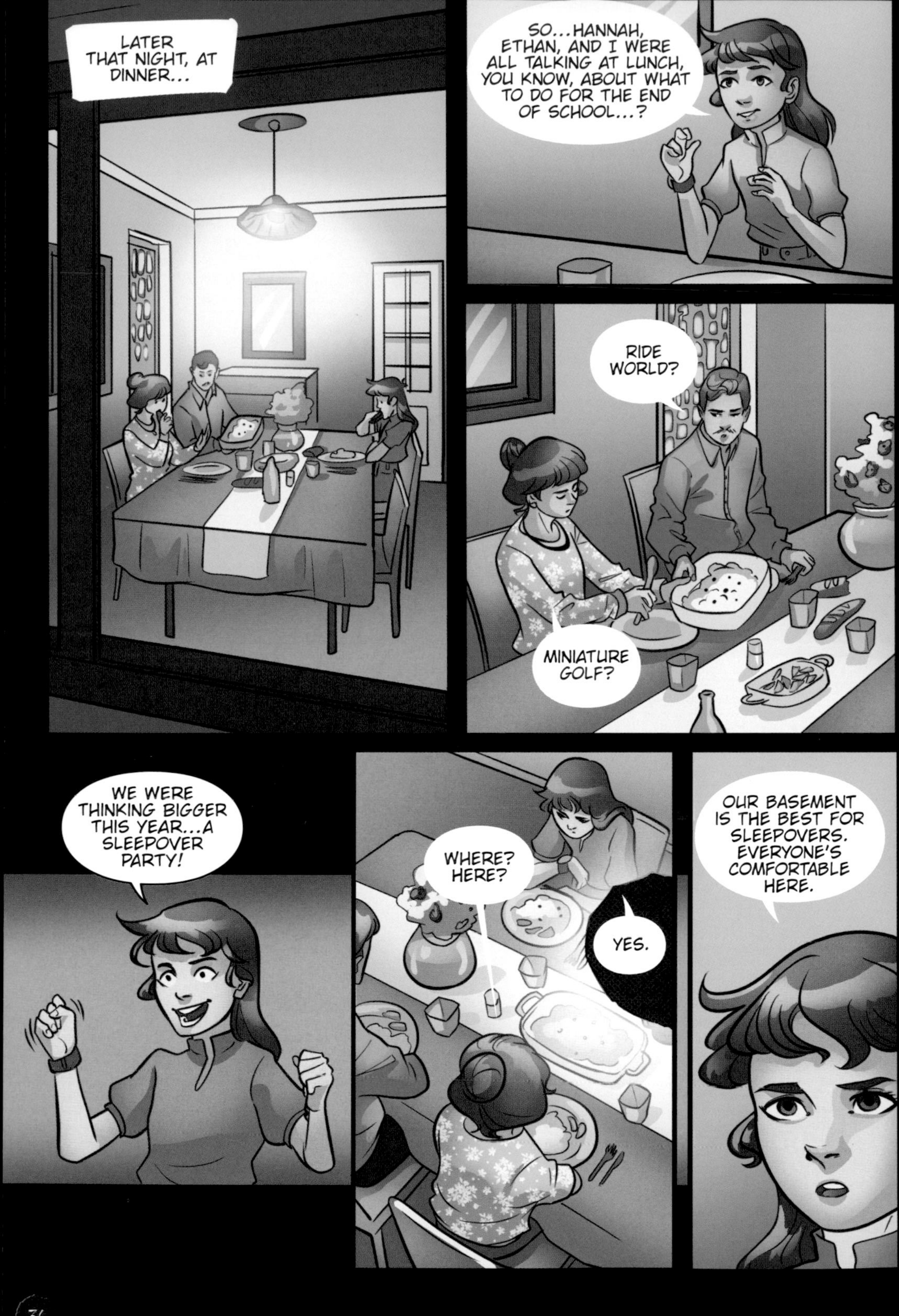
LATER THAT NIGHT, AT DINNER...
SO...HANNAH, ETHAN, AND I WERE ALL TALKING AT LUNCH, YOU KNOW, ABOUT WHAT TO DO FOR THE END OF SCHOOL...?
RIDE WORLD?
MINIATURE GOLF?
WE WERE THINKING BIGGER THIS YEAR...A SLEEPOVER PARTY!
WHERE? HERE?
YES.
OUR BASEMENT IS THE BEST FOR SLEEPOVERS. EVERYONE'S COMFORTABLE HERE.

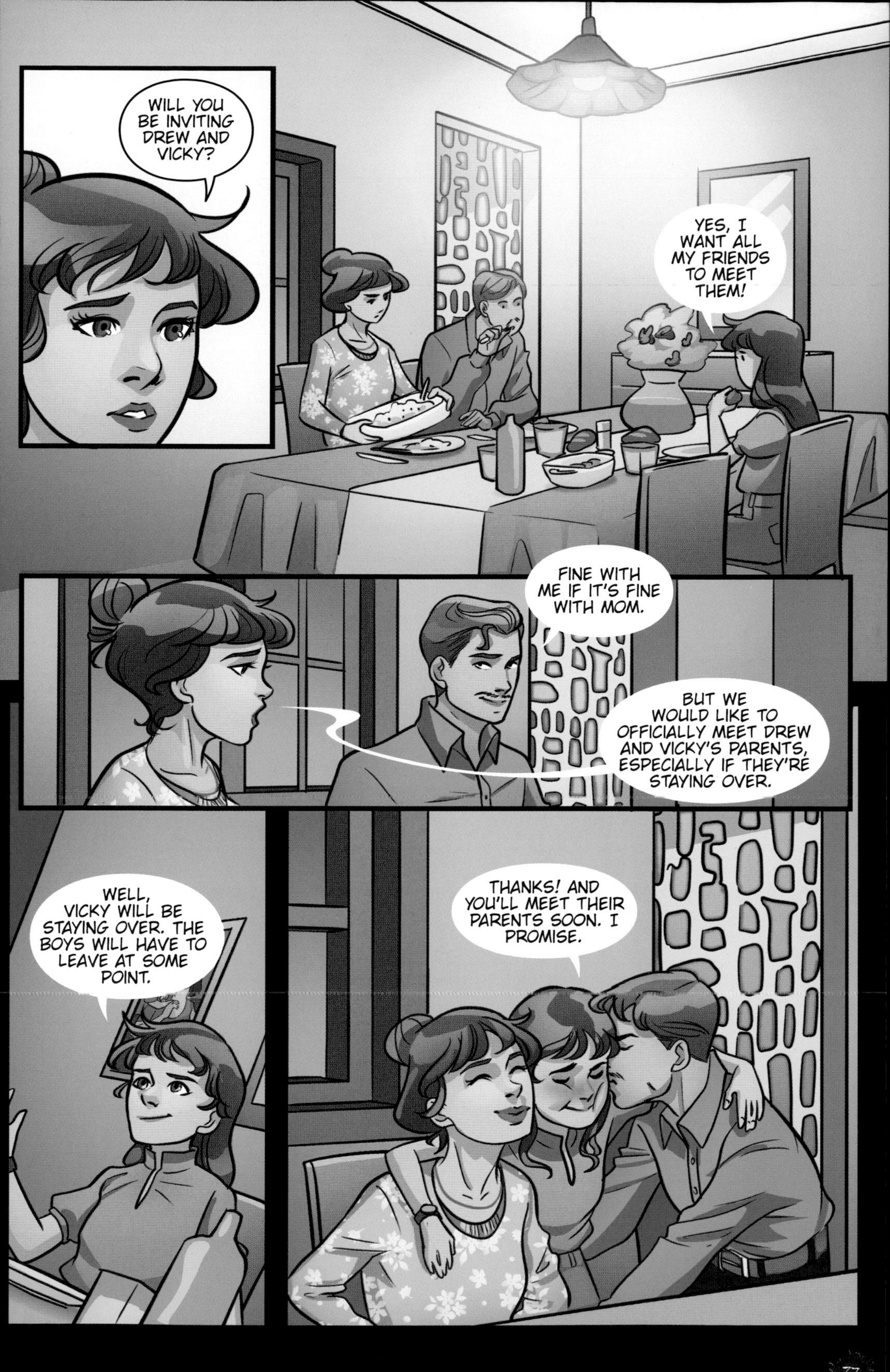
WILL YOU BE INVITING DREW AND VICKY?
YES, I WANT ALL MY FRIENDS TO MEET THEM!
FINE WITH ME IF IT'S FINE WITH MOM.
BUT WE WOULD LIKE TO OFFICIALLY MEET DREW AND VICKY'S PARENTS, ESPECIALLY IF THEY'RE STAYING OVER.
WELL, VICKY WILL BE STAYING OVER. THE BOYS WILL HAVE TO LEAVE AT SOME POINT.
THANKS! AND YOU'LL MEET THEIR PARENTS SOON. I PROMISE.

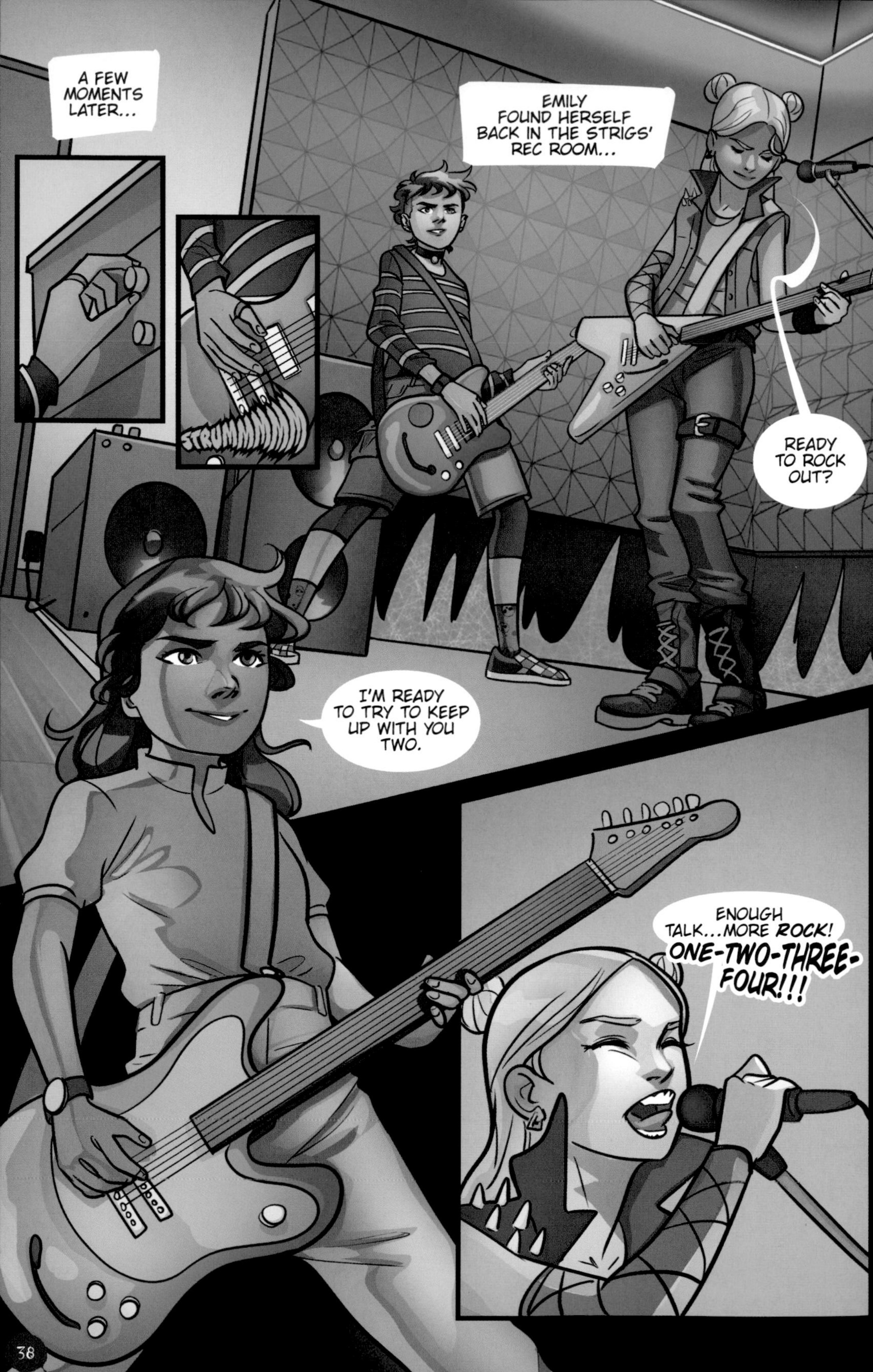
A FEW MOMENTS LATER...
EMILY FOUND HERSELF BACK IN THE STRIGS' REC ROOM...
STRUMMMMMM
READY TO ROCK OUT?
I'M READY TO TRY TO KEEP UP WITH YOU TWO.
ENOUGH TALK...MORE ROCK! ONE-TWO-THREE-FOUR!!!

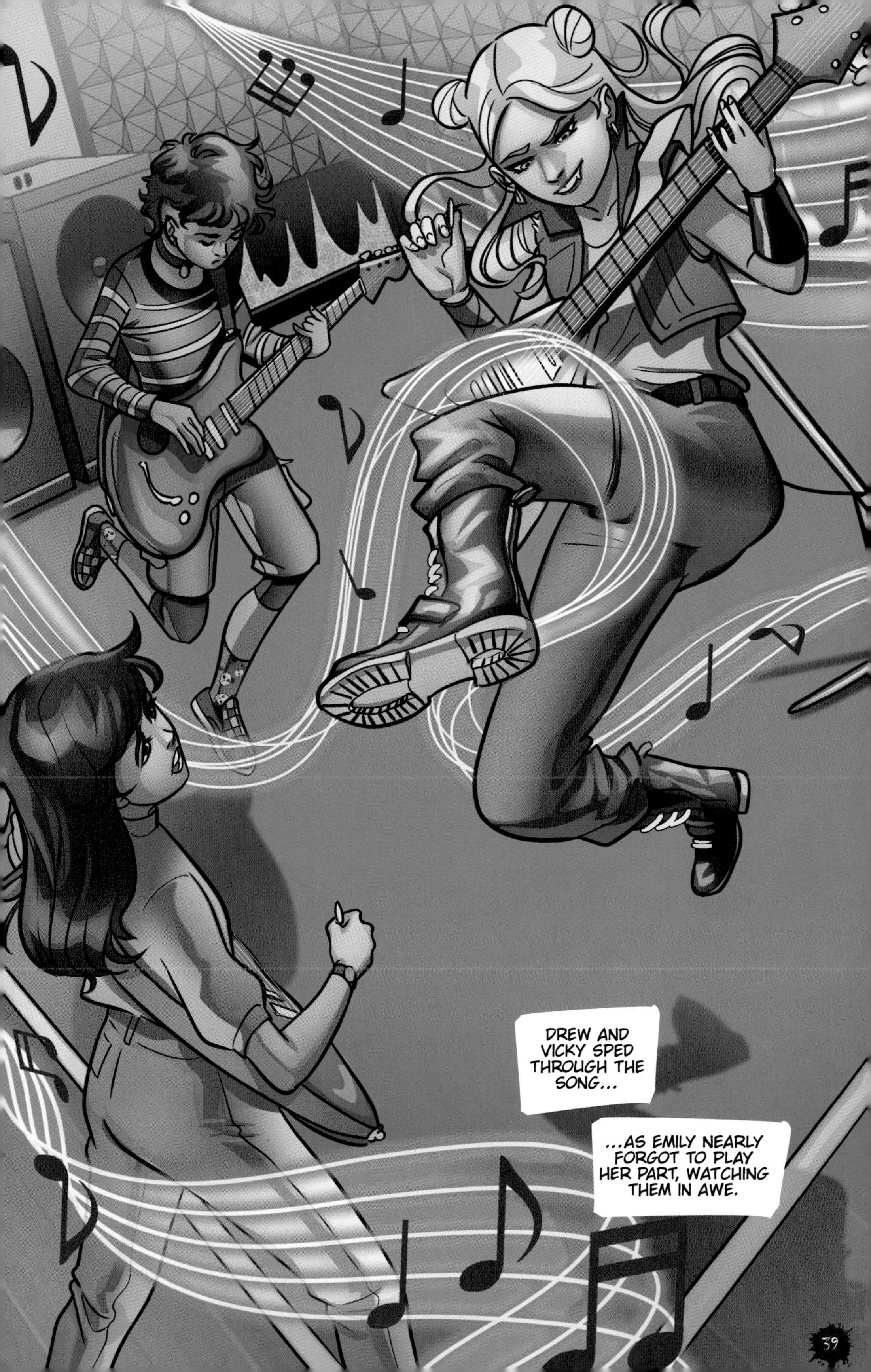
DREW AND VICKY SPED THROUGH THE SONG...
...AS EMILY NEARLY FORGOT TO PLAY HER PART, WATCHING THEM IN AWE.

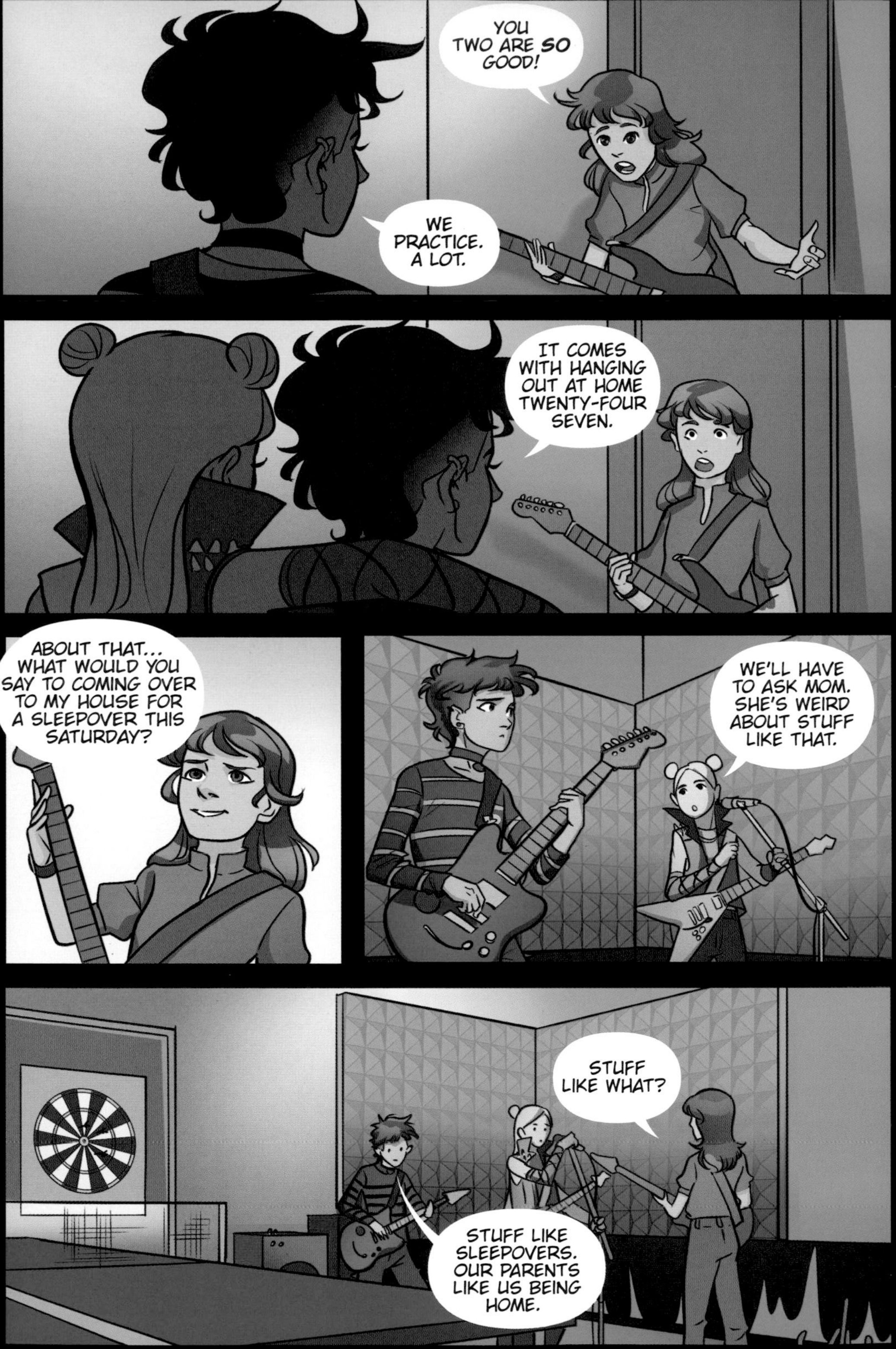
YOU TWO ARE SO GOOD!
WE PRACTICE. A LOT.
IT COMES WITH HANGING OUT AT HOME TWENTY-FOUR SEVEN.
ABOUT THAT... WHAT WOULD YOU SAY TO COMING OVER TO MY HOUSE FOR A SLEEPOVER THIS SATURDAY?
WE'LL HAVE TO ASK MOM. SHE'S WEIRD ABOUT STUFF LIKE THAT.
STUFF LIKE WHAT?
STUFF LIKE SLEEPOVERS. OUR PARENTS LIKE US BEING HOME.

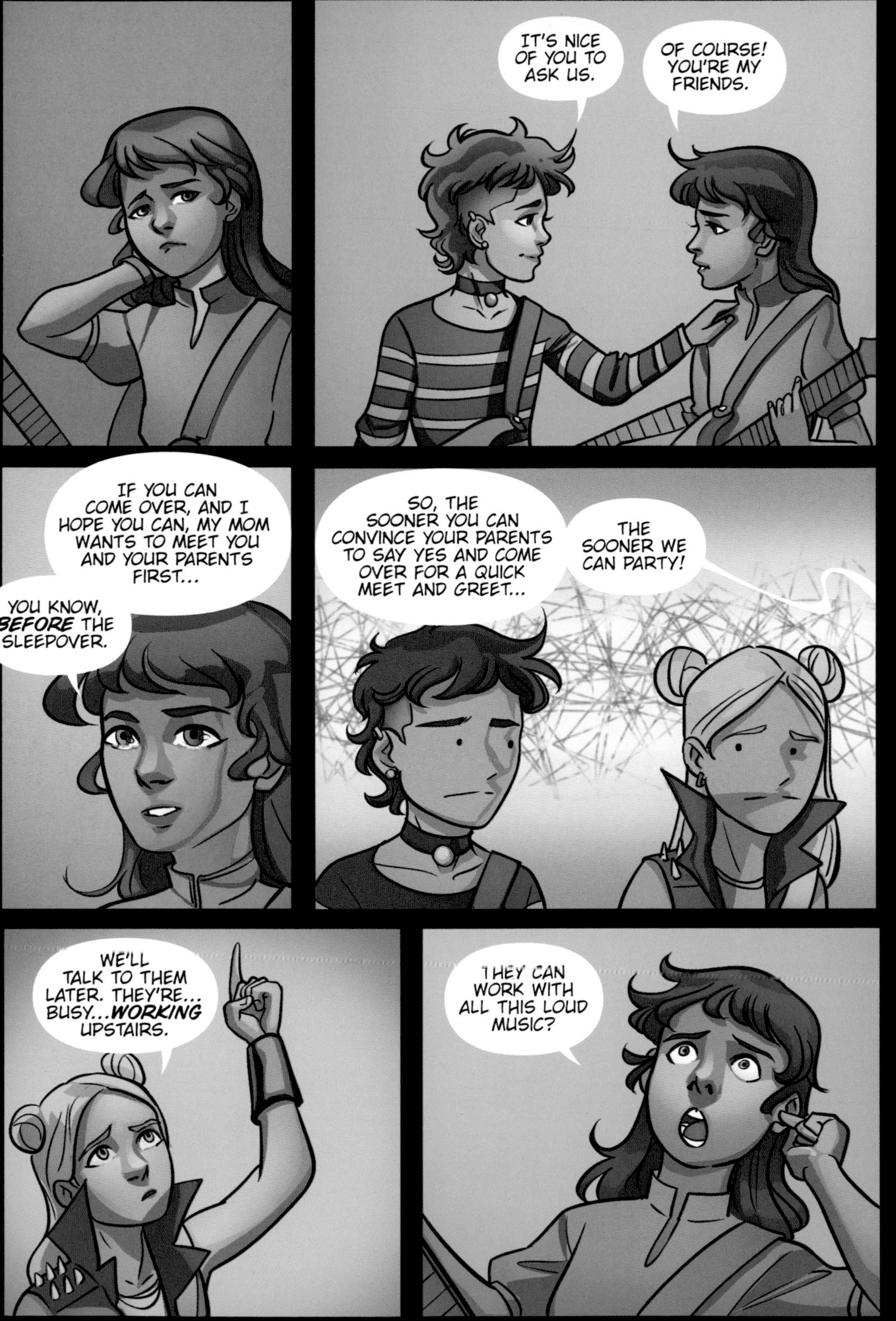
IT'S NICE OF YOU TO ASK US.
OF COURSE! YOU'RE MY FRIENDS.
IF YOU CAN COME OVER, AND I HOPE YOU CAN, MY MOM WANTS TO MEET YOU AND YOUR PARENTS FIRST...
YOU KNOW, **BEFORE** THE SLEEPOVER.
SO, THE SOONER YOU CAN CONVINCE YOUR PARENTS TO SAY YES AND COME OVER FOR A QUICK MEET AND GREET...
THE SOONER WE CAN PARTY!
WE'LL TALK TO THEM LATER. THEY'RE... BUSY...**WORKING** UPSTAIRS.
THEY CAN WORK WITH ALL THIS LOUD MUSIC?

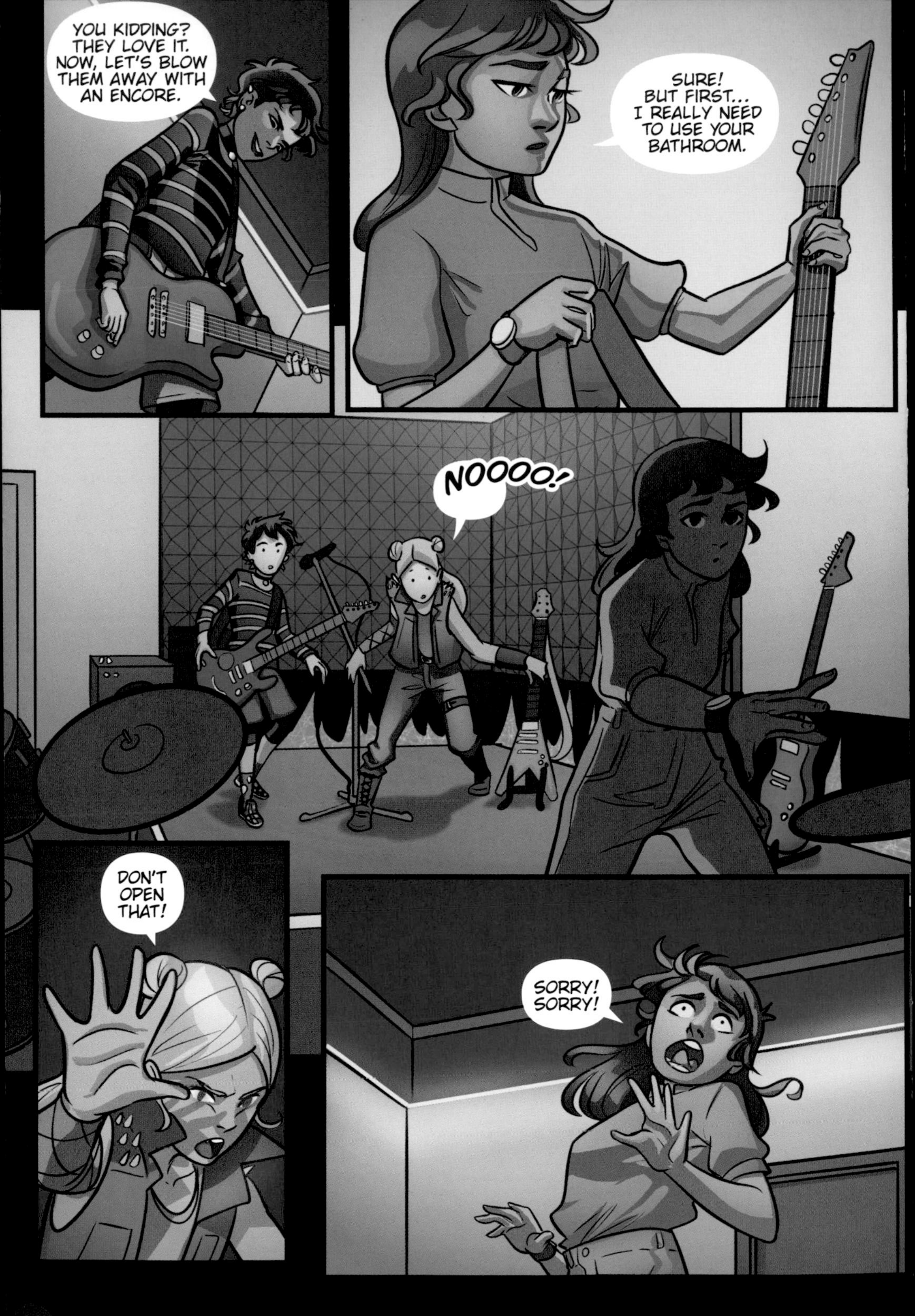
YOU KIDDING? THEY LOVE IT. NOW, LET'S BLOW THEM AWAY WITH AN ENCORE.
SURE! BUT FIRST... I REALLY NEED TO USE YOUR BATHROOM.
NOOOO!
DON'T OPEN THAT!
SORRY! SORRY!

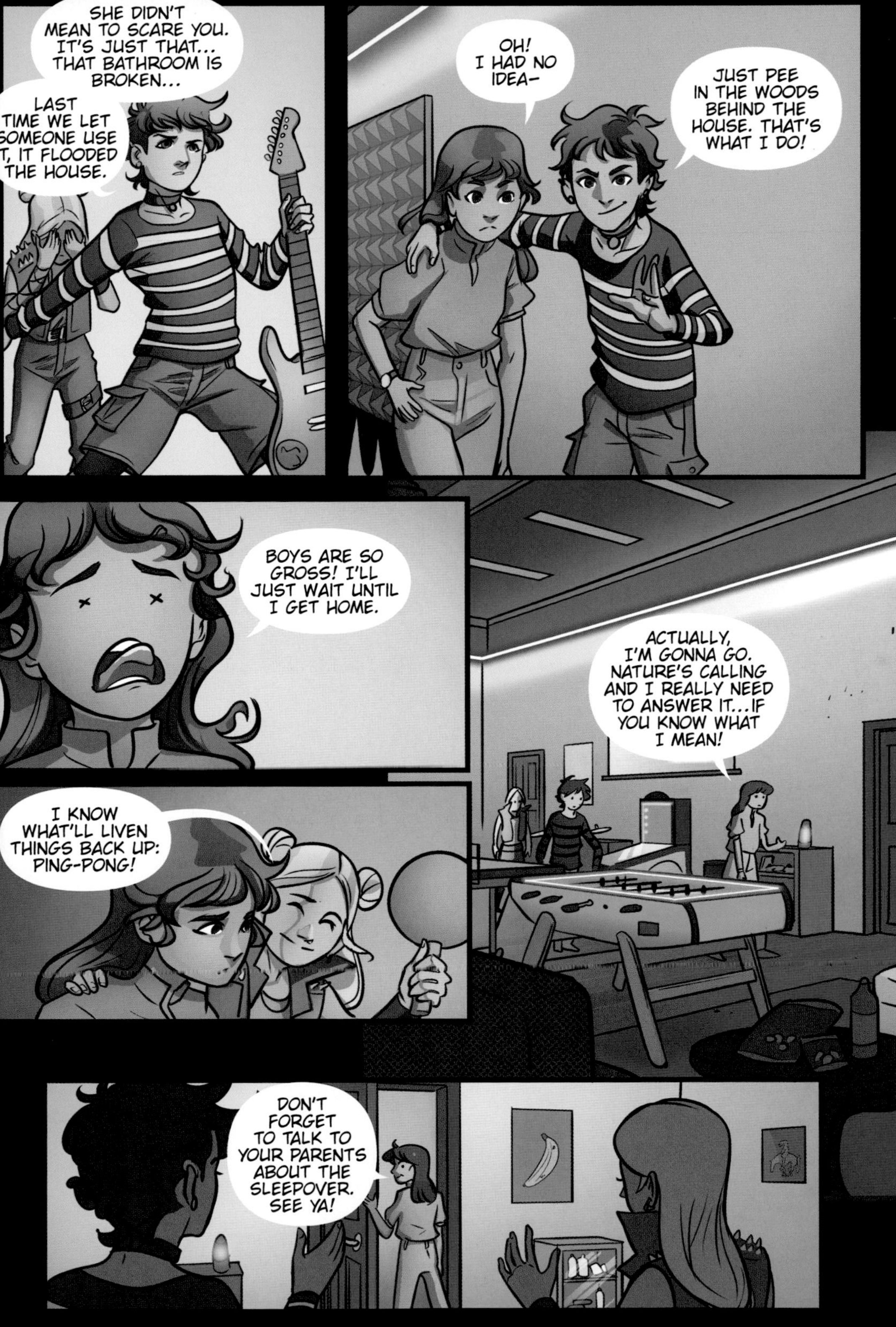
SHE DIDN'T MEAN TO SCARE YOU. IT'S JUST THAT... THAT BATHROOM IS BROKEN...
LAST TIME WE LET SOMEONE USE IT, IT FLOODED THE HOUSE.
OH! I HAD NO IDEA-
JUST PEE IN THE WOODS BEHIND THE HOUSE. THAT'S WHAT I DO!
BOYS ARE SO GROSS! I'LL JUST WAIT UNTIL I GET HOME.
I KNOW WHAT'LL LIVEN THINGS BACK UP: PING-PONG!
ACTUALLY, I'M GONNA GO. NATURE'S CALLING AND I REALLY NEED TO ANSWER IT...IF YOU KNOW WHAT I MEAN!
DON'T FORGET TO TALK TO YOUR PARENTS ABOUT THE SLEEPOVER. SEE YA!

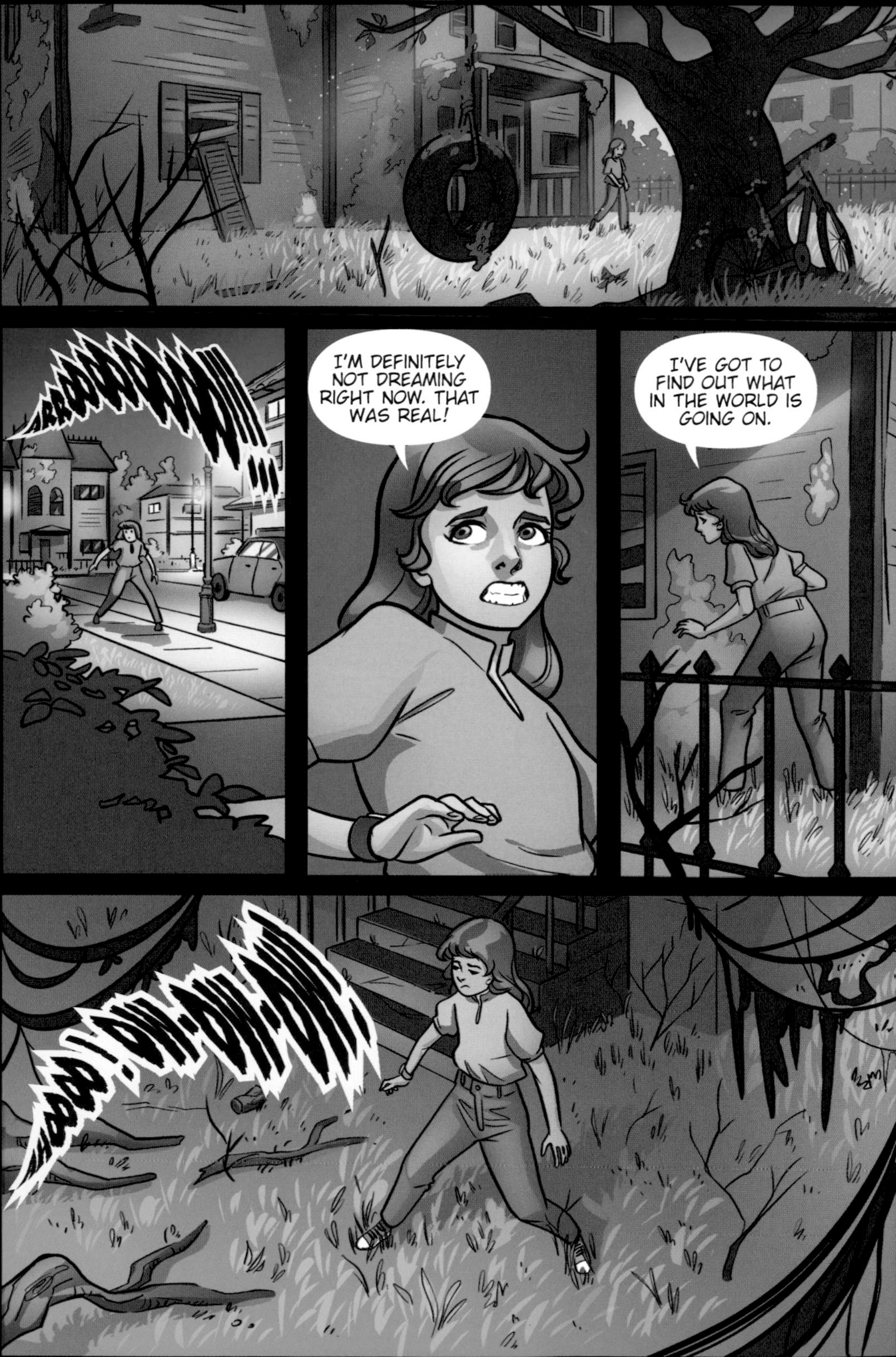
I'M DEFINITELY NOT DREAMING RIGHT NOW. THAT WAS REAL!
I'VE GOT TO FIND OUT WHAT IN THE WORLD IS GOING ON.

CHAPTER 4

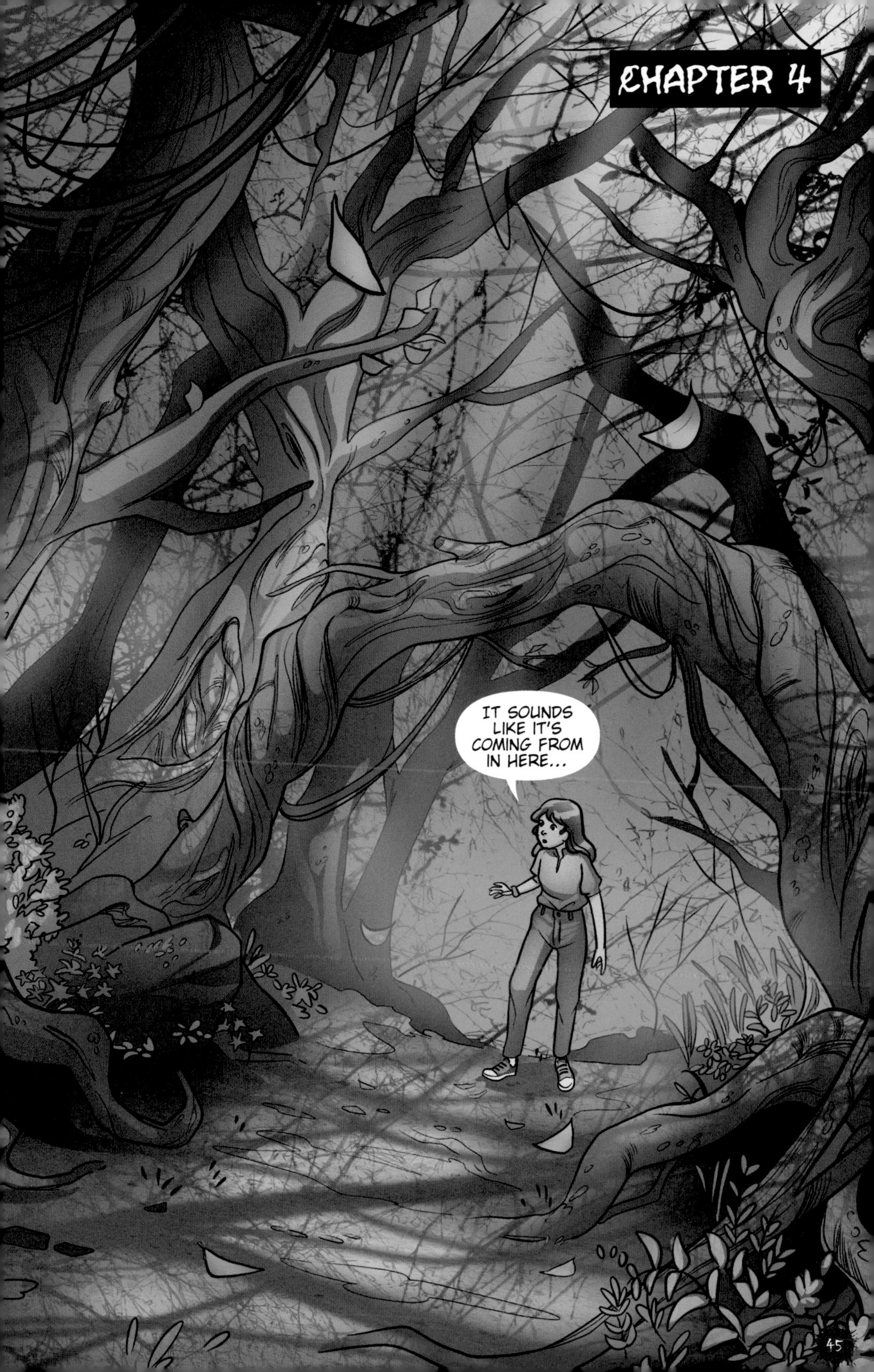
IT SOUNDS LIKE IT'S COMING FROM IN HERE...

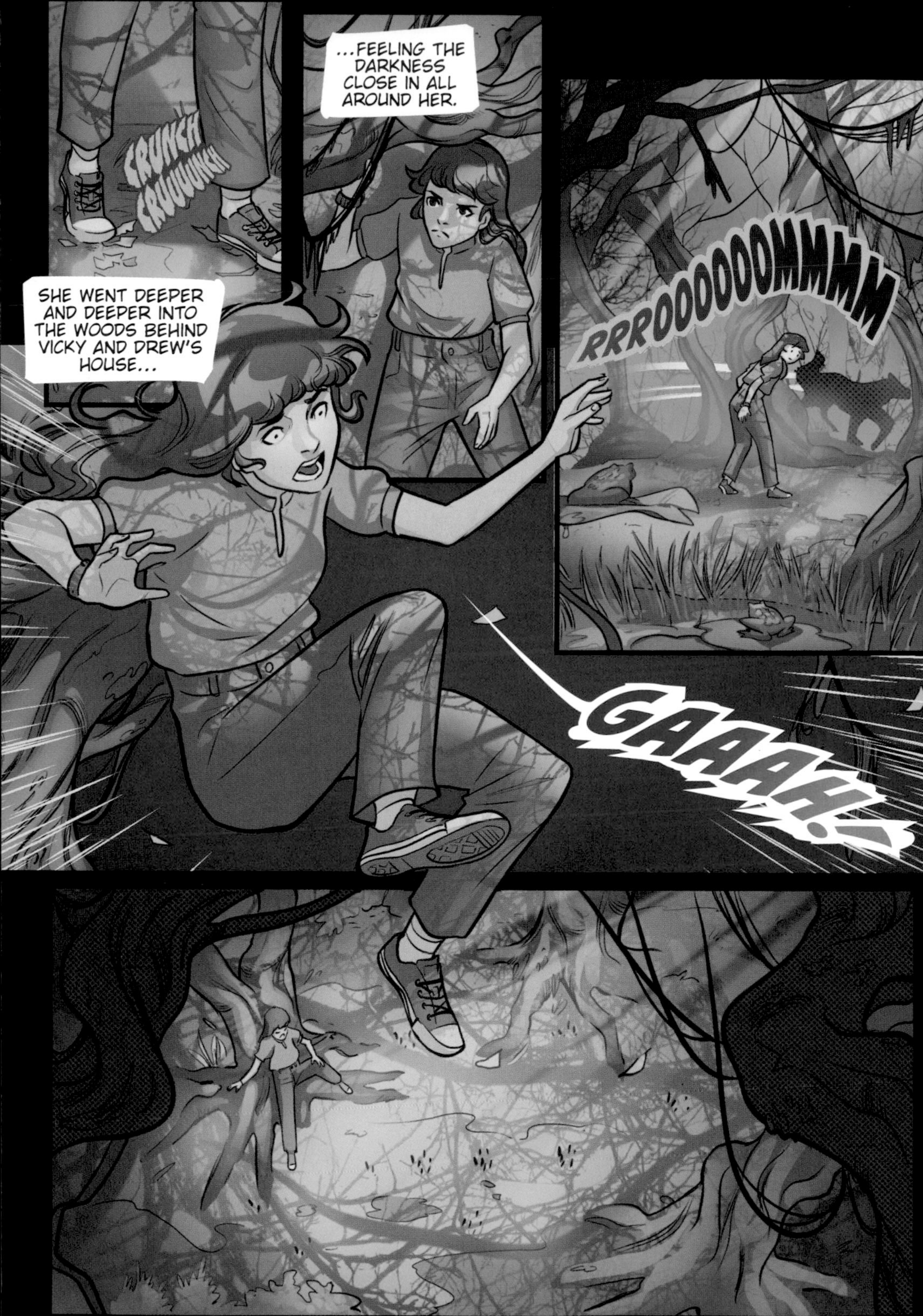
CRUNCH
CRUUUUNCH
...FEELING THE DARKNESS CLOSE IN ALL AROUND HER.
SHE WENT DEEPER AND DEEPER INTO THE WOODS BEHIND VICKY AND DREW'S HOUSE...
RRROOOOOOMMMMM
GAAAH!

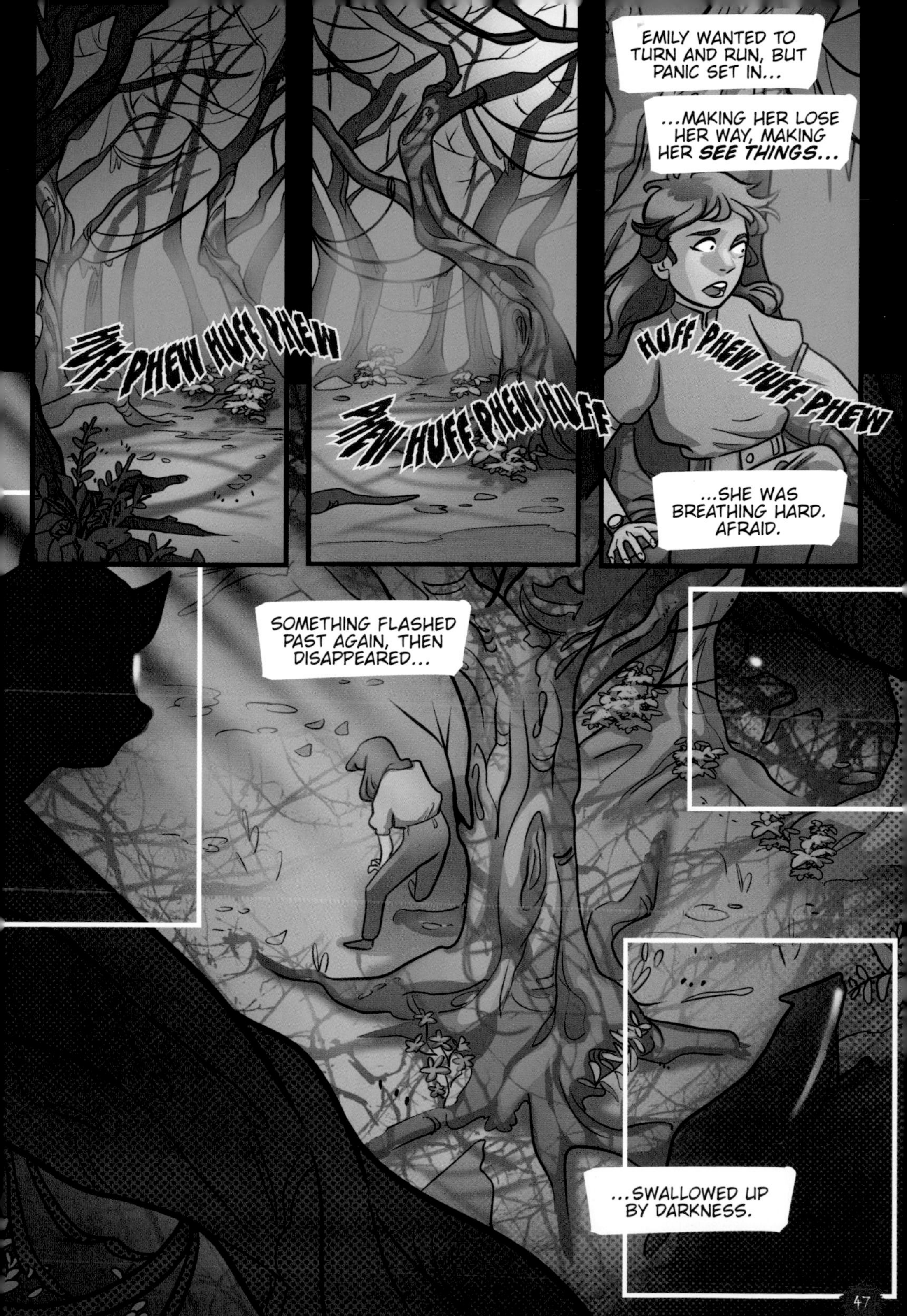
HUFF PHEW HUFF PHEW
PHEW HUFF PHEW HUFF
EMILY WANTED TO TURN AND RUN, BUT PANIC SET IN...
...MAKING HER LOSE HER WAY, MAKING HER ***SEE THINGS...***
HUFF PHEW HUFF PHEW
...SHE WAS BREATHING HARD. AFRAID.
SOMETHING FLASHED PAST AGAIN, THEN DISAPPEARED...
...SWALLOWED UP BY DARKNESS.

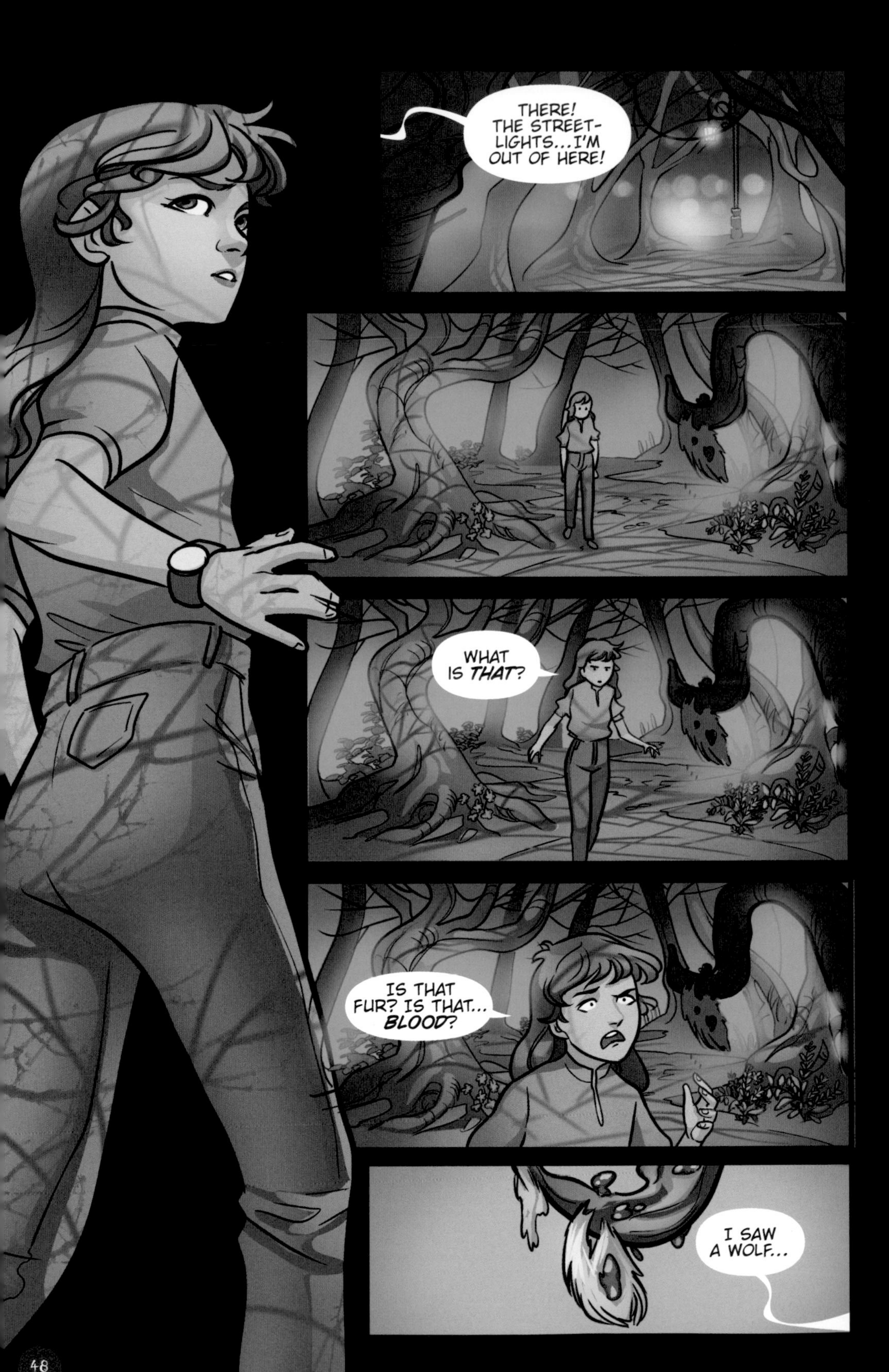
THERE! THE STREET-LIGHTS...I'M OUT OF HERE!
WHAT IS *THAT*?
IS THAT FUR? IS THAT... *BLOOD*?
I SAW A WOLF...

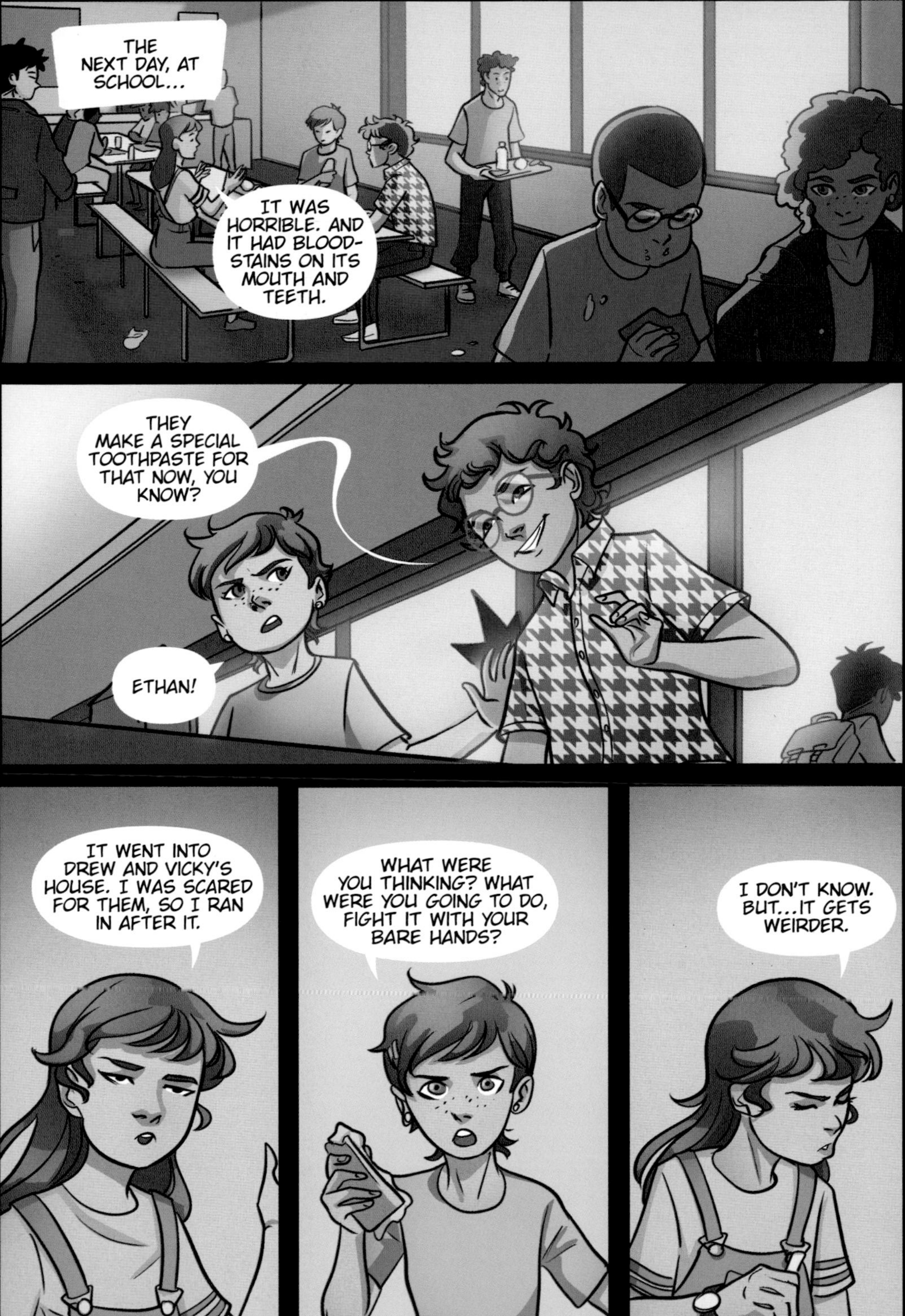
THE NEXT DAY, AT SCHOOL...
IT WAS HORRIBLE. AND IT HAD BLOOD-STAINS ON ITS MOUTH AND TEETH.
THEY MAKE A SPECIAL TOOTHPASTE FOR THAT NOW, YOU KNOW?
ETHAN!
IT WENT INTO DREW AND VICKY'S HOUSE. I WAS SCARED FOR THEM, SO I RAN IN AFTER IT.
WHAT WERE YOU THINKING? WHAT WERE YOU GOING TO DO, FIGHT IT WITH YOUR BARE HANDS?
I DON'T KNOW. BUT...IT GETS WEIRDER.

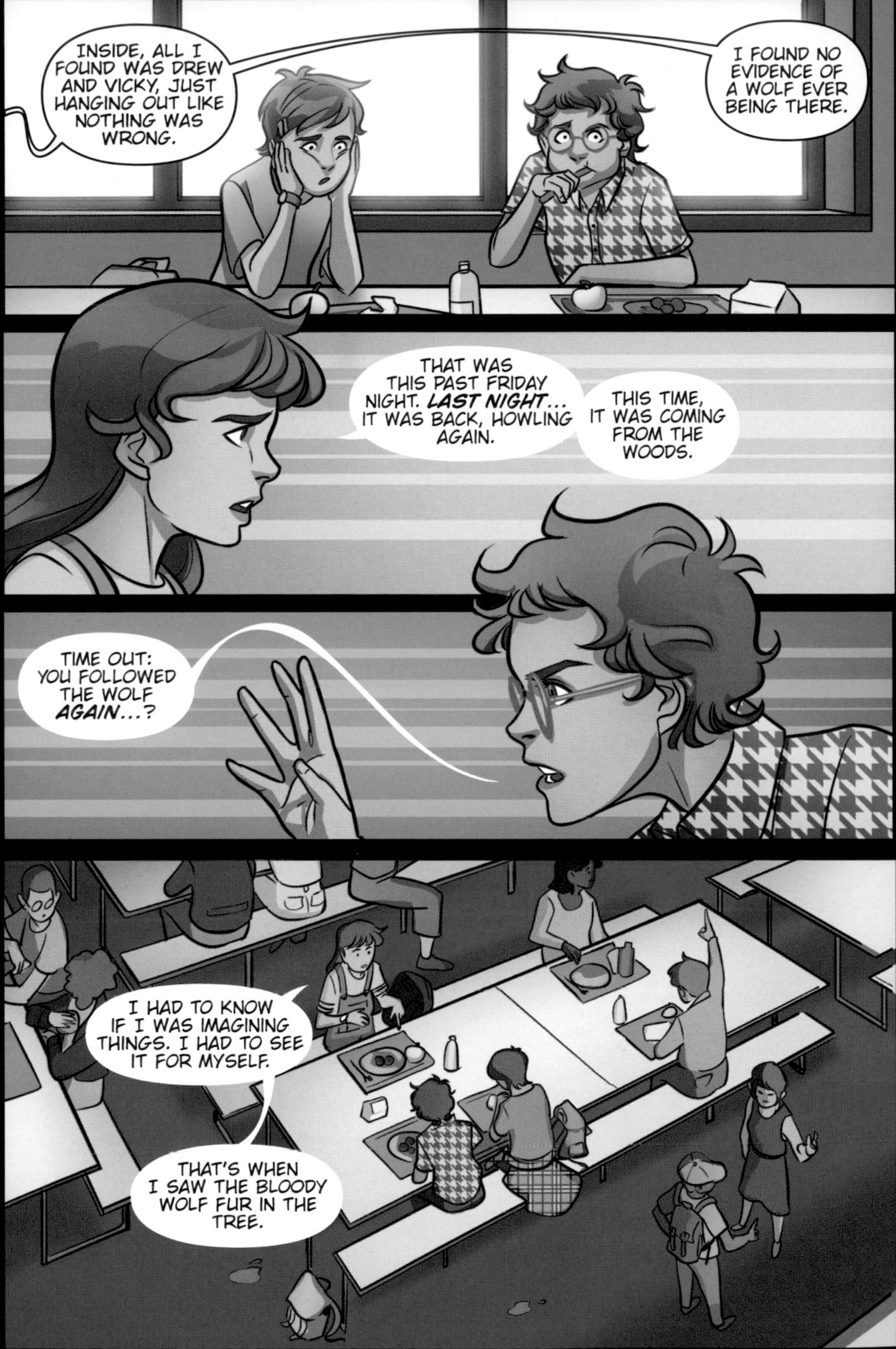
INSIDE, ALL I FOUND WAS DREW AND VICKY, JUST HANGING OUT LIKE NOTHING WAS WRONG.
I FOUND NO EVIDENCE OF A WOLF EVER BEING THERE.
THAT WAS THIS PAST FRIDAY NIGHT. *LAST NIGHT*... IT WAS BACK, HOWLING AGAIN.
THIS TIME, IT WAS COMING FROM THE WOODS.
TIME OUT: YOU FOLLOWED THE WOLF *AGAIN*...?
I HAD TO KNOW IF I WAS IMAGINING THINGS. I HAD TO SEE IT FOR MYSELF.
THAT'S WHEN I SAW THE BLOODY WOLF FUR IN THE TREE.

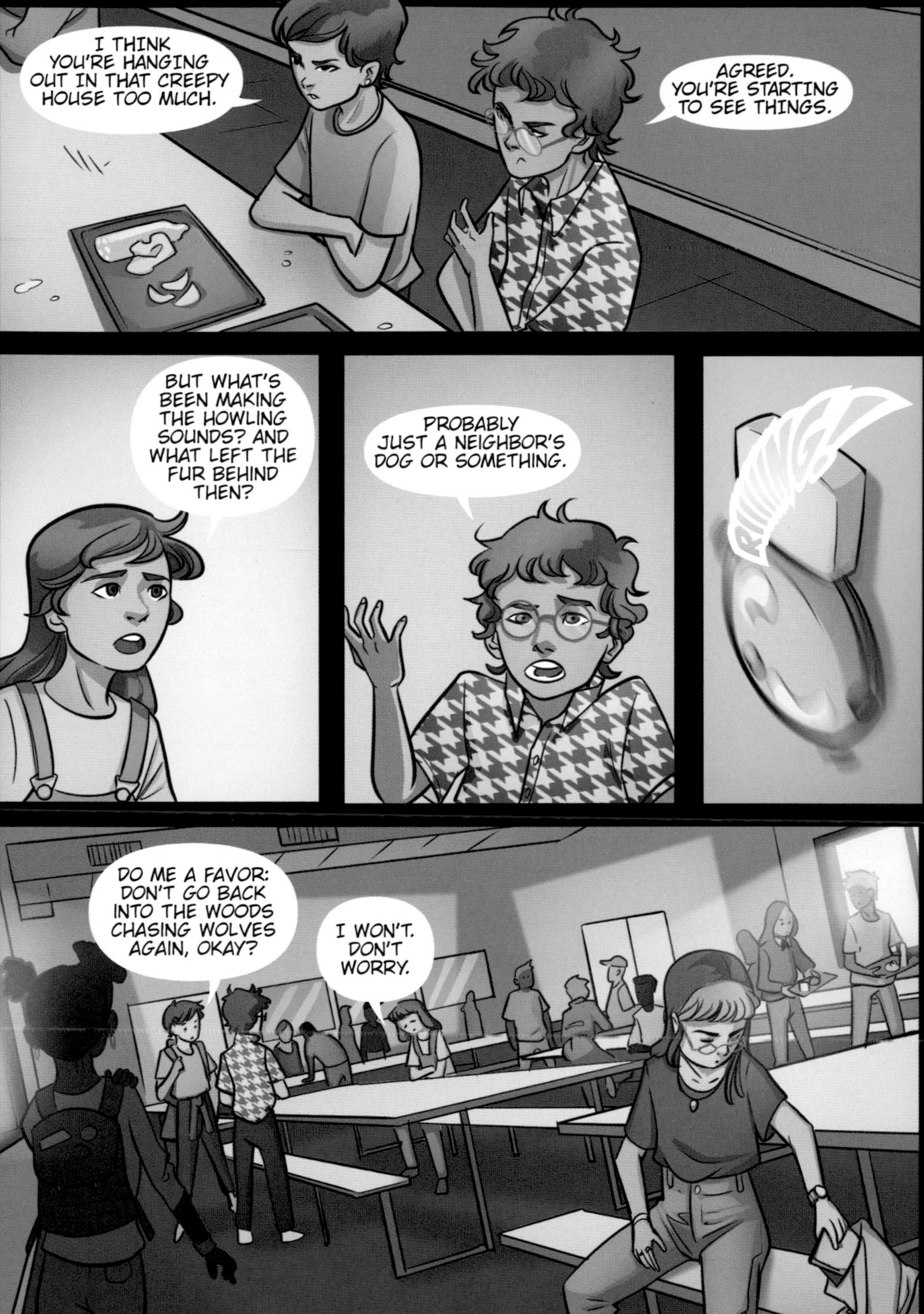

I THINK YOU'RE HANGING OUT IN THAT CREEPY HOUSE TOO MUCH.
AGREED. YOU'RE STARTING TO SEE THINGS.
BUT WHAT'S BEEN MAKING THE HOWLING SOUNDS? AND WHAT LEFT THE FUR BEHIND THEN?
PROBABLY JUST A NEIGHBOR'S DOG OR SOMETHING.
RIIIING!
DO ME A FAVOR: DON'T GO BACK INTO THE WOODS CHASING WOLVES AGAIN, OKAY?
I WON'T. DON'T WORRY.

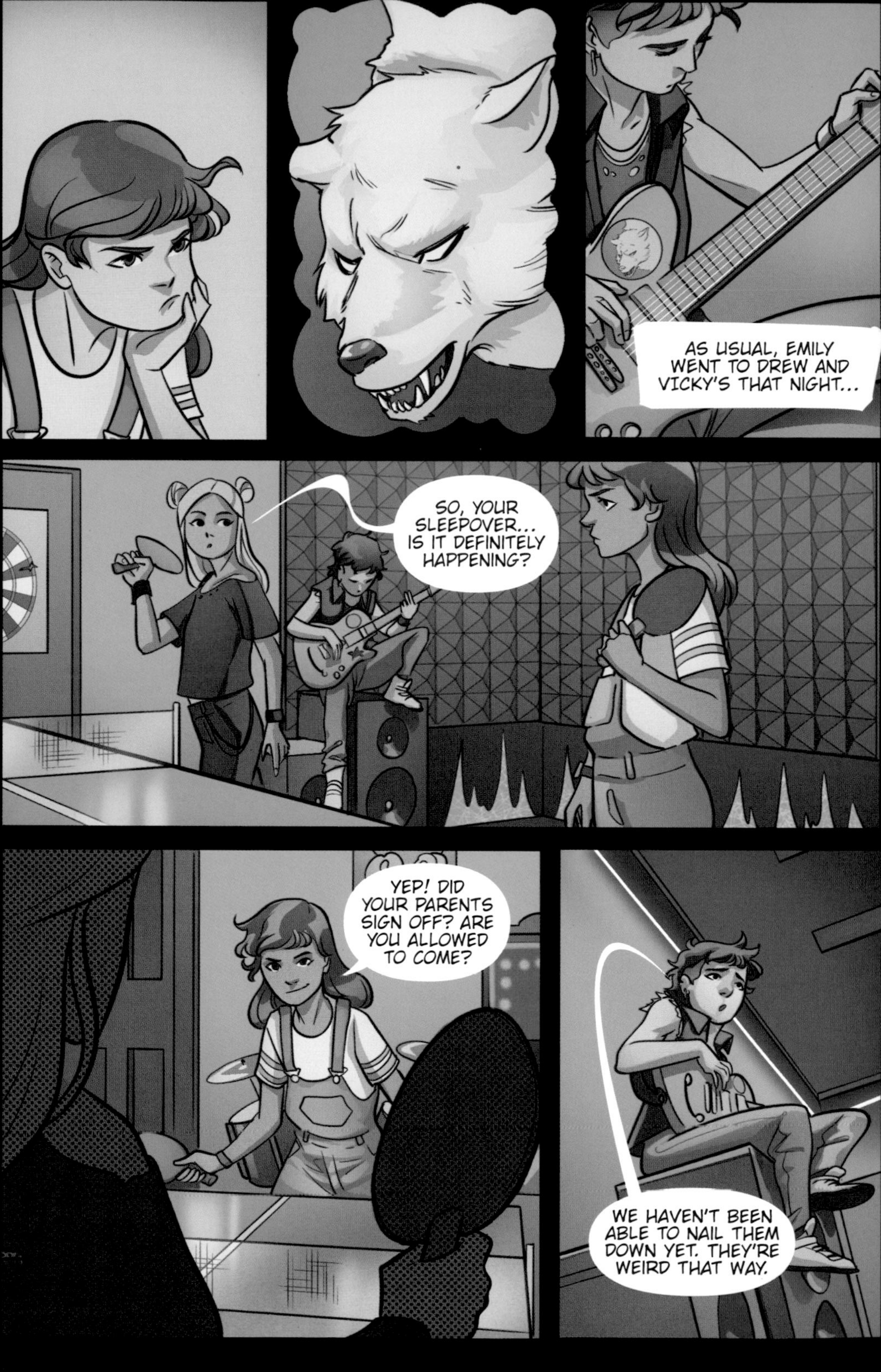
AS USUAL, EMILY WENT TO DREW AND VICKY'S THAT NIGHT...
SO, YOUR SLEEPOVER... IS IT DEFINITELY HAPPENING?
YEP! DID YOUR PARENTS SIGN OFF? ARE YOU ALLOWED TO COME?
WE HAVEN'T BEEN ABLE TO NAIL THEM DOWN YET. THEY'RE WEIRD THAT WAY.

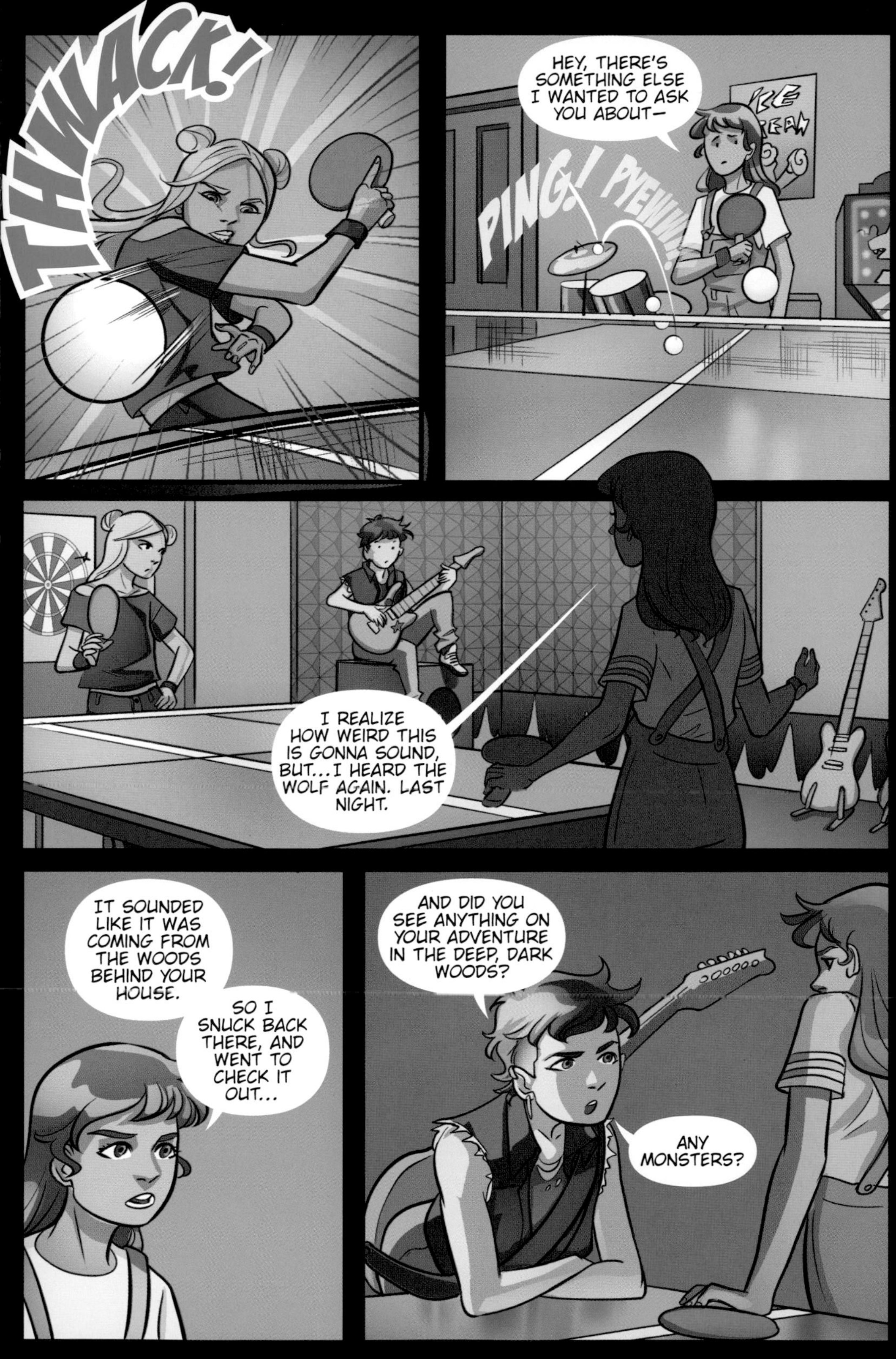
THWACK!
HEY, THERE'S SOMETHING ELSE I WANTED TO ASK YOU ABOUT—
PING!
PYEWWW
I REALIZE HOW WEIRD THIS IS GONNA SOUND, BUT... I HEARD THE WOLF AGAIN. LAST NIGHT.
IT SOUNDED LIKE IT WAS COMING FROM THE WOODS BEHIND YOUR HOUSE.
SO I SNUCK BACK THERE, AND WENT TO CHECK IT OUT...
AND DID YOU SEE ANYTHING ON YOUR ADVENTURE IN THE DEEP, DARK WOODS?
ANY MONSTERS?

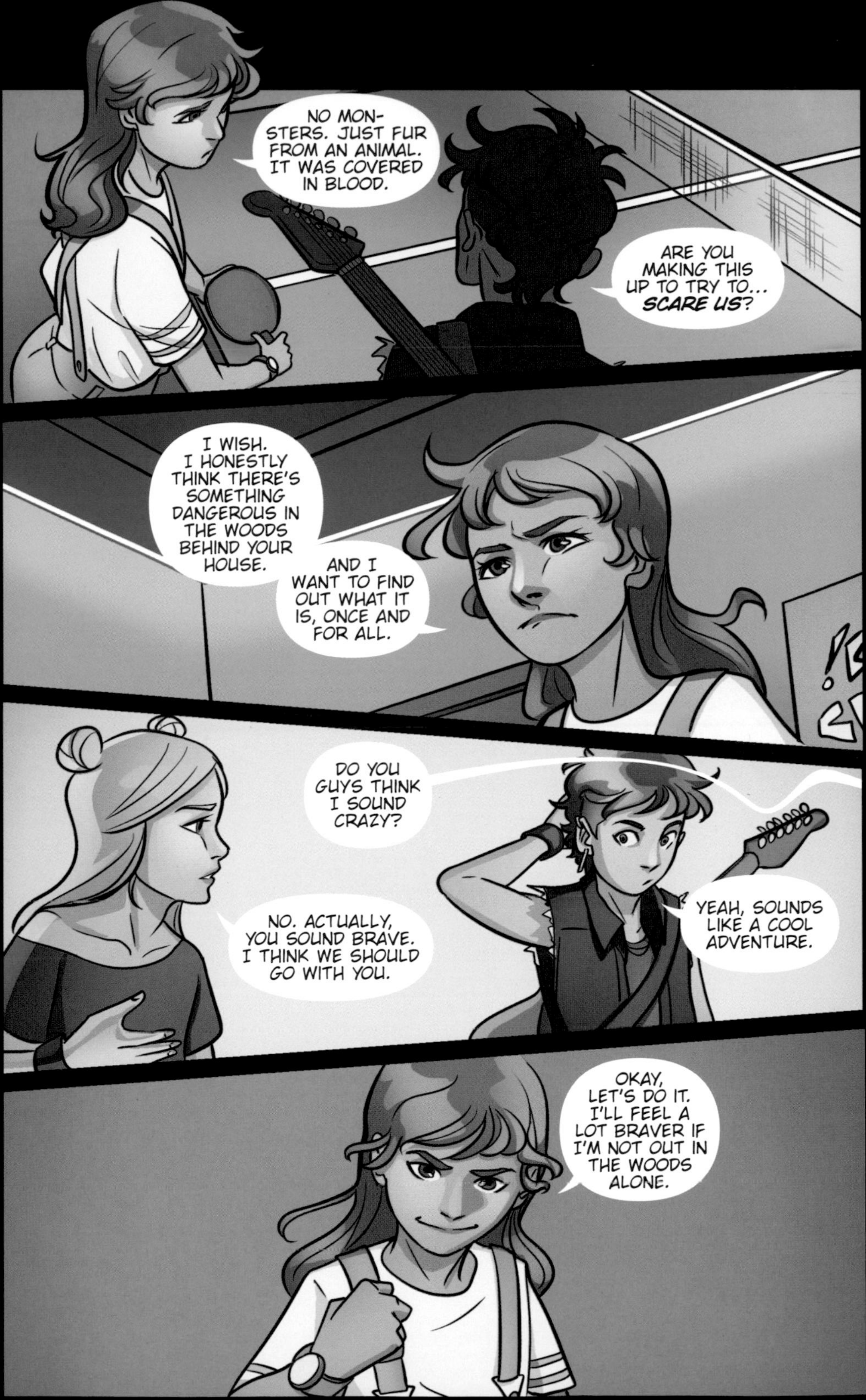
NO MONSTERS. JUST FUR FROM AN ANIMAL. IT WAS COVERED IN BLOOD.
ARE YOU MAKING THIS UP TO TRY TO... **SCARE US**?
I WISH. I HONESTLY THINK THERE'S SOMETHING DANGEROUS IN THE WOODS BEHIND YOUR HOUSE.
AND I WANT TO FIND OUT WHAT IT IS, ONCE AND FOR ALL.
DO YOU GUYS THINK I SOUND CRAZY?
NO. ACTUALLY, YOU SOUND BRAVE. I THINK WE SHOULD GO WITH YOU.
YEAH, SOUNDS LIKE A COOL ADVENTURE.
OKAY, LET'S DO IT. I'LL FEEL A LOT BRAVER IF I'M NOT OUT IN THE WOODS ALONE.

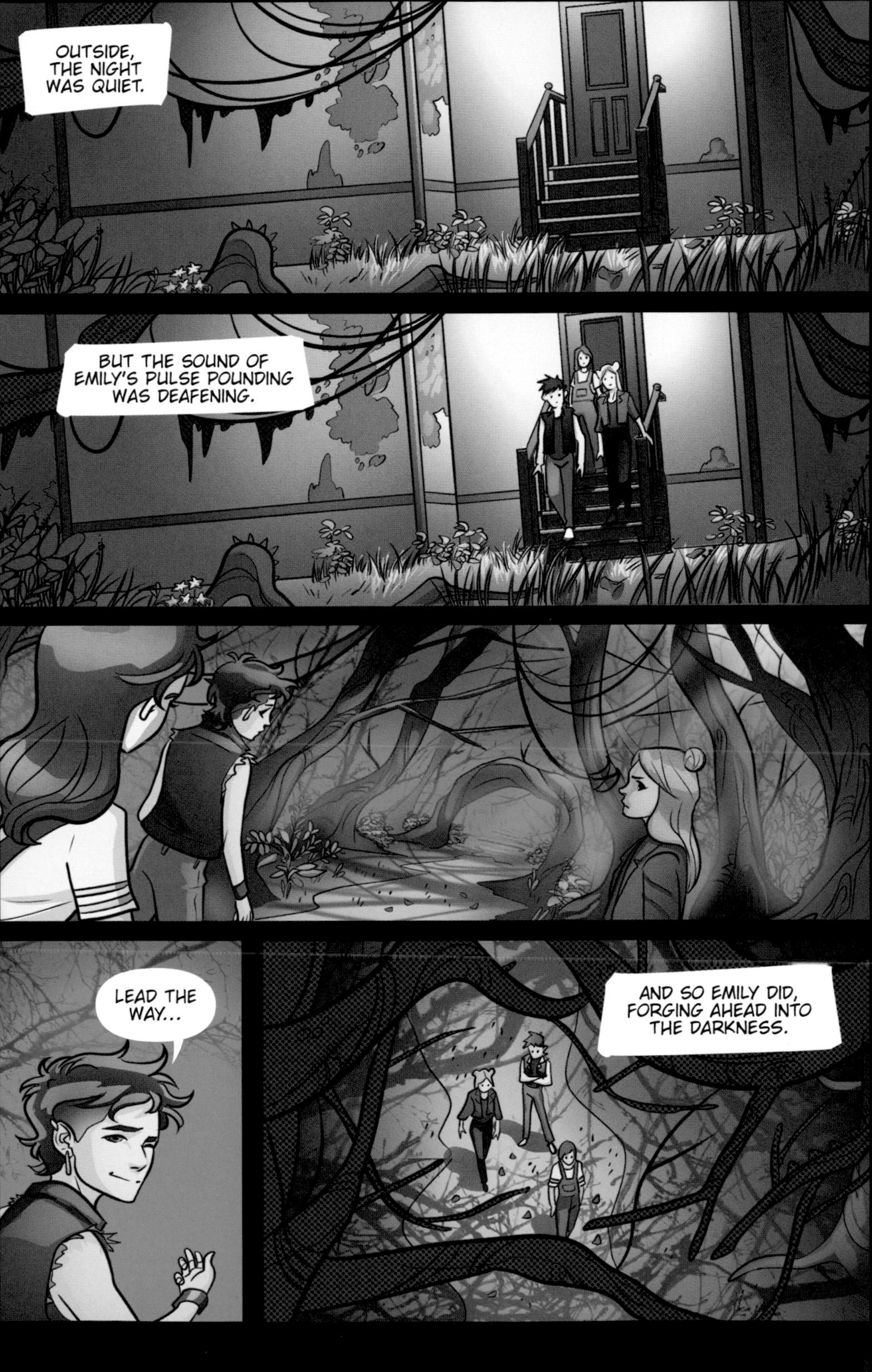
OUTSIDE, THE NIGHT WAS QUIET.
BUT THE SOUND OF EMILY'S PULSE POUNDING WAS DEAFENING.
LEAD THE WAY...
AND SO EMILY DID, FORGING AHEAD INTO THE DARKNESS.

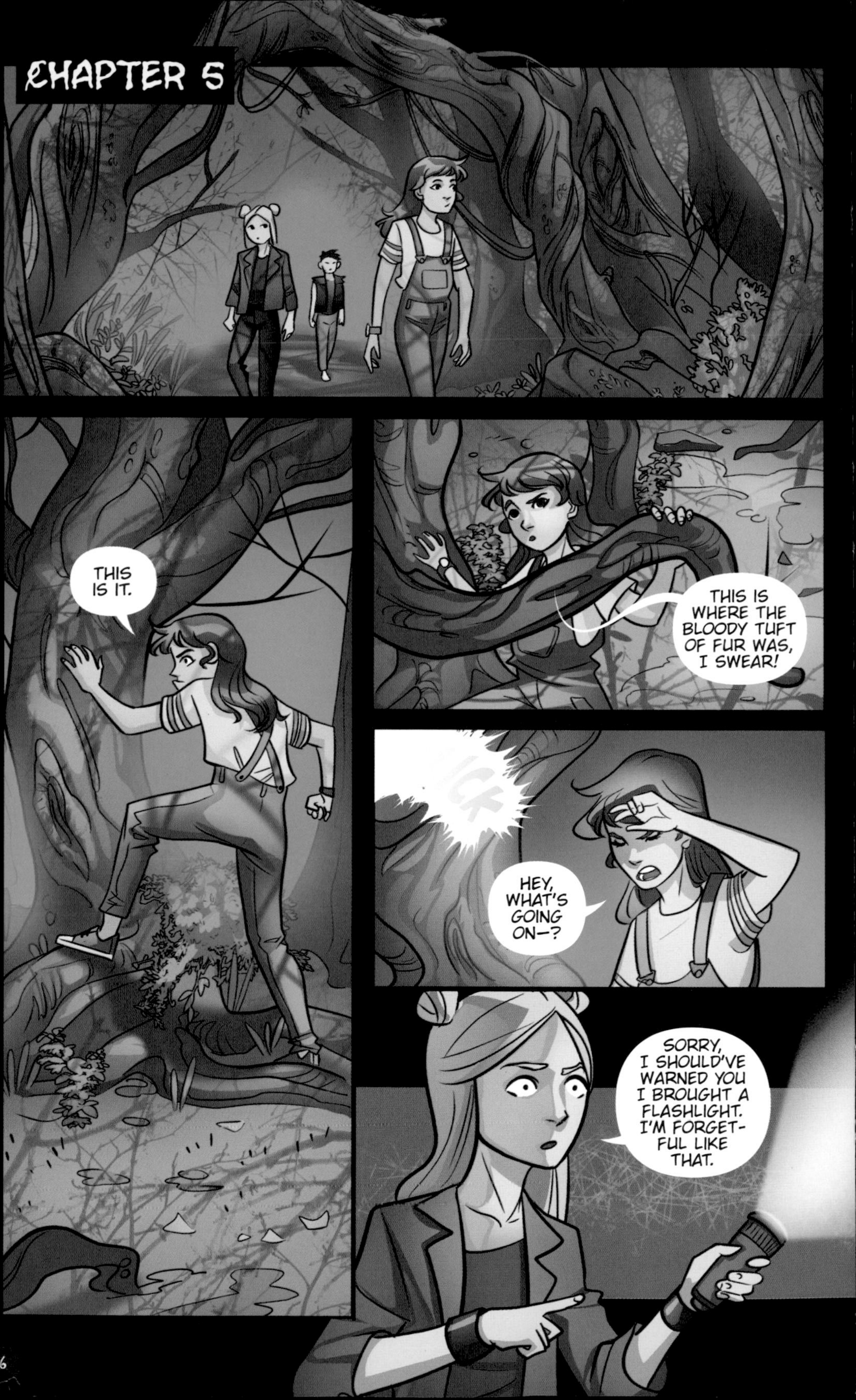

CHAPTER 5
THIS IS IT.
THIS IS WHERE THE BLOODY TUFT OF FUR WAS, I SWEAR!
HEY, WHAT'S GOING ON—?
SORRY, I SHOULD'VE WARNED YOU I BROUGHT A FLASHLIGHT. I'M FORGET-FUL LIKE THAT.

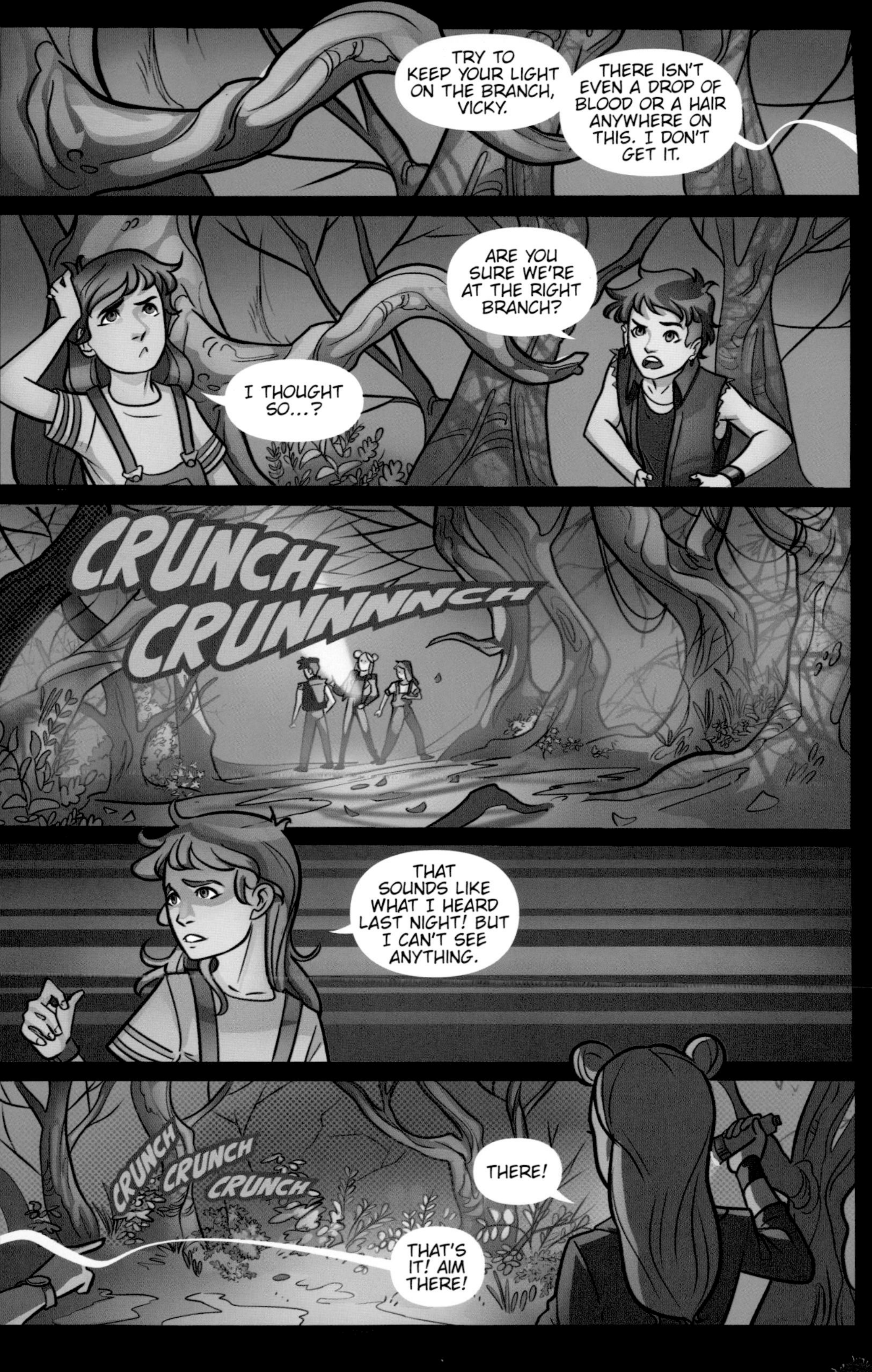
TRY TO KEEP YOUR LIGHT ON THE BRANCH, VICKY.
THERE ISN'T EVEN A DROP OF BLOOD OR A HAIR ANYWHERE ON THIS. I DON'T GET IT.
ARE YOU SURE WE'RE AT THE RIGHT BRANCH?
I THOUGHT SO...?
CRUNCH
CRUNNNNNCH
THAT SOUNDS LIKE WHAT I HEARD LAST NIGHT! BUT I CAN'T SEE ANYTHING.
CRUNCH
CRUNCH
CRUNCH
THERE!
THAT'S IT! AIM THERE!

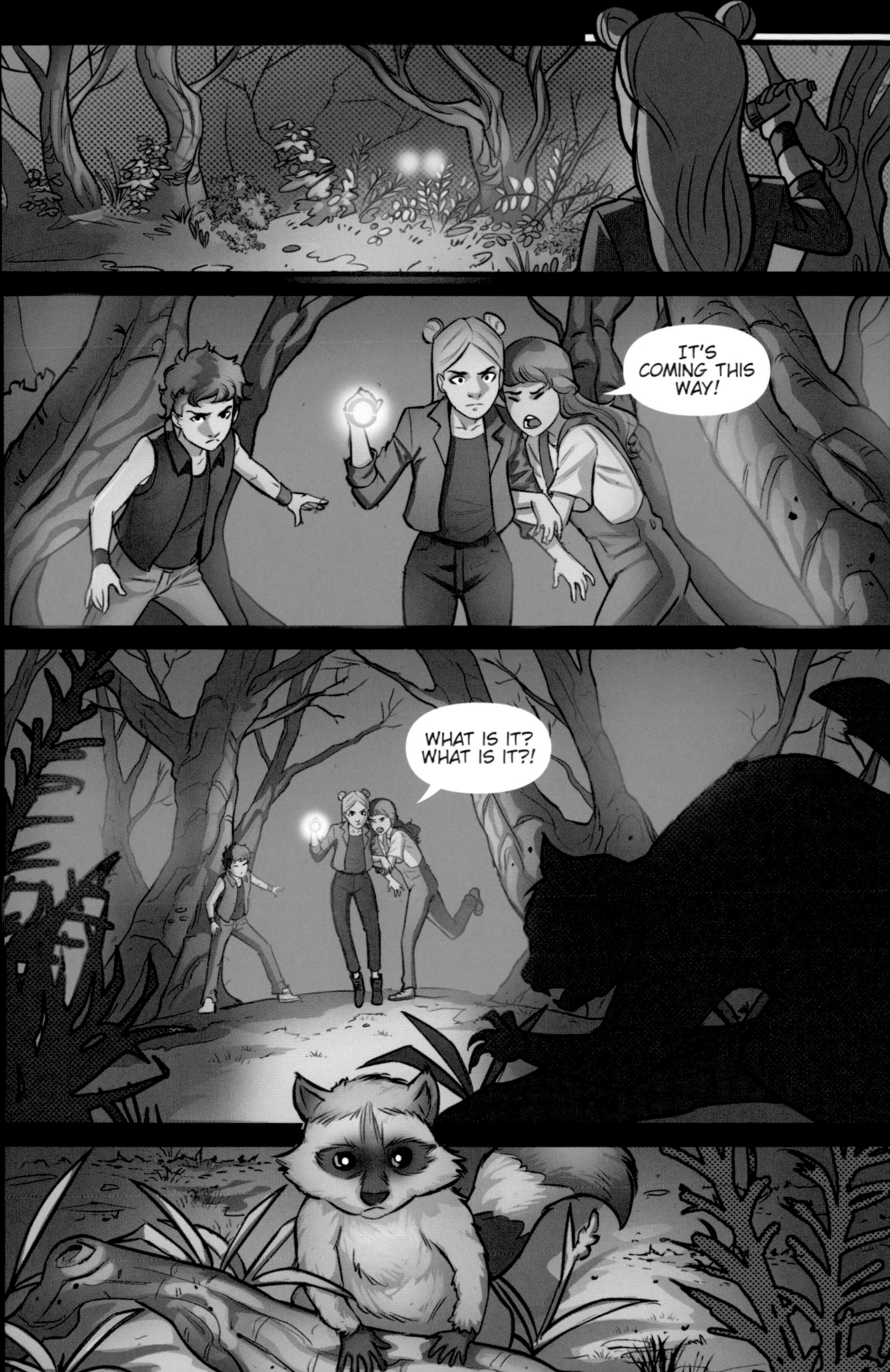
IT'S COMING THIS WAY!
WHAT IS IT? WHAT IS IT?!

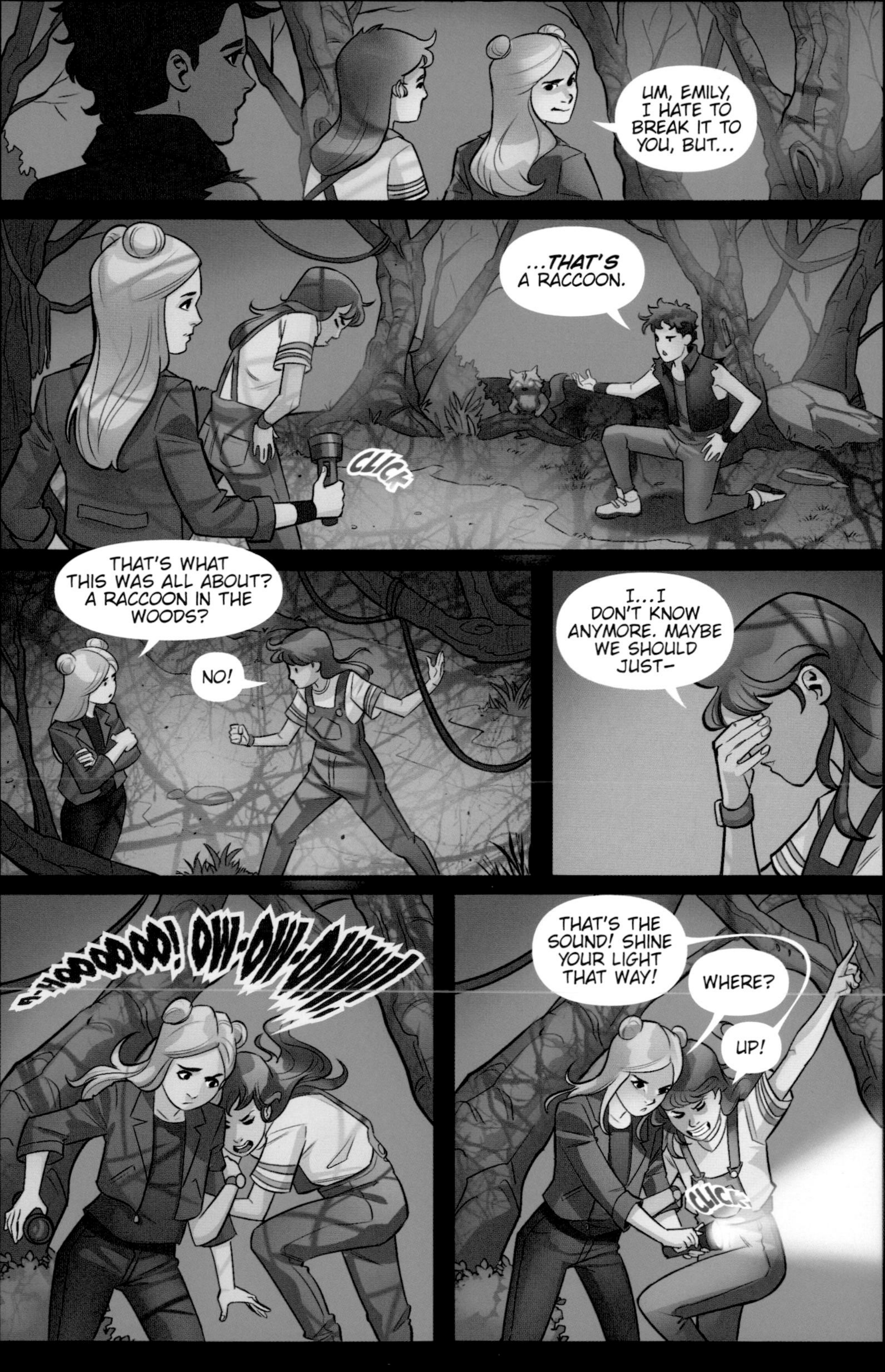
UM, EMILY, I HATE TO BREAK IT TO YOU, BUT...
...THAT'S A RACCOON.
CLICK
THAT'S WHAT THIS WAS ALL ABOUT? A RACCOON IN THE WOODS?
NO!
I...I DON'T KNOW ANYMORE. MAYBE WE SHOULD JUST-
A-HOOOOOO! OW-OW-OWWW!
THAT'S THE SOUND! SHINE YOUR LIGHT THAT WAY!
WHERE?
UP!
CLICK

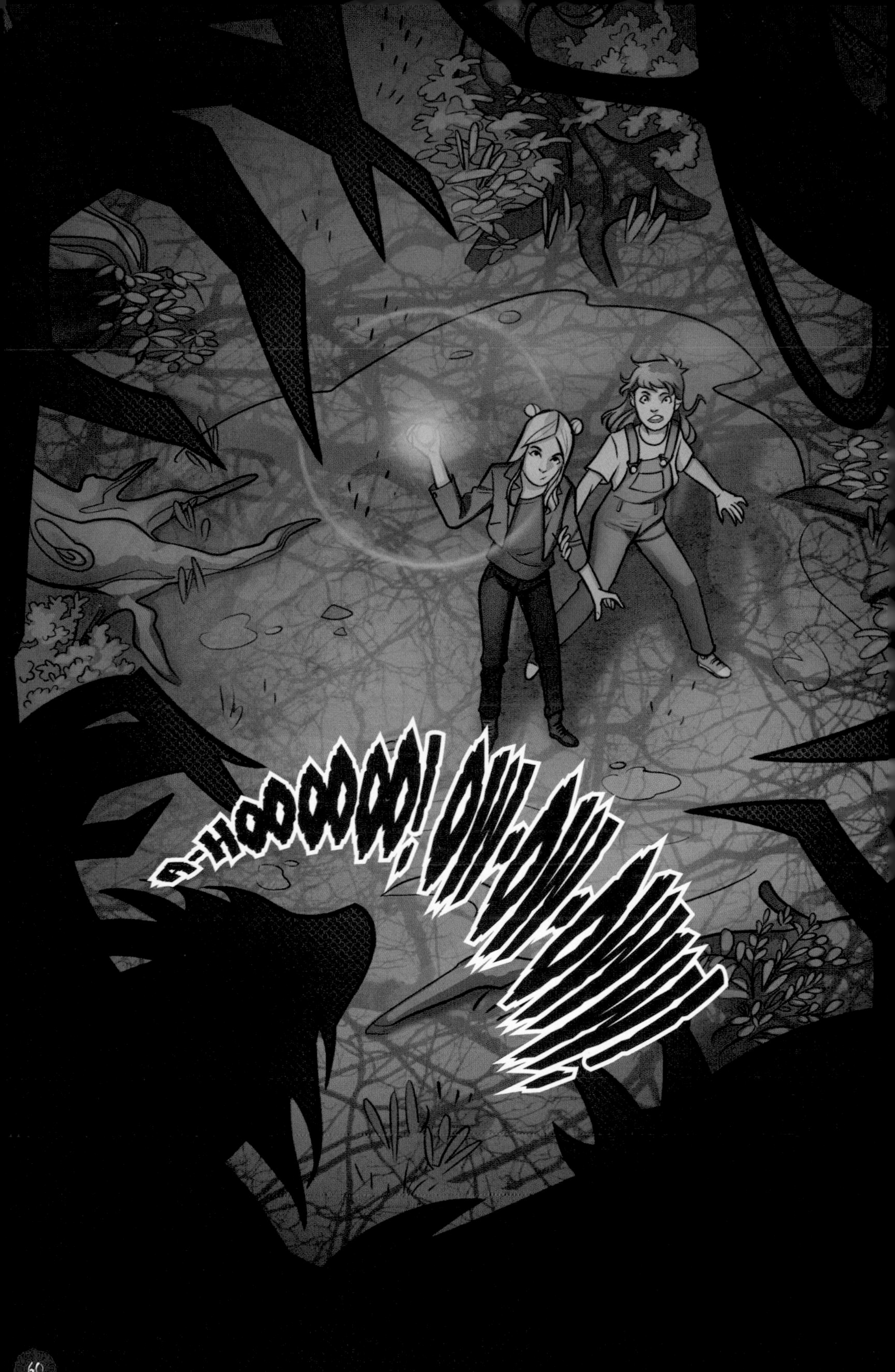
A-HOOOOOO! OW-OW-OW-OWWWW!

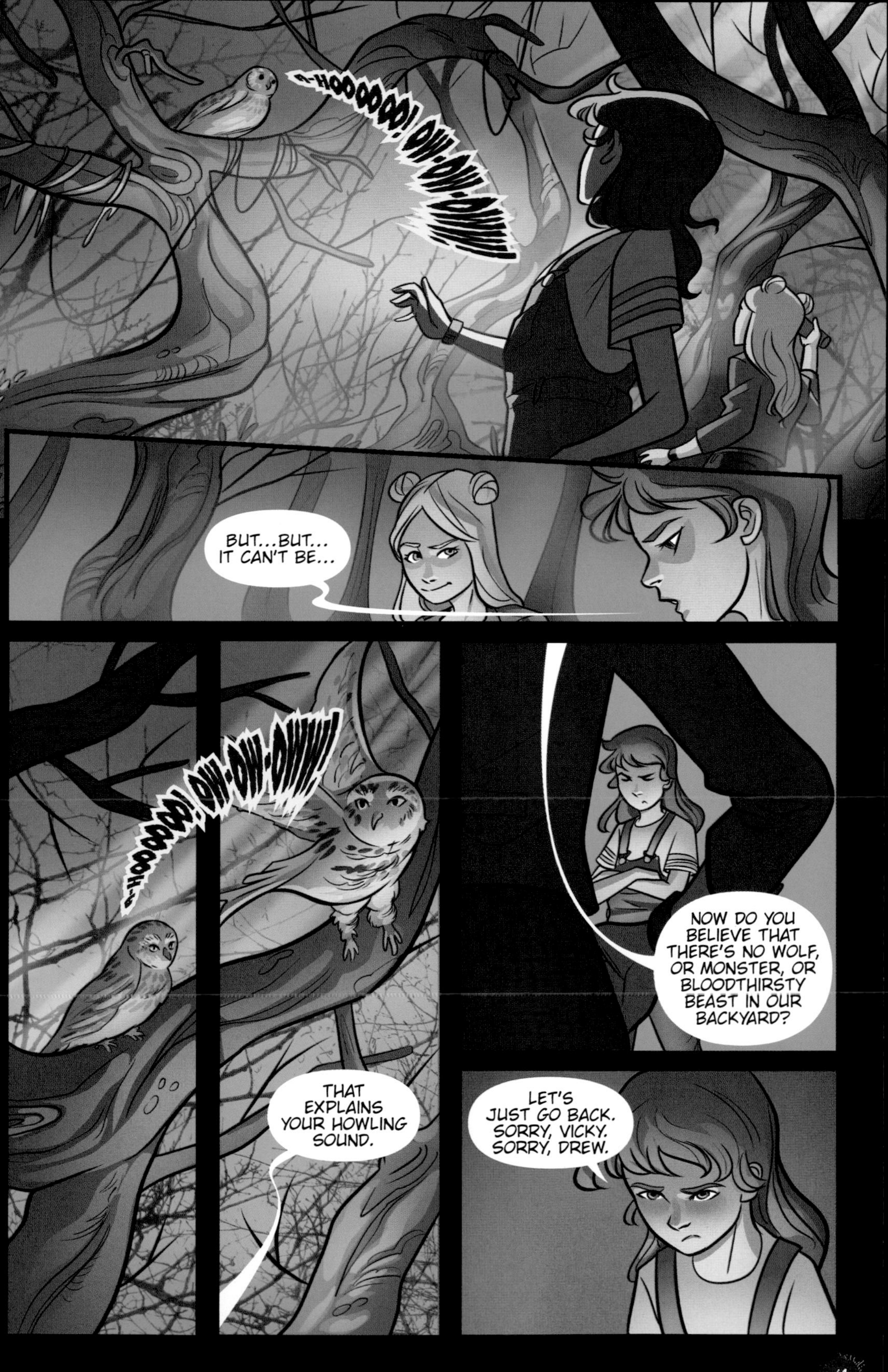

H-OOOOOO! OW-OW-OWW!
BUT...BUT...
IT CAN'T BE...
H-OOOOOO! OW-OW-OWW!
NOW DO YOU BELIEVE THAT THERE'S NO WOLF, OR MONSTER, OR BLOODTHIRSTY BEAST IN OUR BACKYARD?
THAT EXPLAINS YOUR HOWLING SOUND.
LET'S JUST GO BACK. SORRY, VICKY. SORRY, DREW.

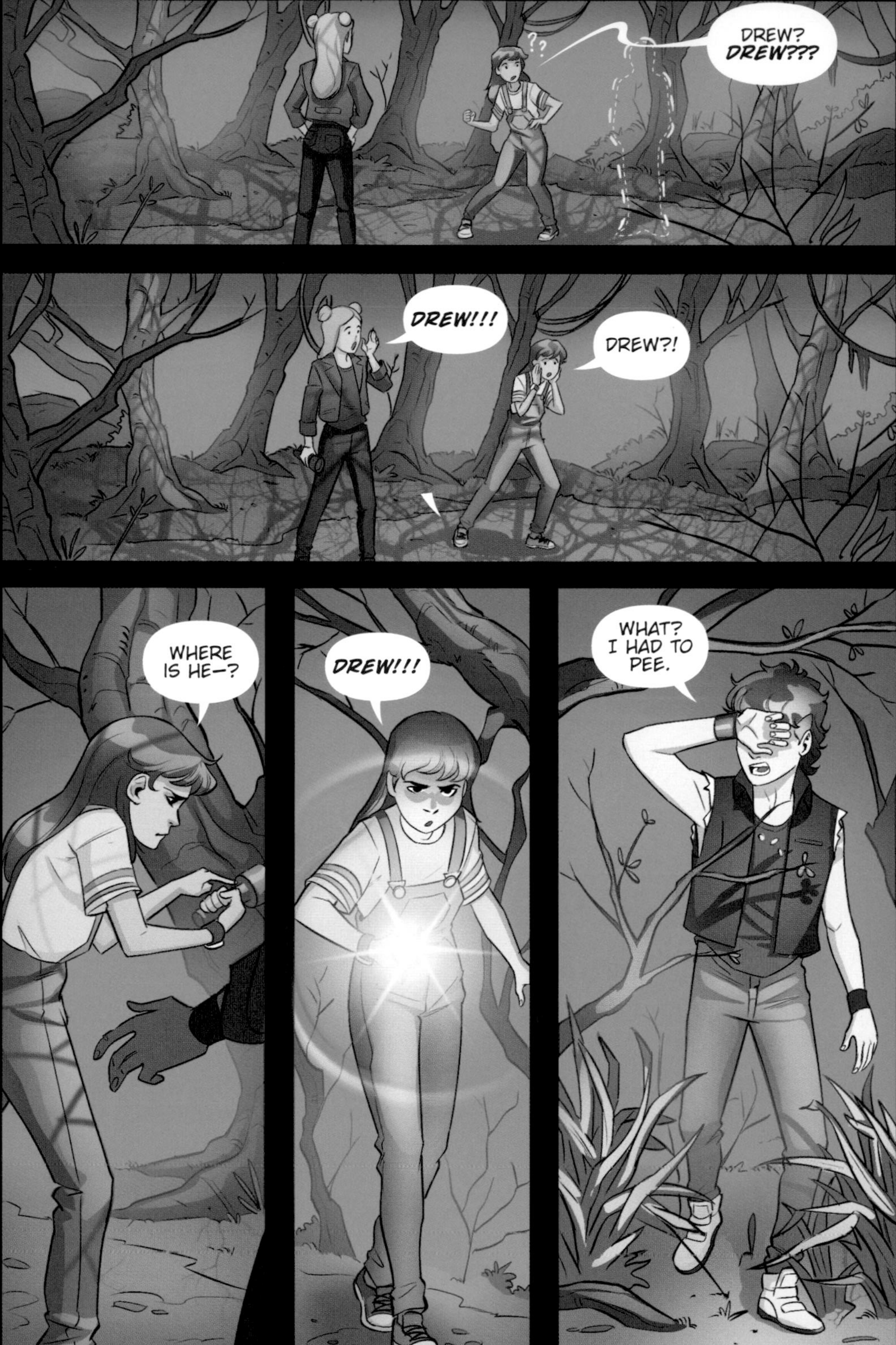
??
DREW?
DREW???
DREW!!!
DREW?!
WHERE IS HE–?
DREW!!!
WHAT? I HAD TO PEE.

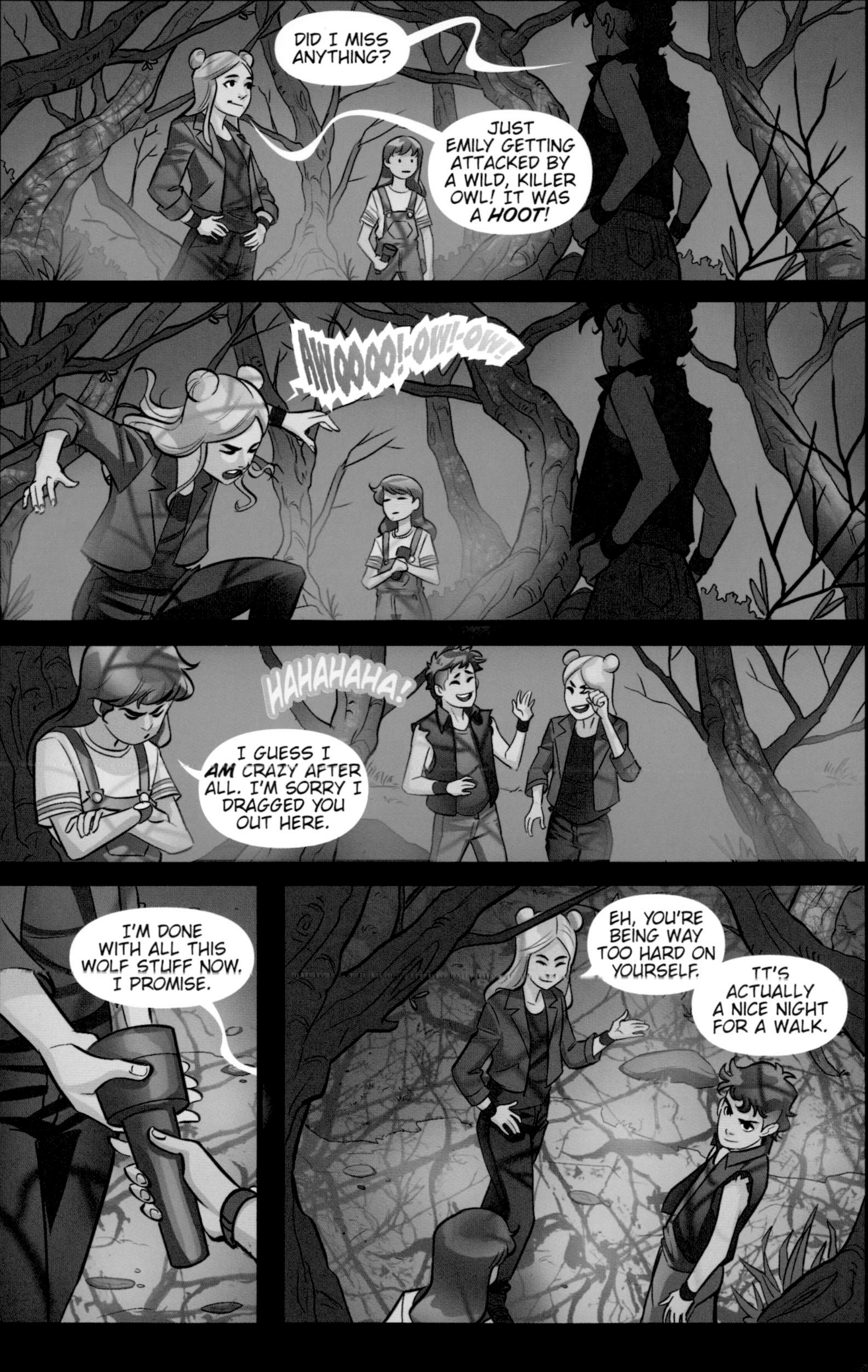
DID I MISS ANYTHING?
JUST EMILY GETTING ATTACKED BY A WILD, KILLER OWL! IT WAS A *HOOT*!
AWOOOO!-OW!-OW!
HAHAHAHA!
I GUESS I *AM* CRAZY AFTER ALL. I'M SORRY I DRAGGED YOU OUT HERE.
I'M DONE WITH ALL THIS WOLF STUFF NOW. I PROMISE.
EH, YOU'RE BEING WAY TOO HARD ON YOURSELF.
IT'S ACTUALLY A NICE NIGHT FOR A WALK.

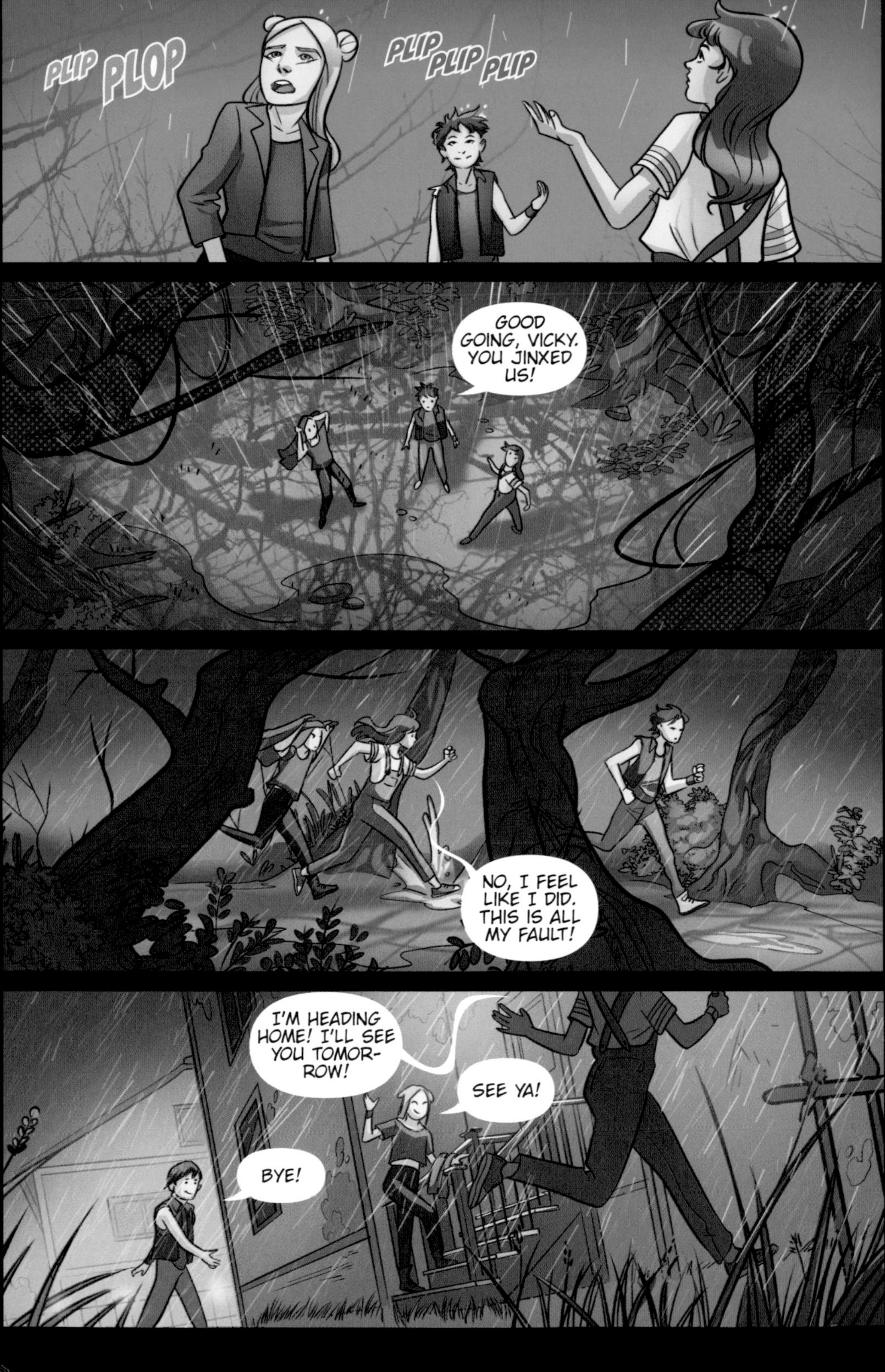
PLIP PLOP
PLIP PLIP PLIP
GOOD GOING, VICKY. YOU JINXED US!
NO, I FEEL LIKE I DID. THIS IS ALL MY FAULT!
I'M HEADING HOME! I'LL SEE YOU TOMOR-ROW!
SEE YA!
BYE!

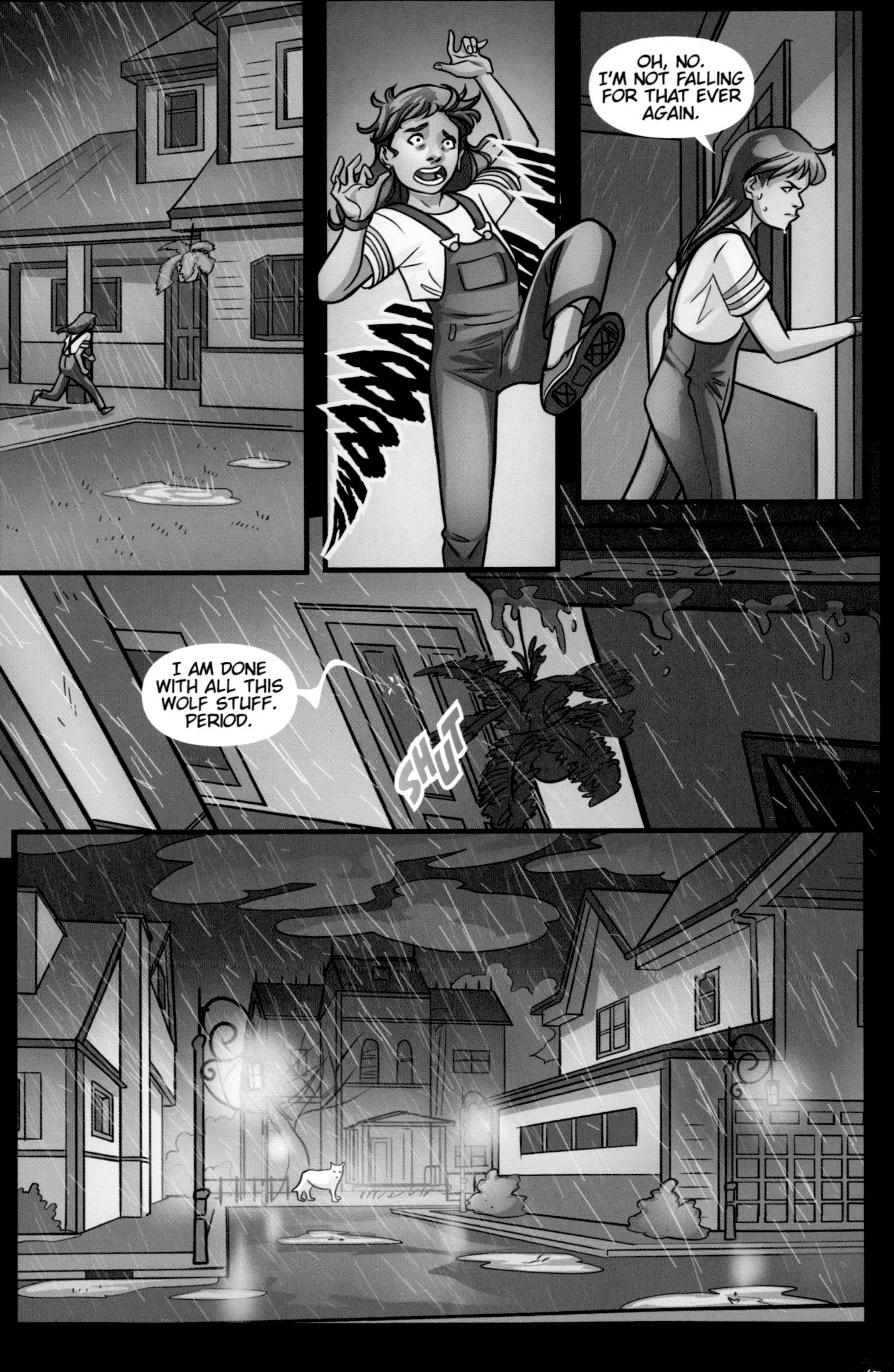
OH, NO. I'M NOT FALLING FOR THAT EVER AGAIN.
I AM DONE WITH ALL THIS WOLF STUFF. PERIOD.
SHUT

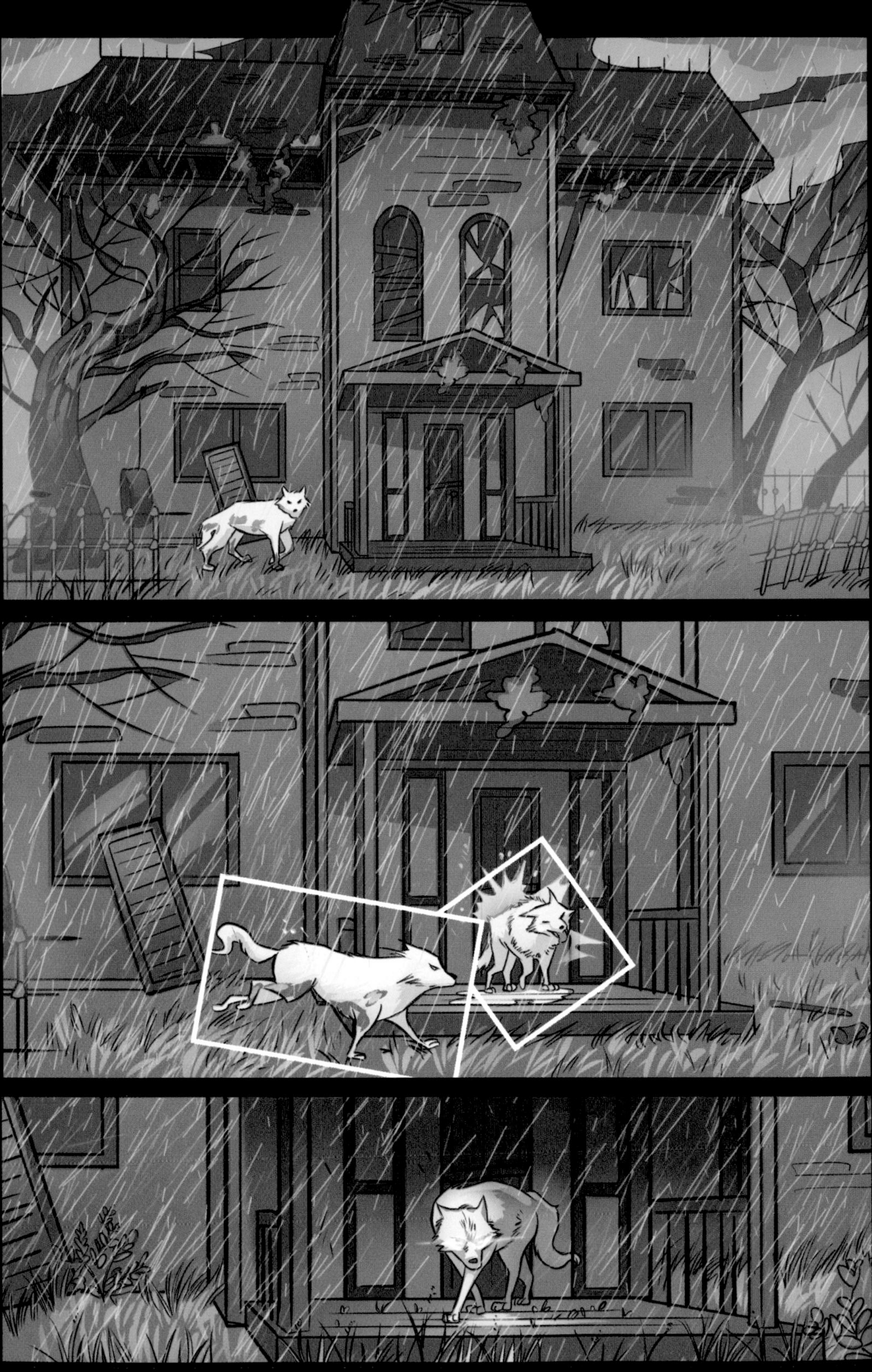

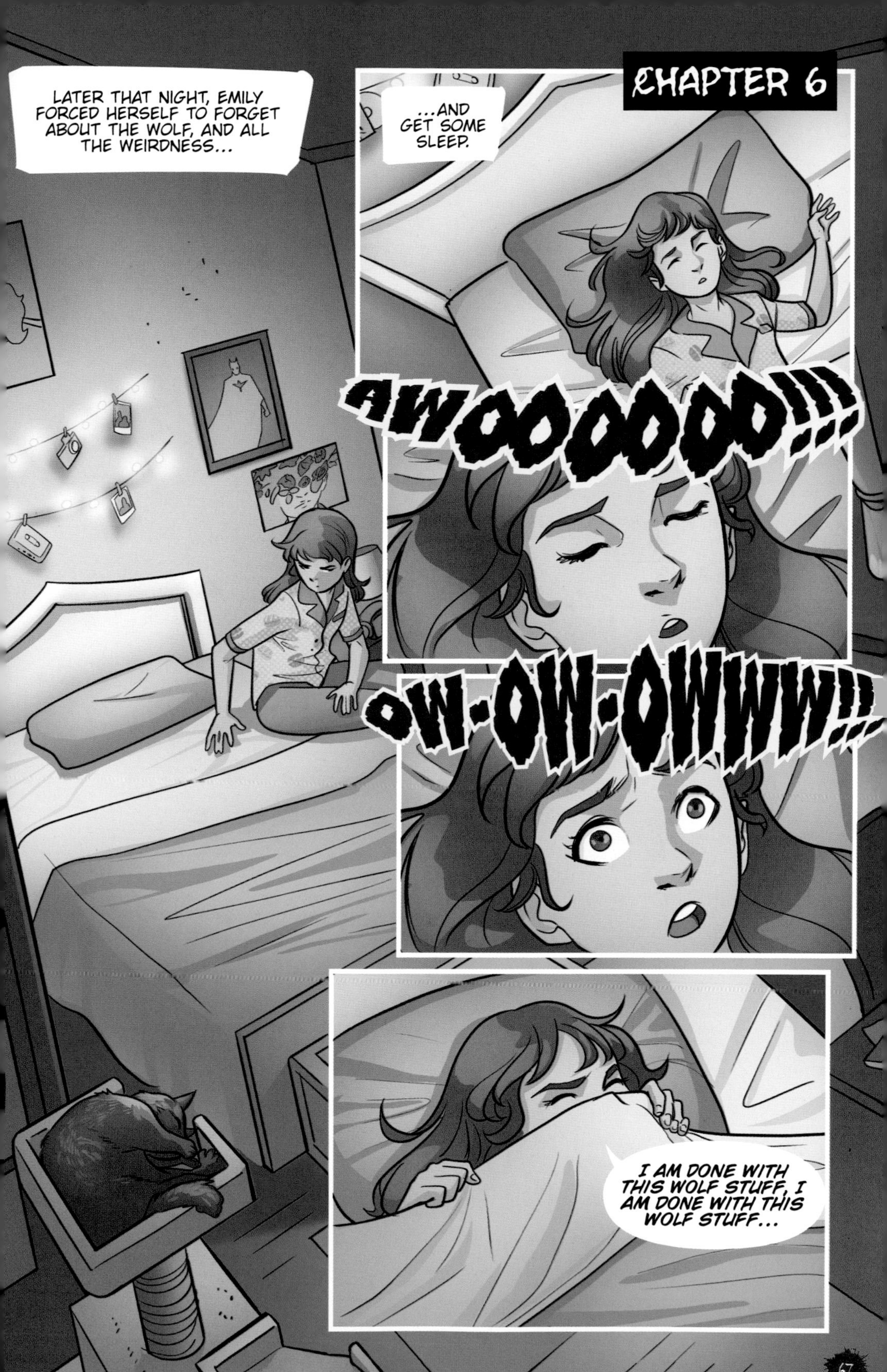
CHAPTER 6
LATER THAT NIGHT, EMILY FORCED HERSELF TO FORGET ABOUT THE WOLF, AND ALL THE WEIRDNESS...
...AND GET SOME SLEEP.
AWOOOOOO!!!
OW-OW-OWWW!!
I AM DONE WITH THIS WOLF STUFF, I AM DONE WITH THIS WOLF STUFF...

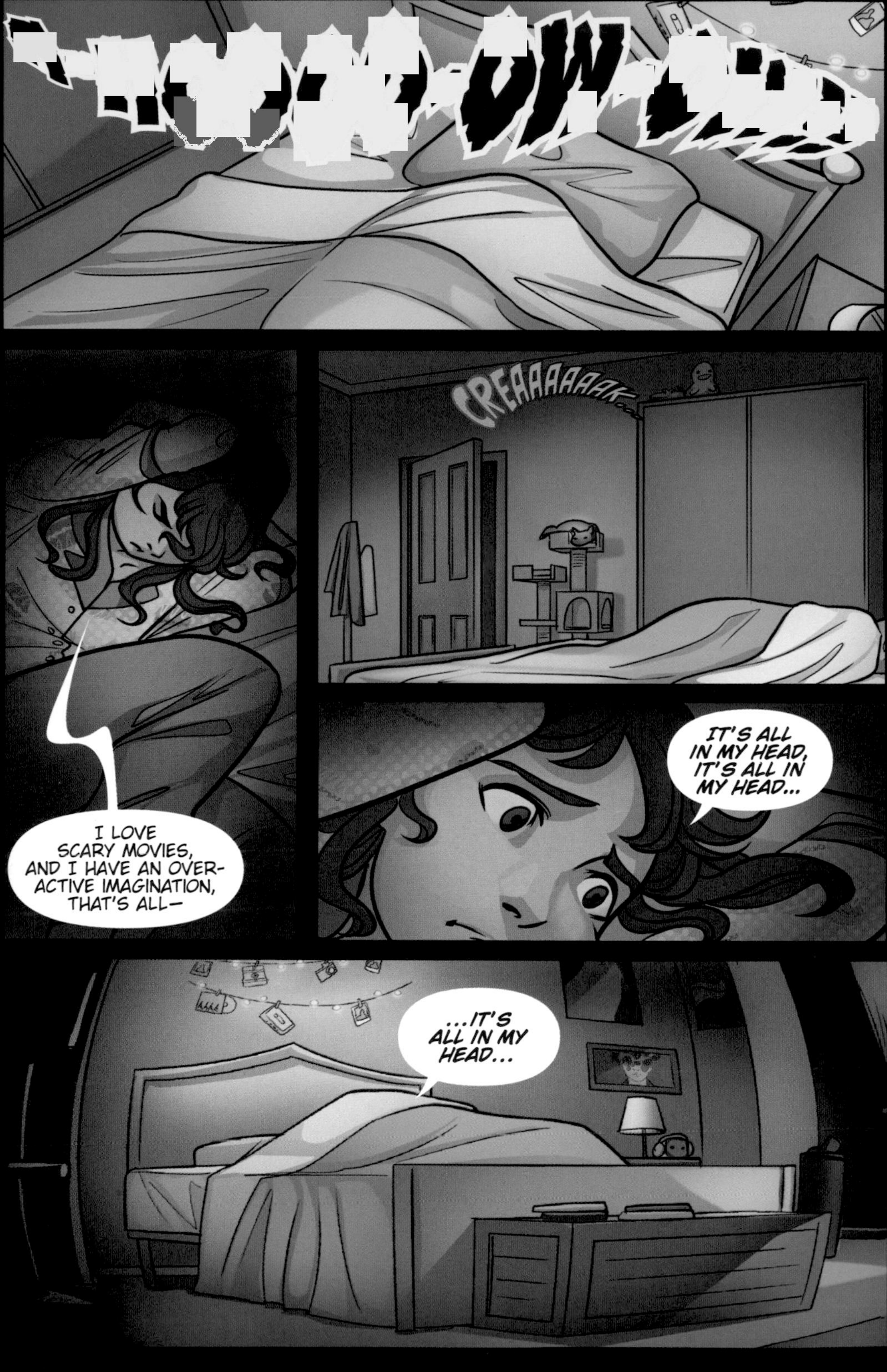
CREAAAAAAK...
I LOVE SCARY MOVIES, AND I HAVE AN OVER-ACTIVE IMAGINATION, THAT'S ALL—
IT'S ALL IN MY HEAD, IT'S ALL IN MY HEAD...
...IT'S ALL IN MY HEAD...

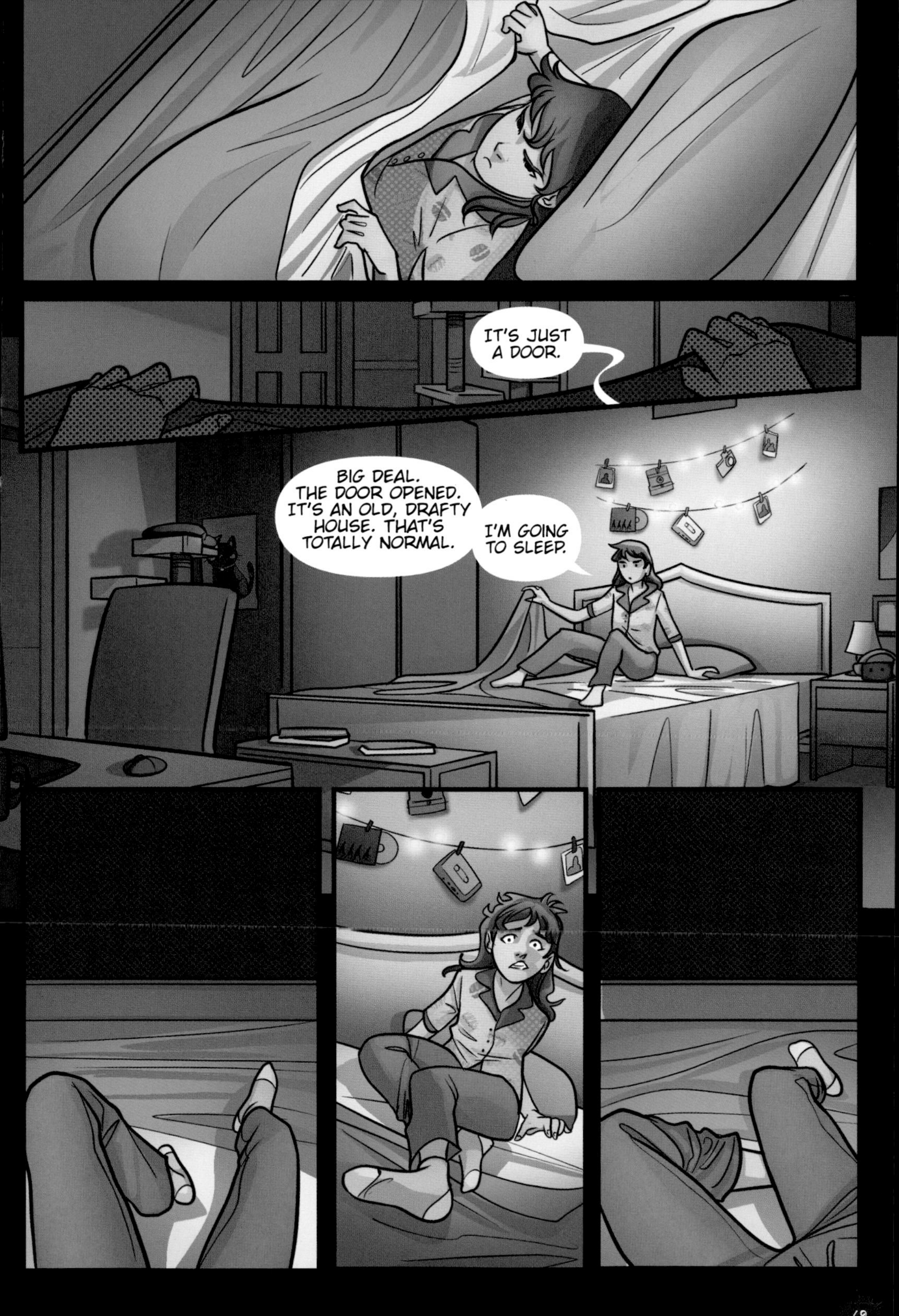
IT'S JUST A DOOR.
BIG DEAL. THE DOOR OPENED. IT'S AN OLD, DRAFTY HOUSE. THAT'S TOTALLY NORMAL.
I'M GOING TO SLEEP.

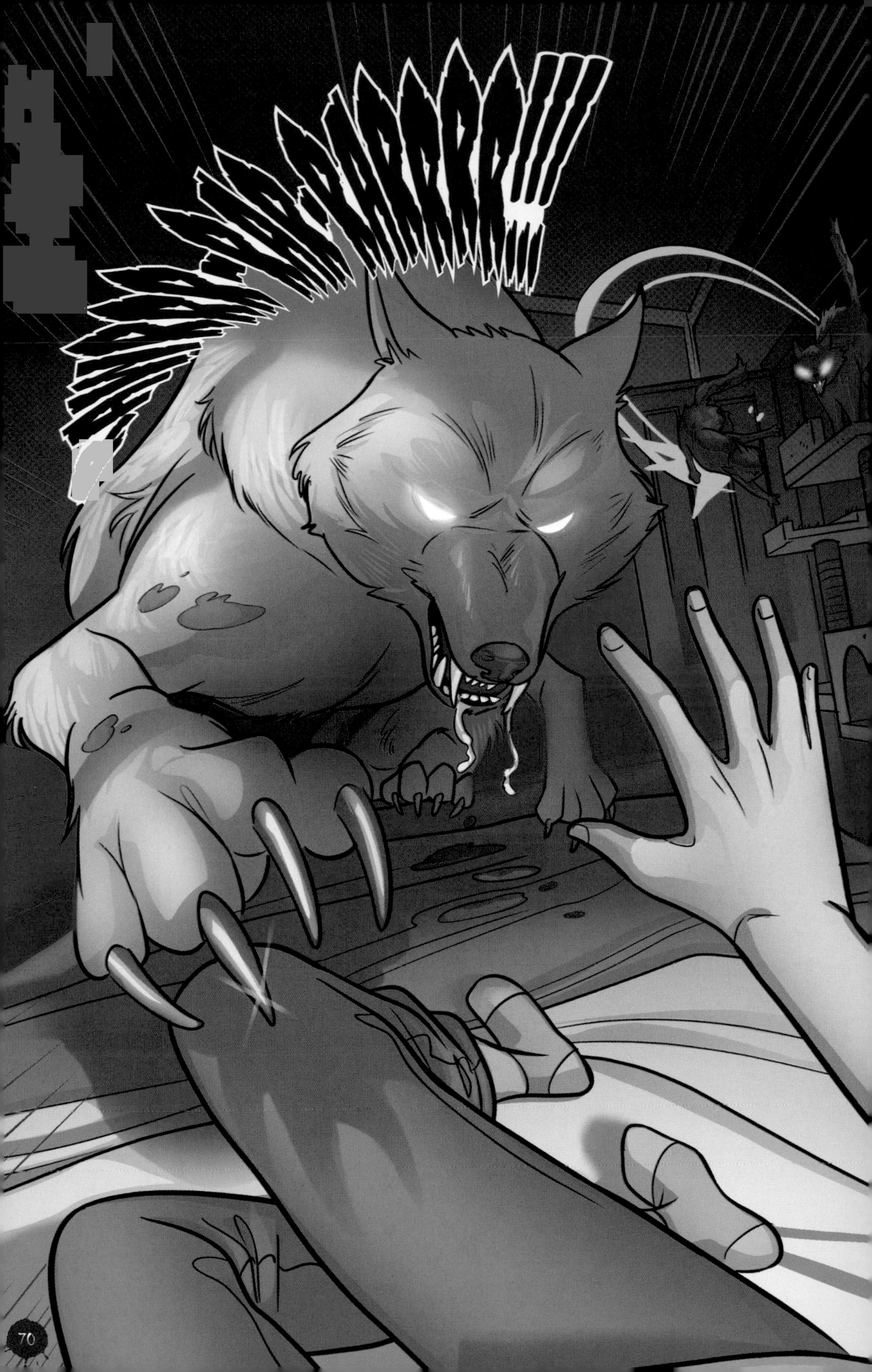

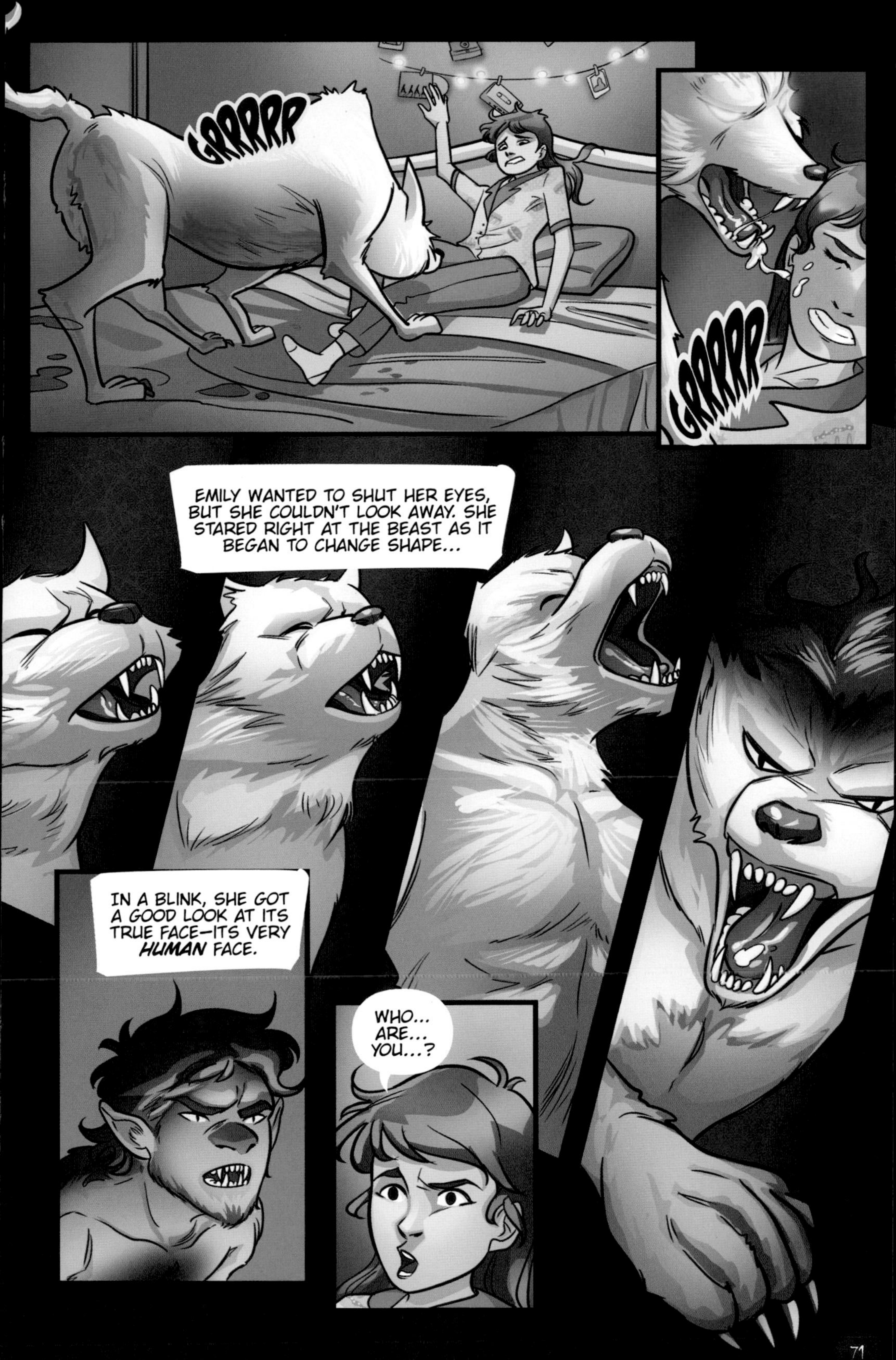
GRRRRR
GRRRRR
EMILY WANTED TO SHUT HER EYES, BUT SHE COULDN'T LOOK AWAY. SHE STARED RIGHT AT THE BEAST AS IT BEGAN TO CHANGE SHAPE...
IN A BLINK, SHE GOT A GOOD LOOK AT ITS TRUE FACE—ITS VERY *HUMAN* FACE.
WHO... ARE... YOU...?

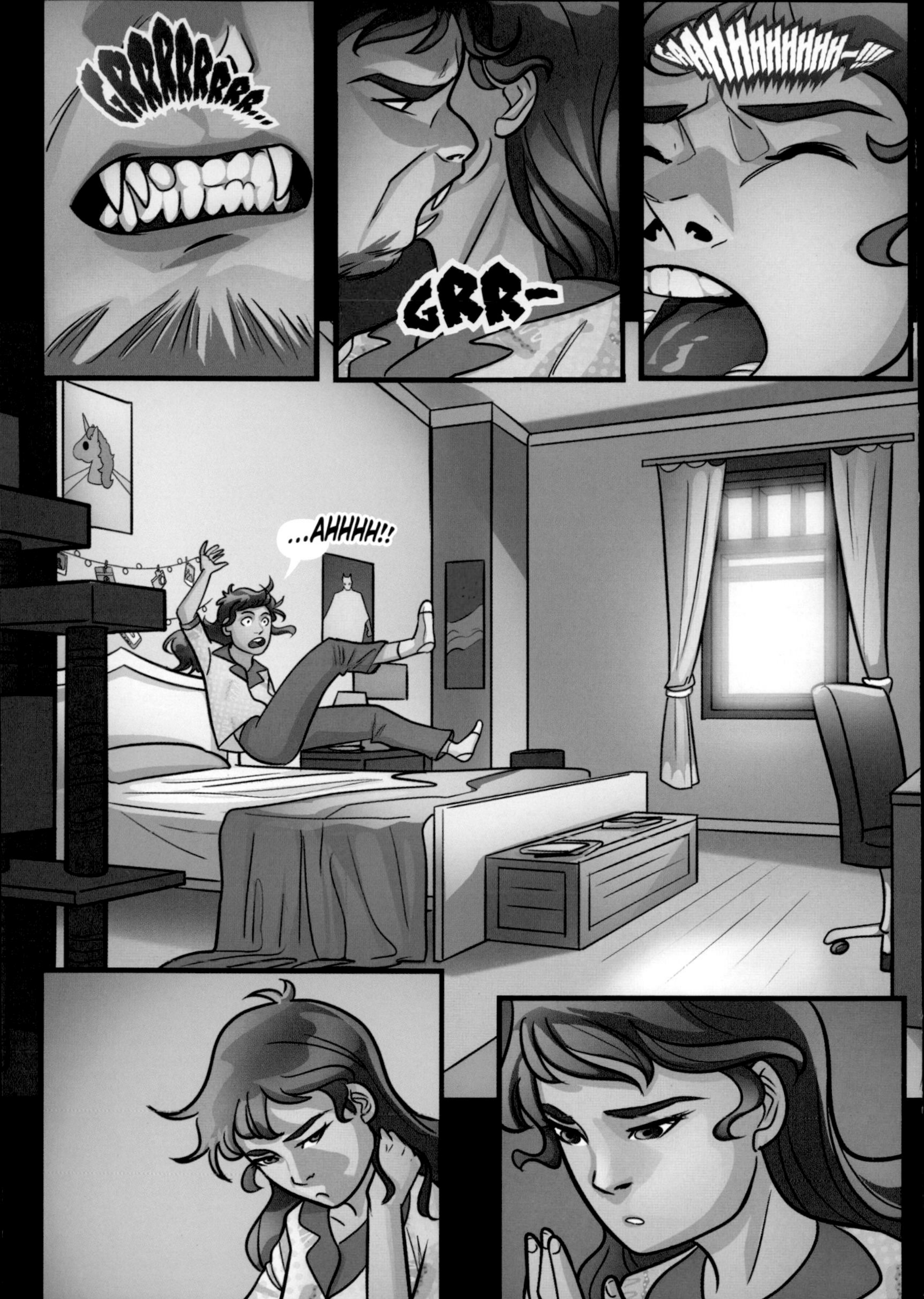
GRRRRRRRR...
GRR-
GAAHHHHHHH-!!!
...AHHHH!!

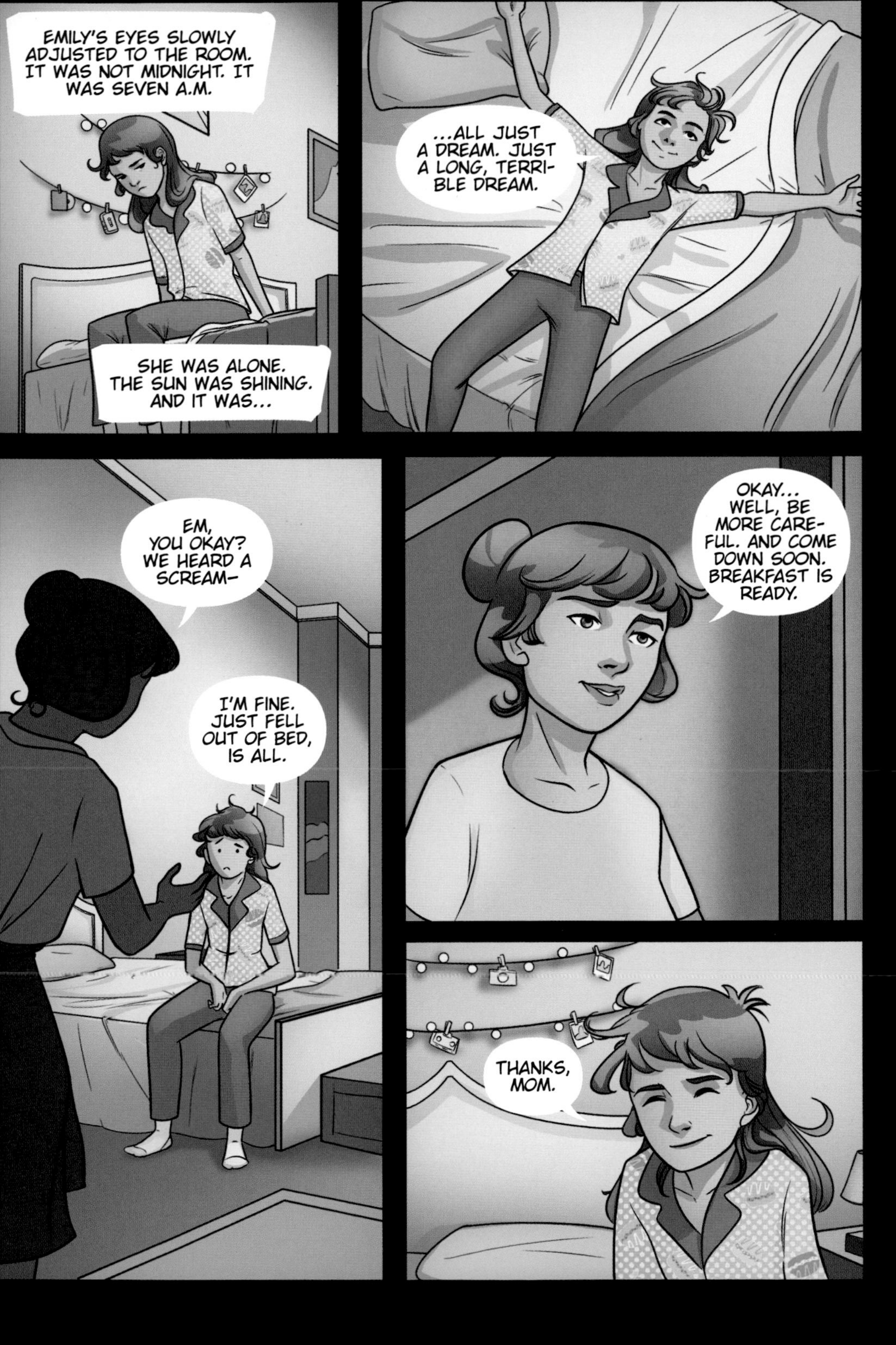
EMILY'S EYES SLOWLY ADJUSTED TO THE ROOM. IT WAS NOT MIDNIGHT. IT WAS SEVEN A.M.
SHE WAS ALONE. THE SUN WAS SHINING. AND IT WAS...
...ALL JUST A DREAM. JUST A LONG, TERRIBLE DREAM.
EM, YOU OKAY? WE HEARD A SCREAM—
I'M FINE. JUST FELL OUT OF BED, IS ALL.
OKAY... WELL, BE MORE CAREFUL. AND COME DOWN SOON. BREAKFAST IS READY.
THANKS, MOM.

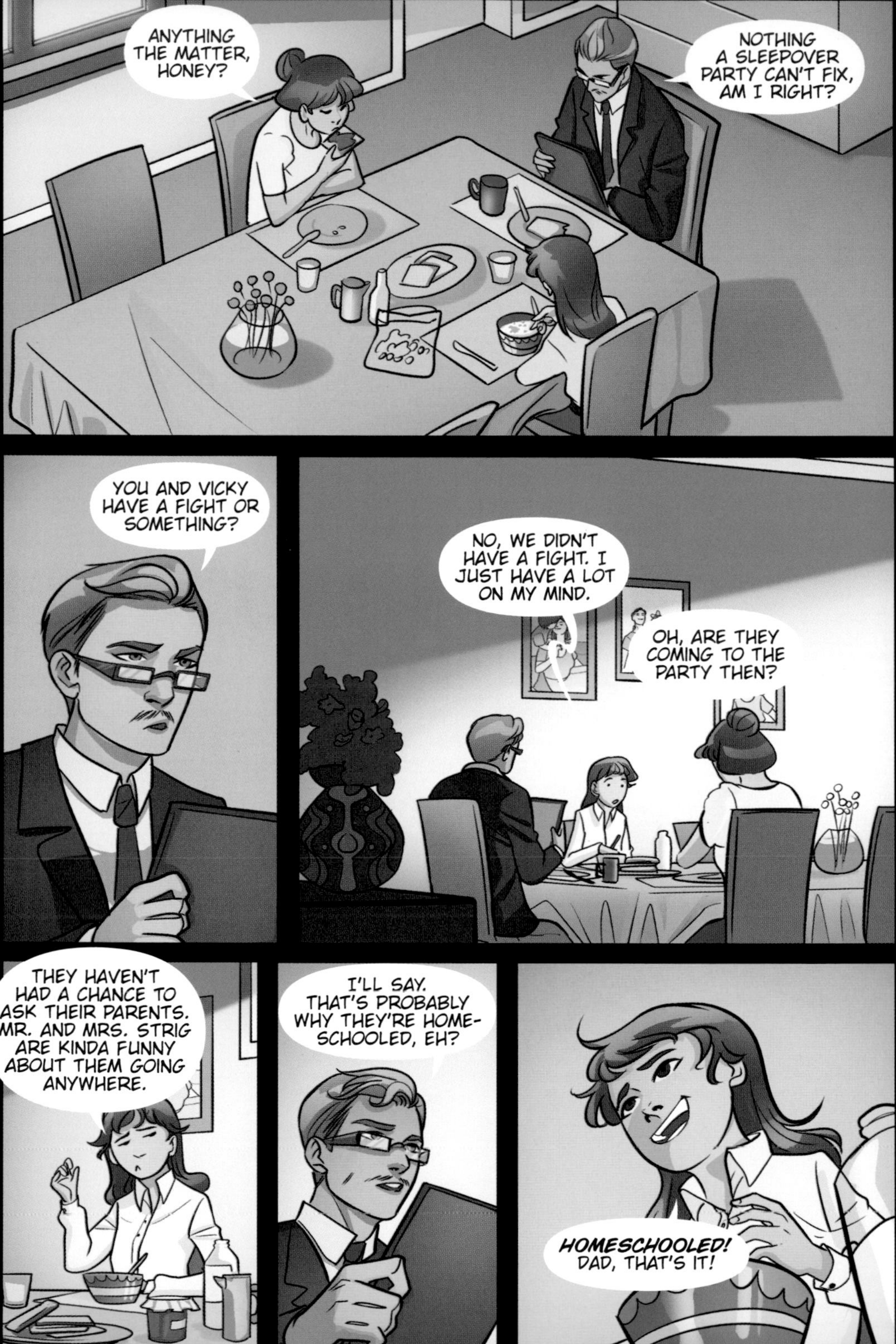
ANYTHING THE MATTER, HONEY?
NOTHING A SLEEPOVER PARTY CAN'T FIX, AM I RIGHT?
YOU AND VICKY HAVE A FIGHT OR SOMETHING?
NO, WE DIDN'T HAVE A FIGHT. I JUST HAVE A LOT ON MY MIND.
OH, ARE THEY COMING TO THE PARTY THEN?
THEY HAVEN'T HAD A CHANCE TO ASK THEIR PARENTS. MR. AND MRS. STRIG ARE KINDA FUNNY ABOUT THEM GOING ANYWHERE.
I'LL SAY. THAT'S PROBABLY WHY THEY'RE HOME-SCHOOLED, EH?
HOMESCHOOLED! DAD, THAT'S IT!

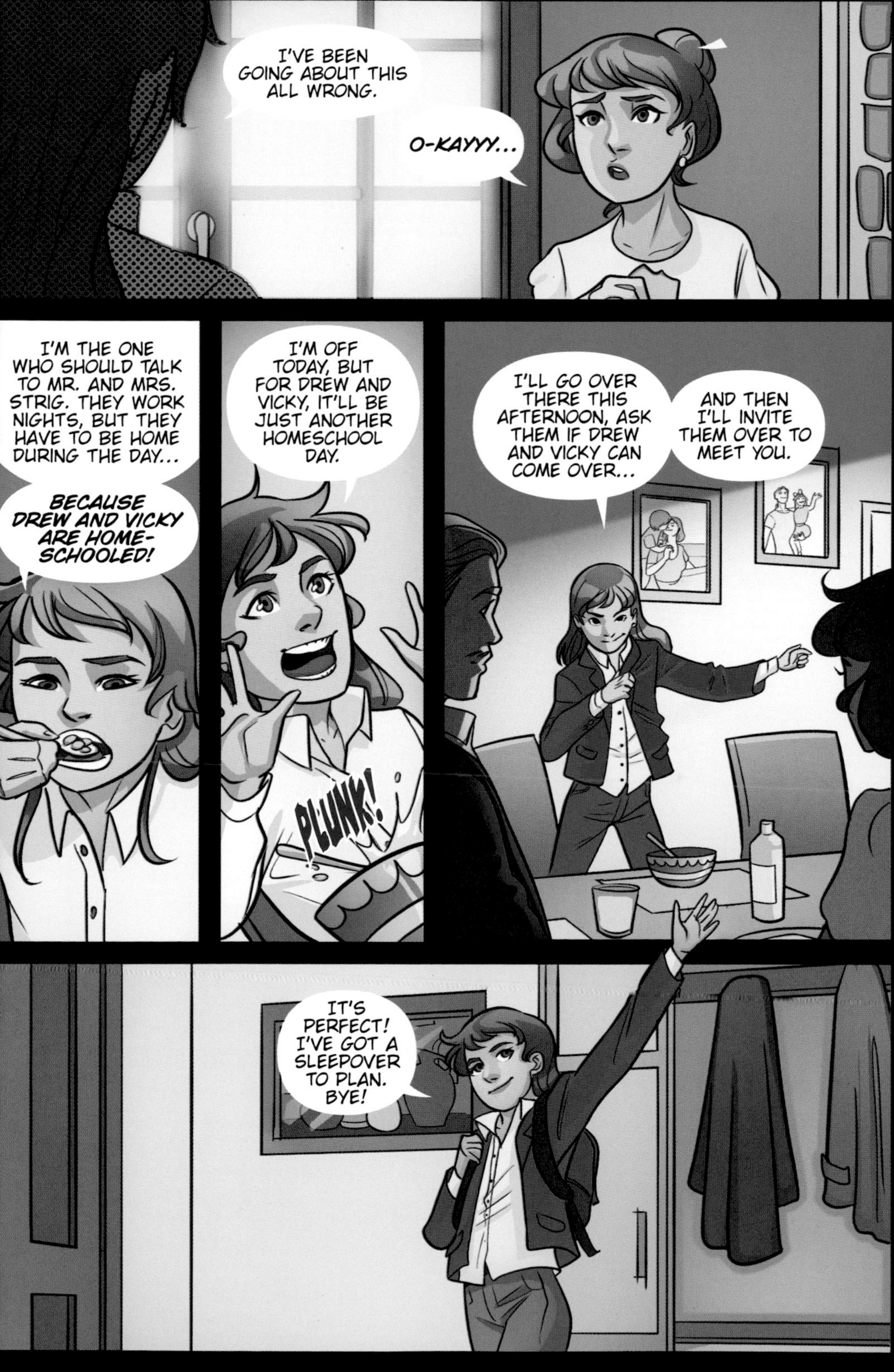
I'VE BEEN GOING ABOUT THIS ALL WRONG.
O-KAYYY...
I'M THE ONE WHO SHOULD TALK TO MR. AND MRS. STRIG. THEY WORK NIGHTS, BUT THEY HAVE TO BE HOME DURING THE DAY...
BECAUSE DREW AND VICKY ARE HOME-SCHOOLED!
I'M OFF TODAY, BUT FOR DREW AND VICKY, IT'LL BE JUST ANOTHER HOMESCHOOL DAY.
PLUNK!
I'LL GO OVER THERE THIS AFTERNOON, ASK THEM IF DREW AND VICKY CAN COME OVER...
AND THEN I'LL INVITE THEM OVER TO MEET YOU.
IT'S PERFECT! I'VE GOT A SLEEPOVER TO PLAN. BYE!

## CHAPTER 7

END OF SCHOOL

# SLEEPOVER PARTY!

(theme coming soon!)

## HOSTS

EMILY
ETHAN · HANNAH

P A R T Y !

Girls will be staying over for the night, so bring a sleeping bag! Boys will leave around 10 or 11

Saturday night
Emily's house

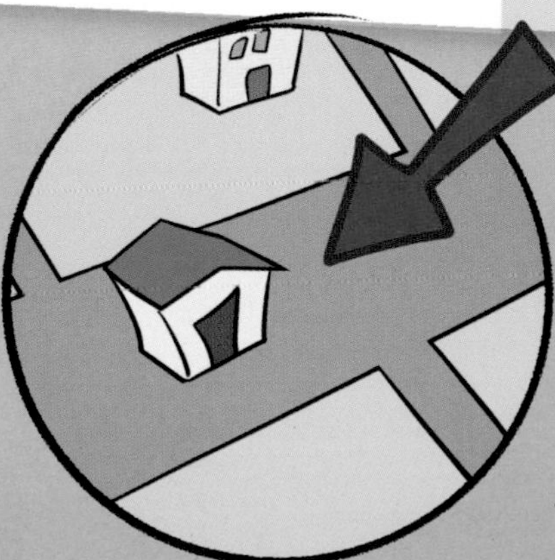

14 GUESTS TOTAL:
12 yes
2 awaiting response

## GOING?

YES
NO
MAYBE

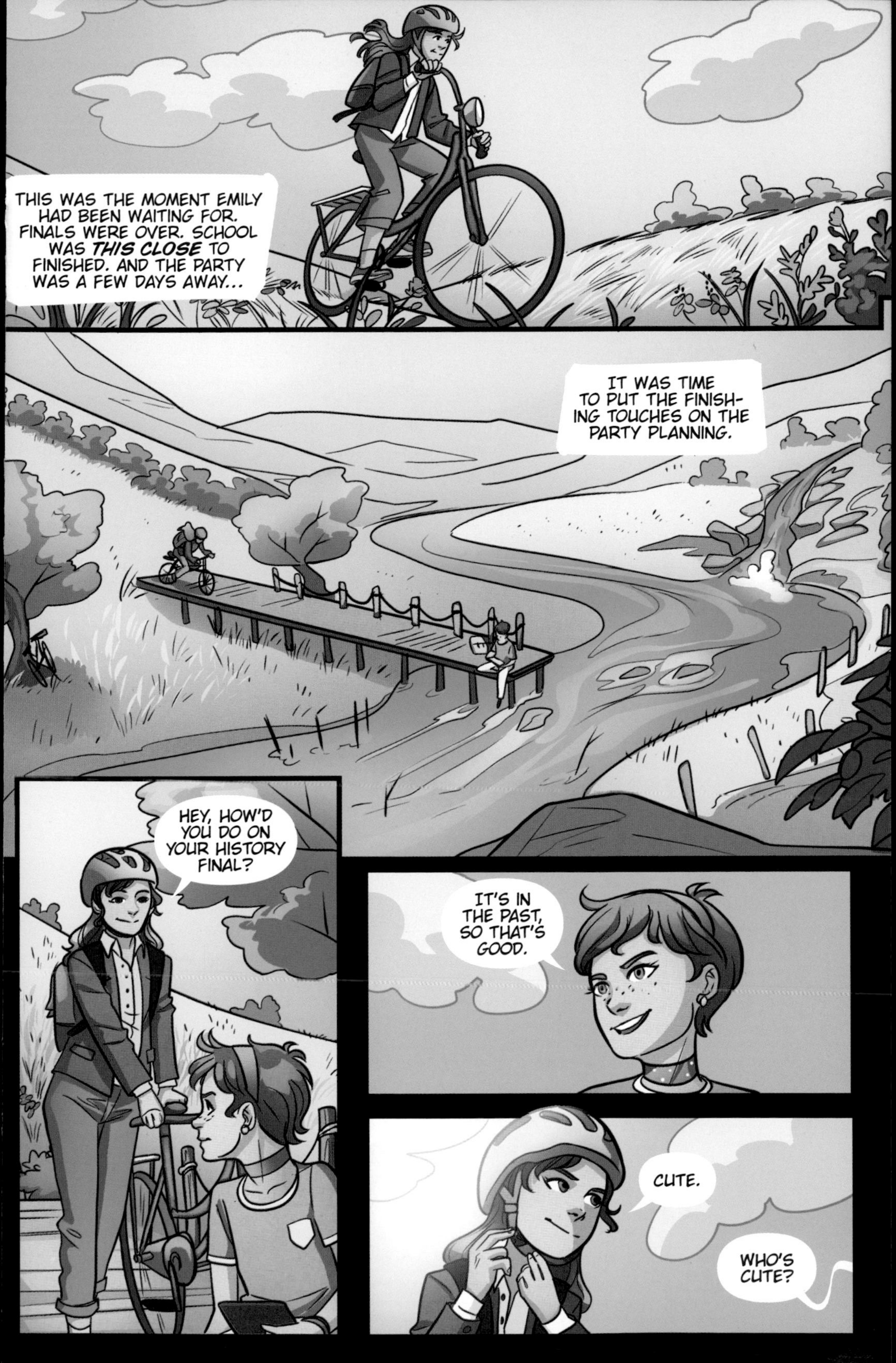
THIS WAS THE MOMENT EMILY HAD BEEN WAITING FOR. FINALS WERE OVER. SCHOOL WAS ***THIS CLOSE*** TO FINISHED. AND THE PARTY WAS A FEW DAYS AWAY...
IT WAS TIME TO PUT THE FINISHING TOUCHES ON THE PARTY PLANNING.
HEY, HOW'D YOU DO ON YOUR HISTORY FINAL?
IT'S IN THE PAST, SO THAT'S GOOD.
CUTE.
WHO'S CUTE?

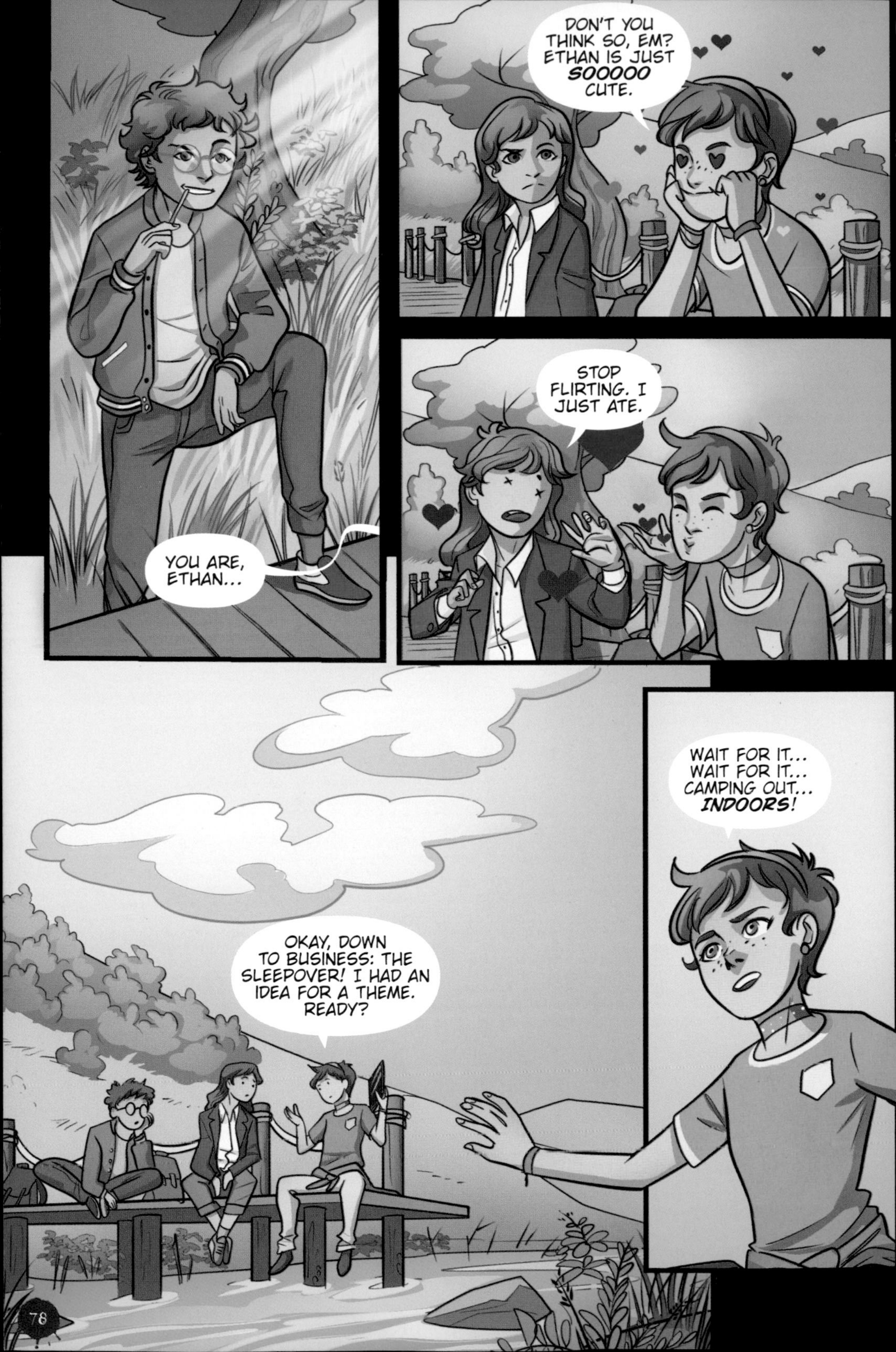
YOU ARE, ETHAN...
DON'T YOU THINK SO, EM? ETHAN IS JUST **SOOOOO** CUTE.
STOP FLIRTING. I JUST ATE.
OKAY, DOWN TO BUSINESS: THE SLEEPOVER! I HAD AN IDEA FOR A THEME. READY?
WAIT FOR IT... WAIT FOR IT... CAMPING OUT... ***INDOORS!***

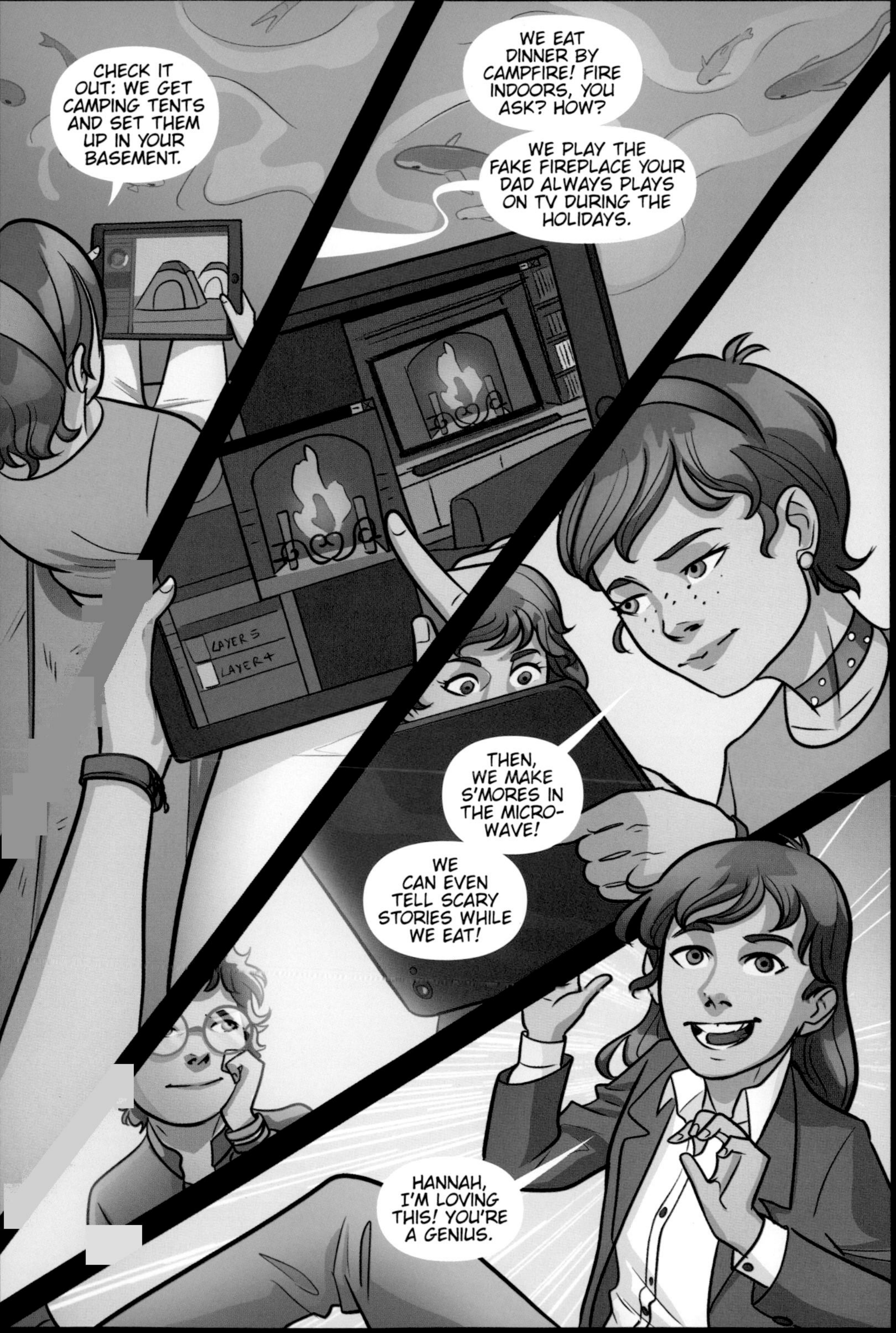
CHECK IT OUT: WE GET CAMPING TENTS AND SET THEM UP IN YOUR BASEMENT.
WE EAT DINNER BY CAMPFIRE! FIRE INDOORS, YOU ASK? HOW?
WE PLAY THE FAKE FIREPLACE YOUR DAD ALWAYS PLAYS ON TV DURING THE HOLIDAYS.
LAYER 5
LAYER 4
THEN, WE MAKE S'MORES IN THE MICRO-WAVE!
WE CAN EVEN TELL SCARY STORIES WHILE WE EAT!
HANNAH, I'M LOVING THIS! YOU'RE A GENIUS.

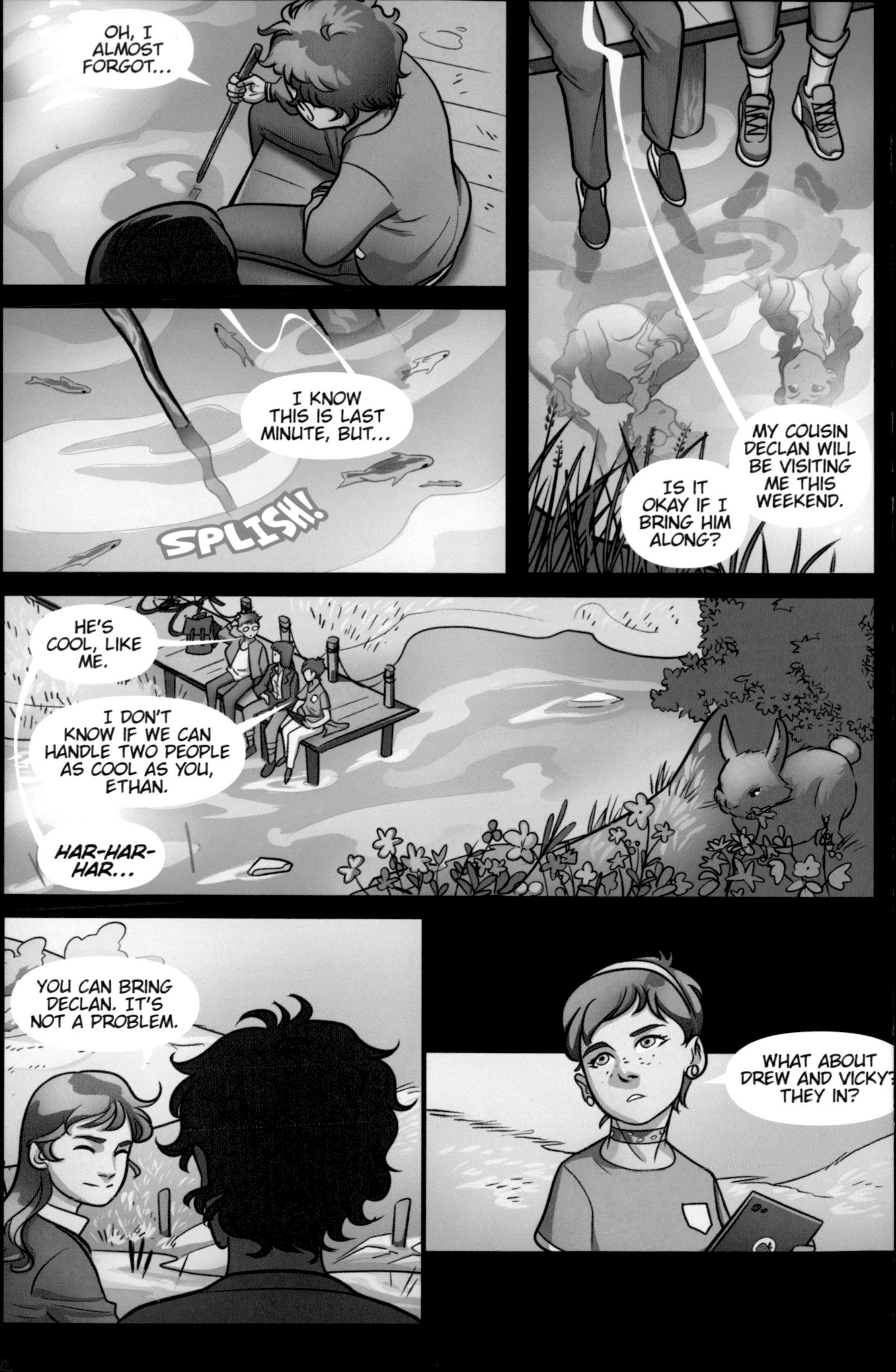
OH, I ALMOST FORGOT...
I KNOW THIS IS LAST MINUTE, BUT...
SPLISH!
MY COUSIN DECLAN WILL BE VISITING ME THIS WEEKEND.
IS IT OKAY IF I BRING HIM ALONG?
HE'S COOL, LIKE ME.
I DON'T KNOW IF WE CAN HANDLE TWO PEOPLE AS COOL AS YOU, ETHAN.
HAR-HAR-HAR...
YOU CAN BRING DECLAN. IT'S NOT A PROBLEM.
WHAT ABOUT DREW AND VICKY? THEY IN?

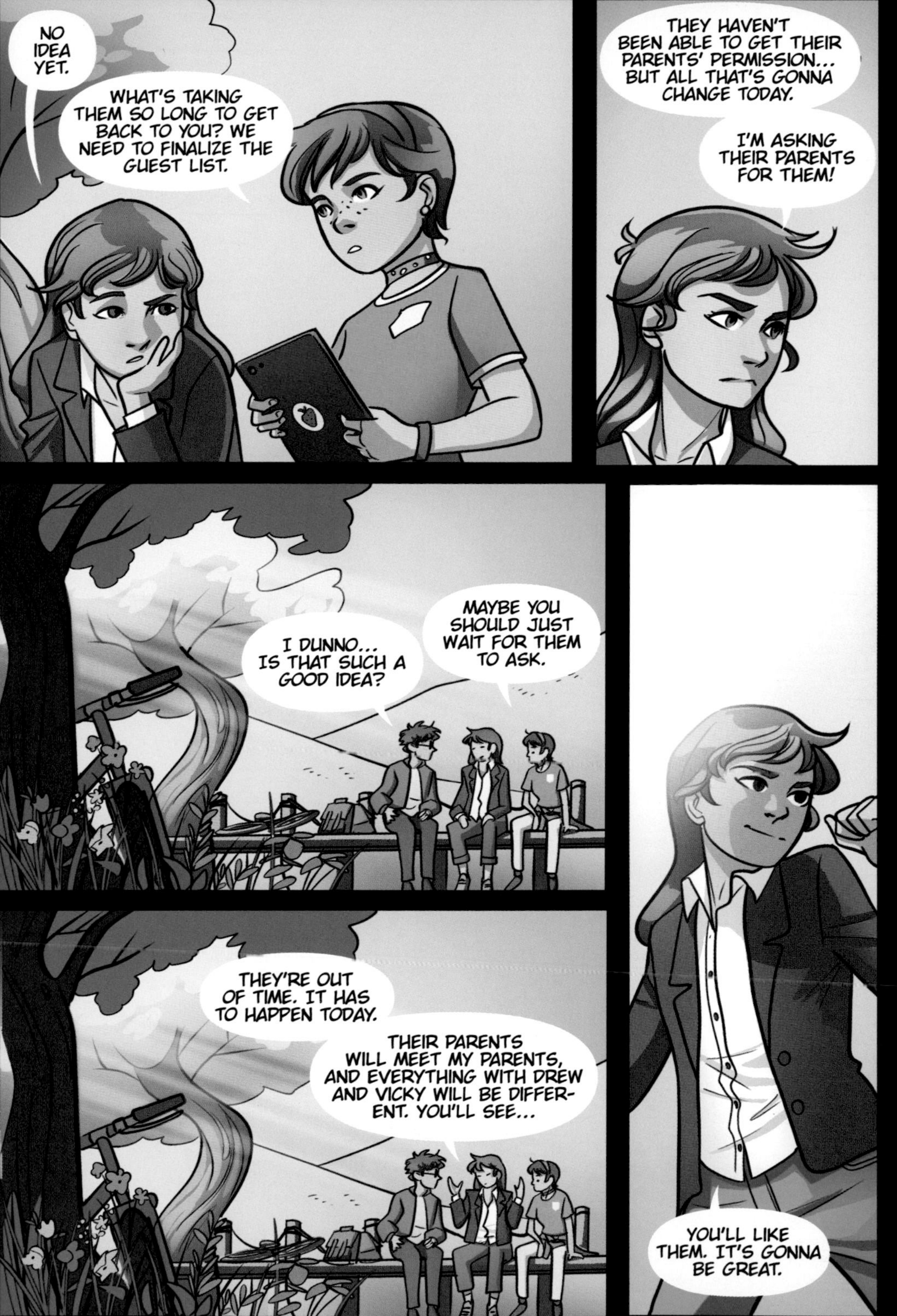
NO IDEA YET.
WHAT'S TAKING THEM SO LONG TO GET BACK TO YOU? WE NEED TO FINALIZE THE GUEST LIST.
THEY HAVEN'T BEEN ABLE TO GET THEIR PARENTS' PERMISSION... BUT ALL THAT'S GONNA CHANGE TODAY.
I'M ASKING THEIR PARENTS FOR THEM!
I DUNNO... IS THAT SUCH A GOOD IDEA?
MAYBE YOU SHOULD JUST WAIT FOR THEM TO ASK.
THEY'RE OUT OF TIME. IT HAS TO HAPPEN TODAY.
THEIR PARENTS WILL MEET MY PARENTS, AND EVERYTHING WITH DREW AND VICKY WILL BE DIFFER-ENT. YOU'LL SEE...
YOU'LL LIKE THEM. IT'S GONNA BE GREAT.

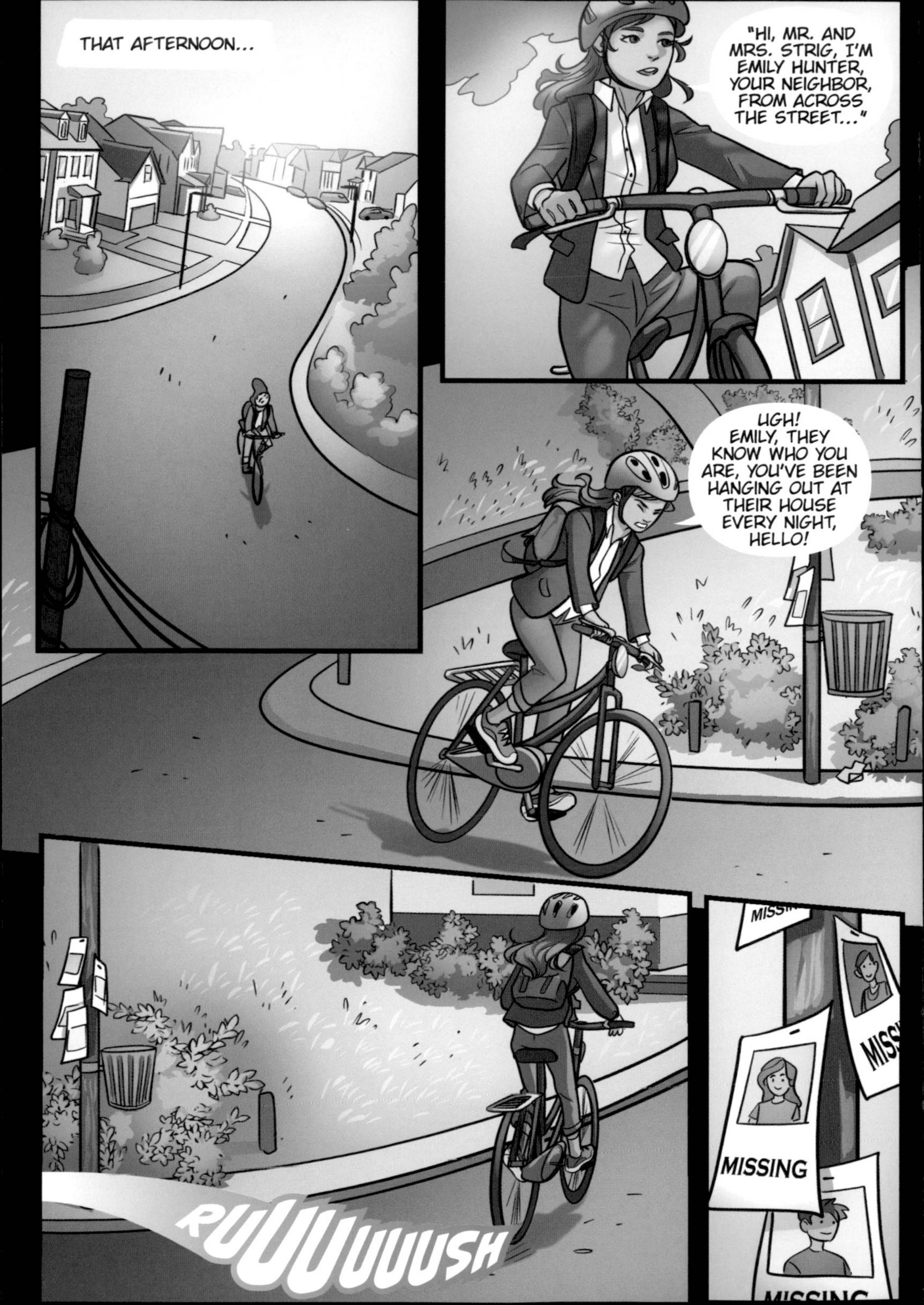
THAT AFTERNOON...
"HI, MR. AND MRS. STRIG, I'M EMILY HUNTER, YOUR NEIGHBOR, FROM ACROSS THE STREET..."
UGH! EMILY, THEY KNOW WHO YOU ARE, YOU'VE BEEN HANGING OUT AT THEIR HOUSE EVERY NIGHT, HELLO!
RUUUUUUUSH
MISSING
MISSING
MISSING

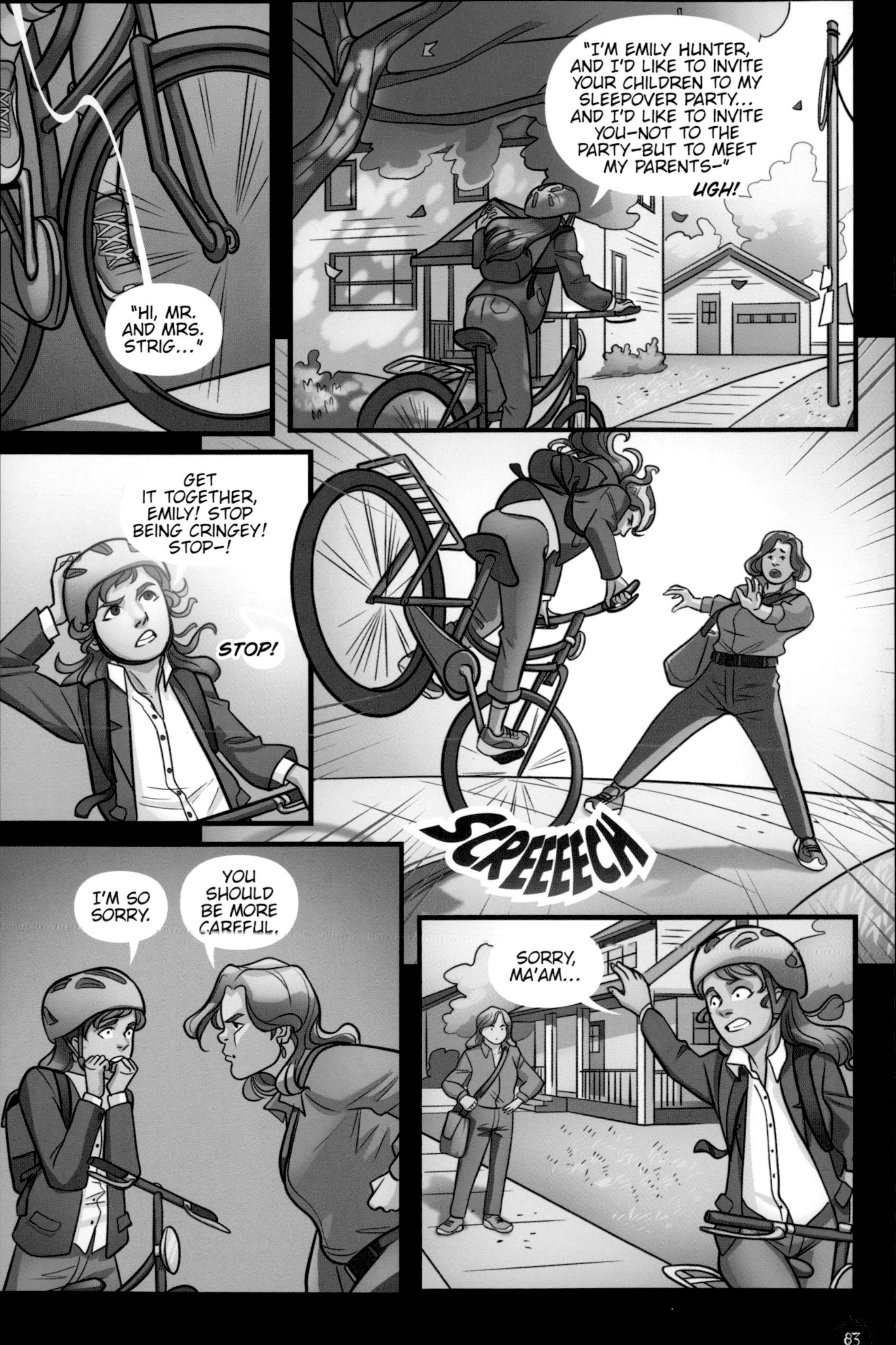
"HI, MR. AND MRS. STRIG..."
"I'M EMILY HUNTER, AND I'D LIKE TO INVITE YOUR CHILDREN TO MY SLEEPOVER PARTY... AND I'D LIKE TO INVITE YOU—NOT TO THE PARTY—BUT TO MEET MY PARENTS—"
UGH!
GET IT TOGETHER, EMILY! STOP BEING CRINGEY! STOP—!
STOP!
SCREEEECH
I'M SO SORRY.
YOU SHOULD BE MORE CAREFUL.
SORRY, MA'AM...

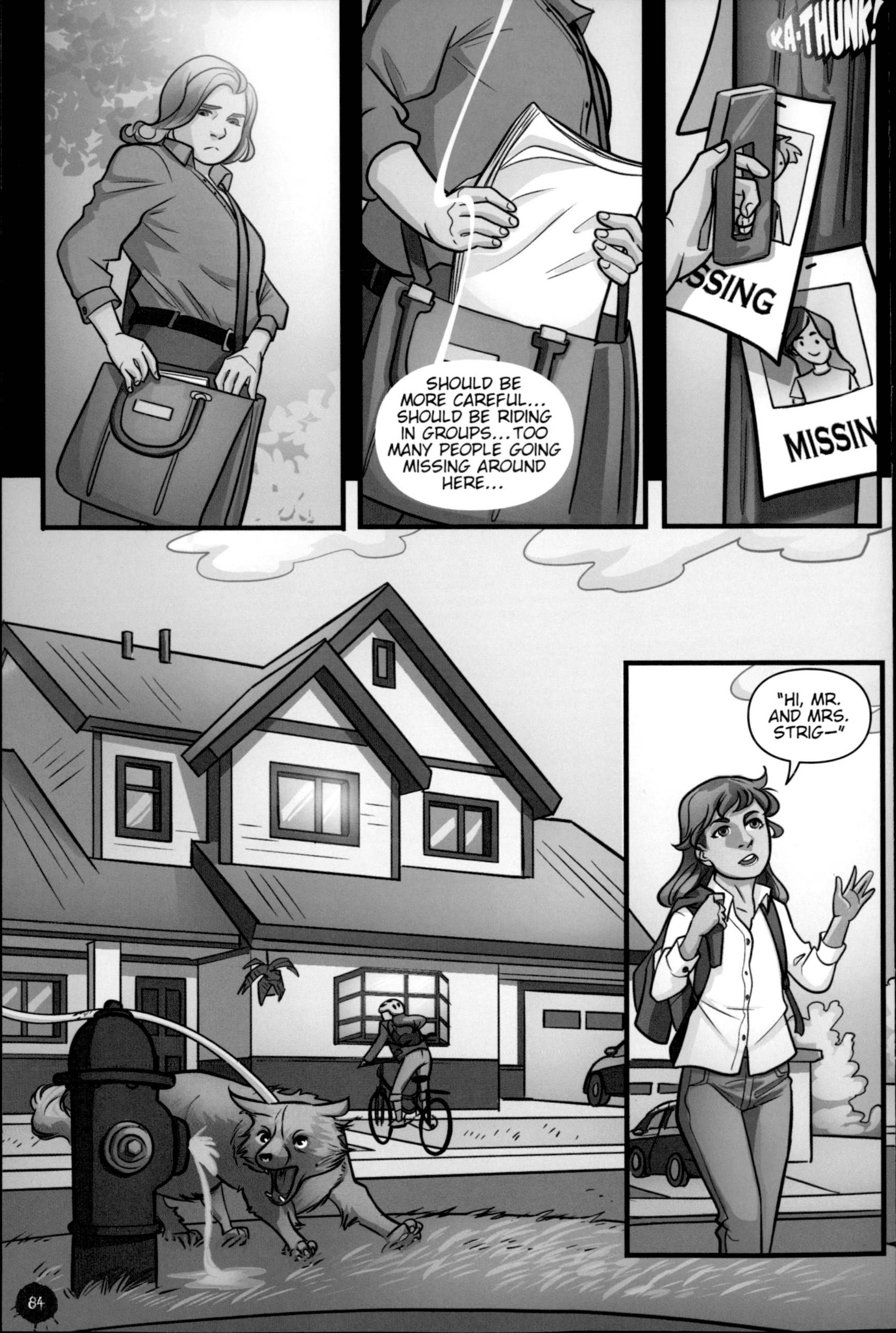
KA-THUNK!
SHOULD BE MORE CAREFUL... SHOULD BE RIDING IN GROUPS...TOO MANY PEOPLE GOING MISSING AROUND HERE...
SSING
MISSIN
"HI, MR. AND MRS. STRIG—"

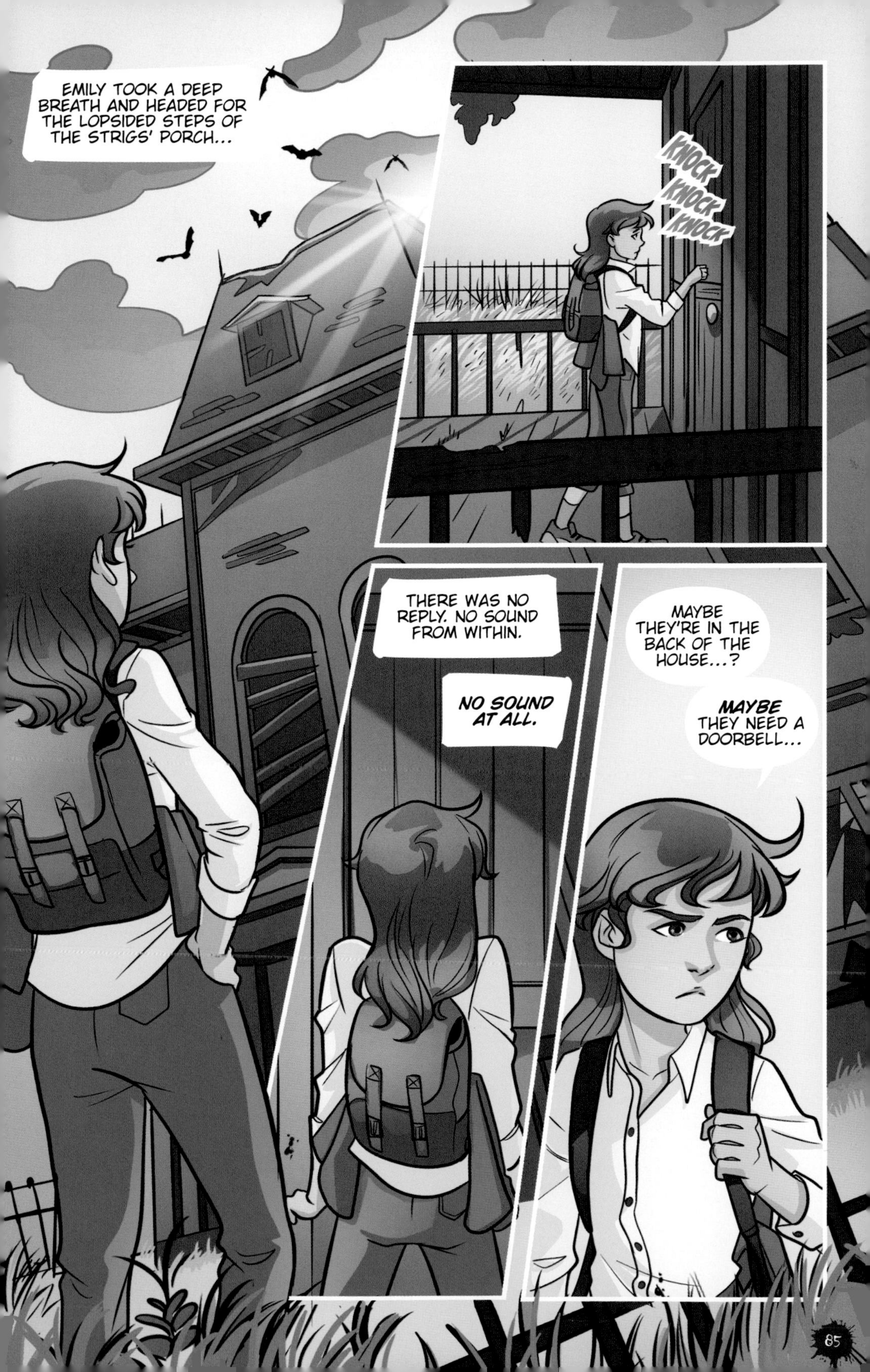
EMILY TOOK A DEEP BREATH AND HEADED FOR THE LOPSIDED STEPS OF THE STRIGS' PORCH...
KNOCK KNOCK KNOCK
THERE WAS NO REPLY. NO SOUND FROM WITHIN.
NO SOUND AT ALL.
MAYBE THEY'RE IN THE BACK OF THE HOUSE...?
MAYBE THEY NEED A DOORBELL...

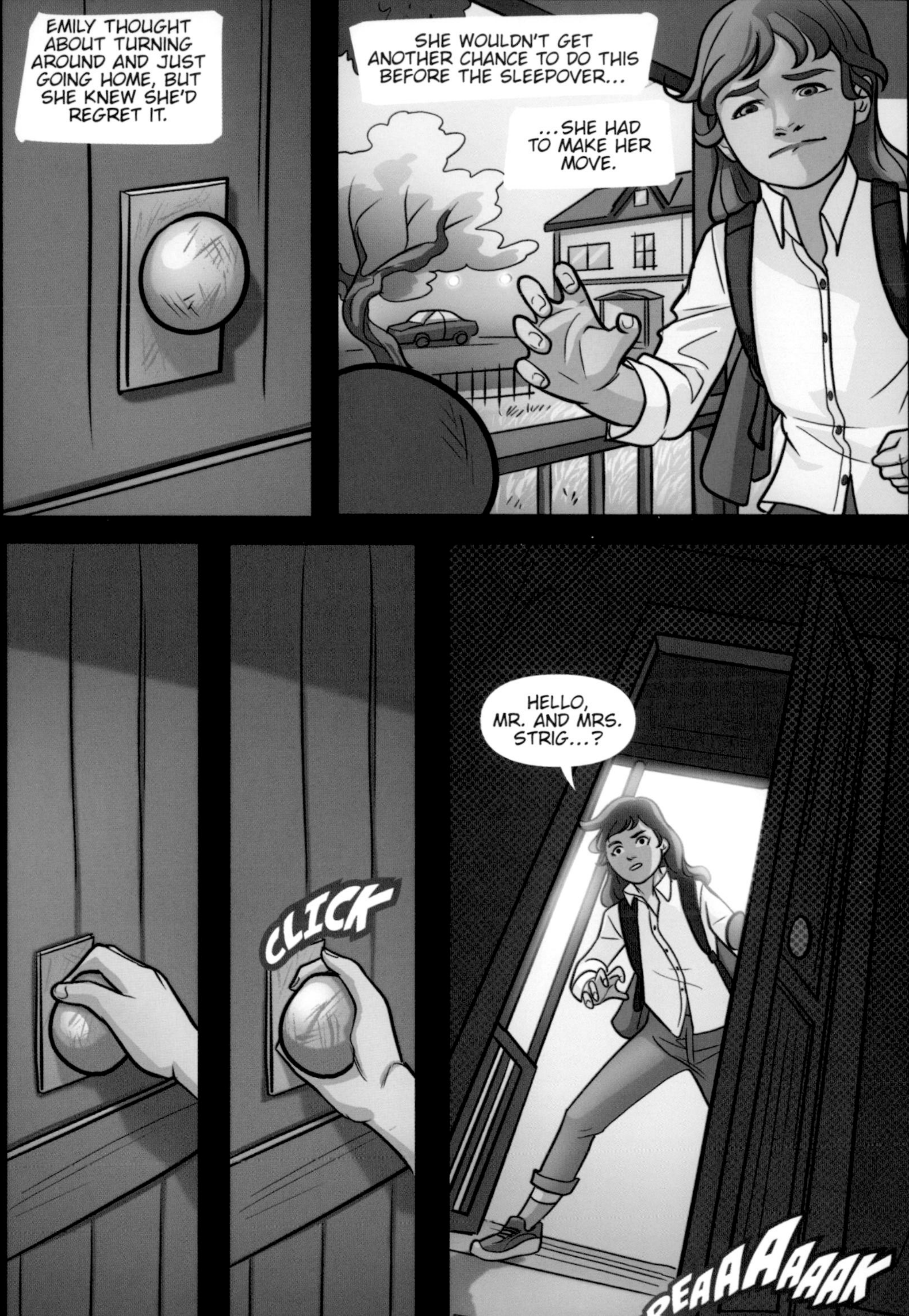
EMILY THOUGHT ABOUT TURNING AROUND AND JUST GOING HOME, BUT SHE KNEW SHE'D REGRET IT.
SHE WOULDN'T GET ANOTHER CHANCE TO DO THIS BEFORE THE SLEEPOVER...
...SHE HAD TO MAKE HER MOVE.
CLICK
HELLO, MR. AND MRS. STRIG...?
CREAAAAAAK

# CHAPTER 8

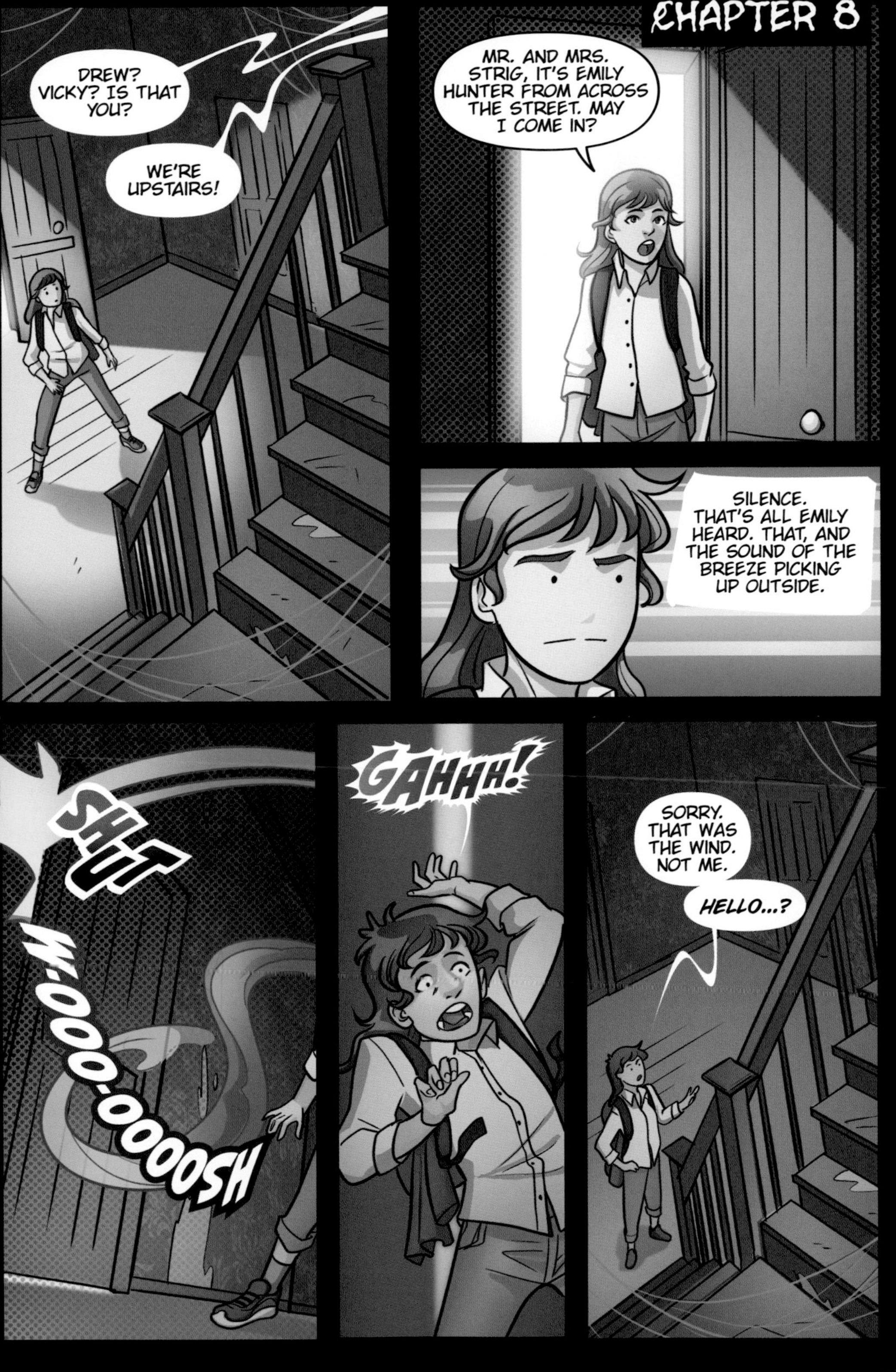

MR. AND MRS. STRIG, IT'S EMILY HUNTER FROM ACROSS THE STREET. MAY I COME IN?
DREW? VICKY? IS THAT YOU?
WE'RE UPSTAIRS!
SILENCE. THAT'S ALL EMILY HEARD. THAT, AND THE SOUND OF THE BREEZE PICKING UP OUTSIDE.
SHUT
W-OOO-OOOOSH
GAHHH!
SORRY. THAT WAS THE WIND. NOT ME.
HELLO...?

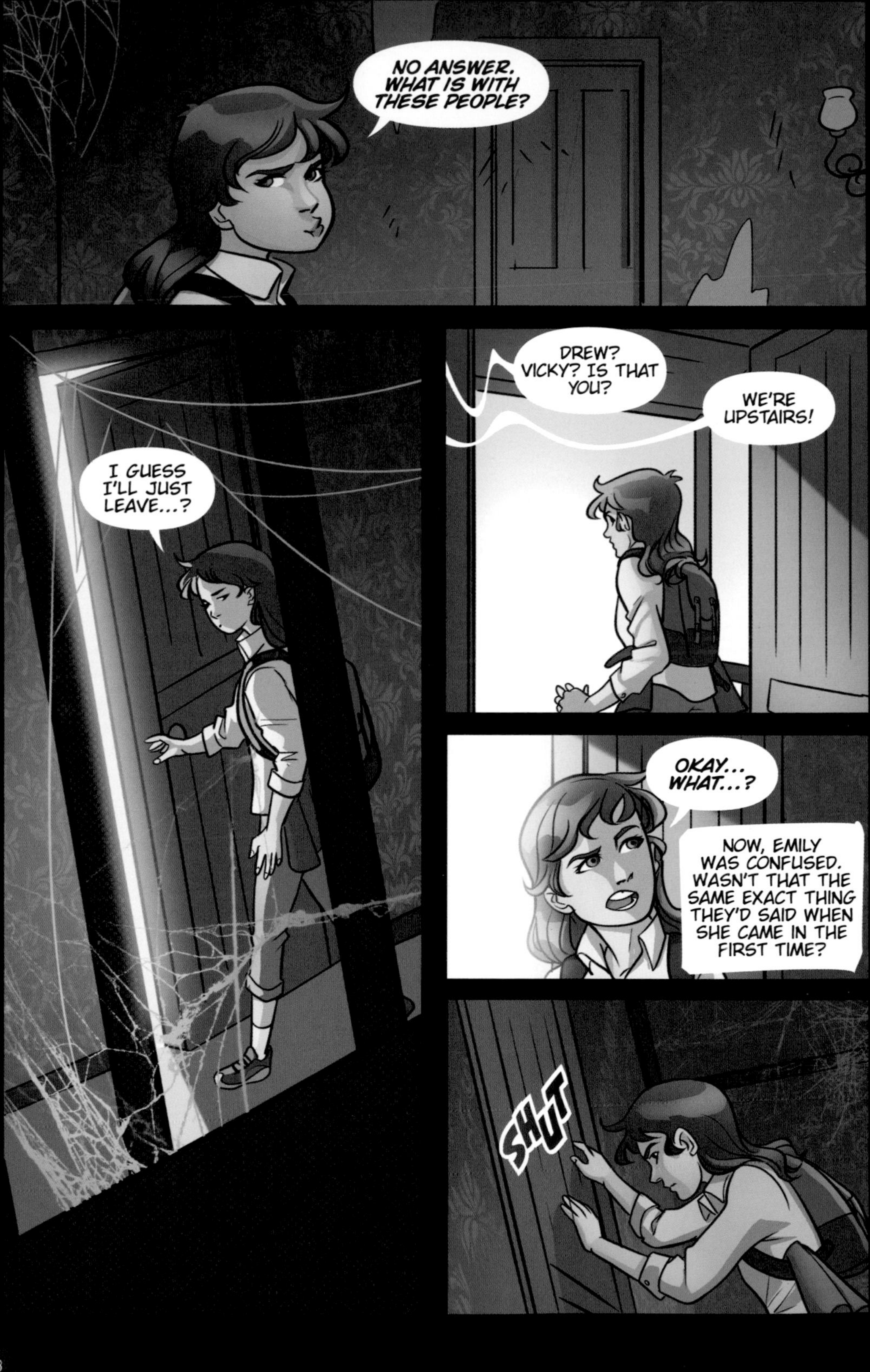
NO ANSWER. WHAT IS WITH THESE PEOPLE?
I GUESS I'LL JUST LEAVE...?
DREW? VICKY? IS THAT YOU?
WE'RE UPSTAIRS!
OKAY... WHAT...?
NOW, EMILY WAS CONFUSED. WASN'T THAT THE SAME EXACT THING THEY'D SAID WHEN SHE CAME IN THE FIRST TIME?
SHUT

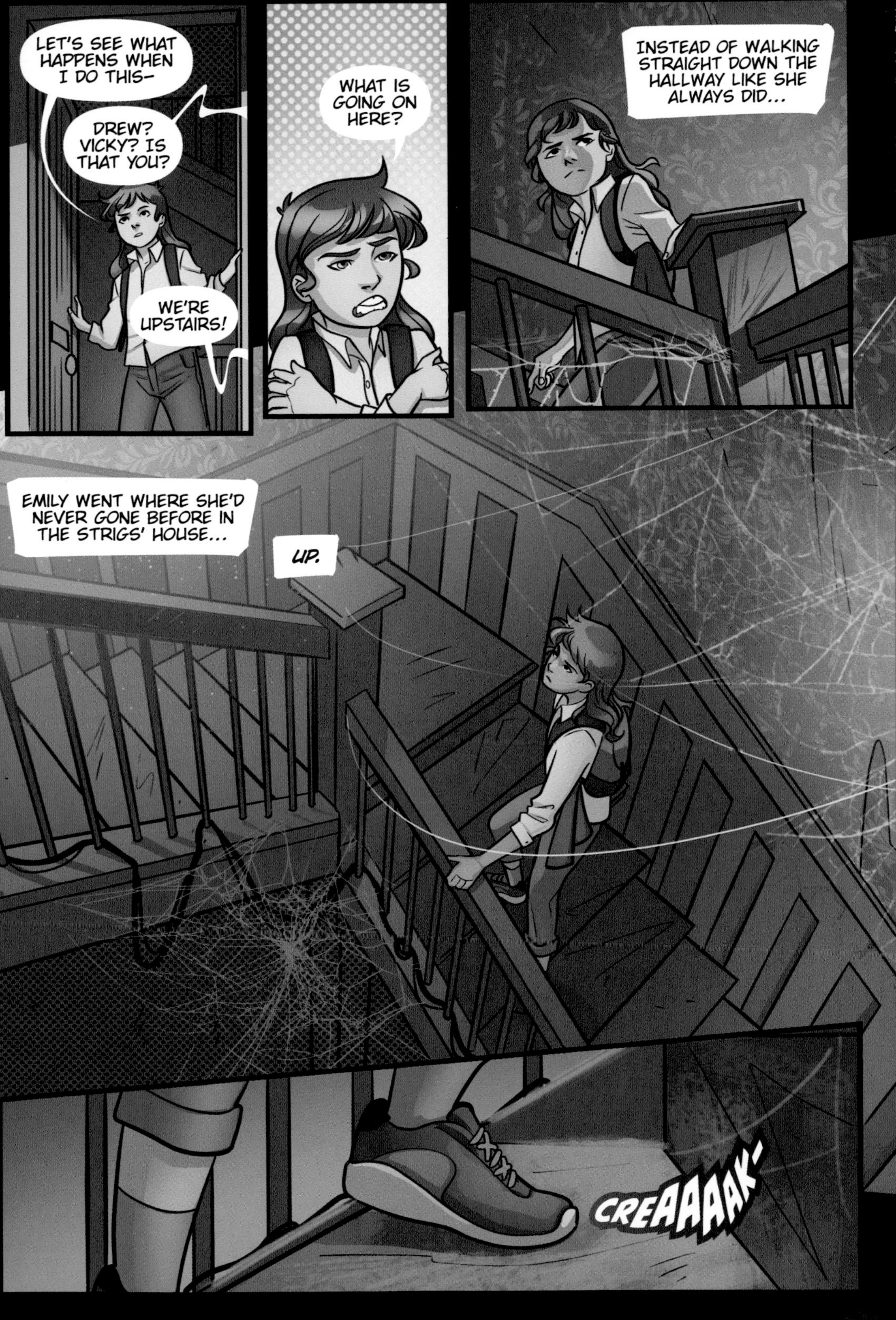
LET'S SEE WHAT HAPPENS WHEN I DO THIS–
DREW? VICKY? IS THAT YOU?
WE'RE UPSTAIRS!
WHAT IS GOING ON HERE?
INSTEAD OF WALKING STRAIGHT DOWN THE HALLWAY LIKE SHE ALWAYS DID...
EMILY WENT WHERE SHE'D NEVER GONE BEFORE IN THE STRIGS' HOUSE...
UP.
CREAAAAK–

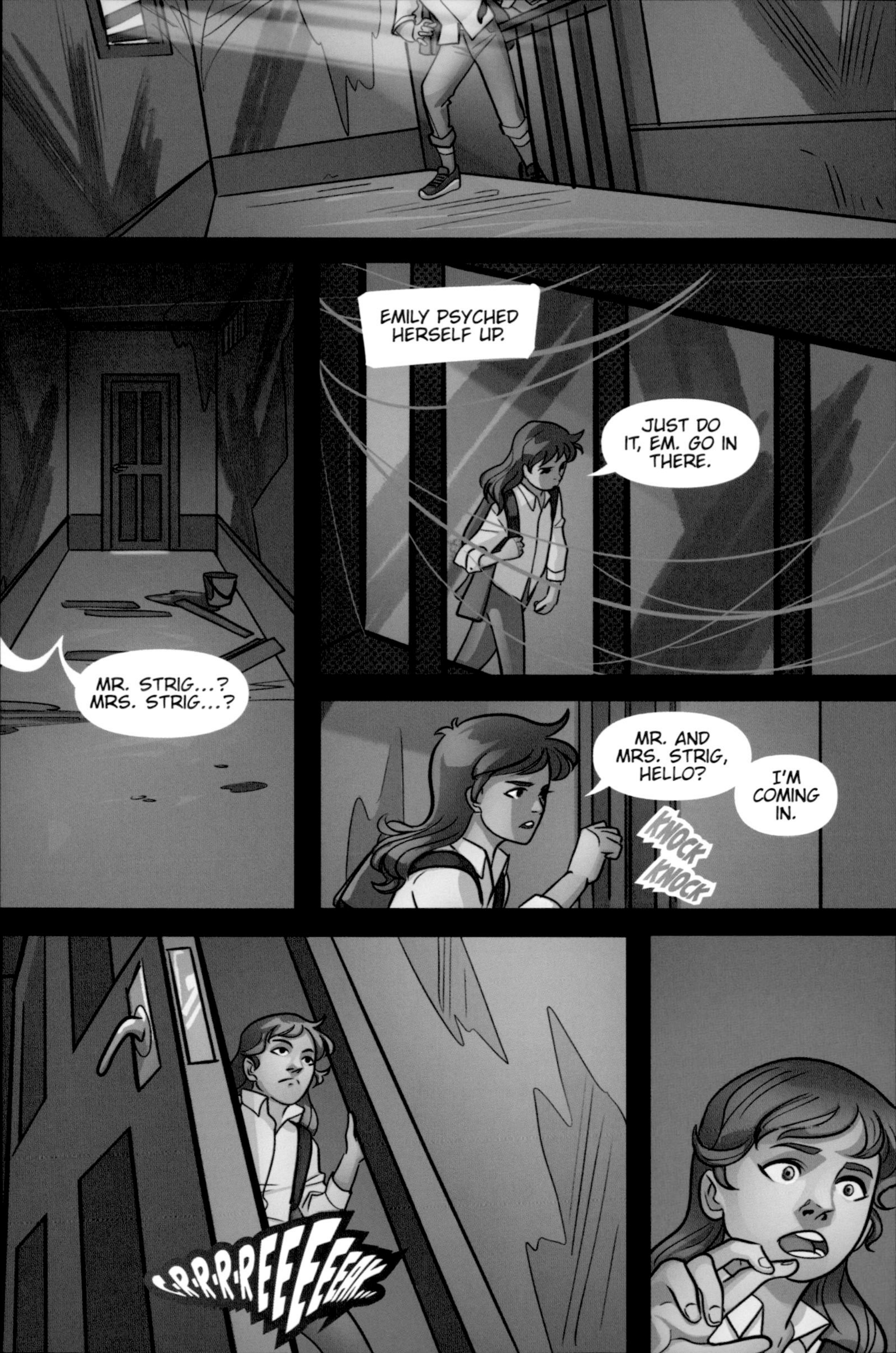
EMILY PSYCHED HERSELF UP.
JUST DO IT, EM. GO IN THERE.
MR. STRIG...? MRS. STRIG...?
MR. AND MRS. STRIG, HELLO?
KNOCK KNOCK
I'M COMING IN.
C-R-R-R-REEEEEEAK...

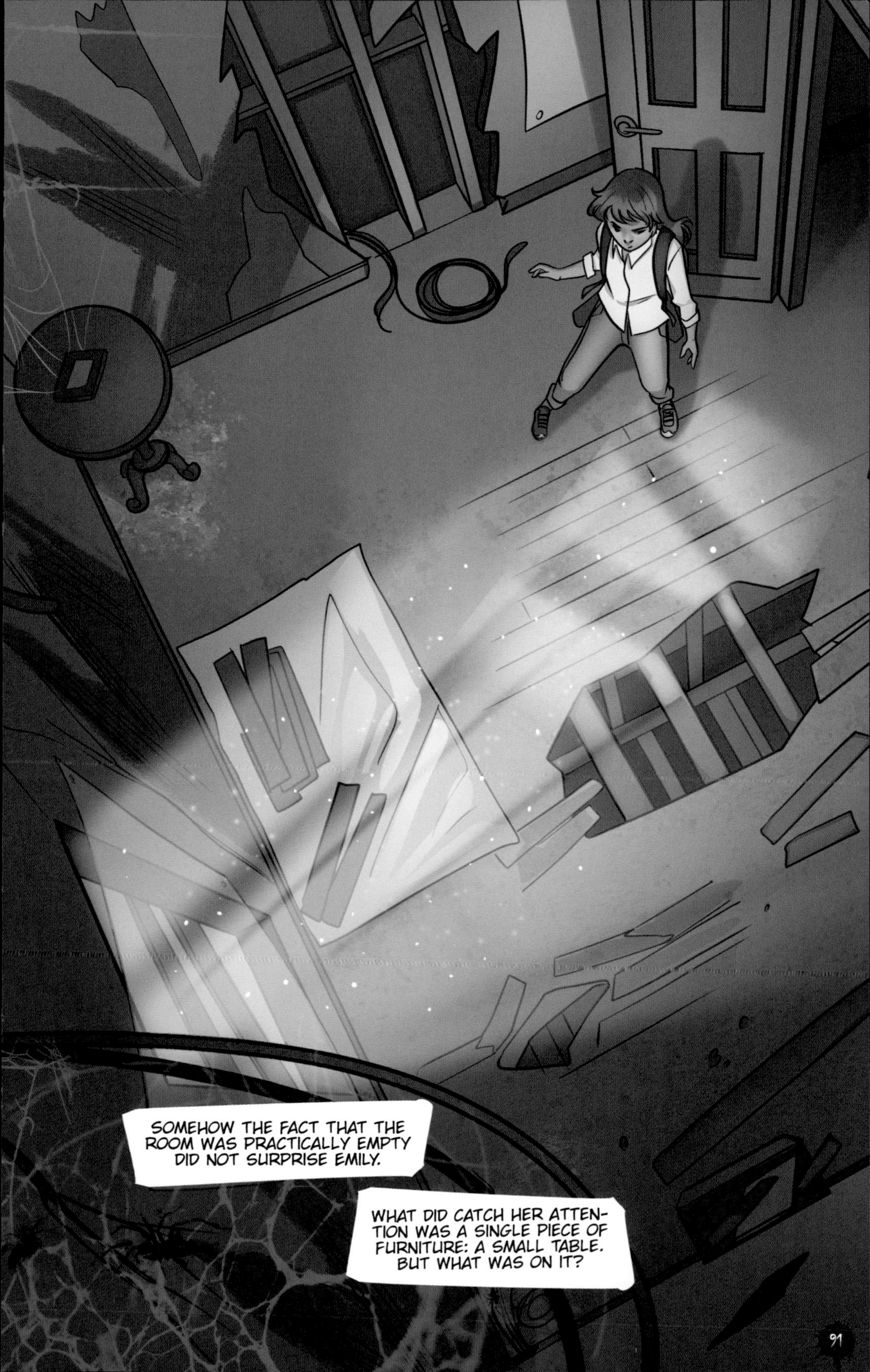
SOMEHOW THE FACT THAT THE ROOM WAS PRACTICALLY EMPTY DID NOT SURPRISE EMILY.
WHAT DID CATCH HER ATTENTION WAS A SINGLE PIECE OF FURNITURE: A SMALL TABLE. BUT WHAT WAS ON IT?

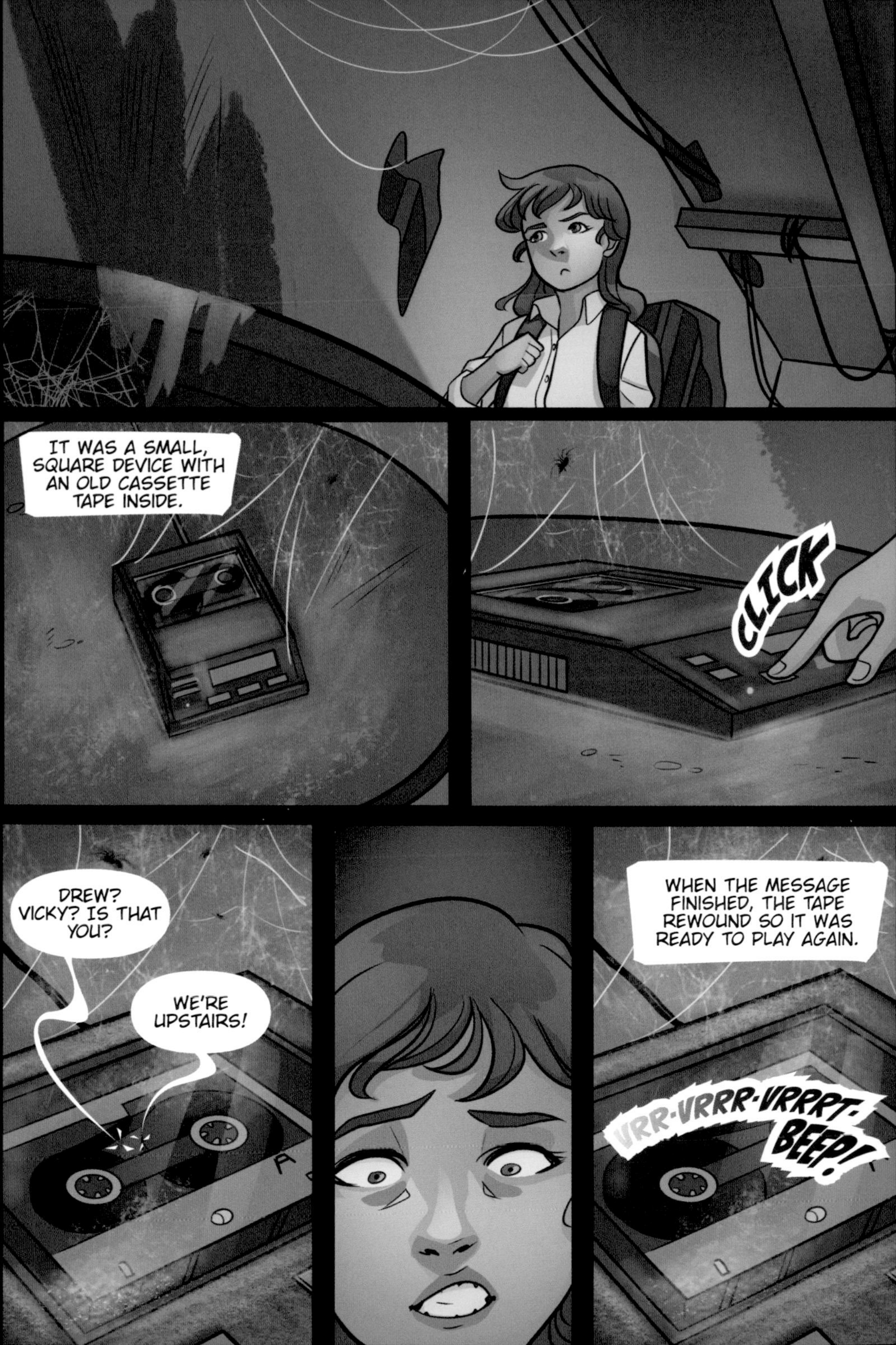
IT WAS A SMALL, SQUARE DEVICE WITH AN OLD CASSETTE TAPE INSIDE.
CLICK
DREW? VICKY? IS THAT YOU?
WE'RE UPSTAIRS!
WHEN THE MESSAGE FINISHED, THE TAPE REWOUND SO IT WAS READY TO PLAY AGAIN.
VRR-VRRR-VRRRT-BEEP!

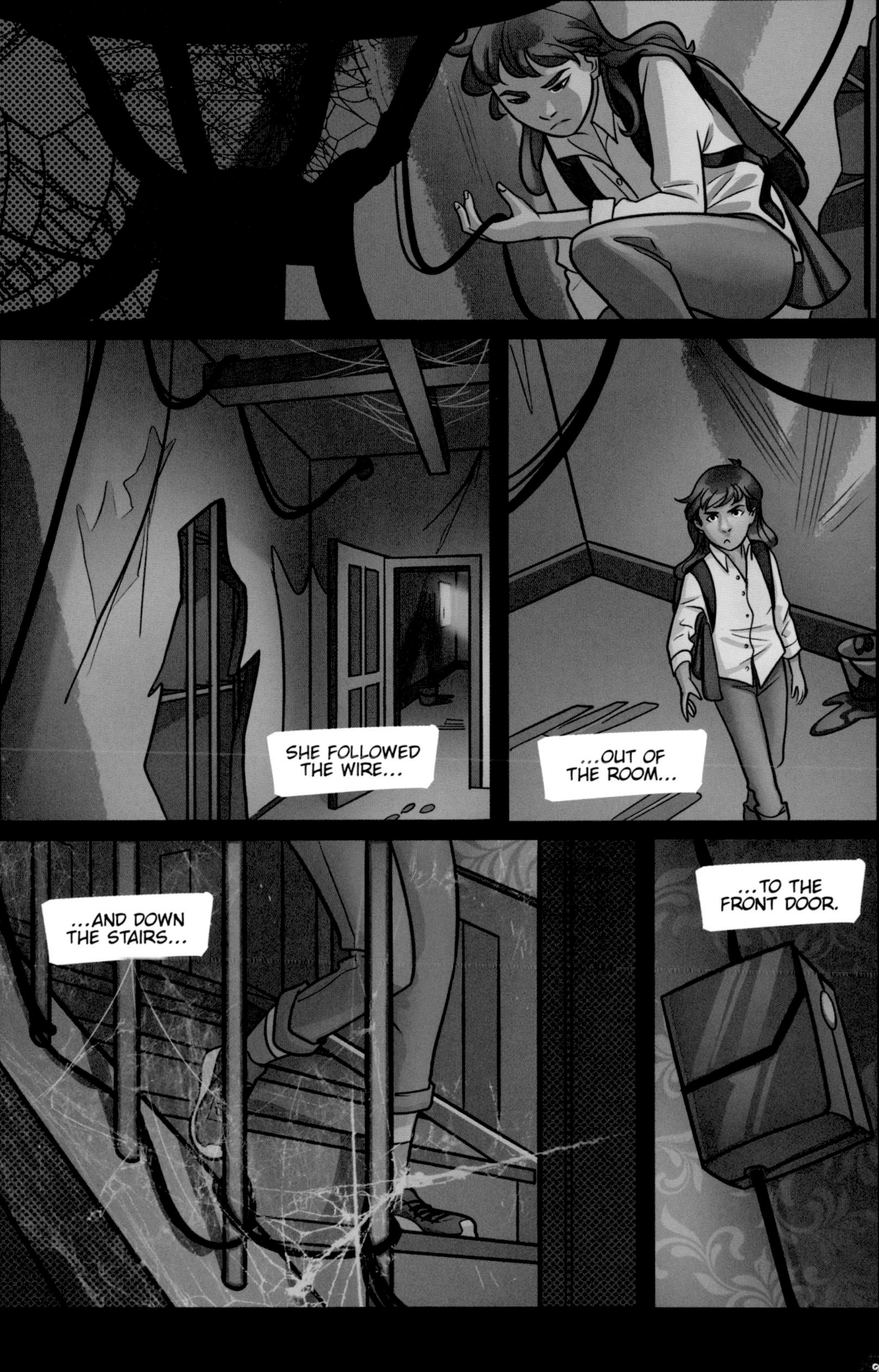
SHE FOLLOWED THE WIRE...
...OUT OF THE ROOM...
...AND DOWN THE STAIRS...
...TO THE FRONT DOOR.

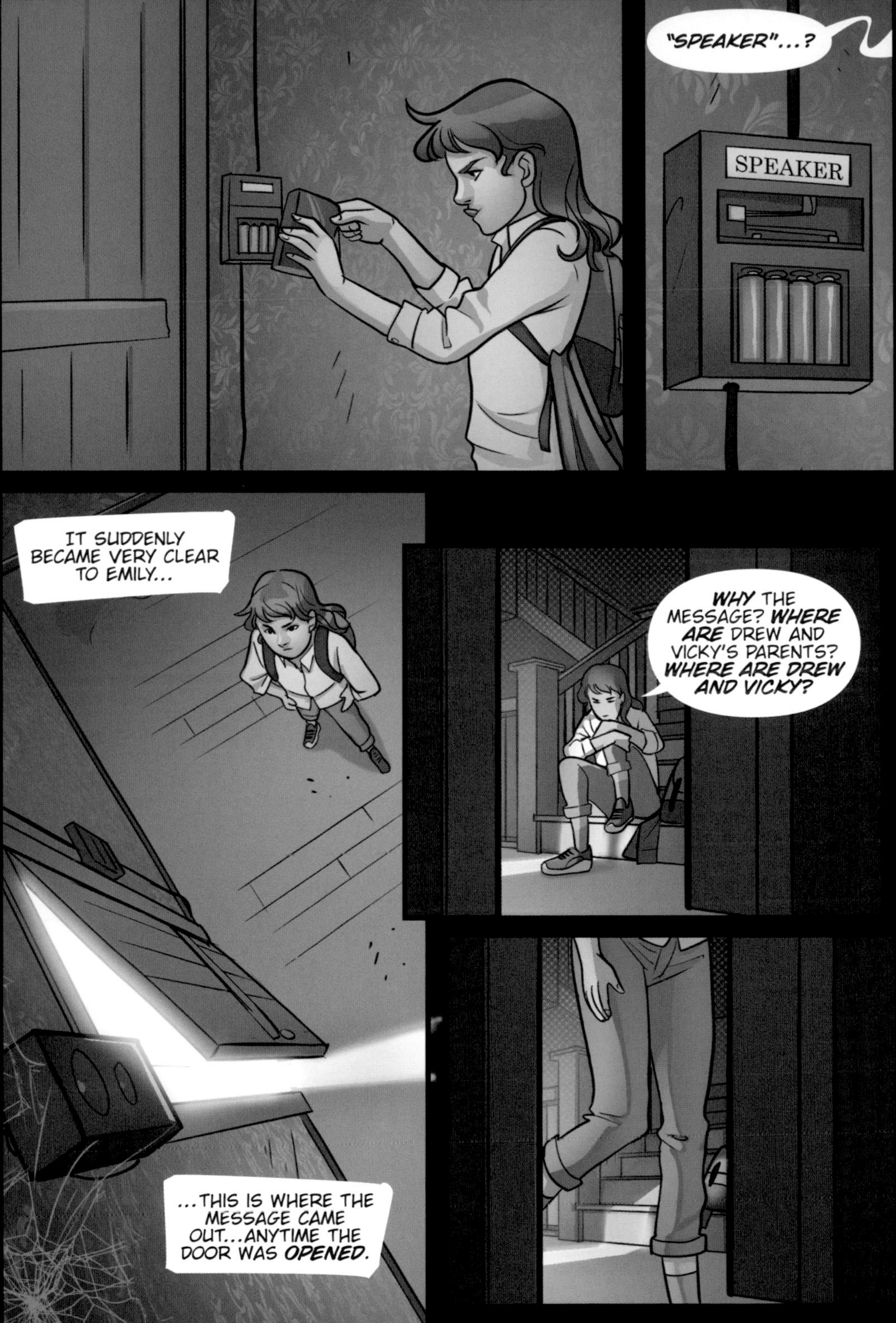
"SPEAKER"...?
SPEAKER
IT SUDDENLY BECAME VERY CLEAR TO EMILY...
WHY THE MESSAGE? WHERE ARE DREW AND VICKY'S PARENTS? WHERE ARE DREW AND VICKY?
...THIS IS WHERE THE MESSAGE CAME OUT...ANYTIME THE DOOR WAS OPENED.

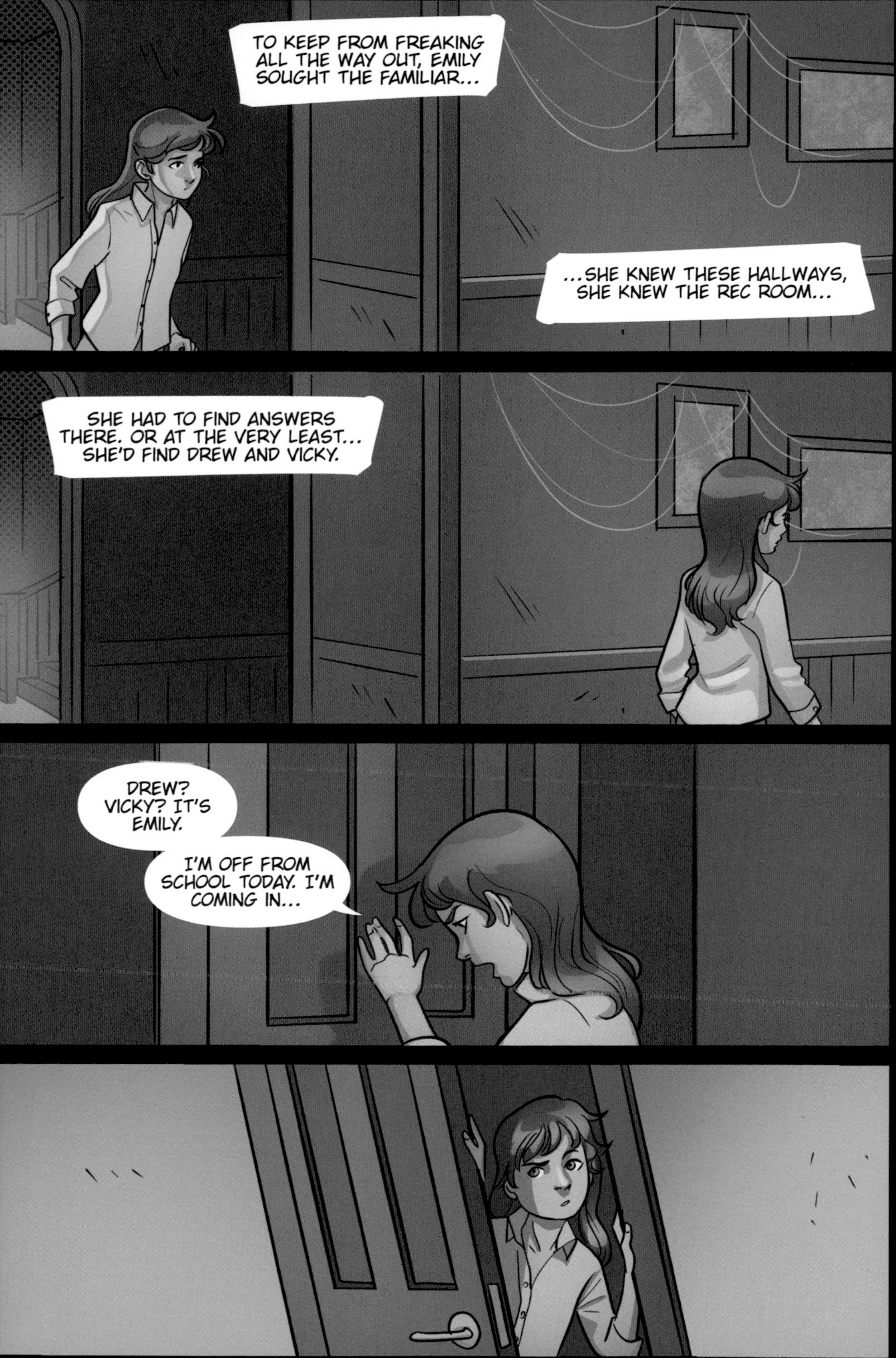
TO KEEP FROM FREAKING ALL THE WAY OUT, EMILY SOUGHT THE FAMILIAR...
...SHE KNEW THESE HALLWAYS, SHE KNEW THE REC ROOM...
SHE HAD TO FIND ANSWERS THERE. OR AT THE VERY LEAST... SHE'D FIND DREW AND VICKY.
DREW? VICKY? IT'S EMILY.
I'M OFF FROM SCHOOL TODAY. I'M COMING IN...

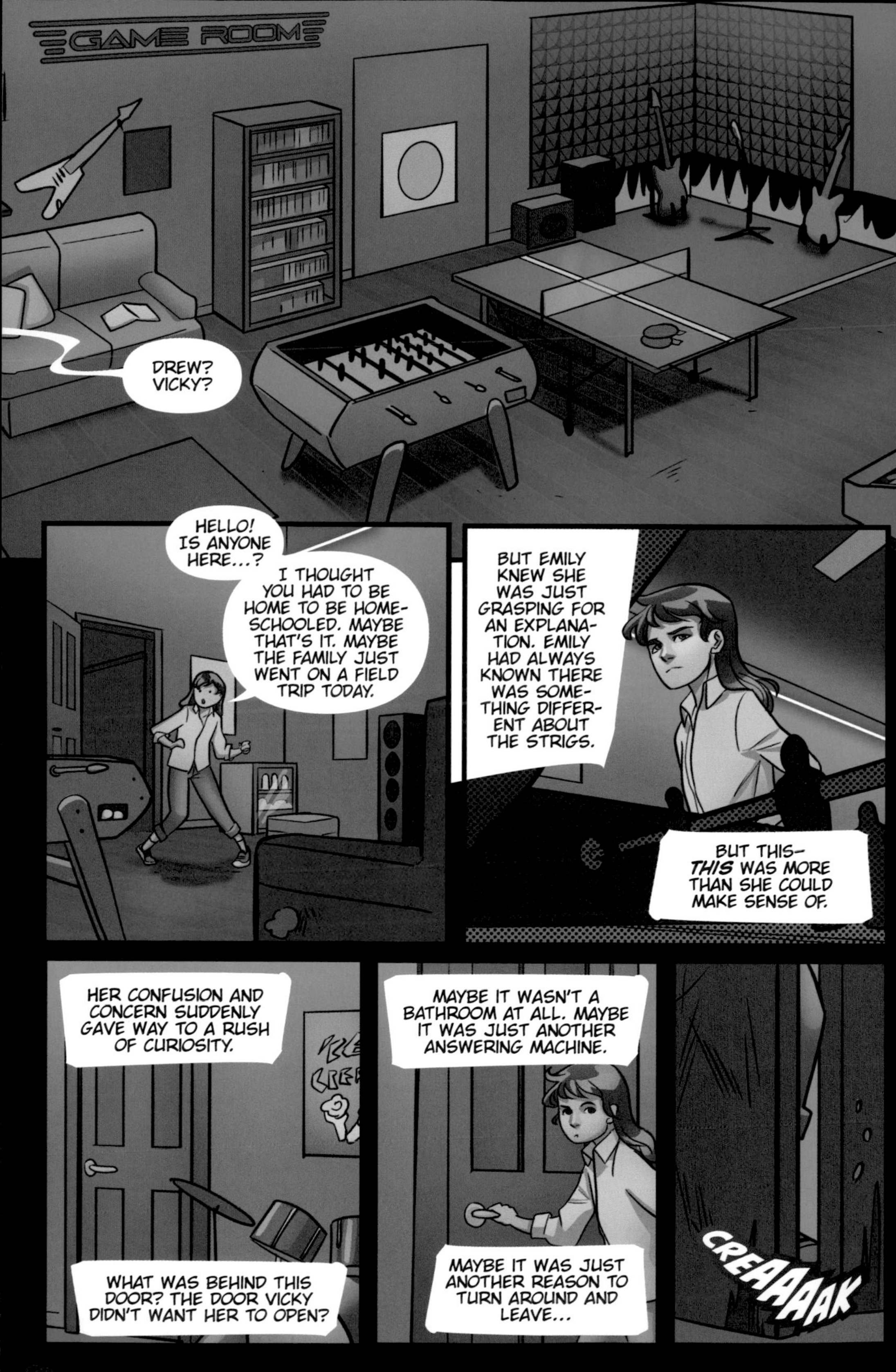
GAME ROOM
DREW? VICKY?
HELLO! IS ANYONE HERE...?
I THOUGHT YOU HAD TO BE HOME TO BE HOME-SCHOOLED. MAYBE THAT'S IT. MAYBE THE FAMILY JUST WENT ON A FIELD TRIP TODAY.
BUT EMILY KNEW SHE WAS JUST GRASPING FOR AN EXPLANATION. EMILY HAD ALWAYS KNOWN THERE WAS SOMETHING DIFFERENT ABOUT THE STRIGS.
BUT THIS— *THIS* WAS MORE THAN SHE COULD MAKE SENSE OF.
HER CONFUSION AND CONCERN SUDDENLY GAVE WAY TO A RUSH OF CURIOSITY.
WHAT WAS BEHIND THIS DOOR? THE DOOR VICKY DIDN'T WANT HER TO OPEN?
MAYBE IT WASN'T A BATHROOM AT ALL. MAYBE IT WAS JUST ANOTHER ANSWERING MACHINE.
MAYBE IT WAS JUST ANOTHER REASON TO TURN AROUND AND LEAVE...
CREAAAAK

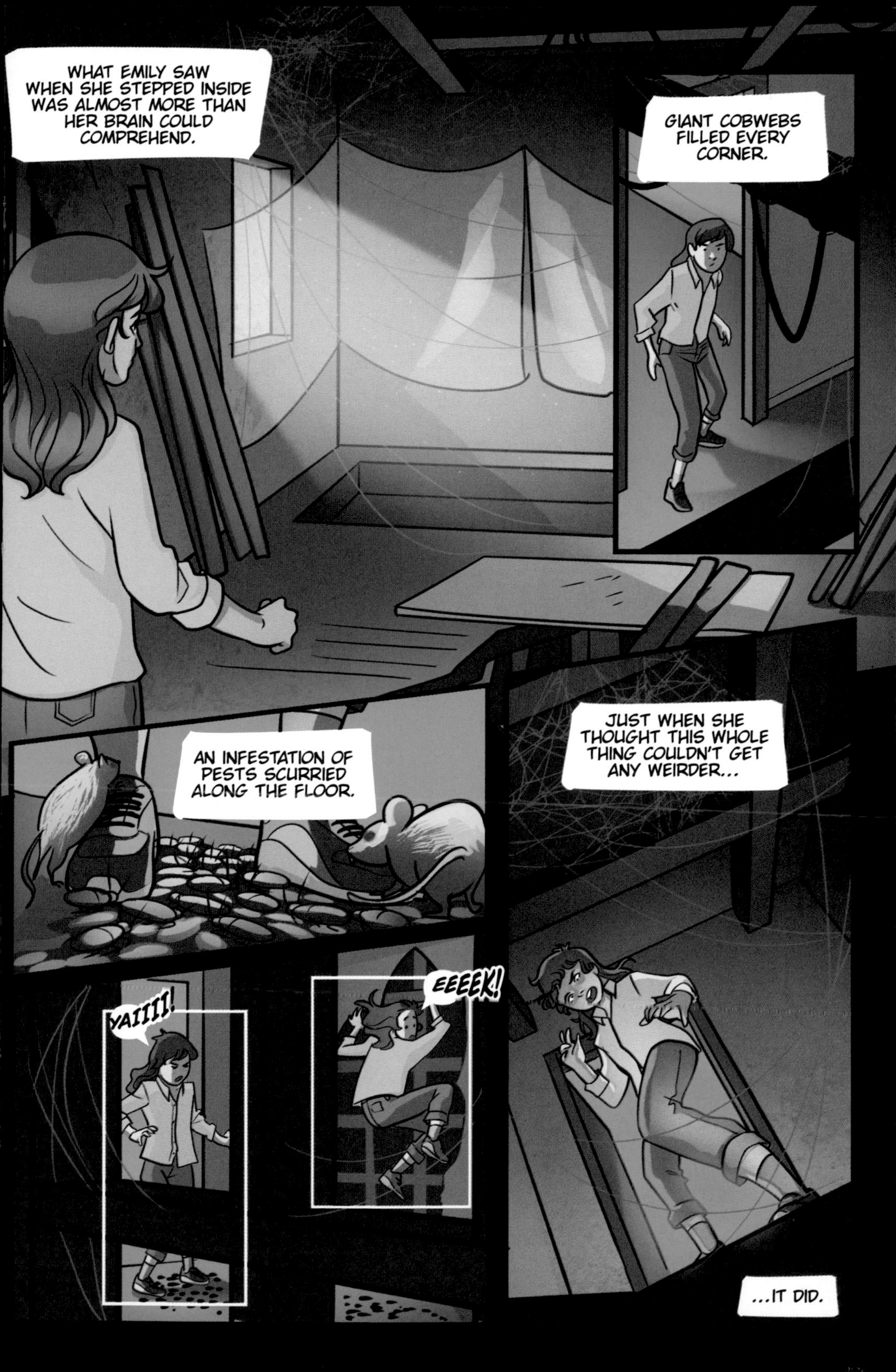
WHAT EMILY SAW WHEN SHE STEPPED INSIDE WAS ALMOST MORE THAN HER BRAIN COULD COMPREHEND.
GIANT COBWEBS FILLED EVERY CORNER.
AN INFESTATION OF PESTS SCURRIED ALONG THE FLOOR.
JUST WHEN SHE THOUGHT THIS WHOLE THING COULDN'T GET ANY WEIRDER...
YAIIII!
EEEEK!
...IT DID.

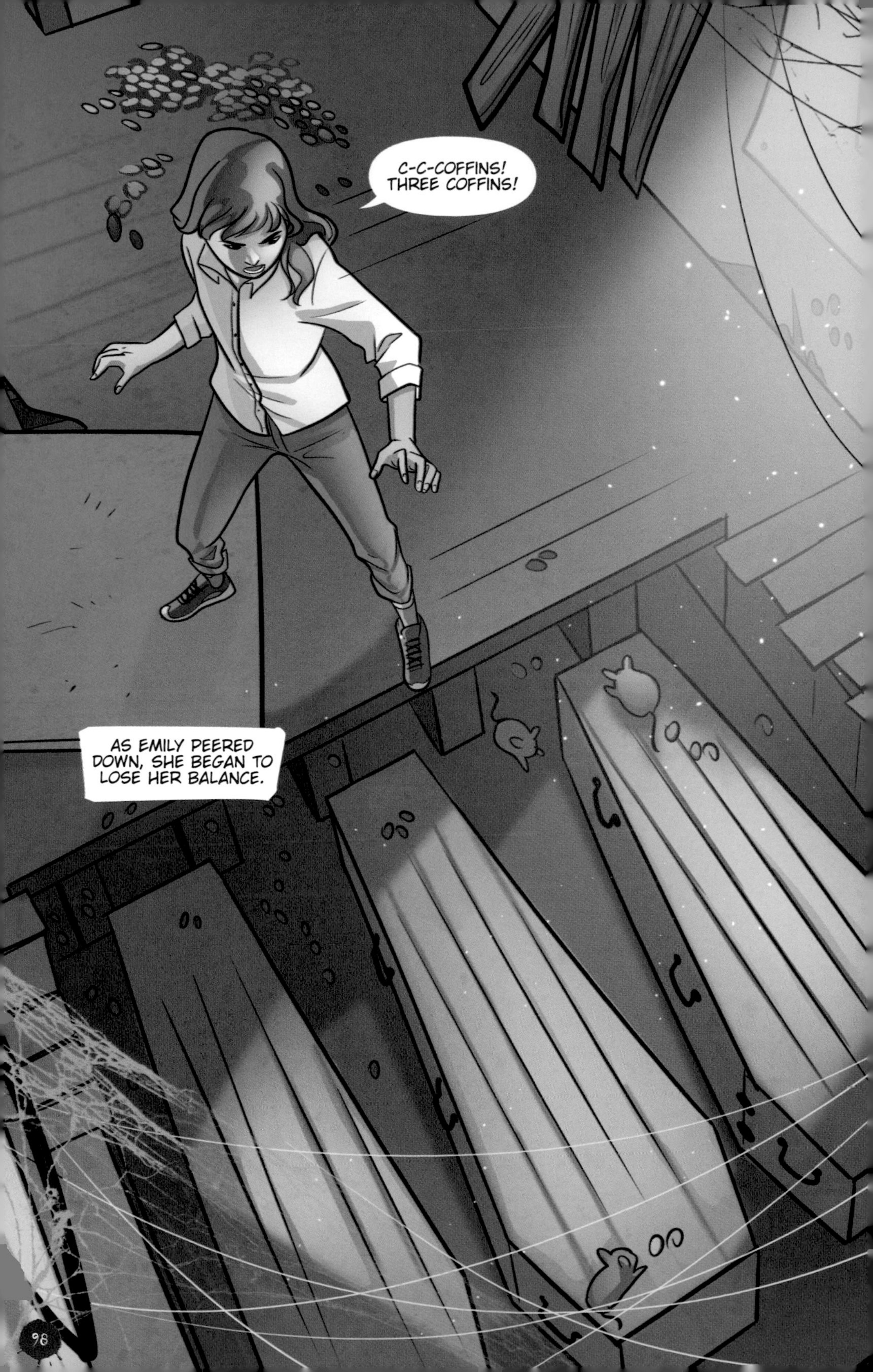
C-C-COFFINS! THREE COFFINS!
AS EMILY PEERED DOWN, SHE BEGAN TO LOSE HER BALANCE.

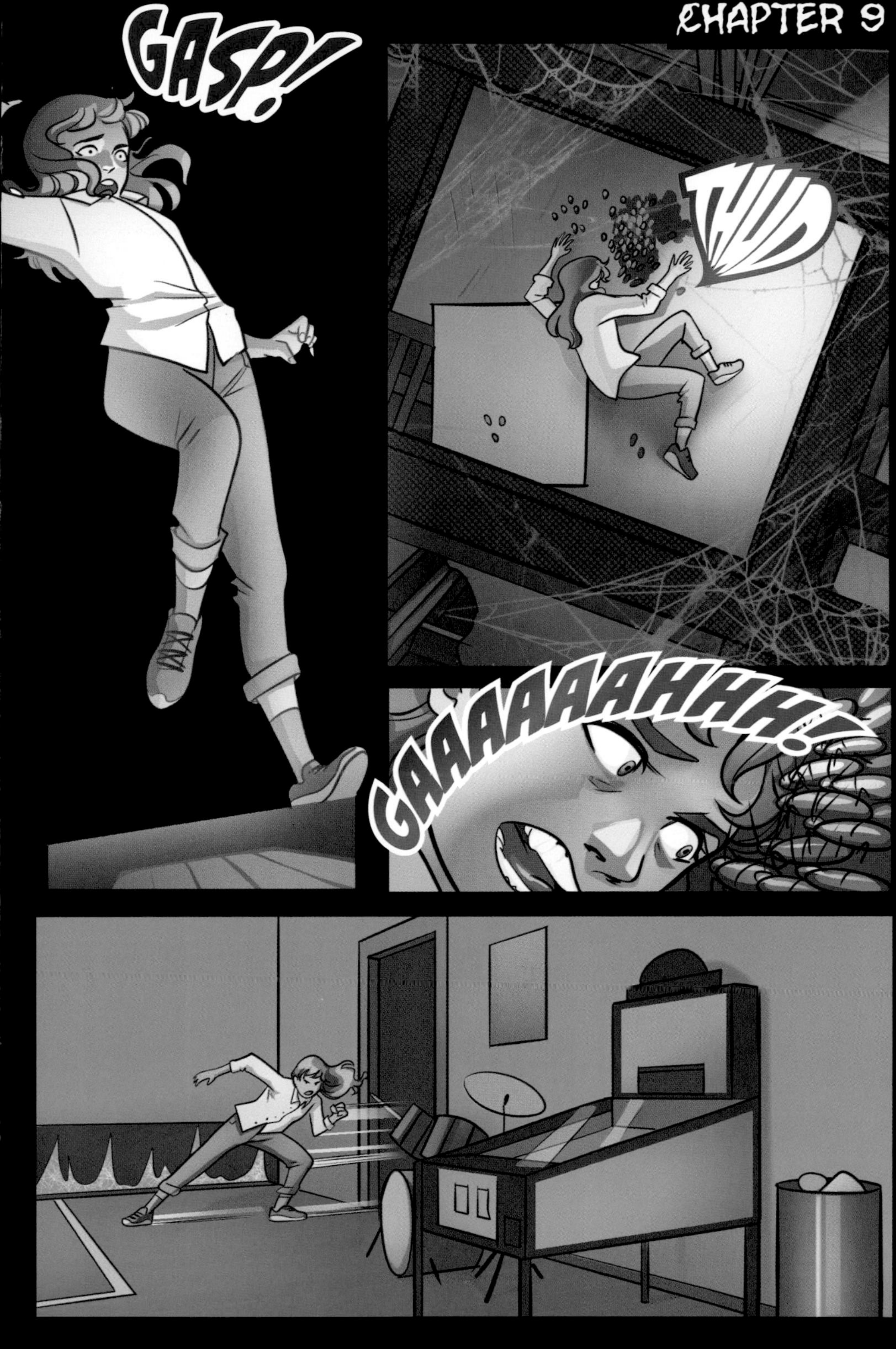
GASP!
THUD
GAAAAAAAHHH!

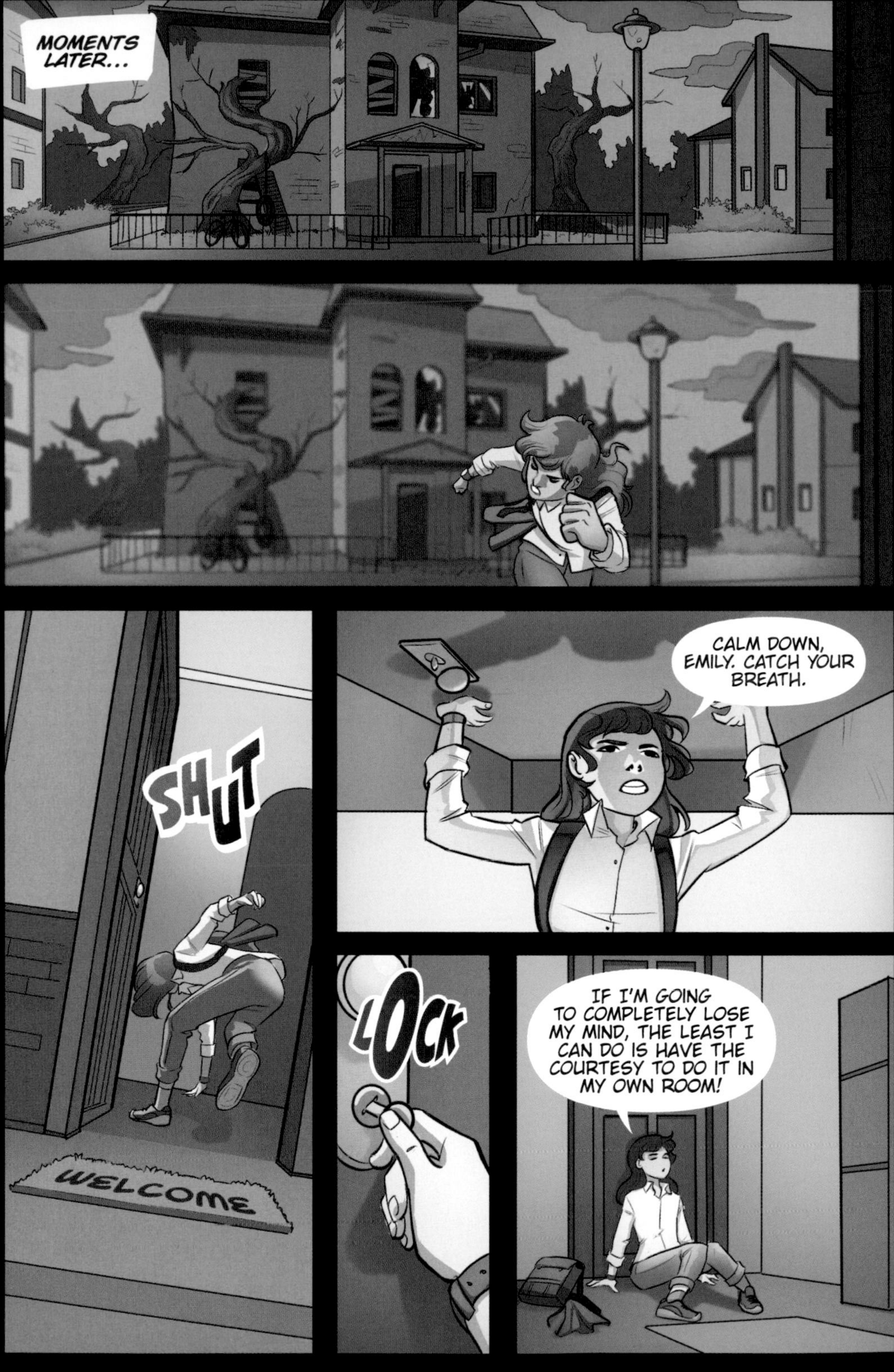
MOMENTS LATER...
SHUT
CALM DOWN, EMILY. CATCH YOUR BREATH.
WELCOME
LOCK
IF I'M GOING TO COMPLETELY LOSE MY MIND, THE LEAST I CAN DO IS HAVE THE COURTESY TO DO IT IN MY OWN ROOM!

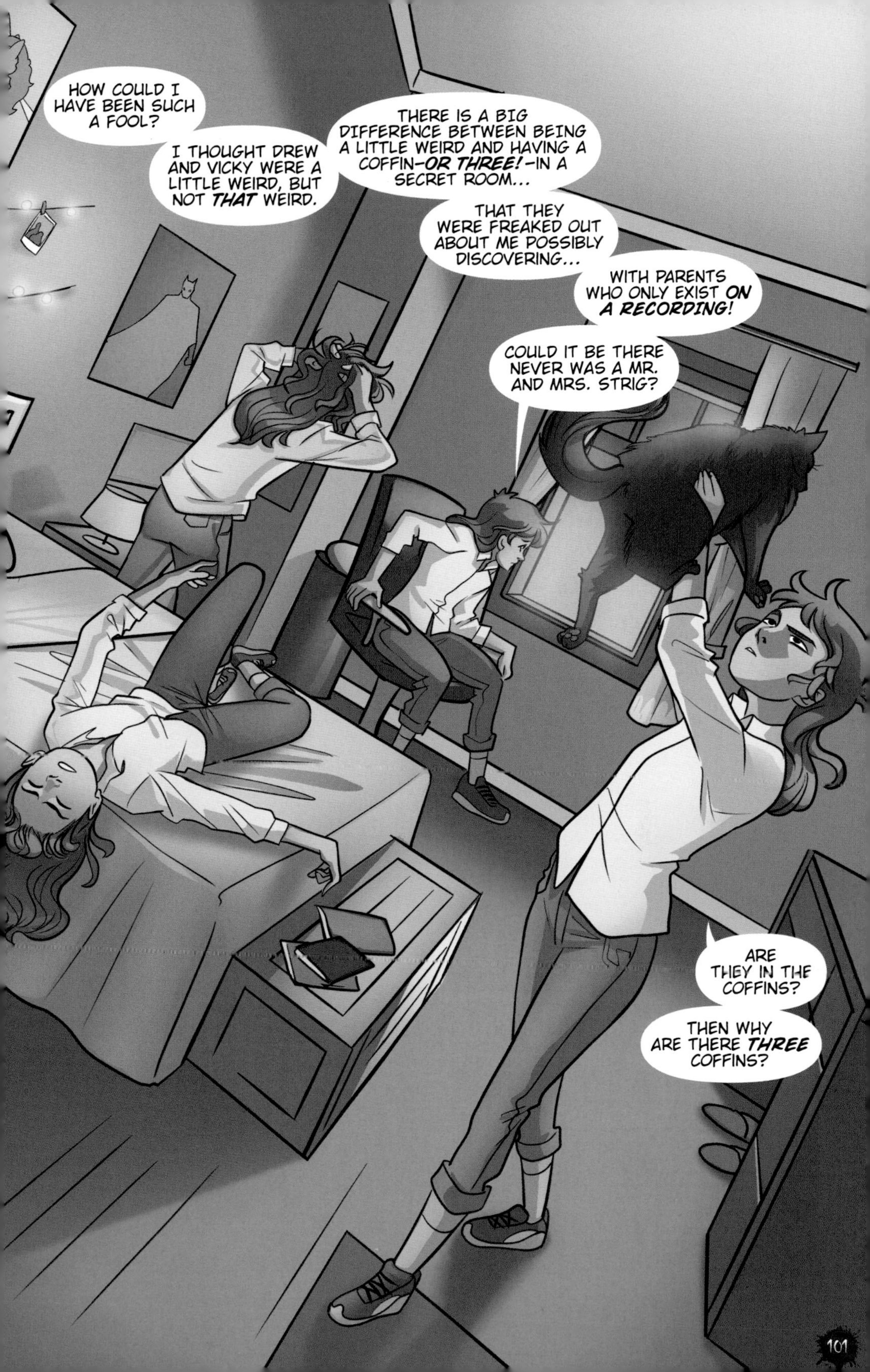
HOW COULD I HAVE BEEN SUCH A FOOL?
I THOUGHT DREW AND VICKY WERE A LITTLE WEIRD, BUT NOT *THAT* WEIRD.
THERE IS A BIG DIFFERENCE BETWEEN BEING A LITTLE WEIRD AND HAVING A COFFIN—***OR THREE!***—IN A SECRET ROOM...
THAT THEY WERE FREAKED OUT ABOUT ME POSSIBLY DISCOVERING...
WITH PARENTS WHO ONLY EXIST ***ON A RECORDING***!
COULD IT BE THERE NEVER WAS A MR. AND MRS. STRIG?
ARE THEY IN THE COFFINS?
THEN WHY ARE THERE ***THREE*** COFFINS?

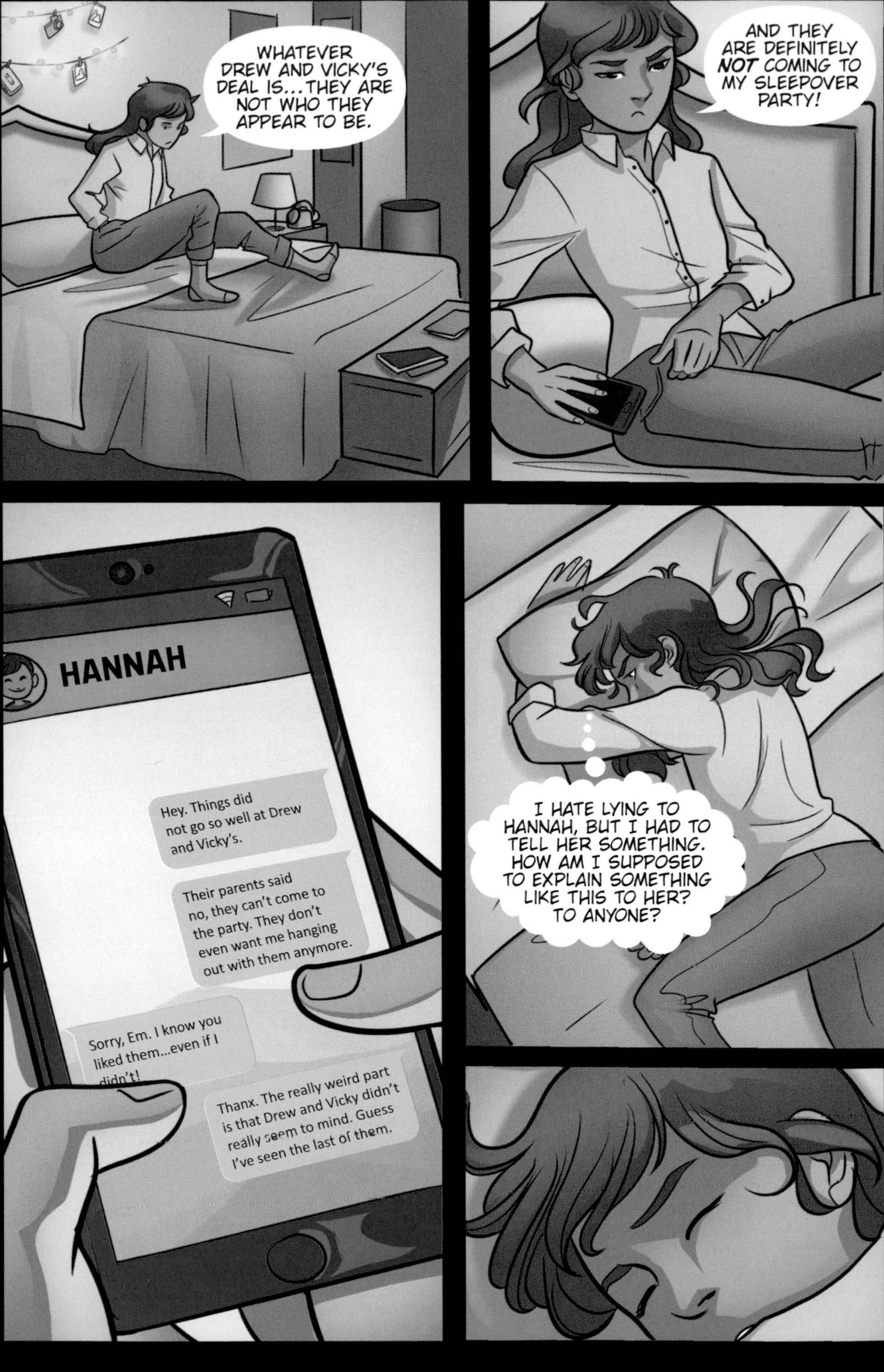
WHATEVER DREW AND VICKY'S DEAL IS...THEY ARE NOT WHO THEY APPEAR TO BE.
AND THEY ARE DEFINITELY *NOT* COMING TO MY SLEEPOVER PARTY!
HANNAH
Hey. Things did not go so well at Drew and Vicky's.
Their parents said no, they can't come to the party. They don't even want me hanging out with them anymore.
Sorry, Em. I know you liked them...even if I didn't!
Thanx. The really weird part is that Drew and Vicky didn't really seem to mind. Guess I've seen the last of them.
I HATE LYING TO HANNAH, BUT I HAD TO TELL HER SOMETHING. HOW AM I SUPPOSED TO EXPLAIN SOMETHING LIKE THIS TO HER? TO ANYONE?

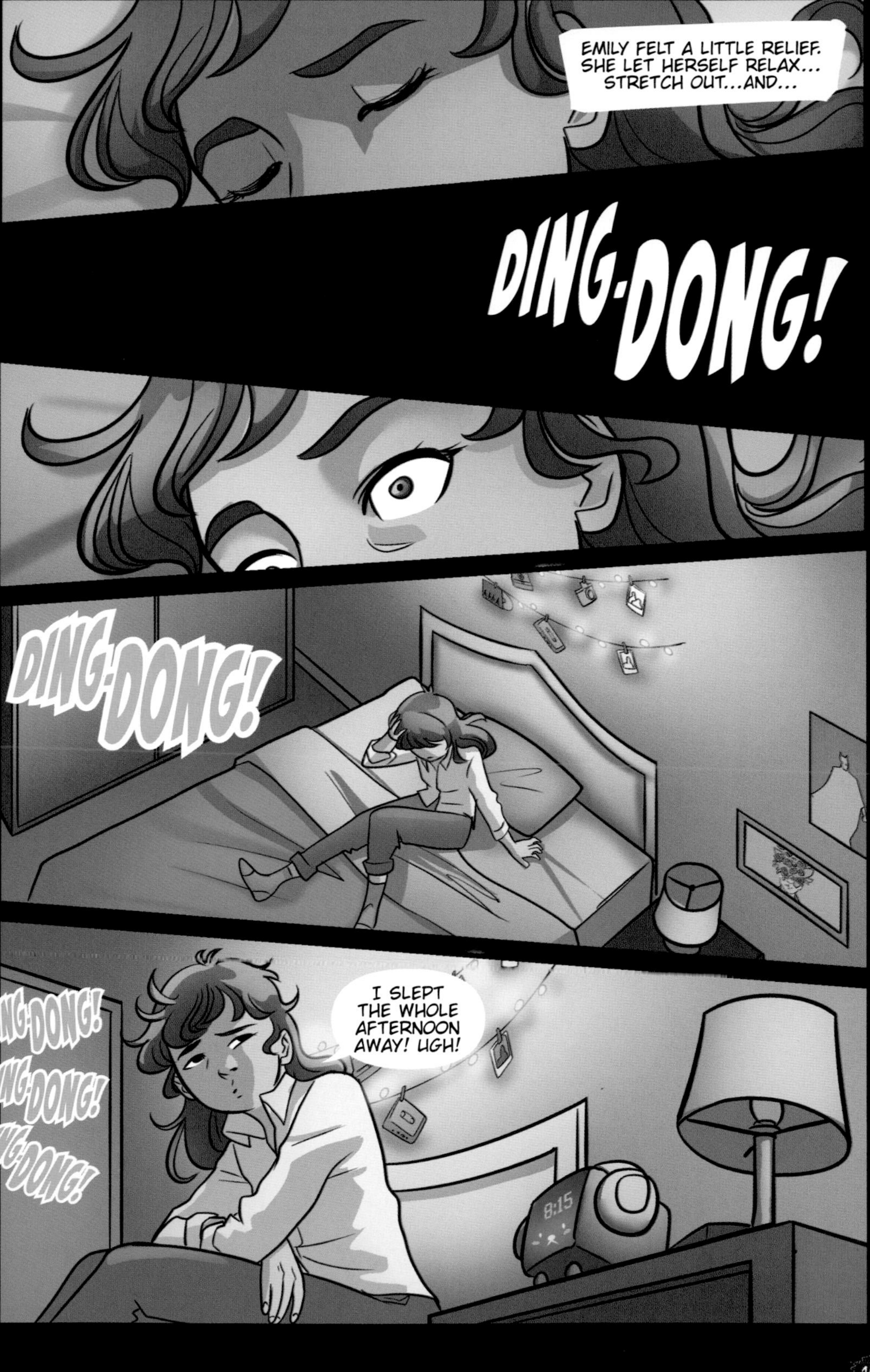
EMILY FELT A LITTLE RELIEF. SHE LET HERSELF RELAX... STRETCH OUT...AND...
DING-DONG!
DING-DONG!
DING-DONG!
DING-DONG!
DING-DONG!
I SLEPT THE WHOLE AFTERNOON AWAY! UGH!
8:15

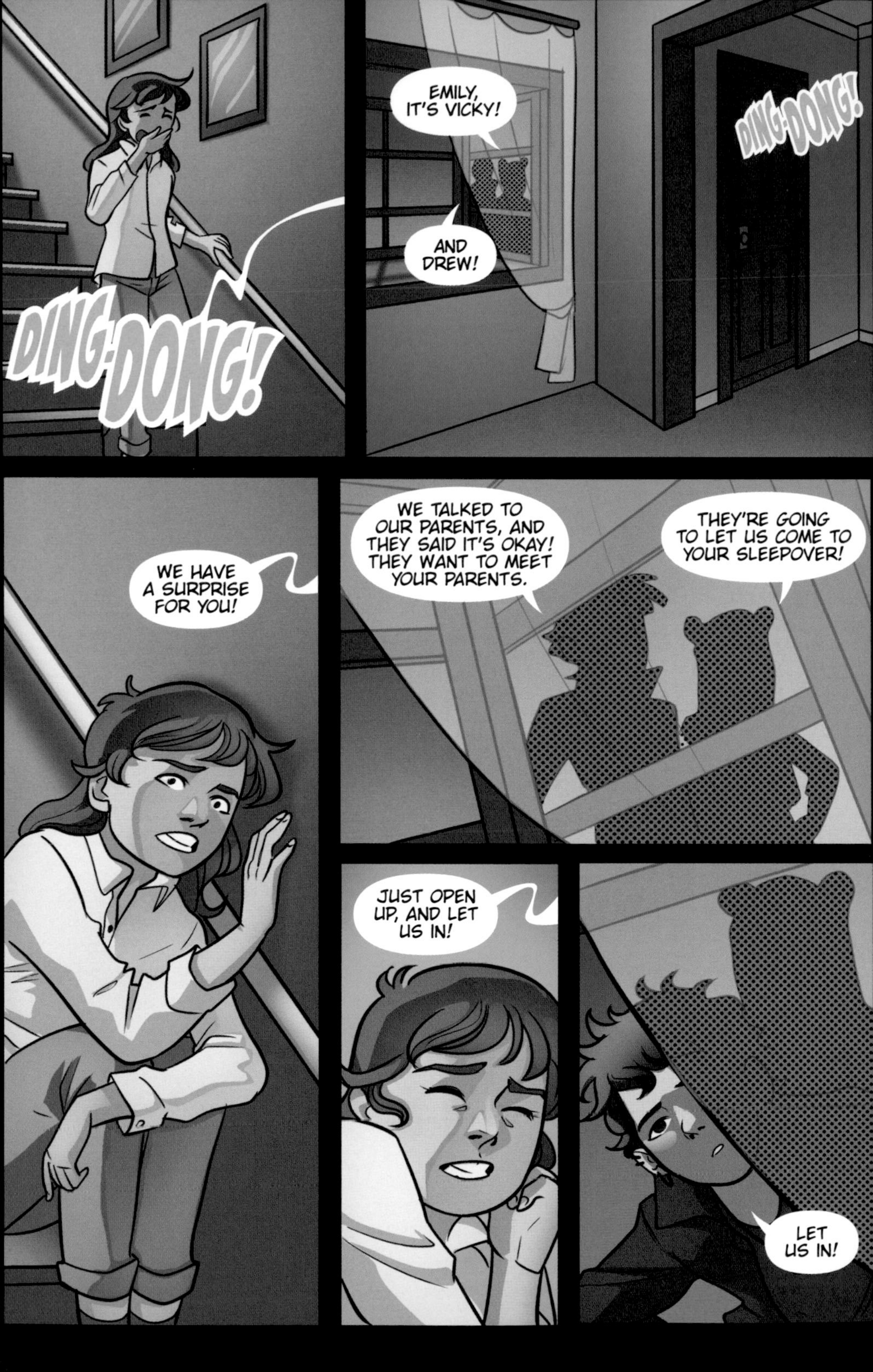
DING-DONG!
EMILY, IT'S VICKY!
AND DREW!
DING-DONG!
WE HAVE A SURPRISE FOR YOU!
WE TALKED TO OUR PARENTS, AND THEY SAID IT'S OKAY! THEY WANT TO MEET YOUR PARENTS.
THEY'RE GOING TO LET US COME TO YOUR SLEEPOVER!
JUST OPEN UP, AND LET US IN!
LET US IN!

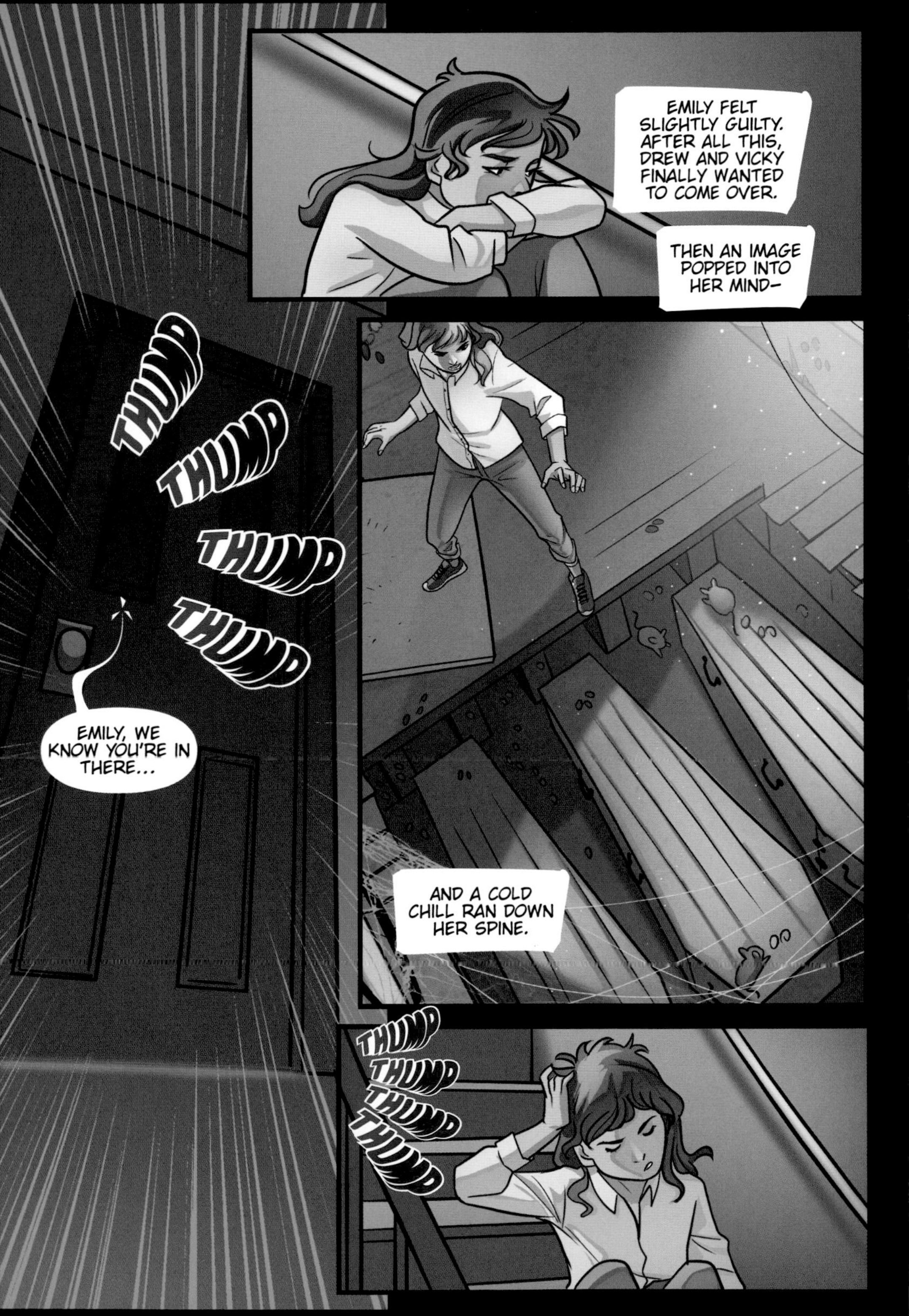
EMILY FELT SLIGHTLY GUILTY. AFTER ALL THIS, DREW AND VICKY FINALLY WANTED TO COME OVER.
THEN AN IMAGE POPPED INTO HER MIND–
THUMP
THUMP
THUMP
THUMP
EMILY, WE KNOW YOU'RE IN THERE...
AND A COLD CHILL RAN DOWN HER SPINE.
THUMP
THUMP
THUMP
THUMP

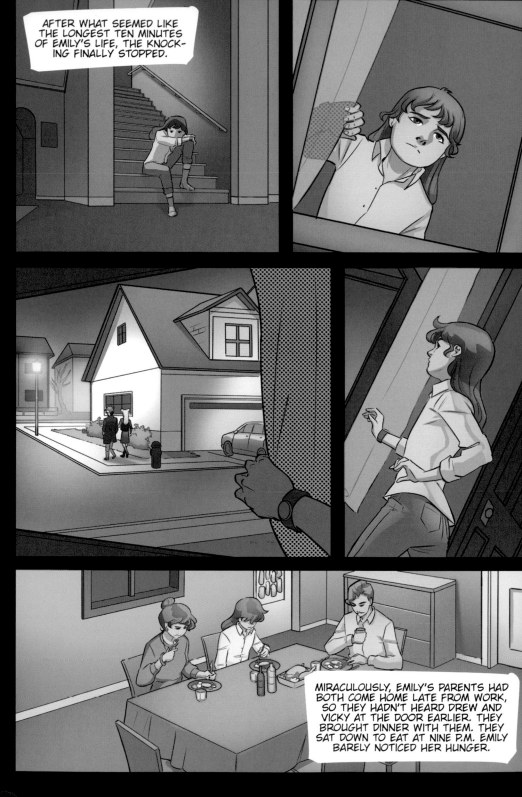

AFTER WHAT SEEMED LIKE THE LONGEST TEN MINUTES OF EMILY'S LIFE, THE KNOCKING FINALLY STOPPED.

MIRACULOUSLY, EMILY'S PARENTS HAD BOTH COME HOME LATE FROM WORK, SO THEY HADN'T HEARD DREW AND VICKY AT THE DOOR EARLIER. THEY BROUGHT DINNER WITH THEM. THEY SAT DOWN TO EAT AT NINE P.M. EMILY BARELY NOTICED HER HUNGER.

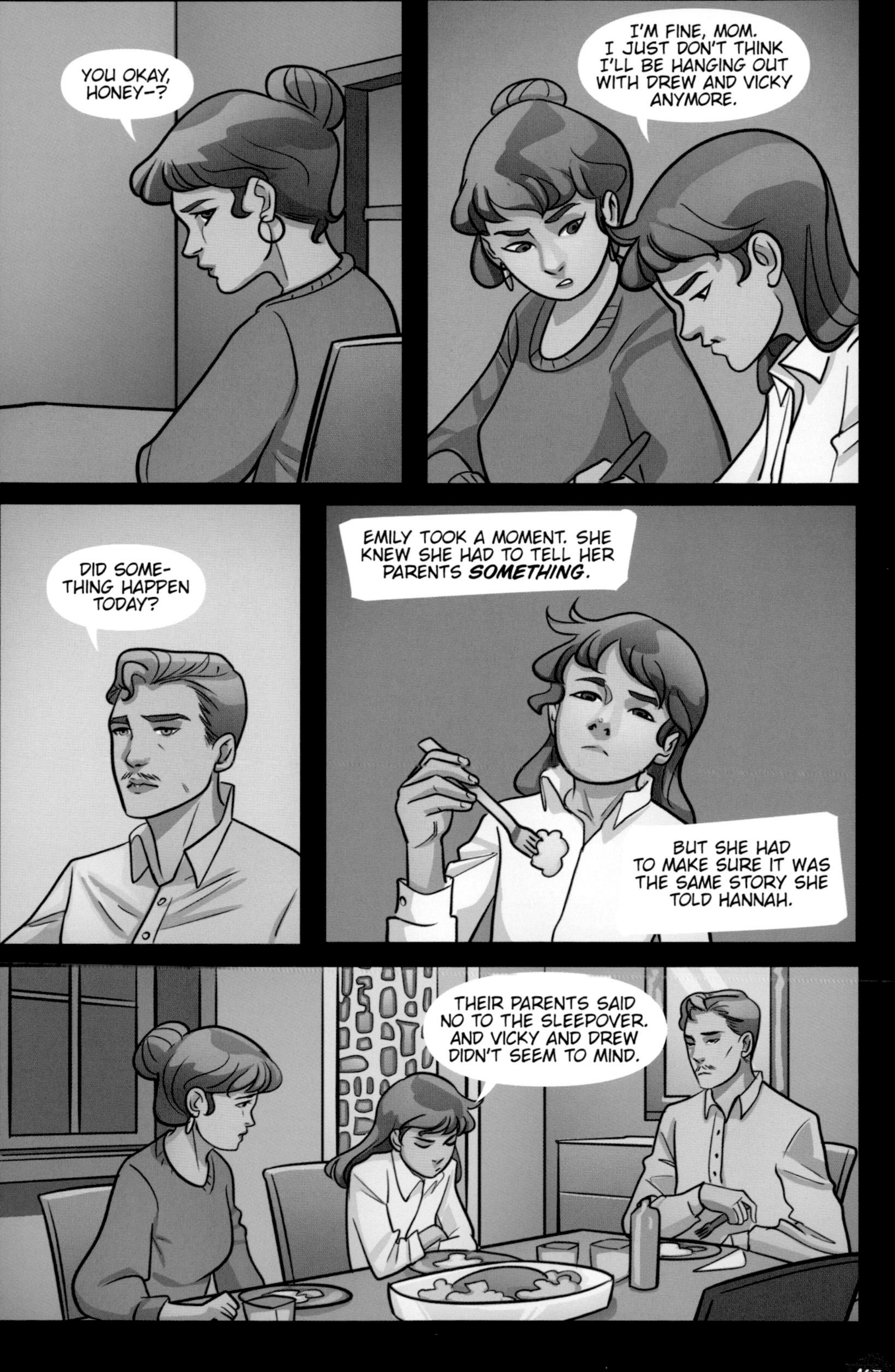
YOU OKAY, HONEY–?
I'M FINE, MOM. I JUST DON'T THINK I'LL BE HANGING OUT WITH DREW AND VICKY ANYMORE.
DID SOME-THING HAPPEN TODAY?
EMILY TOOK A MOMENT. SHE KNEW SHE HAD TO TELL HER PARENTS SOMETHING.
BUT SHE HAD TO MAKE SURE IT WAS THE SAME STORY SHE TOLD HANNAH.
THEIR PARENTS SAID NO TO THE SLEEPOVER. AND VICKY AND DREW DIDN'T SEEM TO MIND.

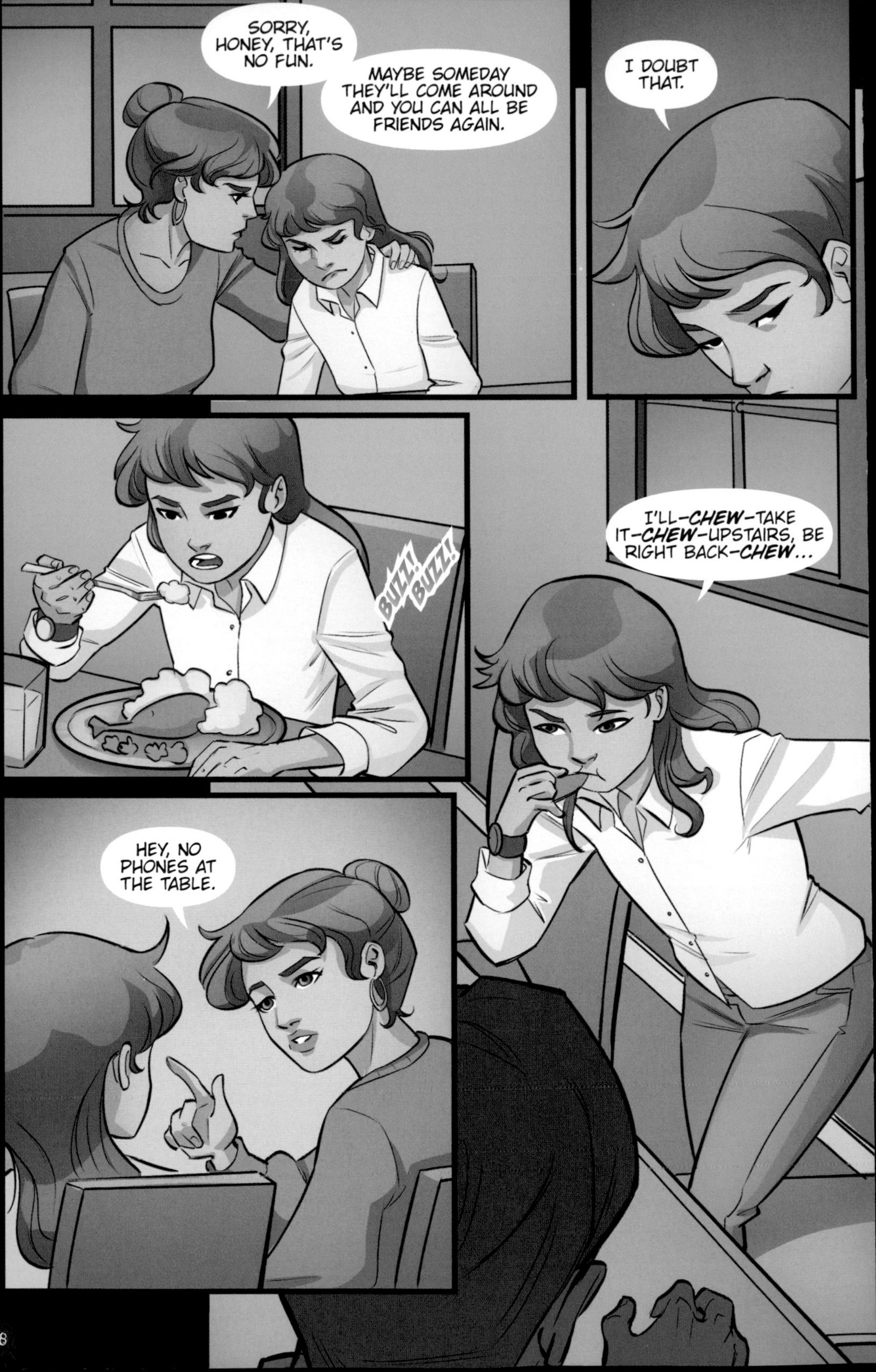
SORRY, HONEY, THAT'S NO FUN.
MAYBE SOMEDAY THEY'LL COME AROUND AND YOU CAN ALL BE FRIENDS AGAIN.
I DOUBT THAT.
BUZZ!! BUZZ!!
I'LL-CHEW-TAKE IT-CHEW-UPSTAIRS, BE RIGHT BACK-CHEW...
HEY, NO PHONES AT THE TABLE.

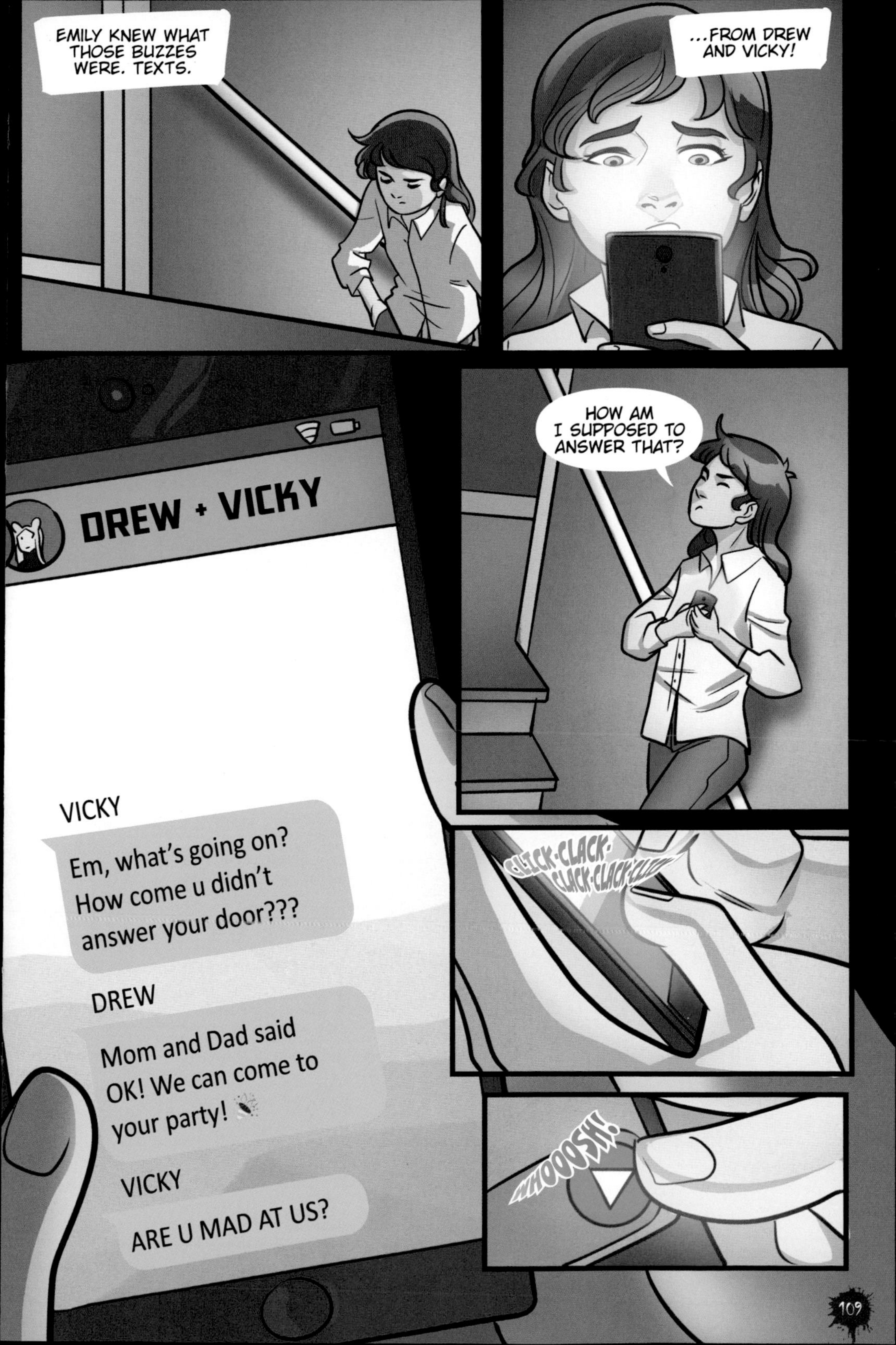
EMILY KNEW WHAT THOSE BUZZES WERE. TEXTS.
...FROM DREW AND VICKY!
DREW + VICKY
VICKY
Em, what's going on? How come u didn't answer your door???
DREW
Mom and Dad said OK! We can come to your party!
VICKY
ARE U MAD AT US?
HOW AM I SUPPOSED TO ANSWER THAT?
WHOOOSH!

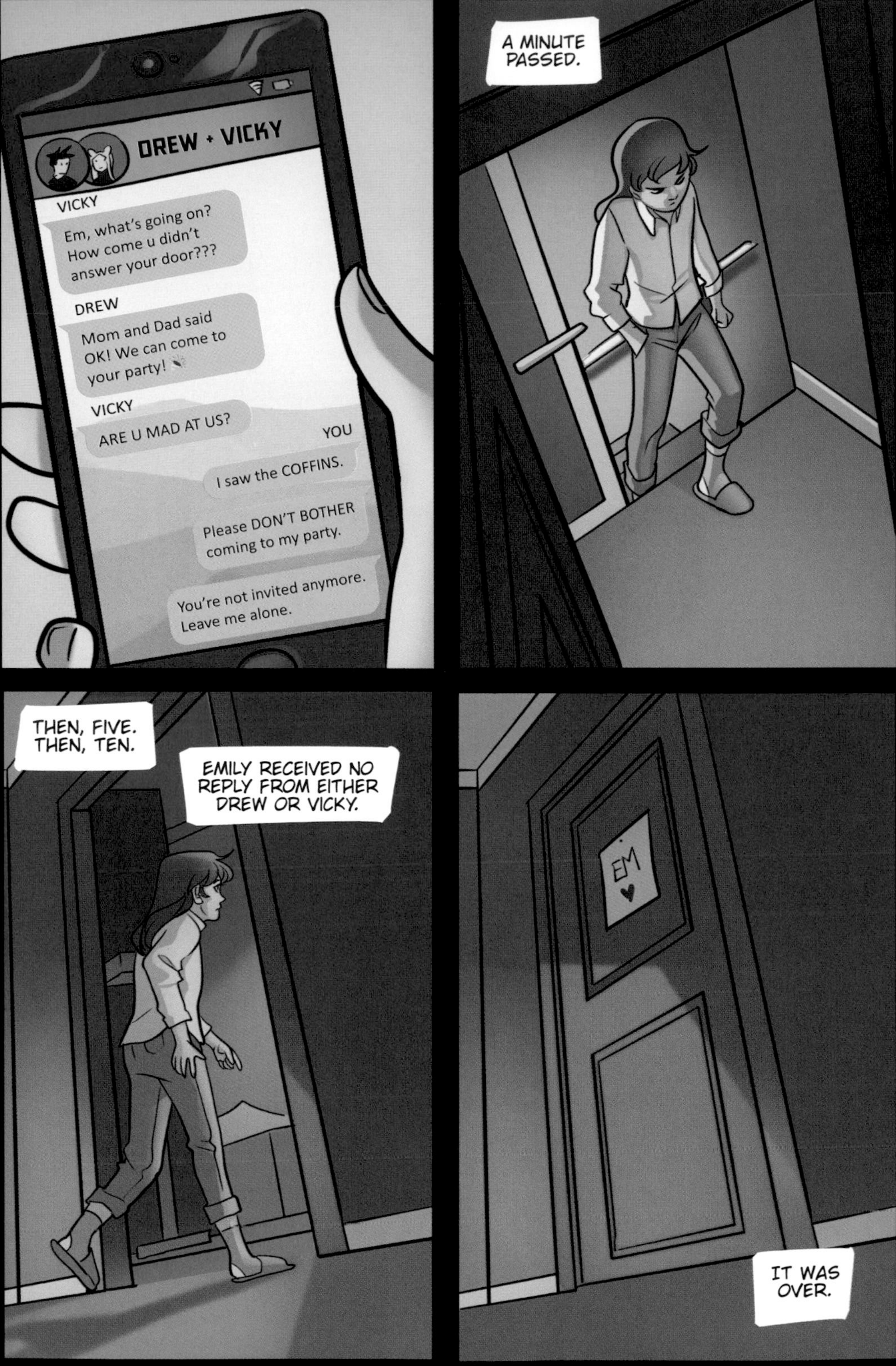
DREW + VICKY
VICKY
Em, what's going on? How come u didn't answer your door???
DREW
Mom and Dad said OK! We can come to your party!
VICKY
ARE U MAD AT US?
YOU
I saw the COFFINS.
Please DON'T BOTHER coming to my party.
You're not invited anymore. Leave me alone.
A MINUTE PASSED.
THEN, FIVE. THEN, TEN.
EMILY RECEIVED NO REPLY FROM EITHER DREW OR VICKY.
EM
IT WAS OVER.

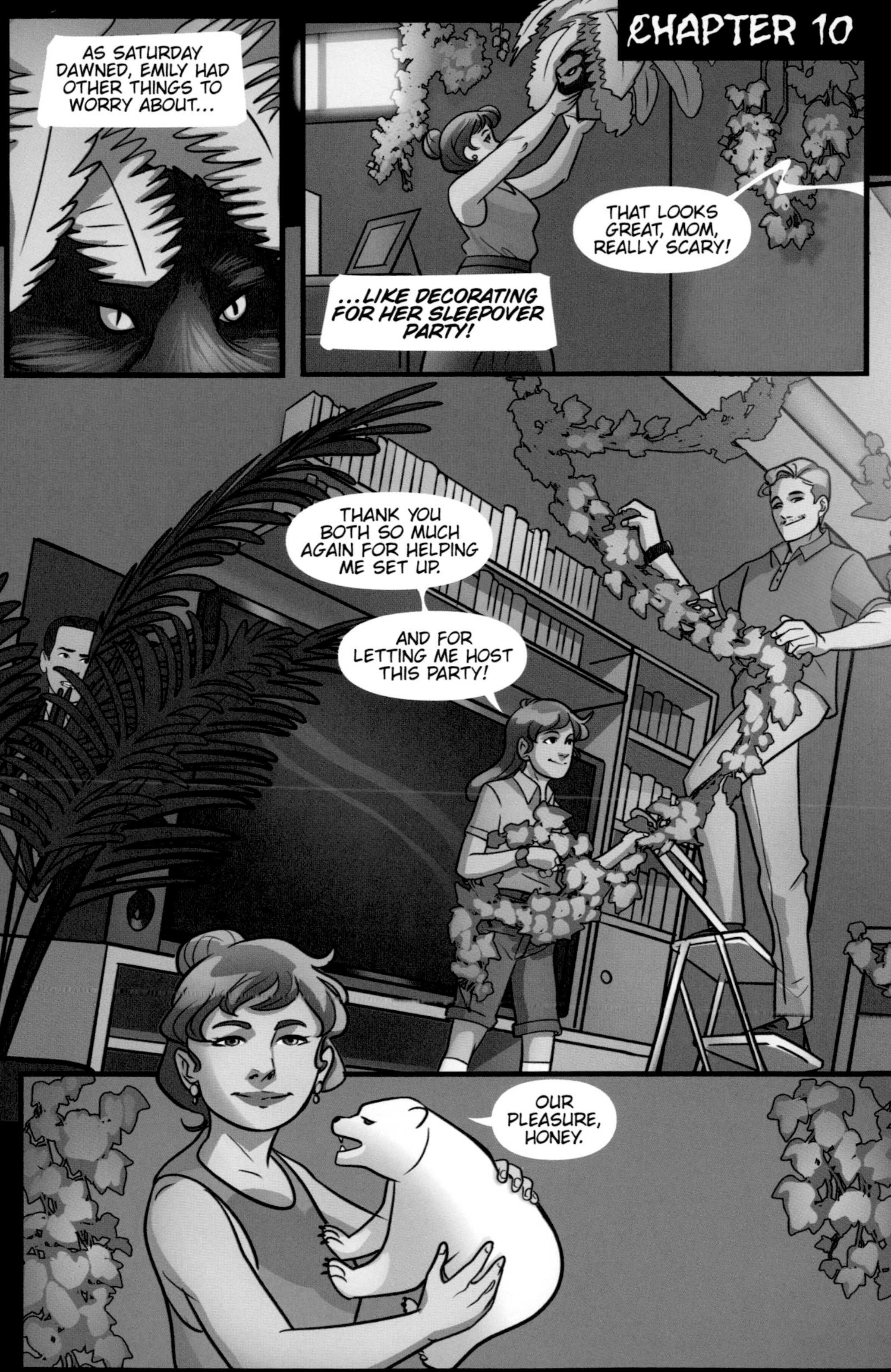
CHAPTER 10
AS SATURDAY DAWNED, EMILY HAD OTHER THINGS TO WORRY ABOUT...
...LIKE DECORATING FOR HER SLEEPOVER PARTY!
THAT LOOKS GREAT, MOM, REALLY SCARY!
THANK YOU BOTH SO MUCH AGAIN FOR HELPING ME SET UP.
AND FOR LETTING ME HOST THIS PARTY!
OUR PLEASURE, HONEY.

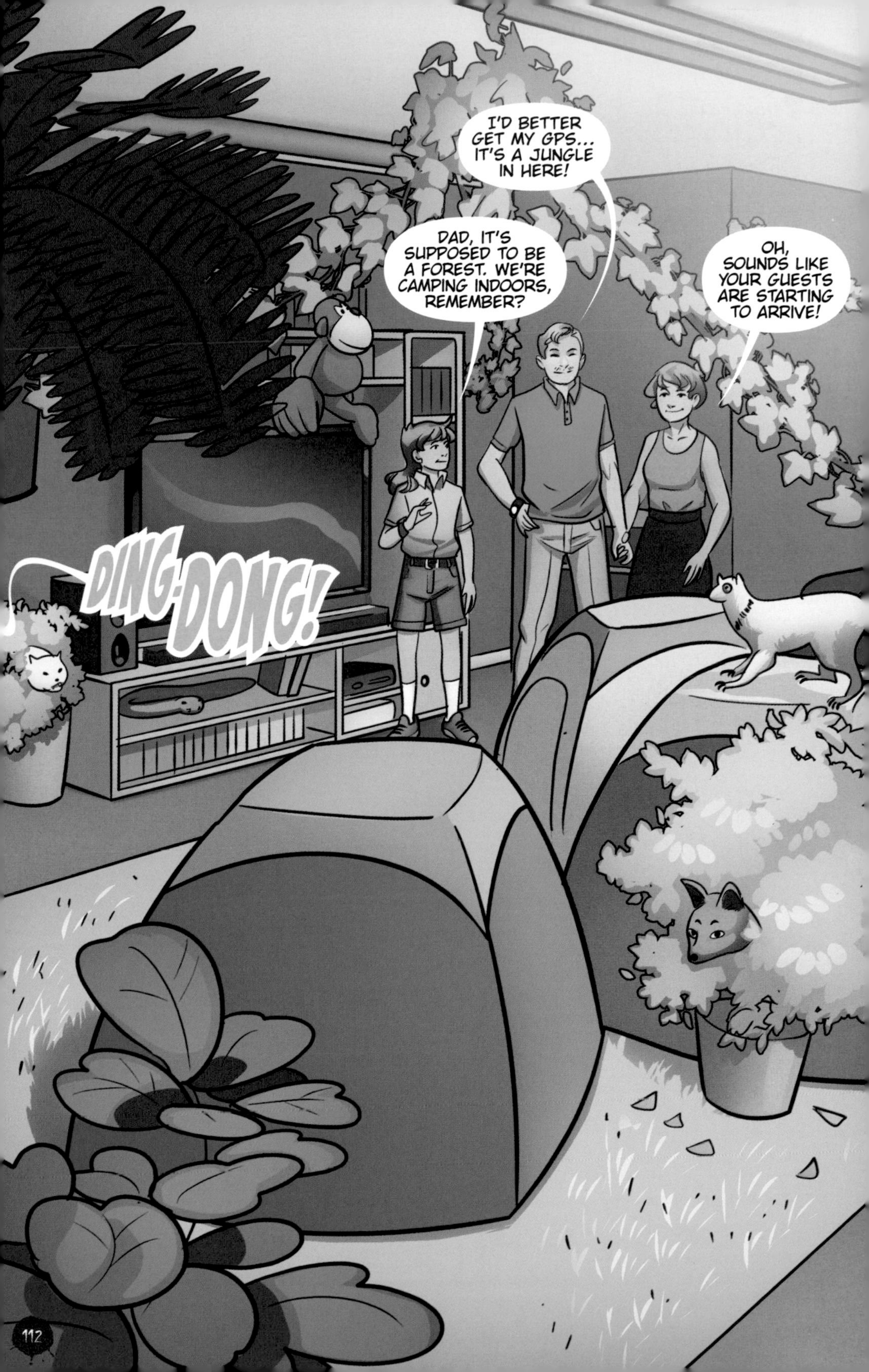
DAD, IT'S SUPPOSED TO BE A FOREST. WE'RE CAMPING INDOORS, REMEMBER?
I'D BETTER GET MY GPS... IT'S A JUNGLE IN HERE!
DING-DONG!
OH, SOUNDS LIKE YOUR GUESTS ARE STARTING TO ARRIVE!

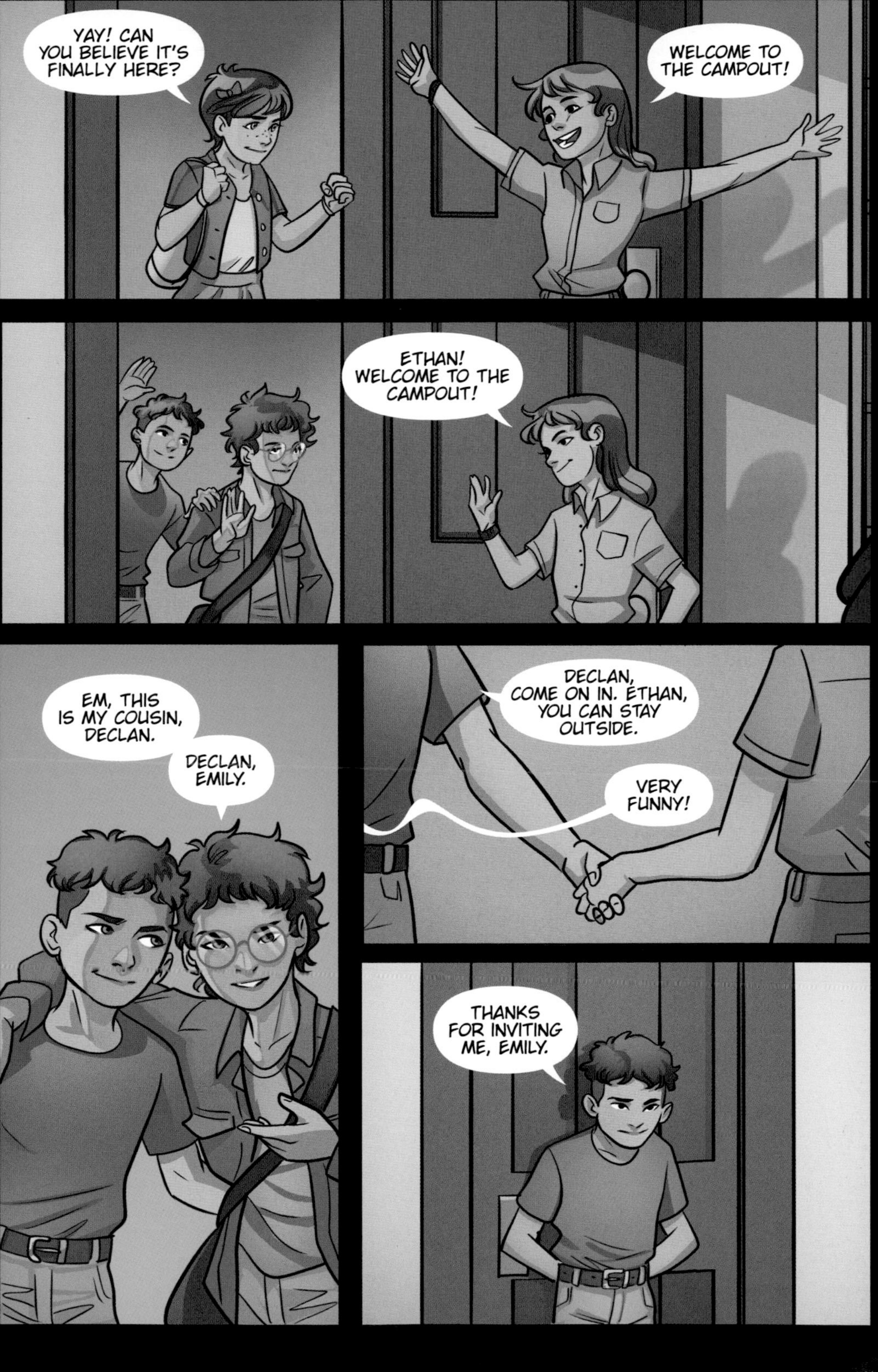
YAY! CAN YOU BELIEVE IT'S FINALLY HERE?
WELCOME TO THE CAMPOUT!
ETHAN! WELCOME TO THE CAMPOUT!
EM, THIS IS MY COUSIN, DECLAN.
DECLAN, EMILY.
DECLAN, COME ON IN. ETHAN, YOU CAN STAY OUTSIDE.
VERY FUNNY!
THANKS FOR INVITING ME, EMILY.

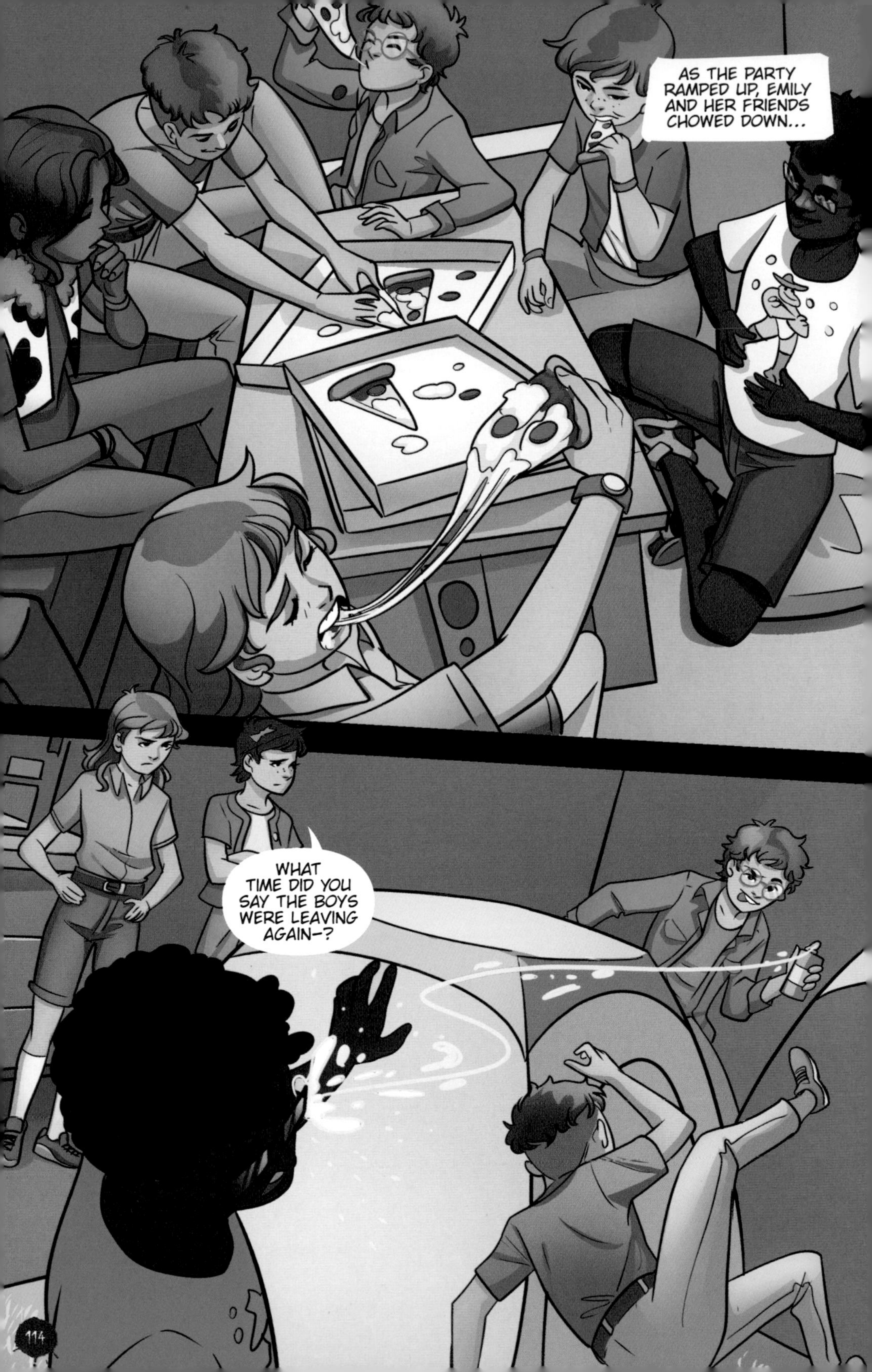
AS THE PARTY RAMPED UP, EMILY AND HER FRIENDS CHOWED DOWN...
WHAT TIME DID YOU SAY THE BOYS WERE LEAVING AGAIN–?

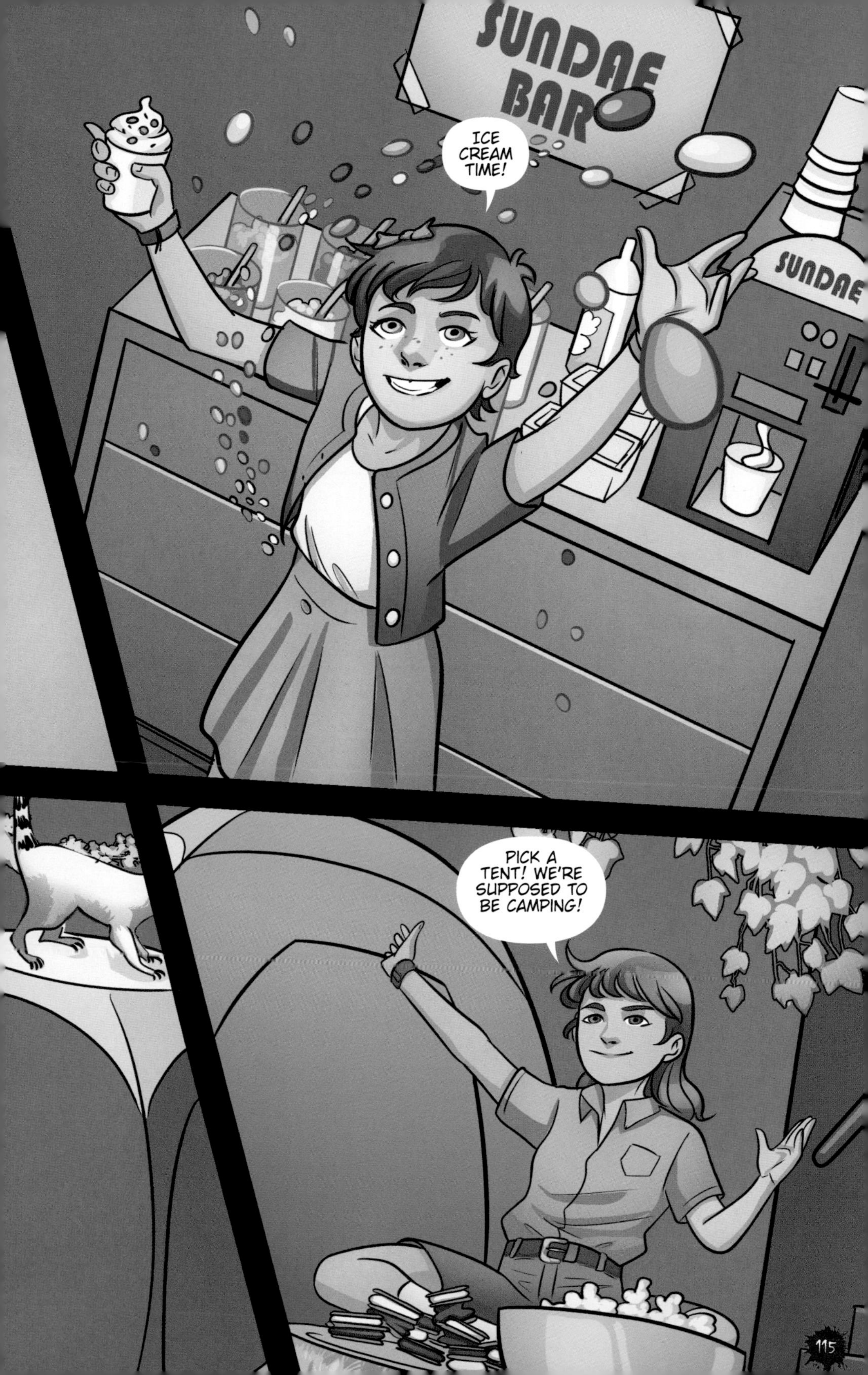
SUNDAE BAR
ICE CREAM TIME!
SUNDAE
PICK A TENT! WE'RE SUPPOSED TO BE CAMPING!

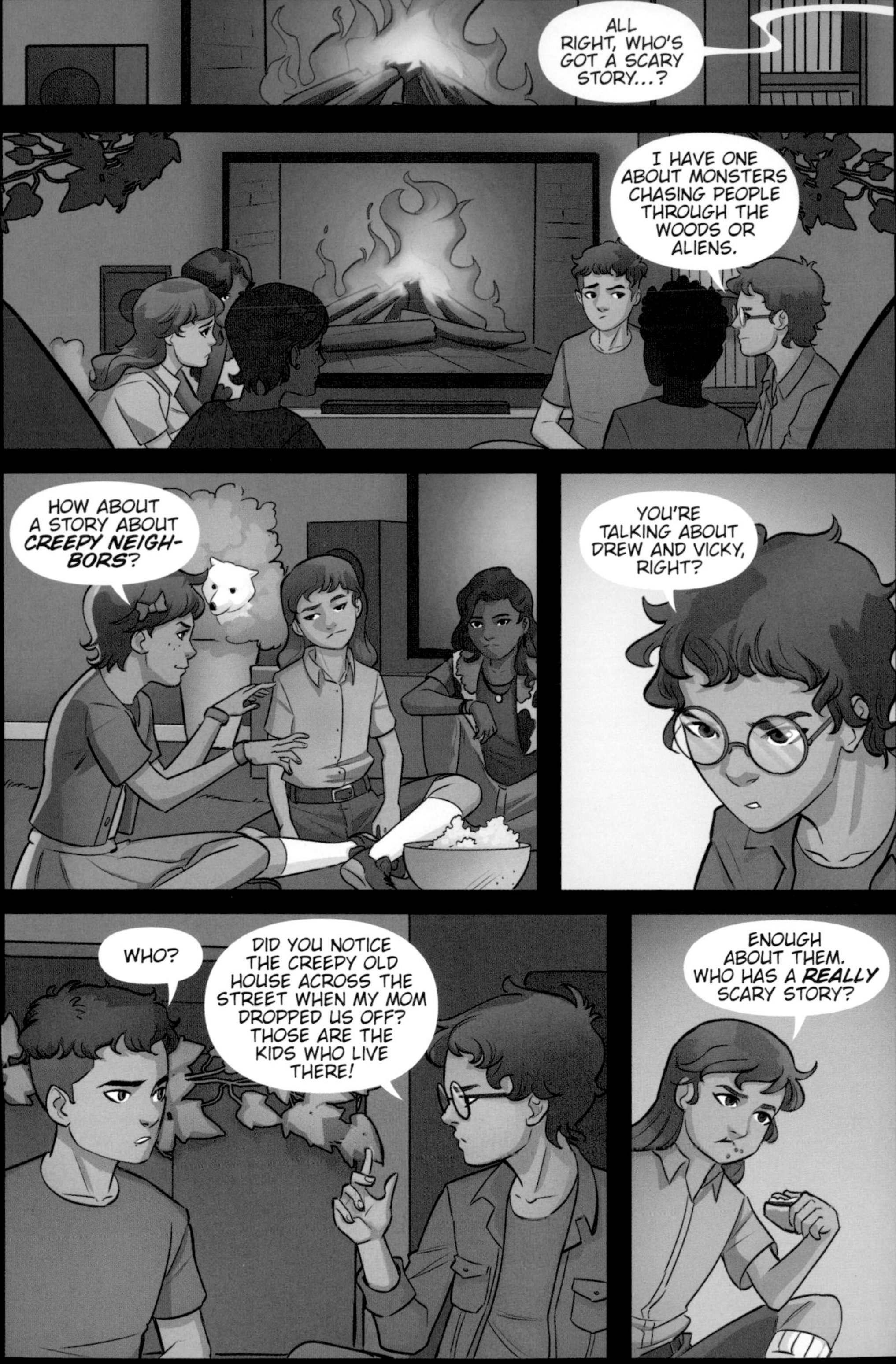
ALL RIGHT, WHO'S GOT A SCARY STORY...?
I HAVE ONE ABOUT MONSTERS CHASING PEOPLE THROUGH THE WOODS OR ALIENS.
HOW ABOUT A STORY ABOUT *CREEPY NEIGH-BORS*?
YOU'RE TALKING ABOUT DREW AND VICKY, RIGHT?
WHO?
DID YOU NOTICE THE CREEPY OLD HOUSE ACROSS THE STREET WHEN MY MOM DROPPED US OFF? THOSE ARE THE KIDS WHO LIVE THERE!
ENOUGH ABOUT THEM. WHO HAS A *REALLY* SCARY STORY?

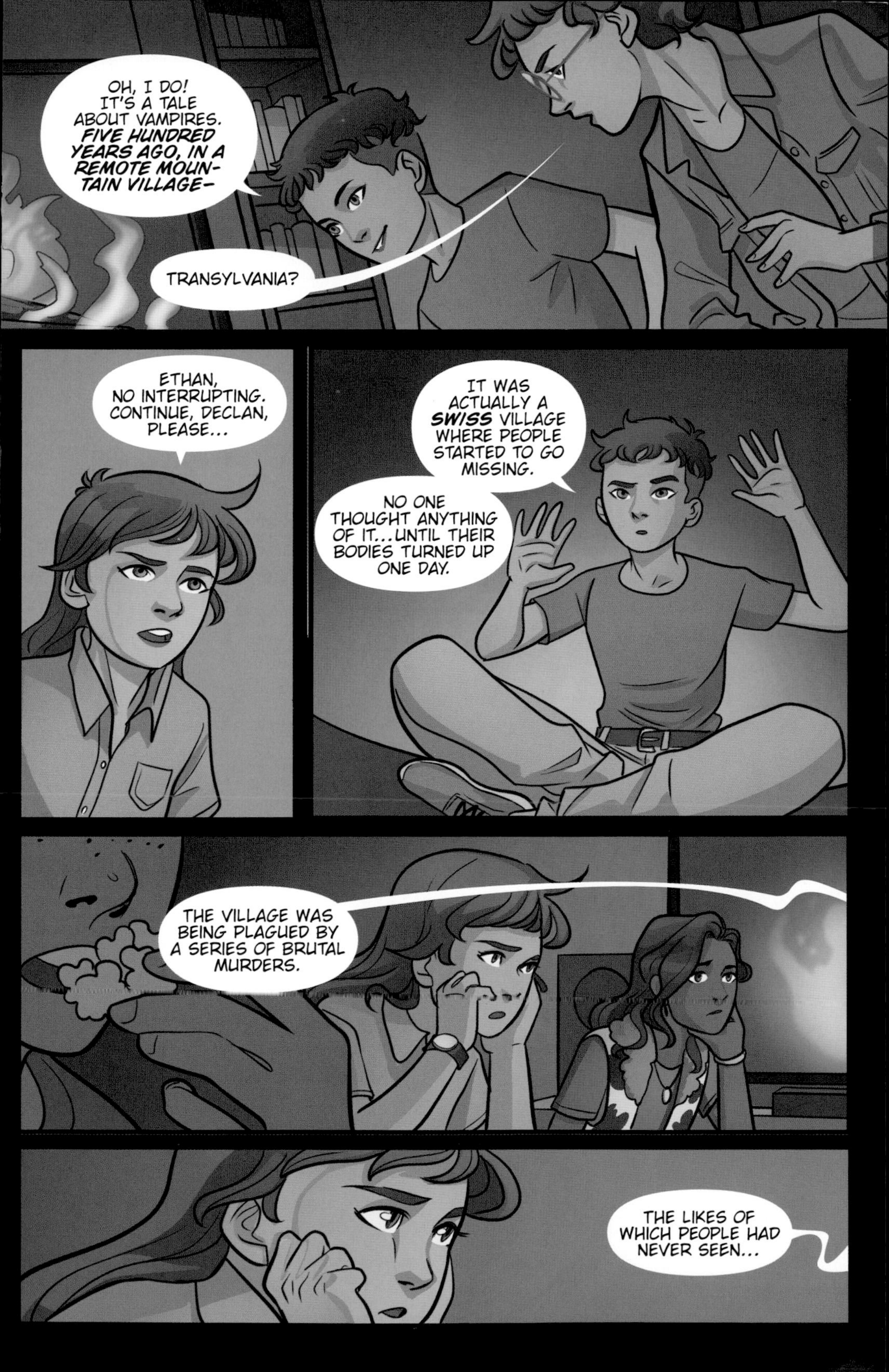
OH, I DO! IT'S A TALE ABOUT VAMPIRES. ***FIVE HUNDRED YEARS AGO, IN A REMOTE MOUNTAIN VILLAGE–***
TRANSYLVANIA?
ETHAN, NO INTERRUPTING. CONTINUE, DECLAN, PLEASE...
IT WAS ACTUALLY A ***SWISS*** VILLAGE WHERE PEOPLE STARTED TO GO MISSING.
NO ONE THOUGHT ANYTHING OF IT...UNTIL THEIR BODIES TURNED UP ONE DAY.
THE VILLAGE WAS BEING PLAGUED BY A SERIES OF BRUTAL MURDERS.
THE LIKES OF WHICH PEOPLE HAD NEVER SEEN...

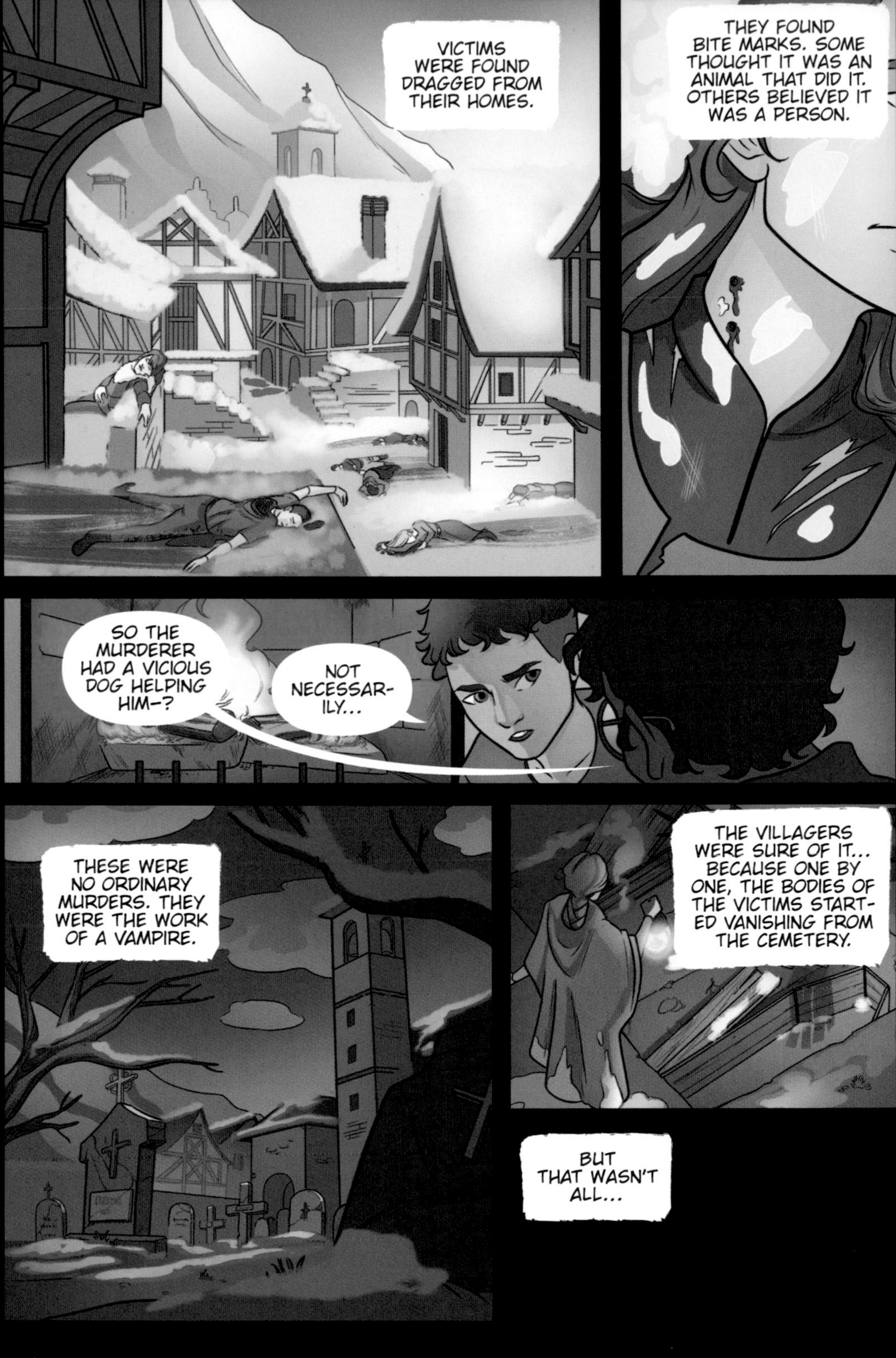
VICTIMS WERE FOUND DRAGGED FROM THEIR HOMES.
THEY FOUND BITE MARKS. SOME THOUGHT IT WAS AN ANIMAL THAT DID IT. OTHERS BELIEVED IT WAS A PERSON.
SO THE MURDERER HAD A VICIOUS DOG HELPING HIM–?
NOT NECESSAR-ILY…
THESE WERE NO ORDINARY MURDERS. THEY WERE THE WORK OF A VAMPIRE.
THE VILLAGERS WERE SURE OF IT… BECAUSE ONE BY ONE, THE BODIES OF THE VICTIMS START-ED VANISHING FROM THE CEMETERY.
BUT THAT WASN'T ALL…

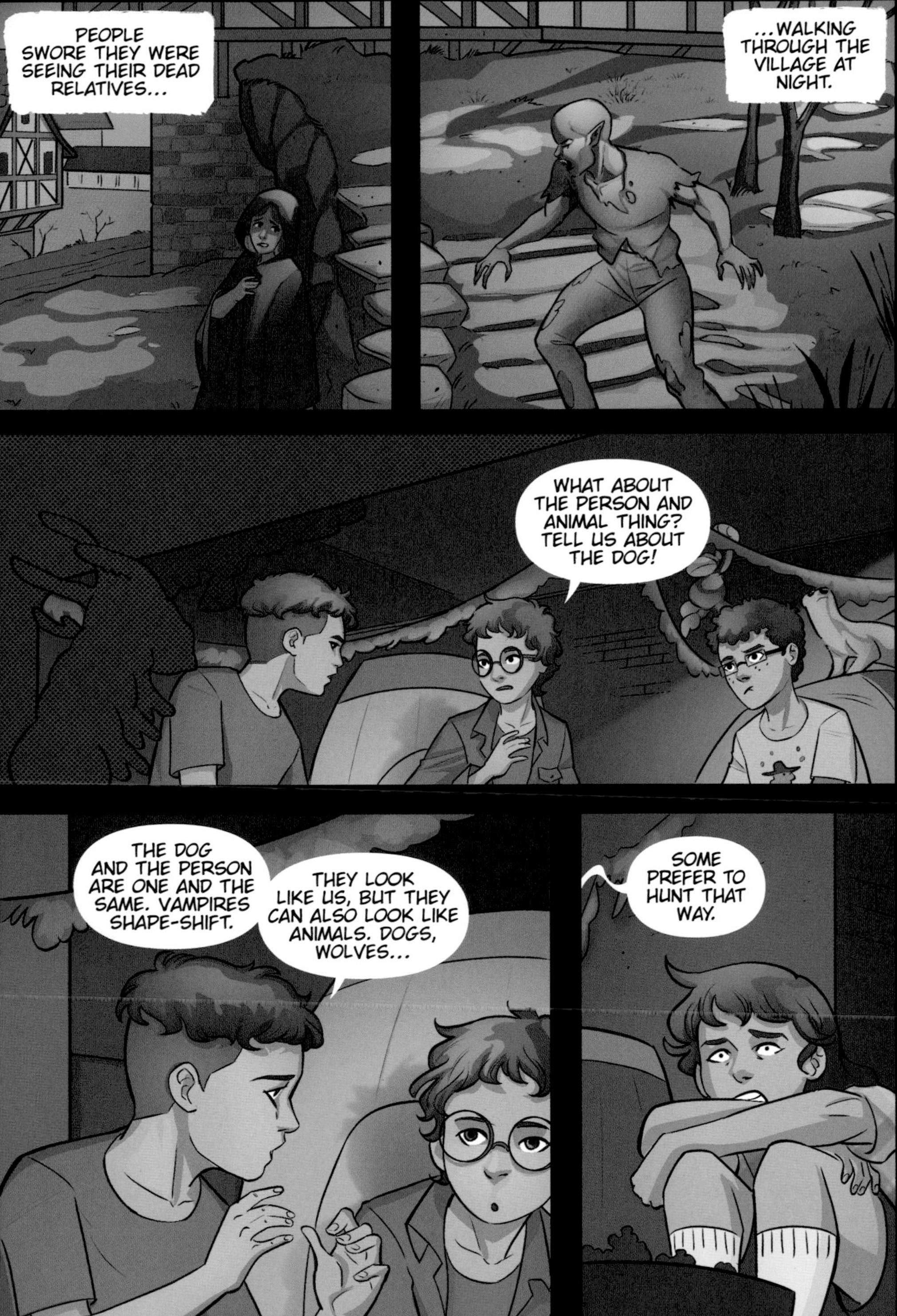
PEOPLE SWORE THEY WERE SEEING THEIR DEAD RELATIVES...
...WALKING THROUGH THE VILLAGE AT NIGHT.
WHAT ABOUT THE PERSON AND ANIMAL THING? TELL US ABOUT THE DOG!
THE DOG AND THE PERSON ARE ONE AND THE SAME. VAMPIRES SHAPE-SHIFT.
THEY LOOK LIKE US, BUT THEY CAN ALSO LOOK LIKE ANIMALS. DOGS, WOLVES...
SOME PREFER TO HUNT THAT WAY.

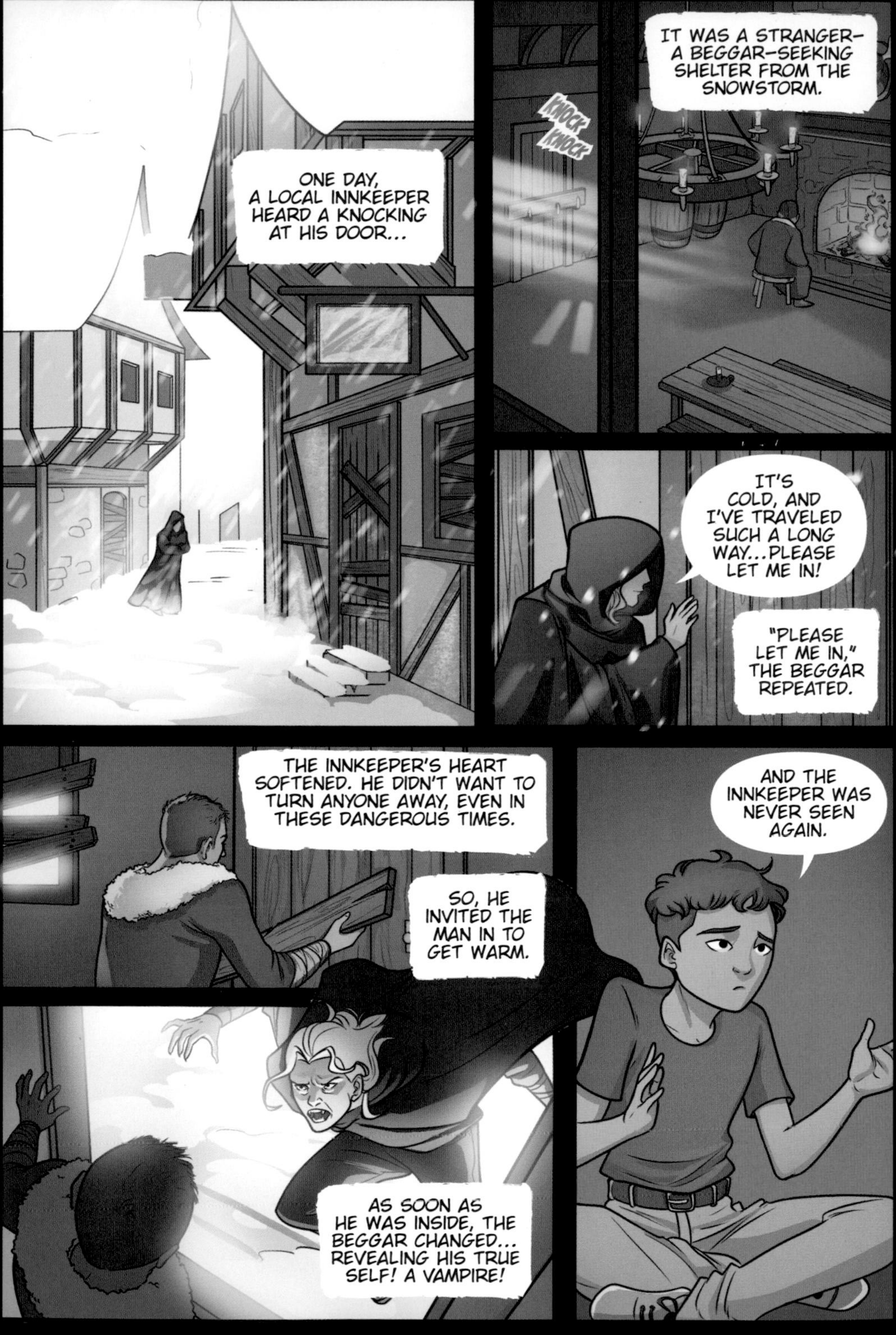
ONE DAY, A LOCAL INNKEEPER HEARD A KNOCKING AT HIS DOOR...
KNOCK KNOCK
IT WAS A STRANGER—A BEGGAR—SEEKING SHELTER FROM THE SNOWSTORM.
IT'S COLD, AND I'VE TRAVELED SUCH A LONG WAY...PLEASE LET ME IN!
"PLEASE LET ME IN," THE BEGGAR REPEATED.
THE INNKEEPER'S HEART SOFTENED. HE DIDN'T WANT TO TURN ANYONE AWAY, EVEN IN THESE DANGEROUS TIMES.
SO, HE INVITED THE MAN IN TO GET WARM.
AS SOON AS HE WAS INSIDE, THE BEGGAR CHANGED... REVEALING HIS TRUE SELF! A VAMPIRE!
AND THE INNKEEPER WAS NEVER SEEN AGAIN.

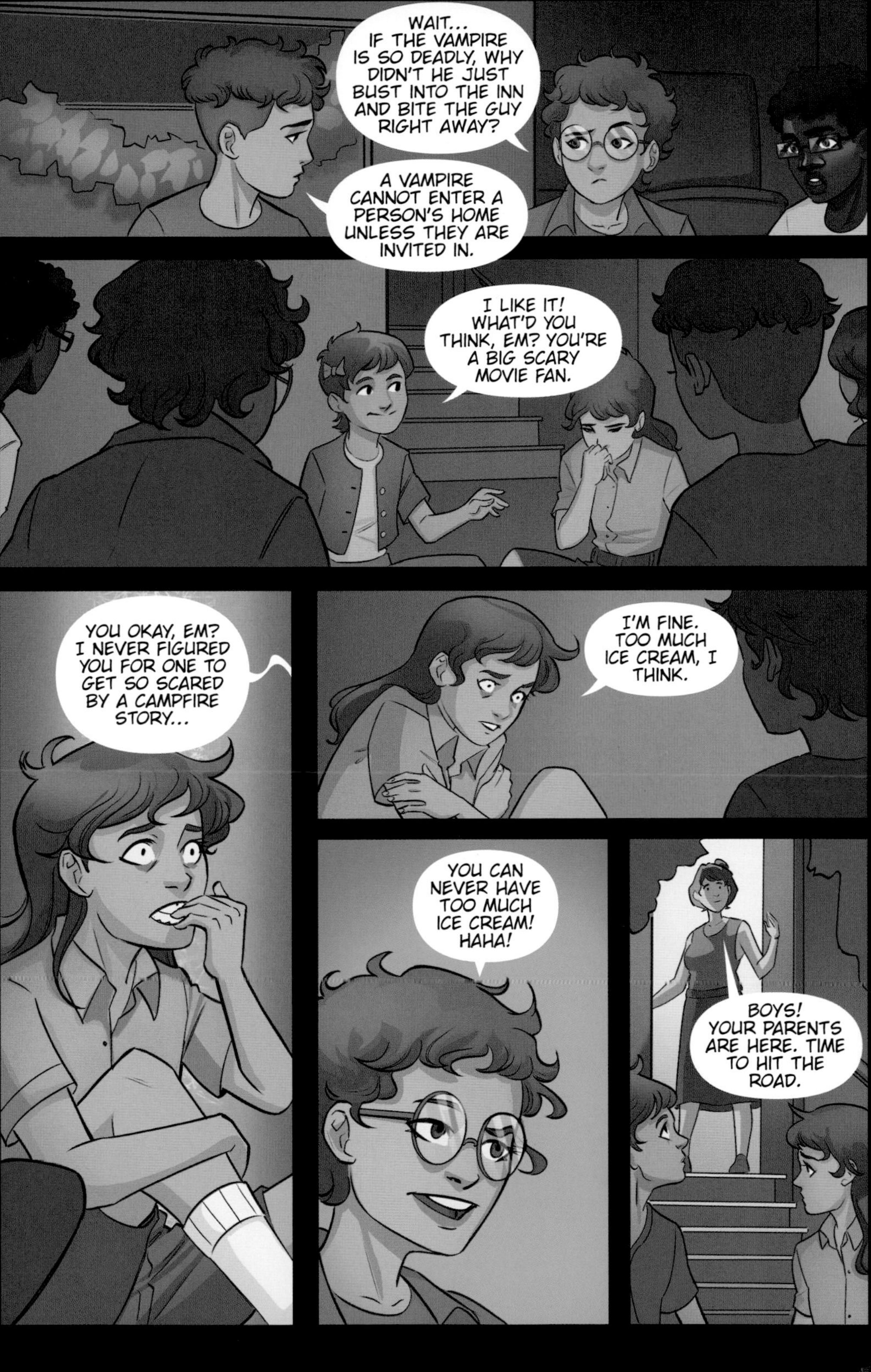
WAIT... IF THE VAMPIRE IS SO DEADLY, WHY DIDN'T HE JUST BUST INTO THE INN AND BITE THE GUY RIGHT AWAY?
A VAMPIRE CANNOT ENTER A PERSON'S HOME UNLESS THEY ARE INVITED IN.
I LIKE IT! WHAT'D YOU THINK, EM? YOU'RE A BIG SCARY MOVIE FAN.
YOU OKAY, EM? I NEVER FIGURED YOU FOR ONE TO GET SO SCARED BY A CAMPFIRE STORY...
I'M FINE. TOO MUCH ICE CREAM, I THINK.
YOU CAN NEVER HAVE TOO MUCH ICE CREAM! HAHA!
BOYS! YOUR PARENTS ARE HERE. TIME TO HIT THE ROAD.

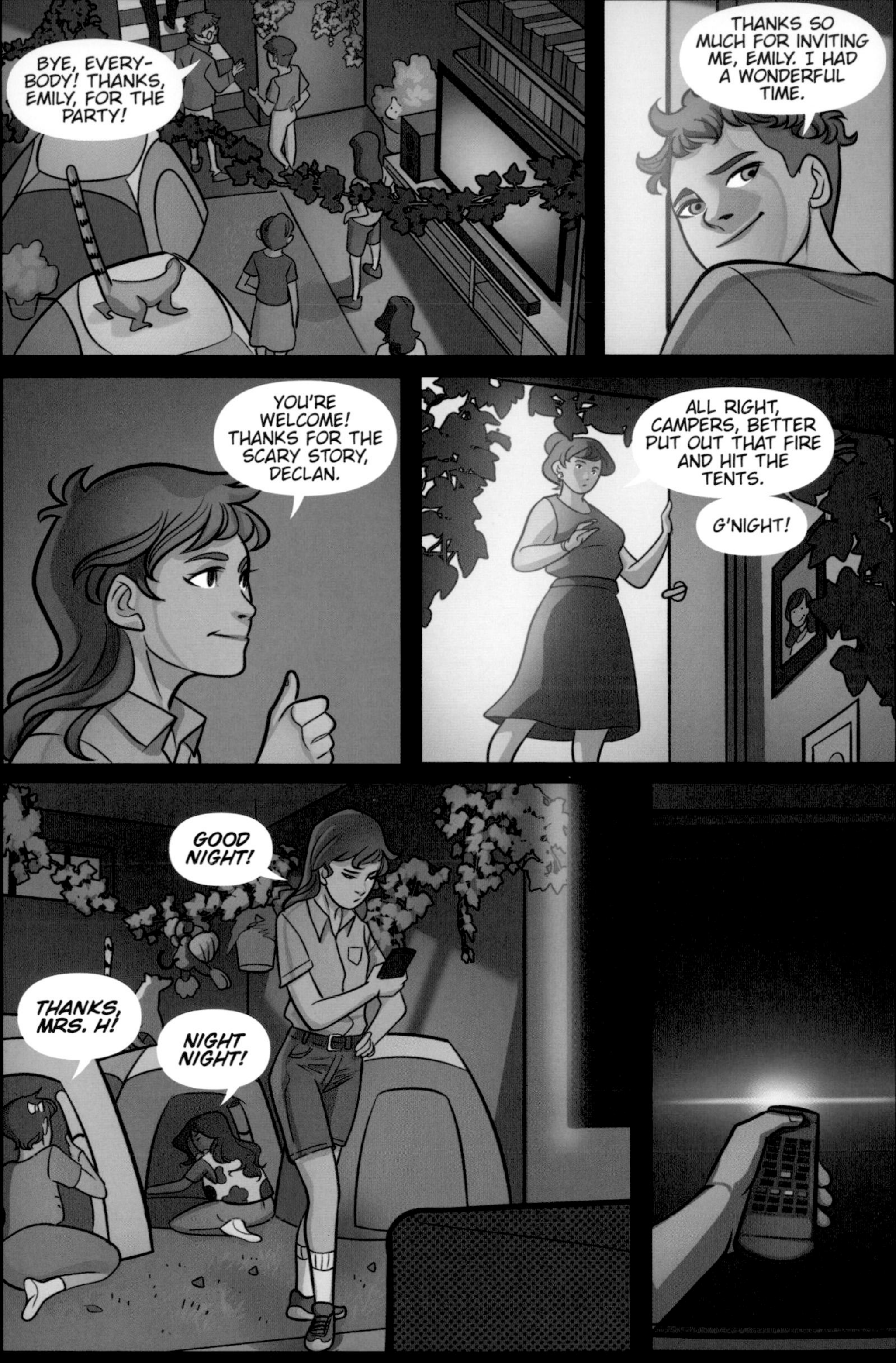
BYE, EVERY-BODY! THANKS, EMILY, FOR THE PARTY!
THANKS SO MUCH FOR INVITING ME, EMILY. I HAD A WONDERFUL TIME.
YOU'RE WELCOME! THANKS FOR THE SCARY STORY, DECLAN.
ALL RIGHT, CAMPERS, BETTER PUT OUT THAT FIRE AND HIT THE TENTS.
G'NIGHT!
GOOD NIGHT!
THANKS, MRS. H!
NIGHT NIGHT!

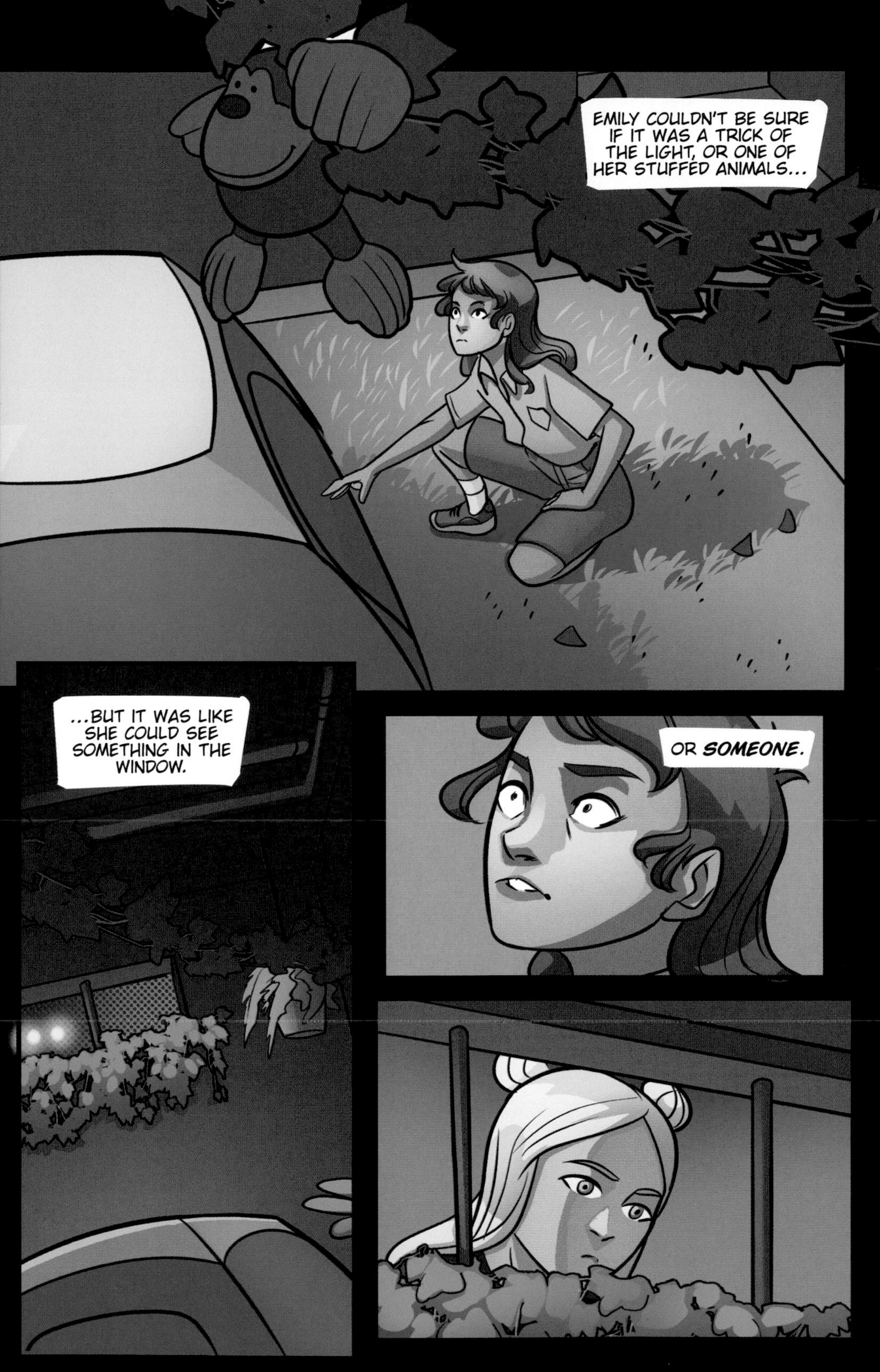
EMILY COULDN'T BE SURE IF IT WAS A TRICK OF THE LIGHT, OR ONE OF HER STUFFED ANIMALS...
...BUT IT WAS LIKE SHE COULD SEE SOMETHING IN THE WINDOW.
OR ***SOMEONE***.

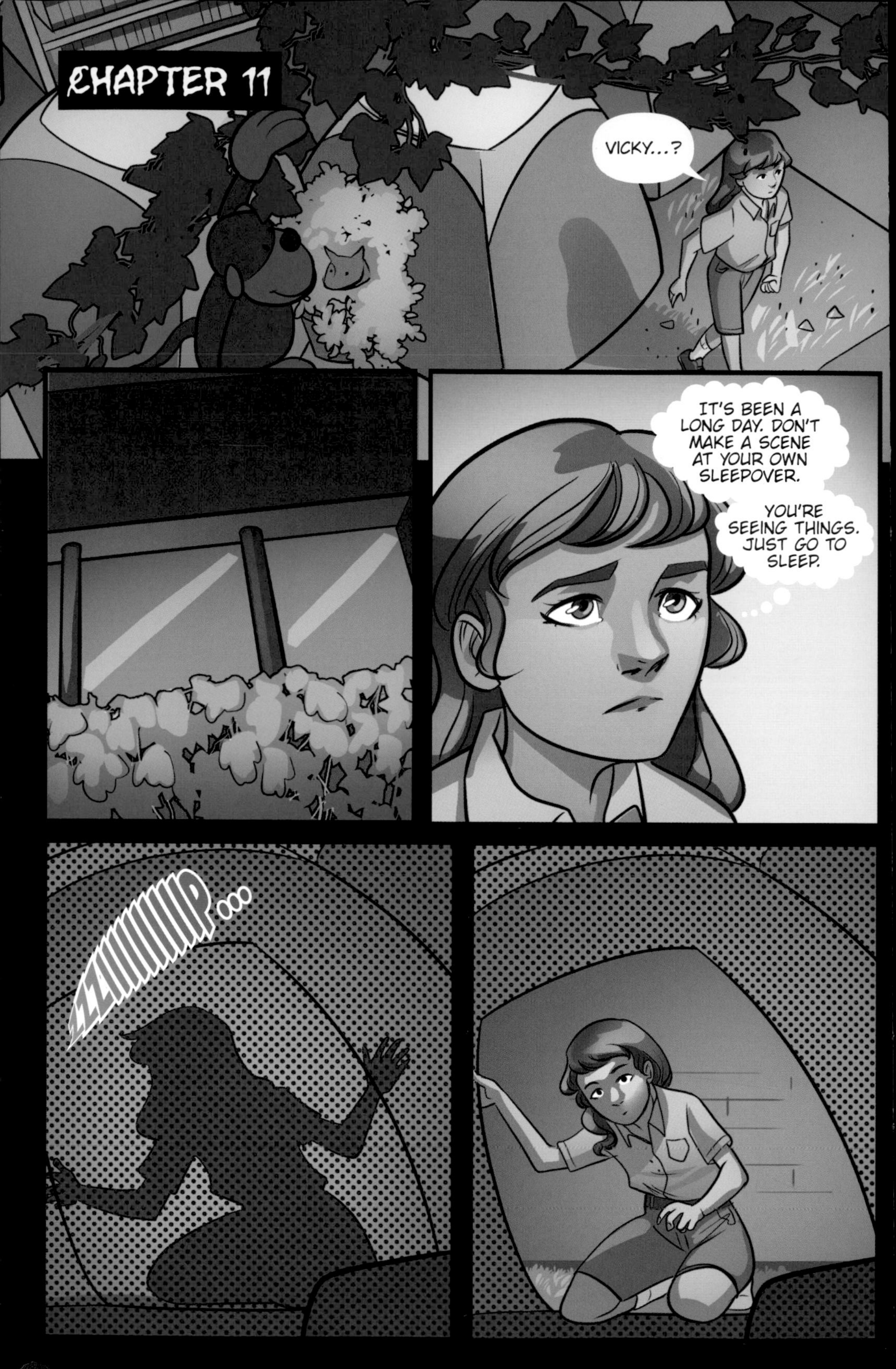
CHAPTER 11
VICKY...?
IT'S BEEN A LONG DAY. DON'T MAKE A SCENE AT YOUR OWN SLEEPOVER.
YOU'RE SEEING THINGS. JUST GO TO SLEEP.
ZZZIIIIIIIIIP...

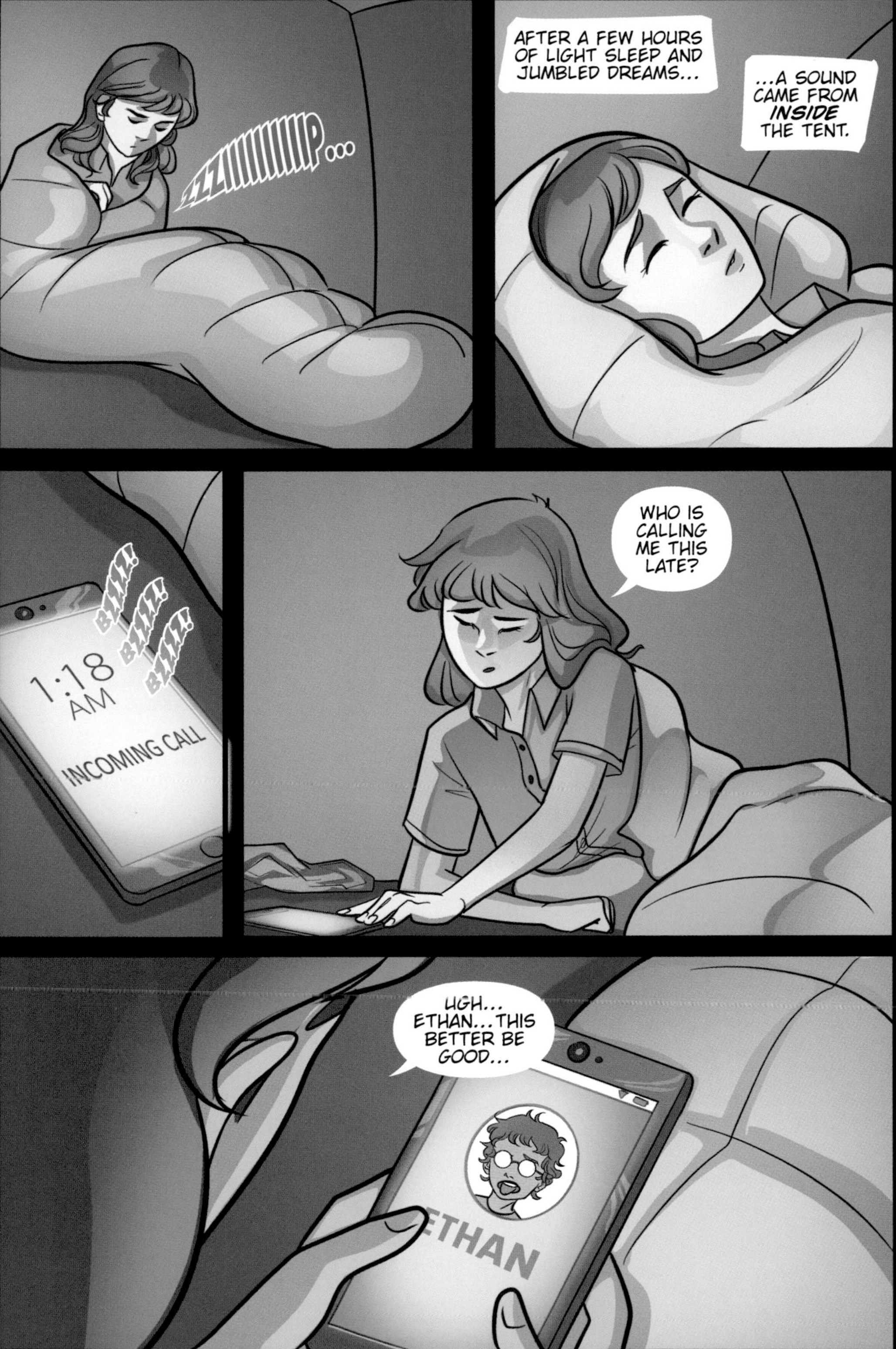
ZZZIIIIIIIIIIIP...
AFTER A FEW HOURS OF LIGHT SLEEP AND JUMBLED DREAMS...
...A SOUND CAME FROM *INSIDE* THE TENT.
BZZZZ! BZZZZ! BZZZZ!
1:18 AM
INCOMING CALL
WHO IS CALLING ME THIS LATE?
UGH... ETHAN... THIS BETTER BE GOOD...
ETHAN

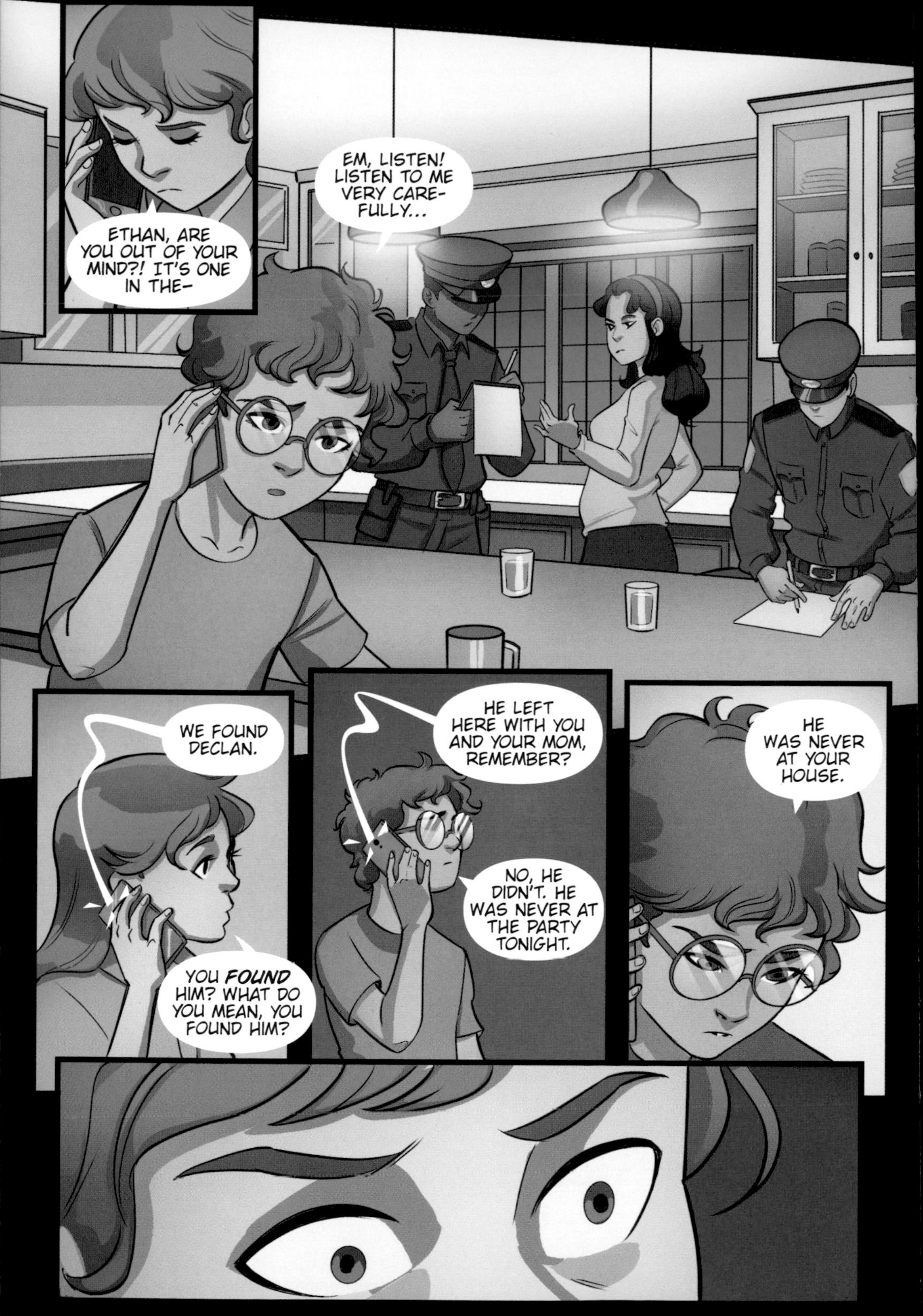
ETHAN, ARE YOU OUT OF YOUR MIND?! IT'S ONE IN THE–
EM, LISTEN! LISTEN TO ME VERY CARE-FULLY...
WE FOUND DECLAN.
YOU *FOUND* HIM? WHAT DO YOU MEAN, YOU FOUND HIM?
HE LEFT HERE WITH YOU AND YOUR MOM, REMEMBER?
NO, HE DIDN'T. HE WAS NEVER AT THE PARTY TONIGHT.
HE WAS NEVER AT YOUR HOUSE.

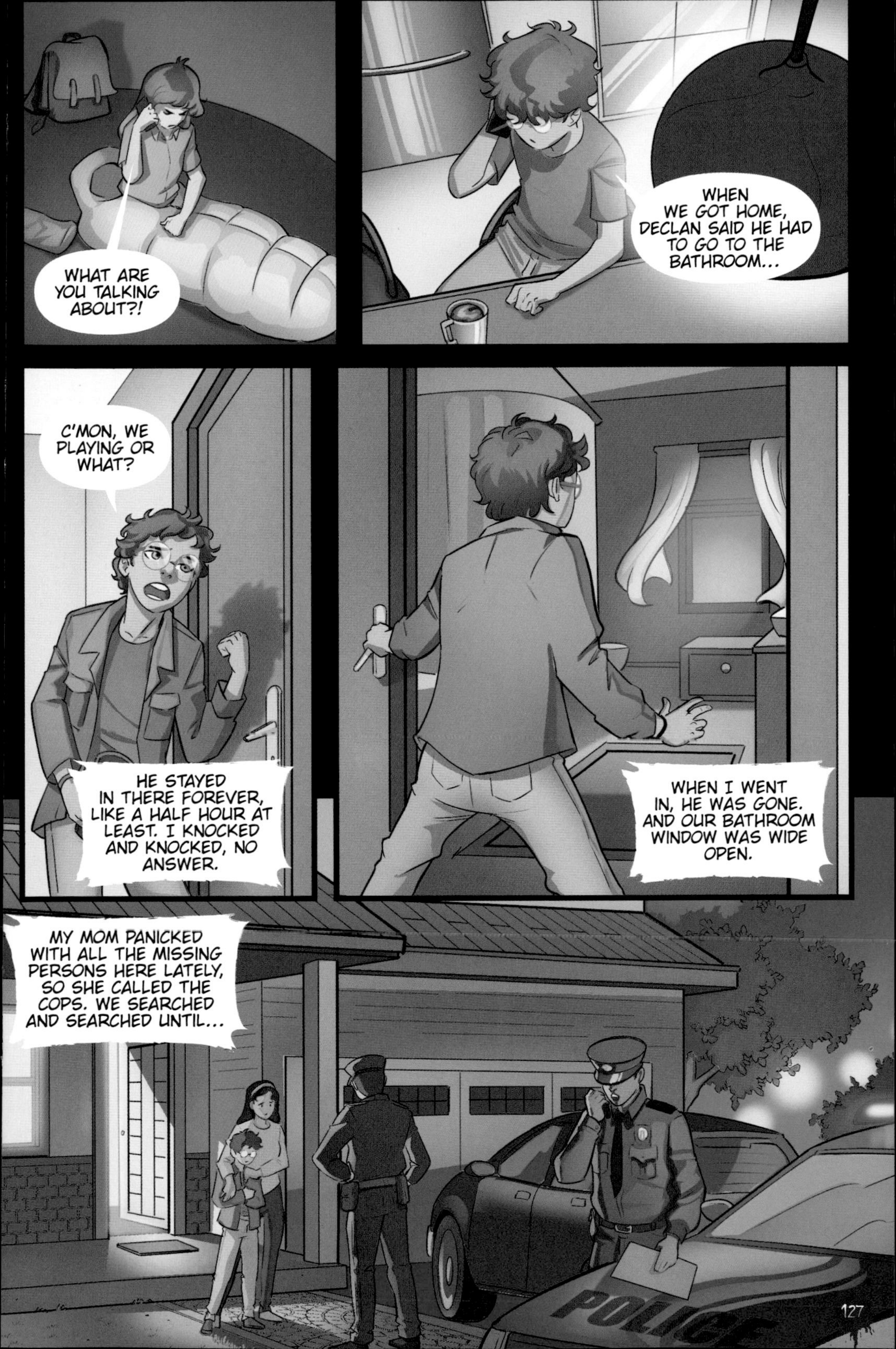
WHAT ARE YOU TALKING ABOUT?!
WHEN WE GOT HOME, DECLAN SAID HE HAD TO GO TO THE BATHROOM...
C'MON, WE PLAYING OR WHAT?
HE STAYED IN THERE FOREVER, LIKE A HALF HOUR AT LEAST. I KNOCKED AND KNOCKED, NO ANSWER.
WHEN I WENT IN, HE WAS GONE. AND OUR BATHROOM WINDOW WAS WIDE OPEN.
MY MOM PANICKED WITH ALL THE MISSING PERSONS HERE LATELY, SO SHE CALLED THE COPS. WE SEARCHED AND SEARCHED UNTIL...
POLICE

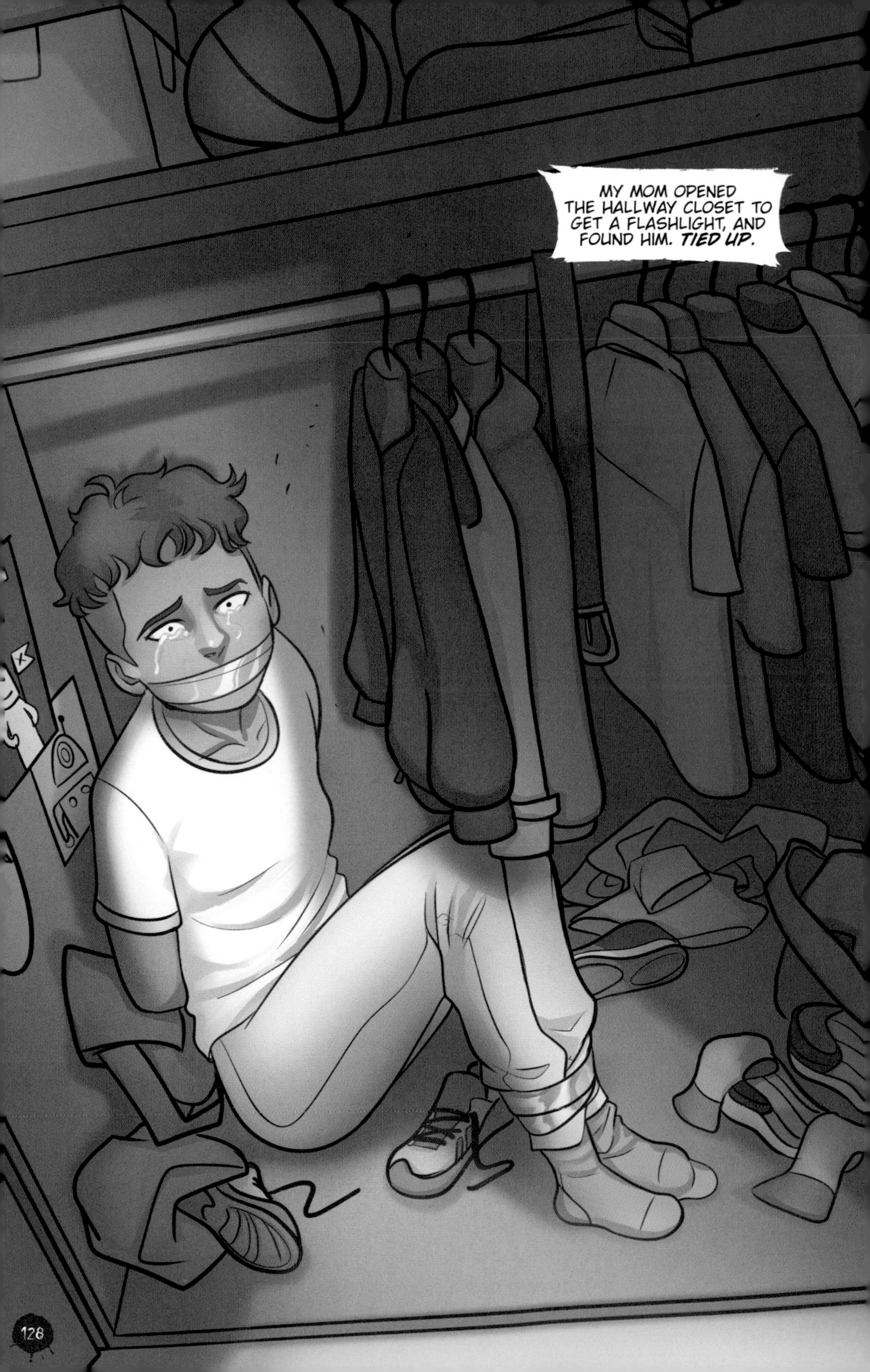
MY MOM OPENED THE HALLWAY CLOSET TO GET A FLASHLIGHT, AND FOUND HIM. *TIED UP.*

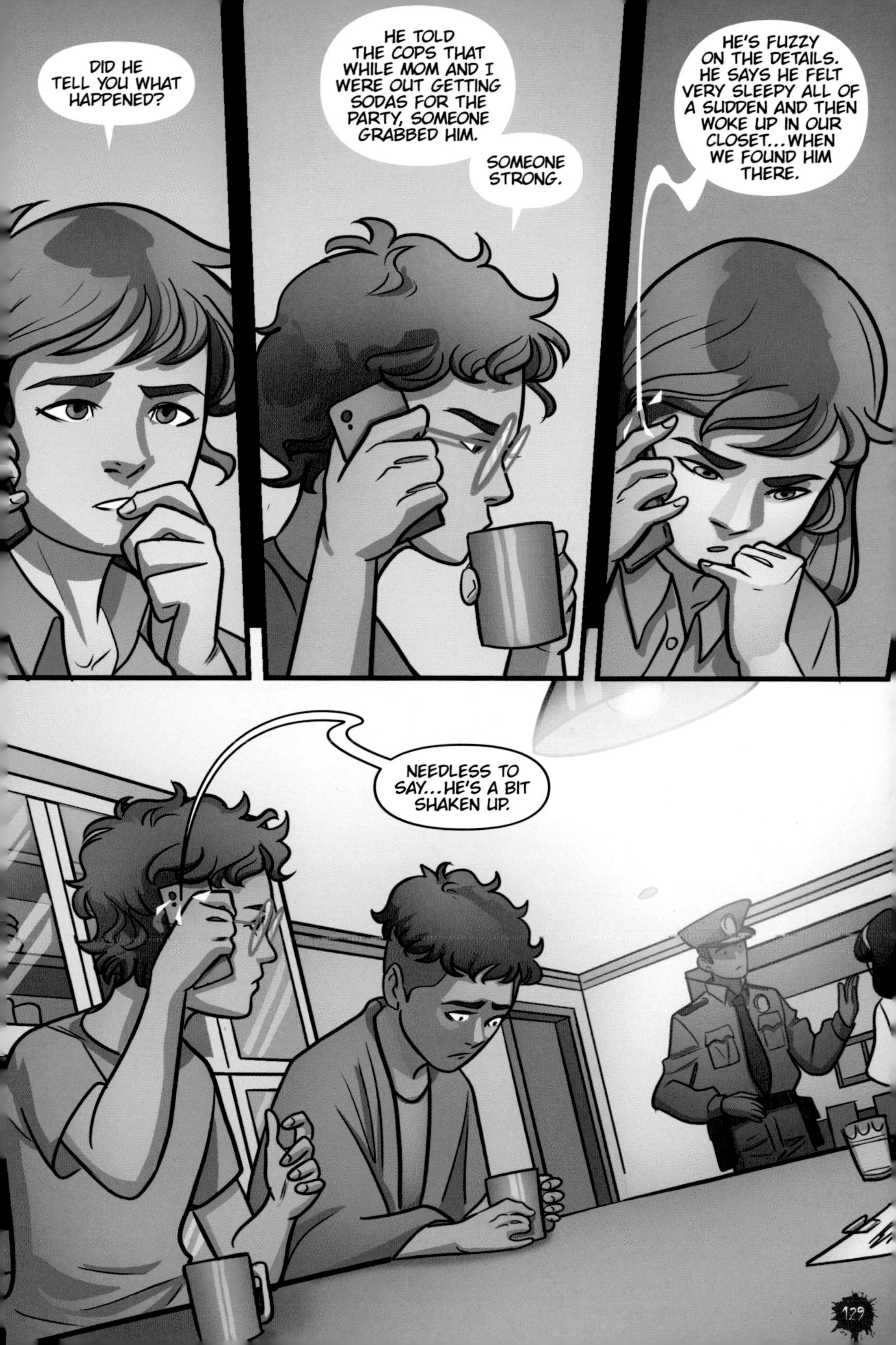
DID HE TELL YOU WHAT HAPPENED?
HE TOLD THE COPS THAT WHILE MOM AND I WERE OUT GETTING SODAS FOR THE PARTY, SOMEONE GRABBED HIM.
SOMEONE STRONG.
HE'S FUZZY ON THE DETAILS. HE SAYS HE FELT VERY SLEEPY ALL OF A SUDDEN AND THEN WOKE UP IN OUR CLOSET...WHEN WE FOUND HIM THERE.
NEEDLESS TO SAY...HE'S A BIT SHAKEN UP.

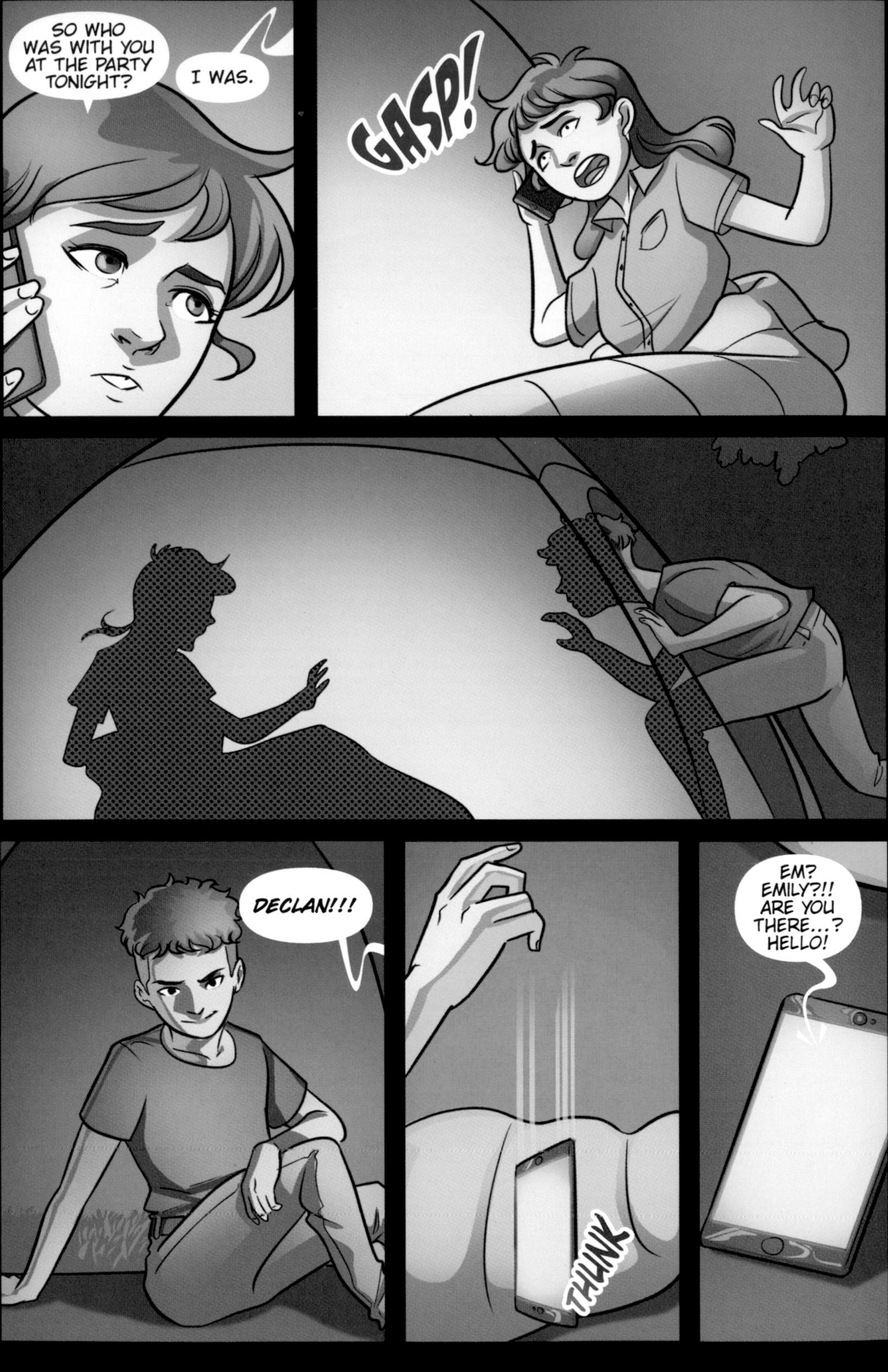
SO WHO WAS WITH YOU AT THE PARTY TONIGHT?
I WAS.
GASP!
DECLAN!!!
THUNK
EM? EMILY?!! ARE YOU THERE...? HELLO!

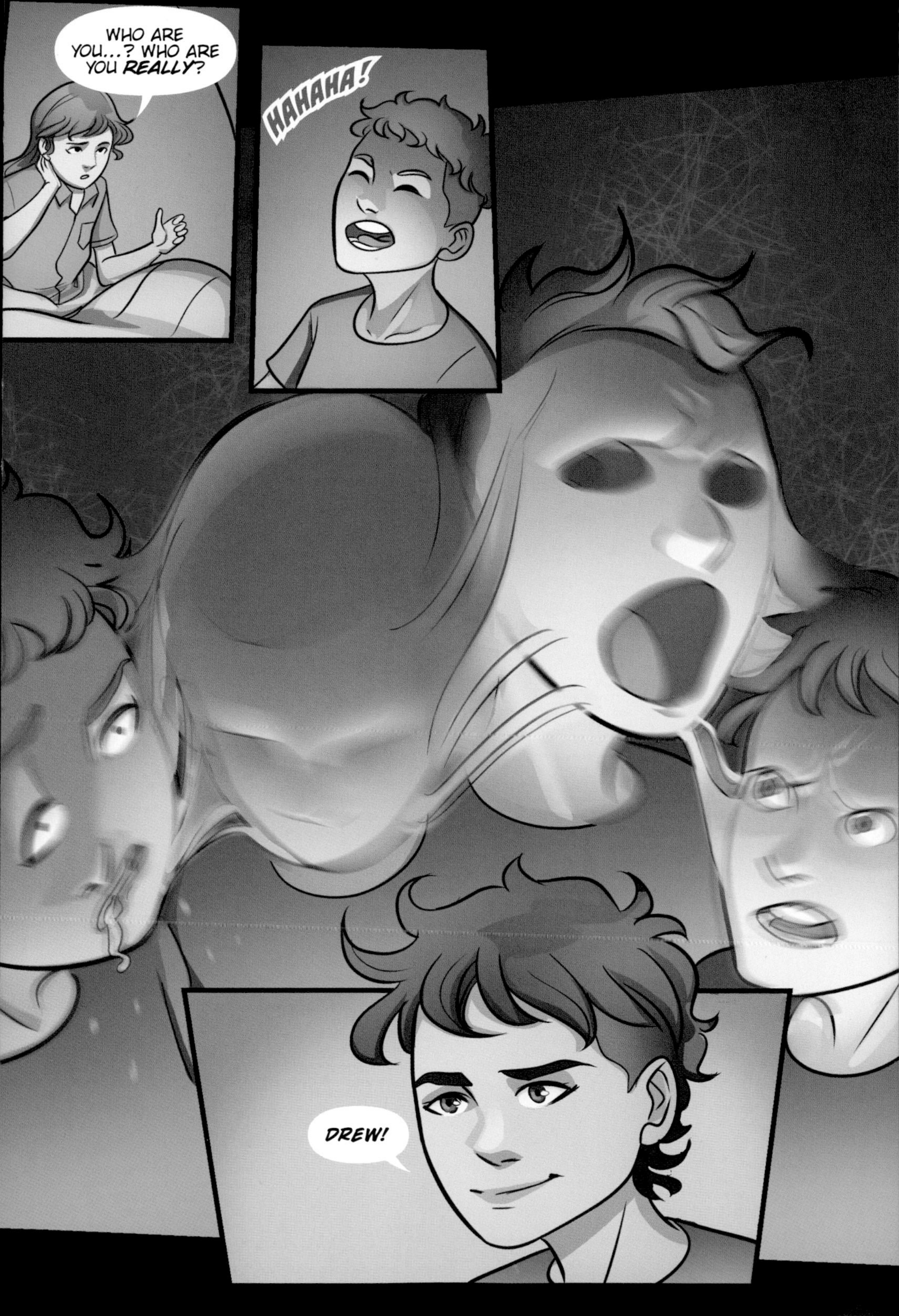
WHO ARE YOU...? WHO ARE YOU REALLY?
HAHAHA!
DREW!

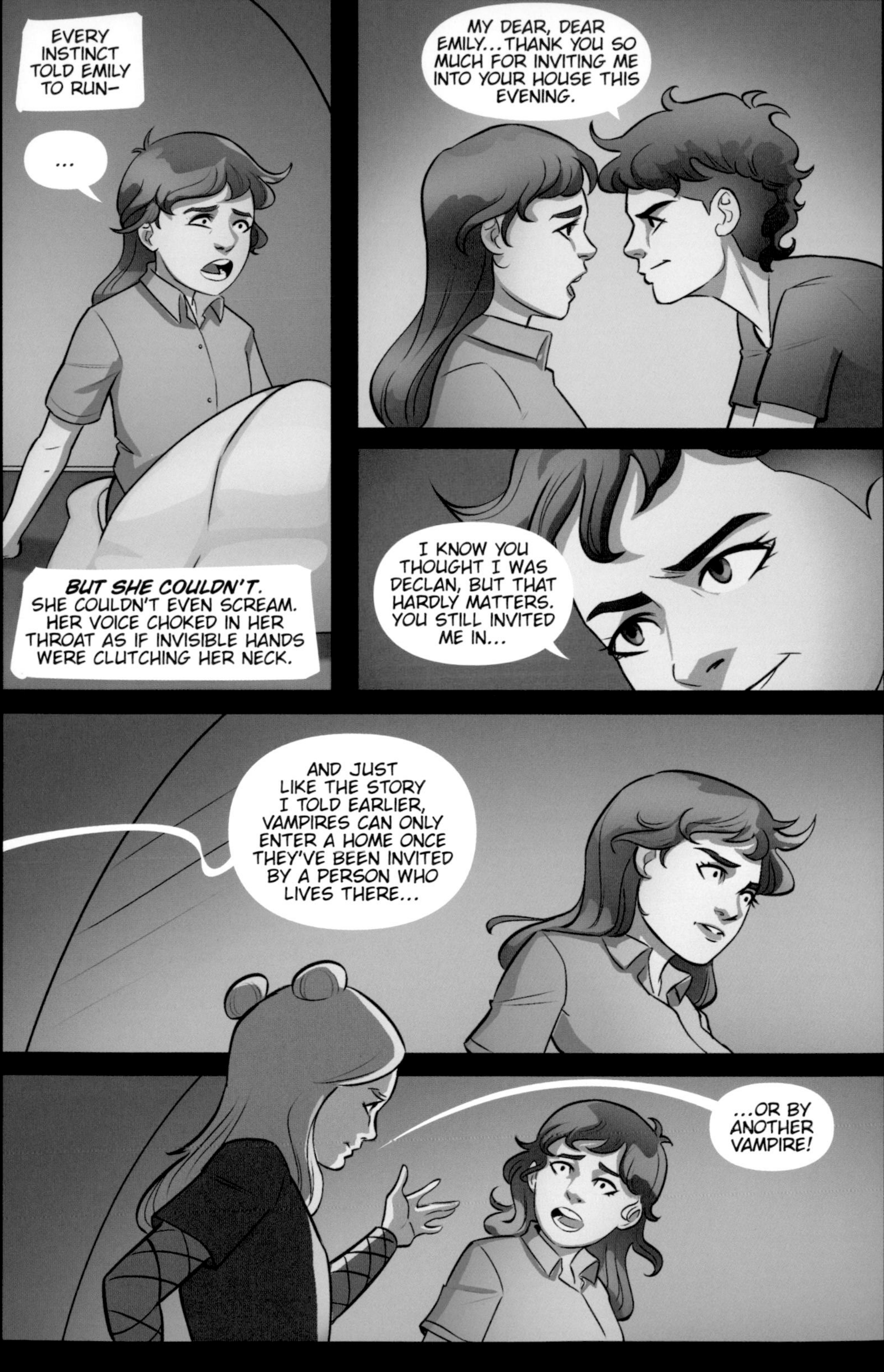
EVERY INSTINCT TOLD EMILY TO RUN–
...
MY DEAR, DEAR EMILY...THANK YOU SO MUCH FOR INVITING ME INTO YOUR HOUSE THIS EVENING.
BUT SHE COULDN'T. SHE COULDN'T EVEN SCREAM. HER VOICE CHOKED IN HER THROAT AS IF INVISIBLE HANDS WERE CLUTCHING HER NECK.
I KNOW YOU THOUGHT I WAS DECLAN, BUT THAT HARDLY MATTERS. YOU STILL INVITED ME IN...
AND JUST LIKE THE STORY I TOLD EARLIER, VAMPIRES CAN ONLY ENTER A HOME ONCE THEY'VE BEEN INVITED BY A PERSON WHO LIVES THERE...
...OR BY ANOTHER VAMPIRE!

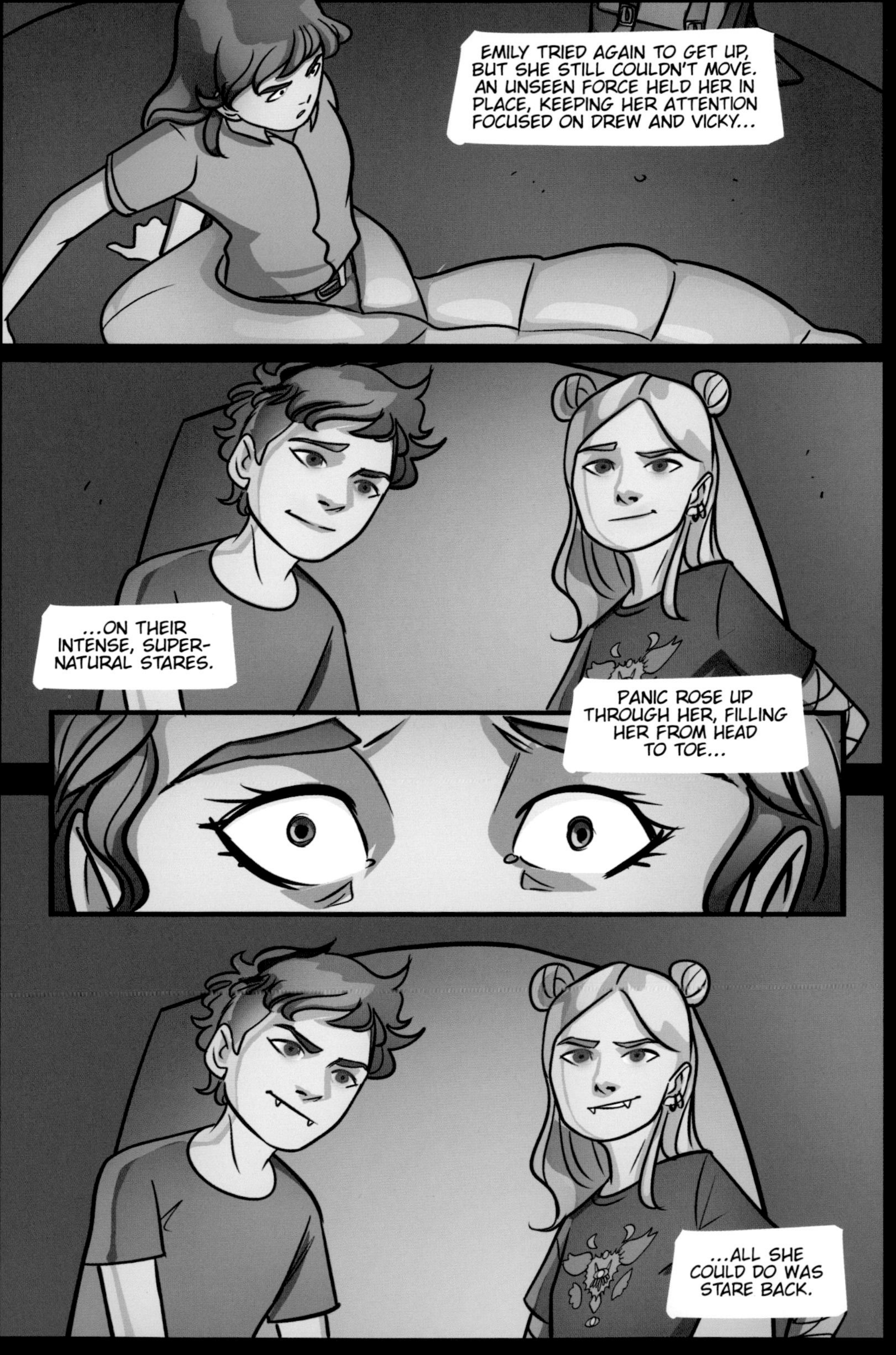
EMILY TRIED AGAIN TO GET UP, BUT SHE STILL COULDN'T MOVE. AN UNSEEN FORCE HELD HER IN PLACE, KEEPING HER ATTENTION FOCUSED ON DREW AND VICKY...
...ON THEIR INTENSE, SUPER-NATURAL STARES.
PANIC ROSE UP THROUGH HER, FILLING HER FROM HEAD TO TOE...
...ALL SHE COULD DO WAS STARE BACK.

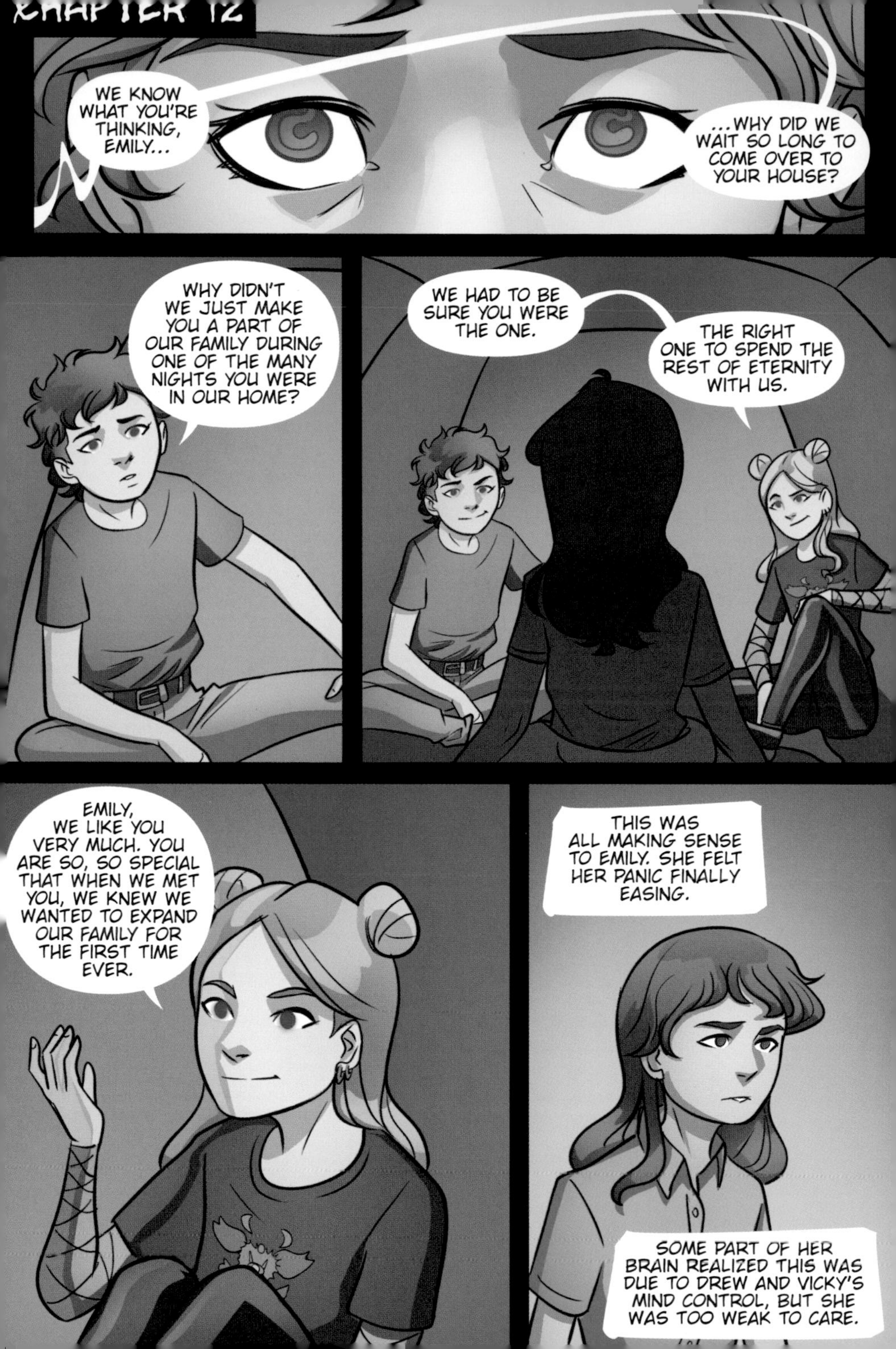
CHAPTER 12
WE KNOW WHAT YOU'RE THINKING, EMILY...
...WHY DID WE WAIT SO LONG TO COME OVER TO YOUR HOUSE?
WHY DIDN'T WE JUST MAKE YOU A PART OF OUR FAMILY DURING ONE OF THE MANY NIGHTS YOU WERE IN OUR HOME?
WE HAD TO BE SURE YOU WERE THE ONE.
THE RIGHT ONE TO SPEND THE REST OF ETERNITY WITH US.
EMILY, WE LIKE YOU VERY MUCH. YOU ARE SO, SO SPECIAL THAT WHEN WE MET YOU, WE KNEW WE WANTED TO EXPAND OUR FAMILY FOR THE FIRST TIME EVER.
THIS WAS ALL MAKING SENSE TO EMILY. SHE FELT HER PANIC FINALLY EASING.
SOME PART OF HER BRAIN REALIZED THIS WAS DUE TO DREW AND VICKY'S MIND CONTROL, BUT SHE WAS TOO WEAK TO CARE.

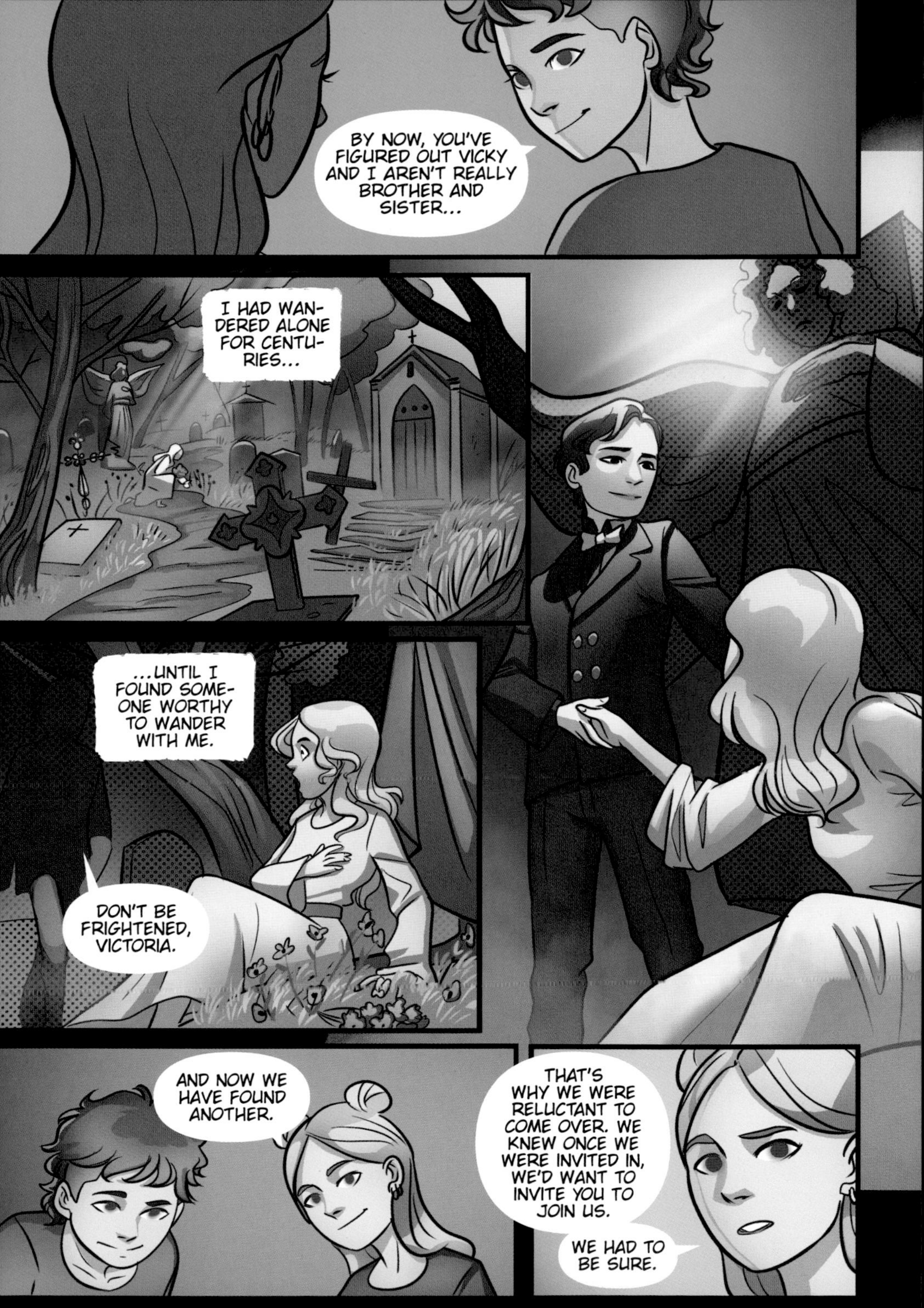
BY NOW, YOU'VE FIGURED OUT VICKY AND I AREN'T REALLY BROTHER AND SISTER...
I HAD WANDERED ALONE FOR CENTURIES...
...UNTIL I FOUND SOMEONE WORTHY TO WANDER WITH ME.
DON'T BE FRIGHTENED, VICTORIA.
AND NOW WE HAVE FOUND ANOTHER.
THAT'S WHY WE WERE RELUCTANT TO COME OVER. WE KNEW ONCE WE WERE INVITED IN, WE'D WANT TO INVITE YOU TO JOIN US.
WE HAD TO BE SURE.

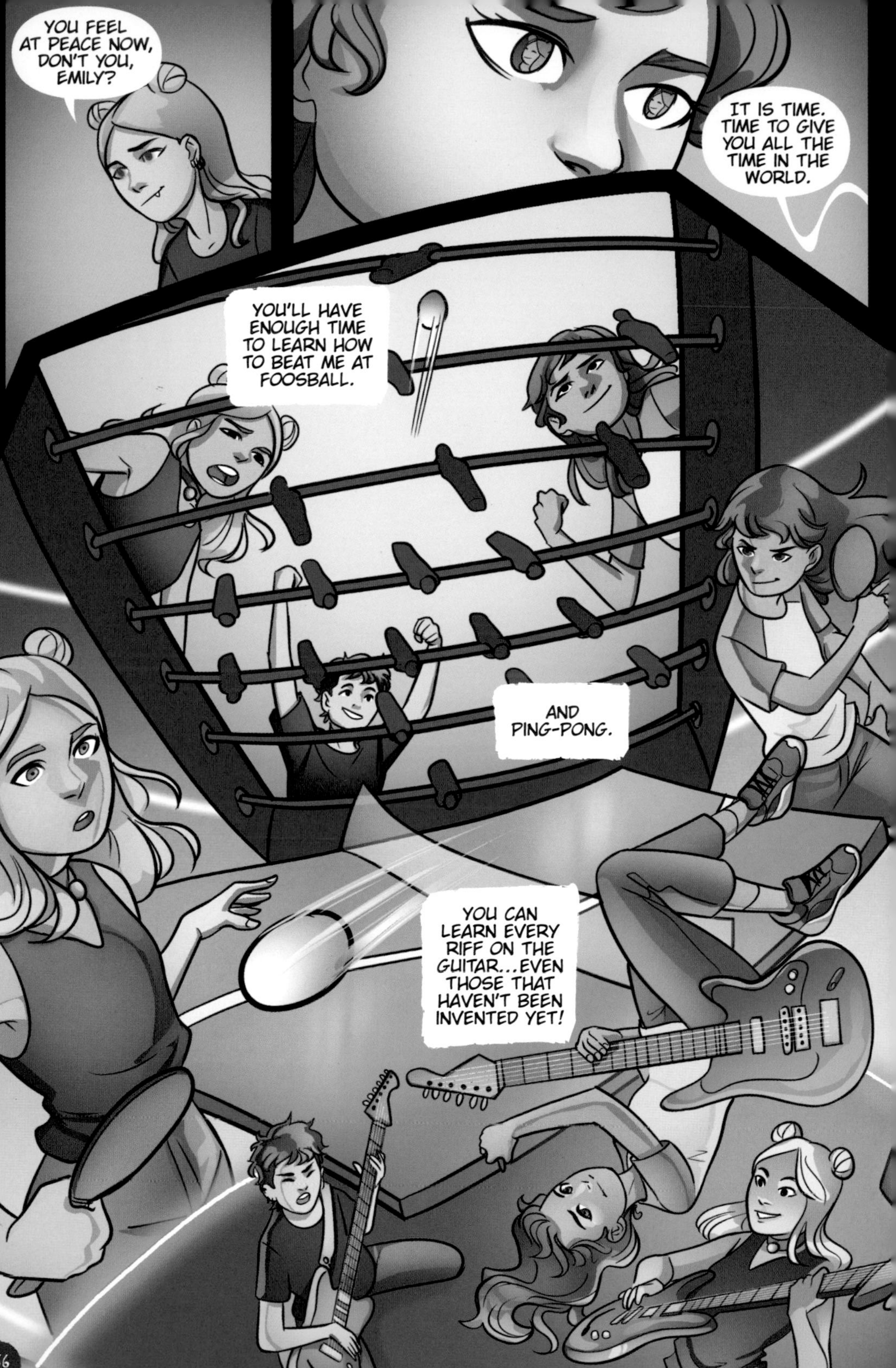
YOU FEEL AT PEACE NOW, DON'T YOU, EMILY?
IT IS TIME. TIME TO GIVE YOU ALL THE TIME IN THE WORLD.
YOU'LL HAVE ENOUGH TIME TO LEARN HOW TO BEAT ME AT FOOSBALL.
AND PING-PONG.
YOU CAN LEARN EVERY RIFF ON THE GUITAR...EVEN THOSE THAT HAVEN'T BEEN INVENTED YET!

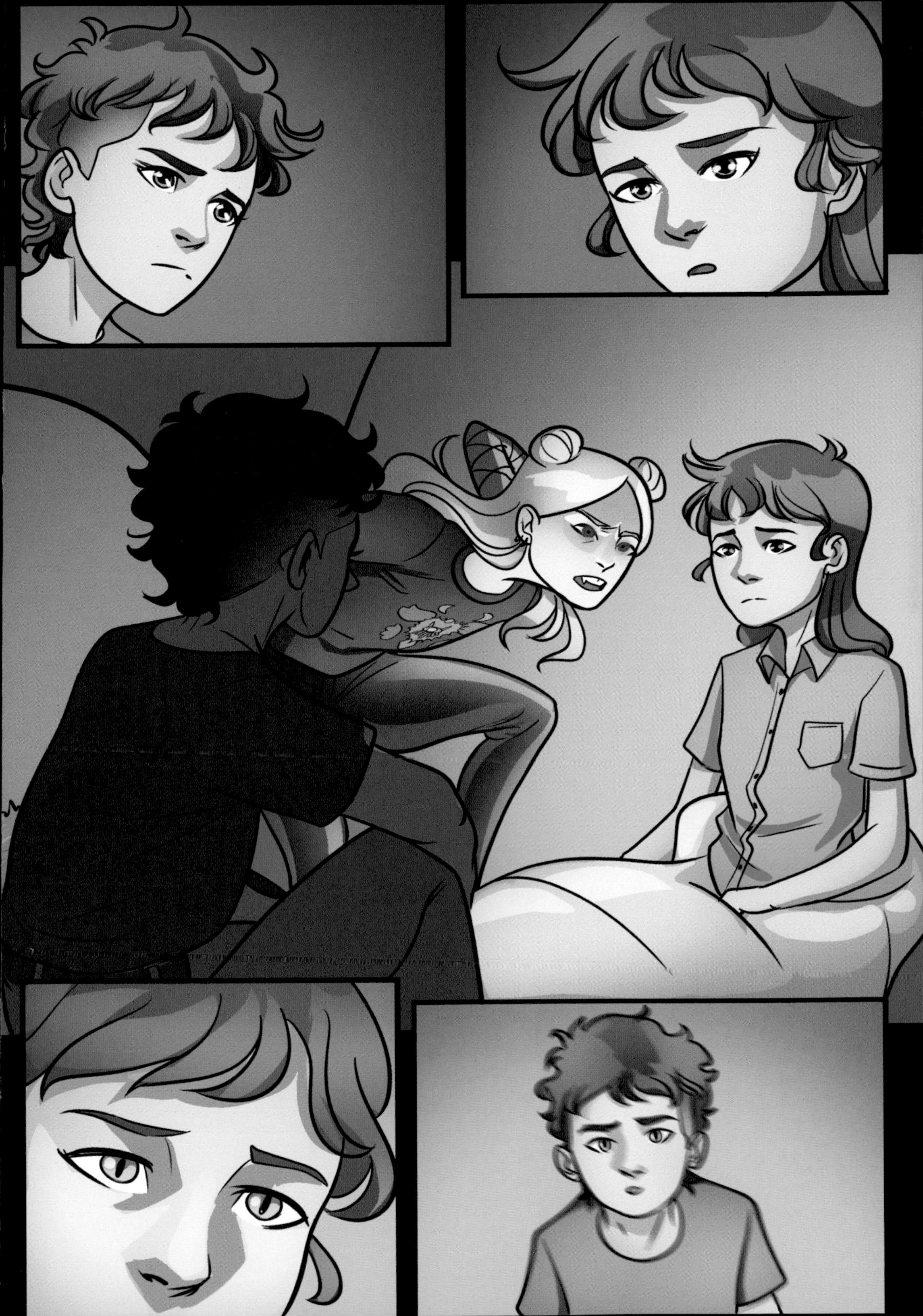

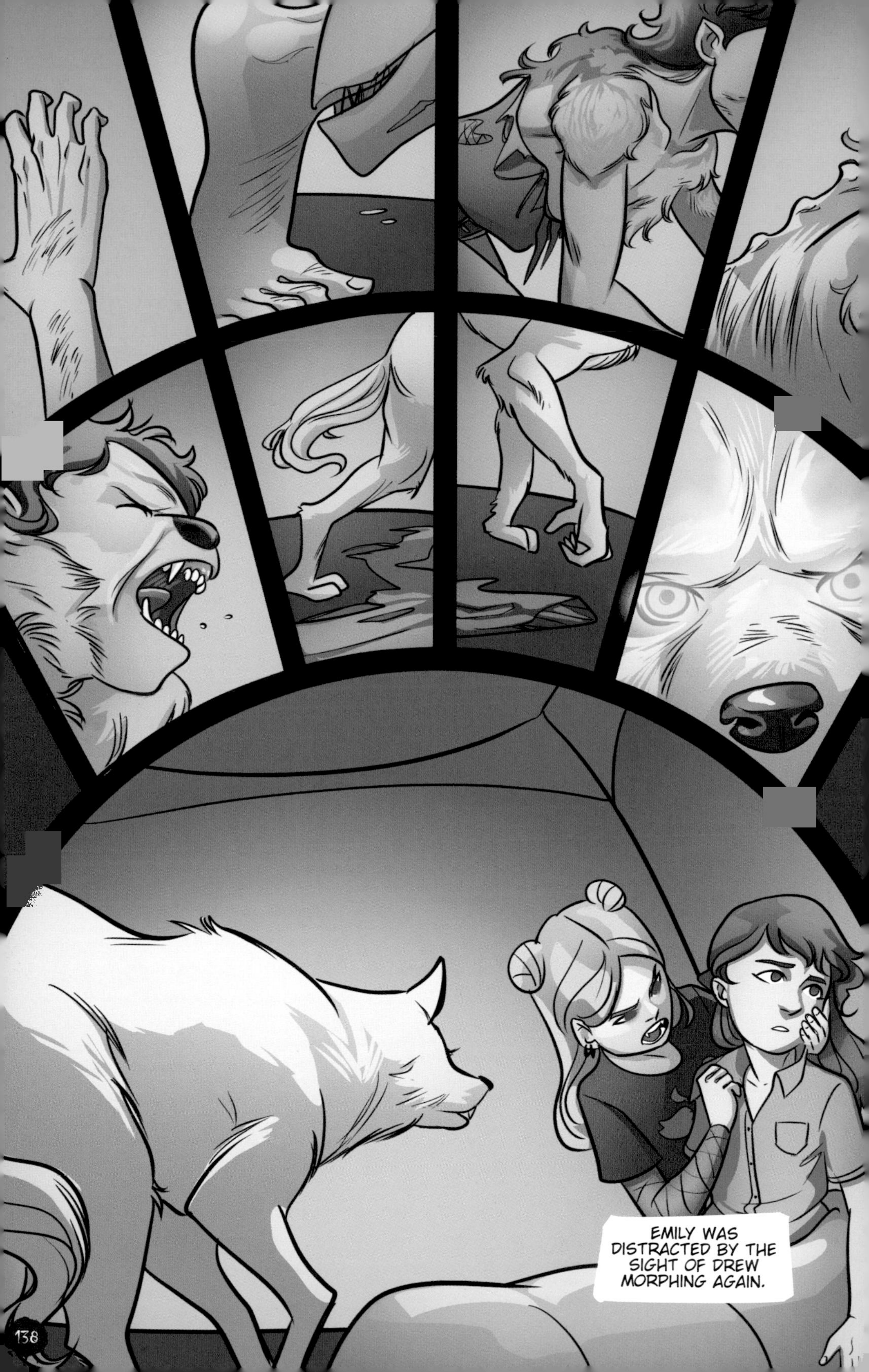
EMILY WAS DISTRACTED BY THE SIGHT OF DREW MORPHING AGAIN.

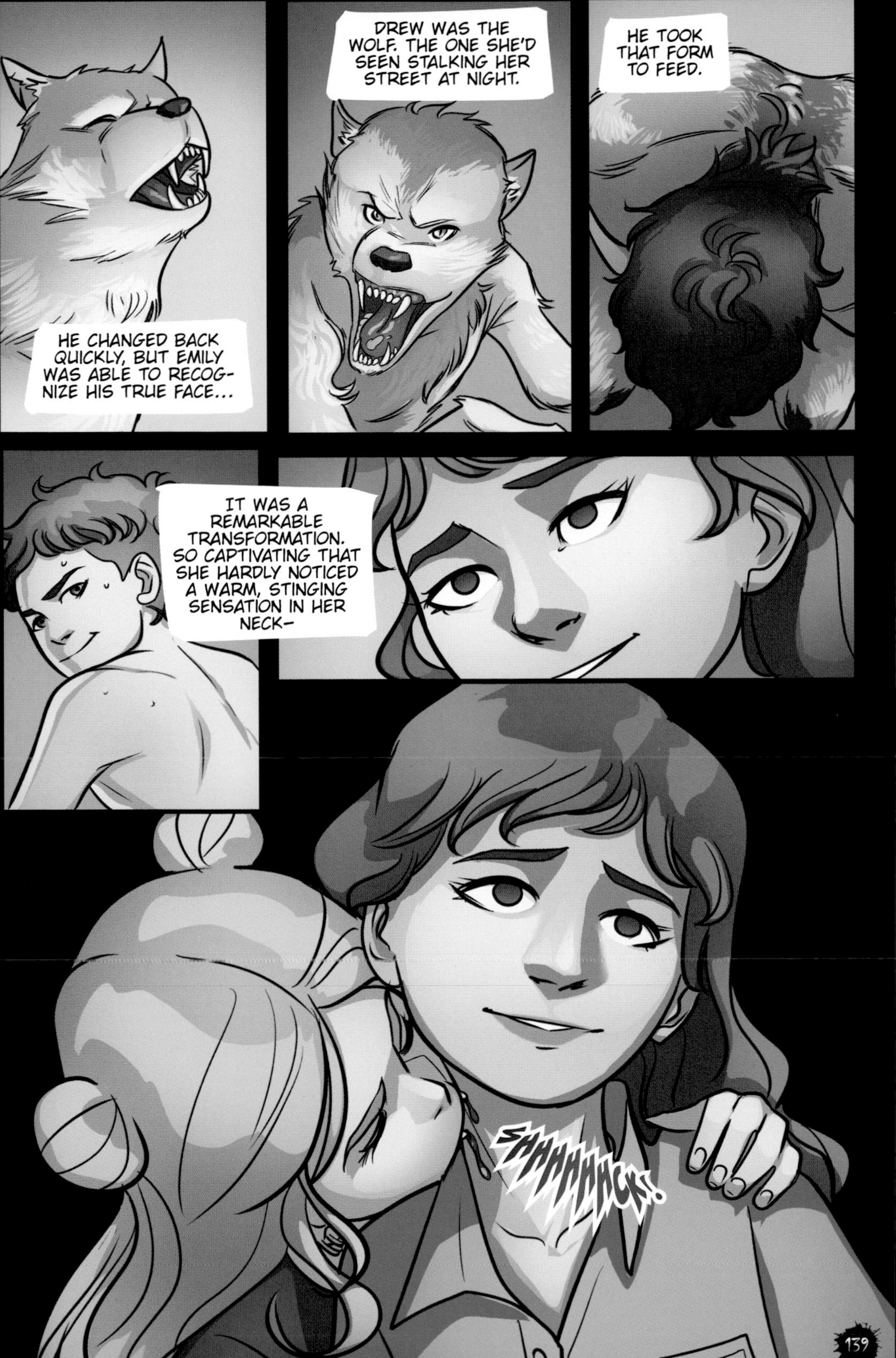
HE CHANGED BACK QUICKLY, BUT EMILY WAS ABLE TO RECOG-NIZE HIS TRUE FACE...
DREW WAS THE WOLF. THE ONE SHE'D SEEN STALKING HER STREET AT NIGHT.
HE TOOK THAT FORM TO FEED.
IT WAS A REMARKABLE TRANSFORMATION. SO CAPTIVATING THAT SHE HARDLY NOTICED A WARM, STINGING SENSATION IN HER NECK–
SHHHHHHCK!

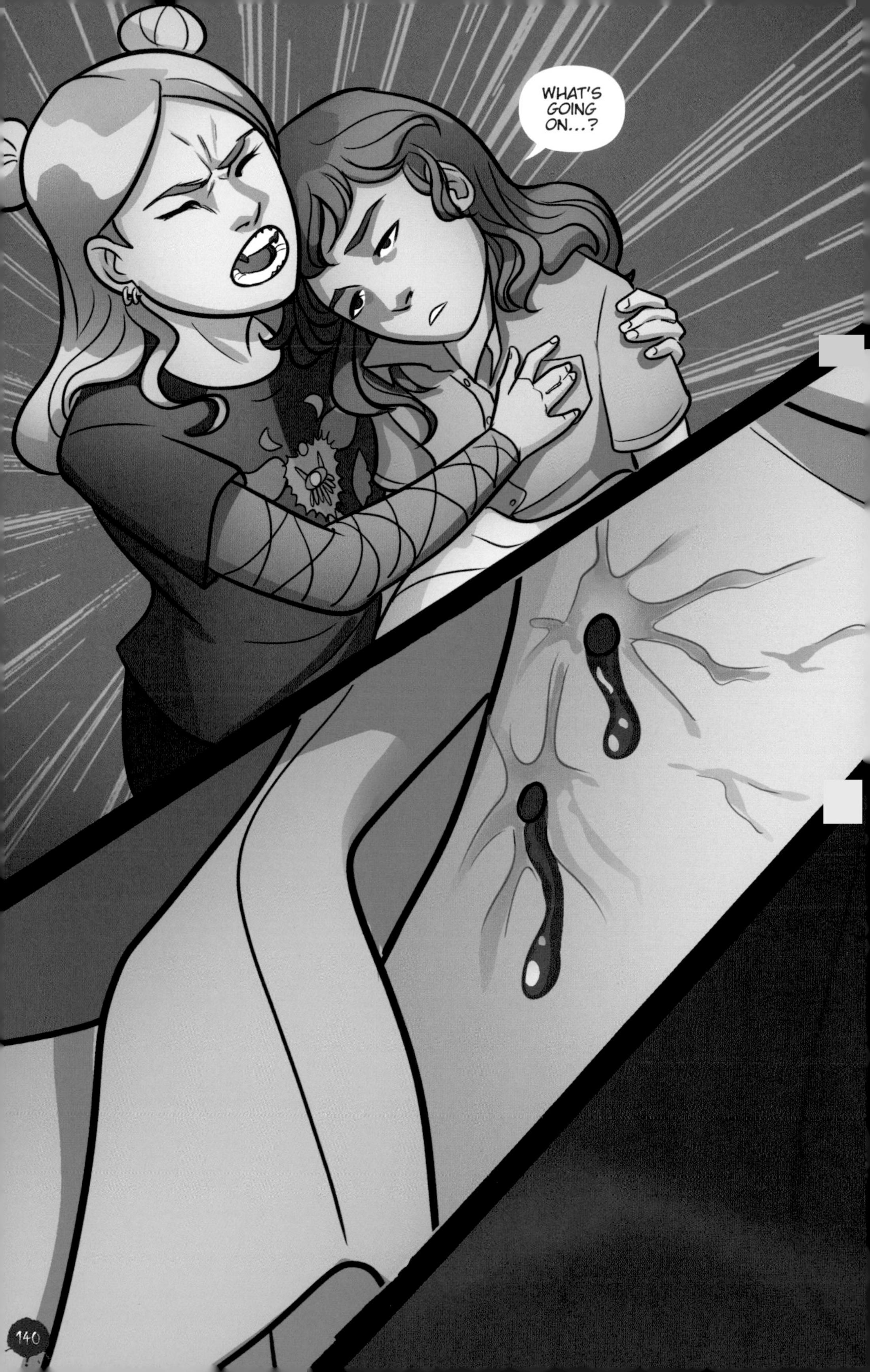
WHAT'S GOING ON...?

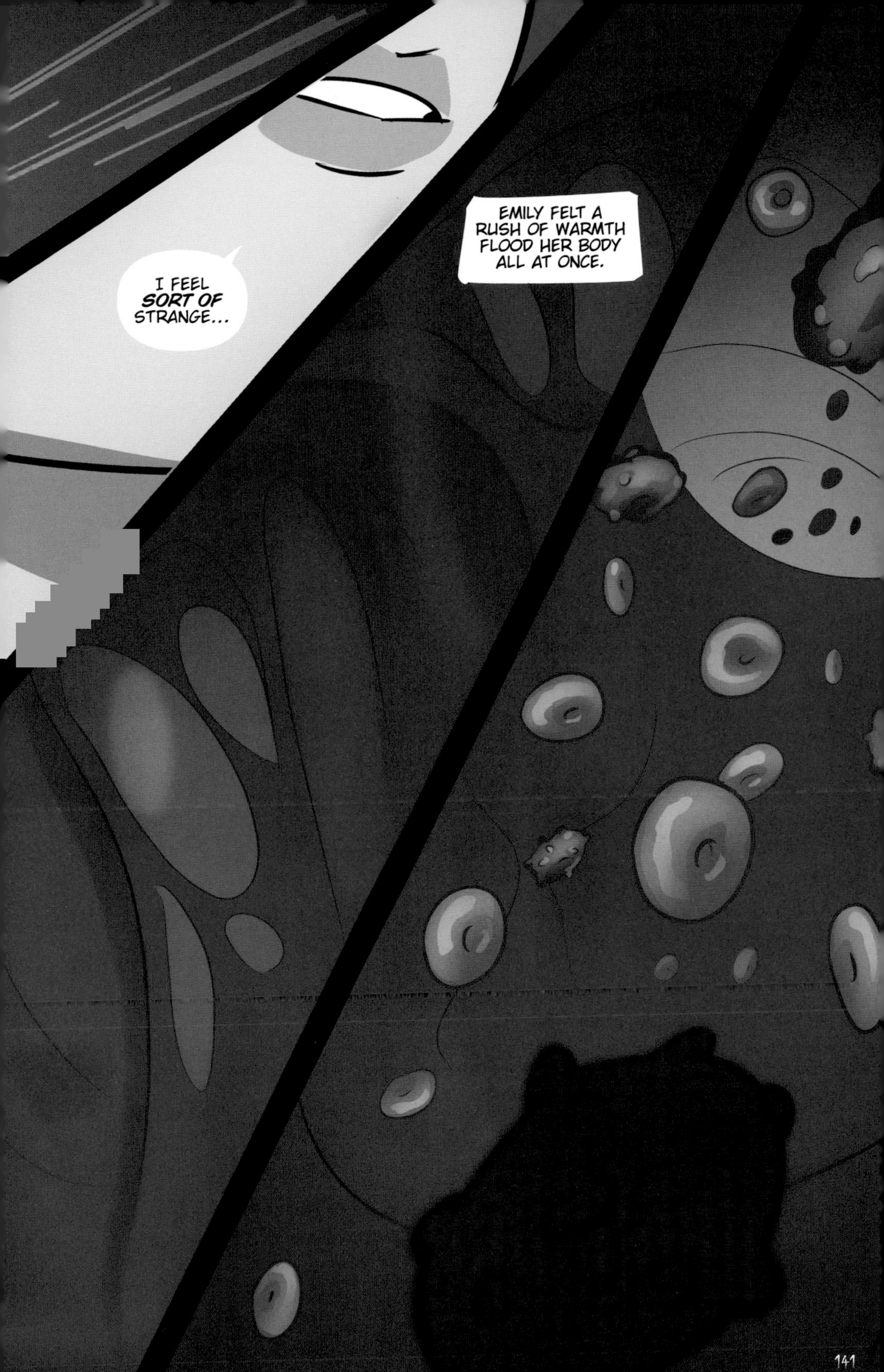
I FEEL **SORT OF** STRANGE...
EMILY FELT A RUSH OF WARMTH FLOOD HER BODY ALL AT ONCE.

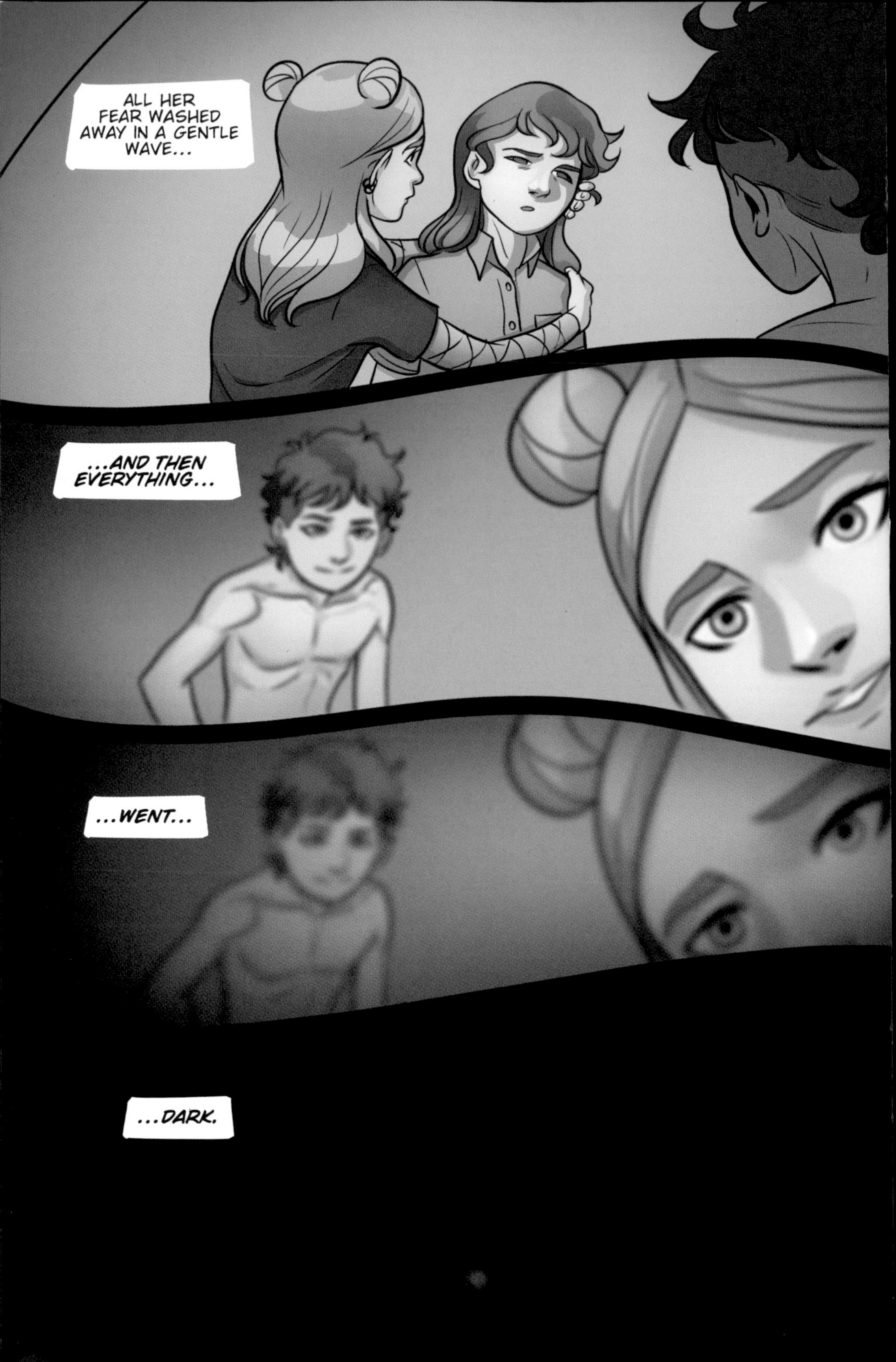
ALL HER FEAR WASHED AWAY IN A GENTLE WAVE...
...AND THEN EVERYTHING...
...WENT...
...DARK.

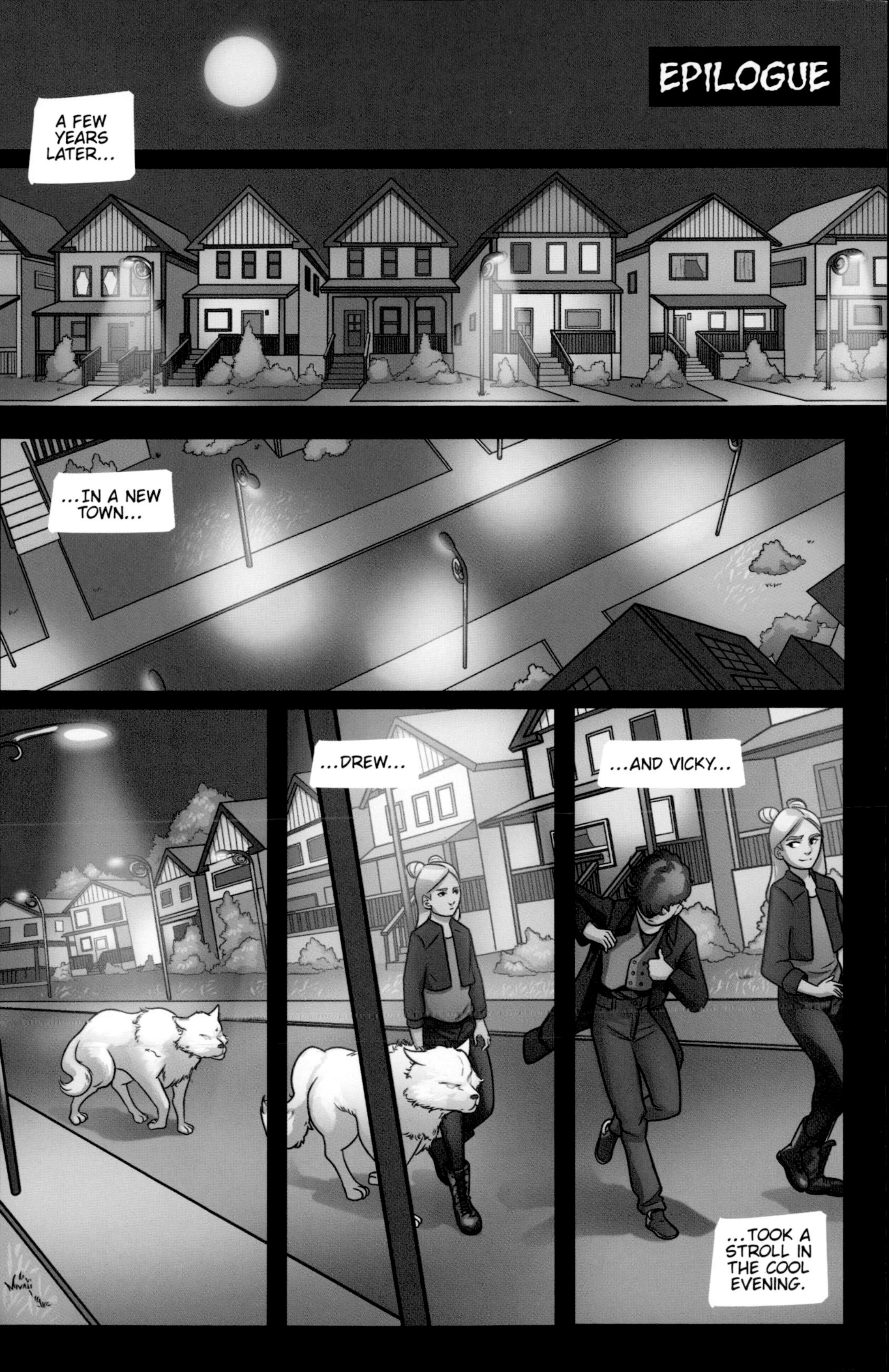
EPILOGUE
A FEW YEARS LATER...
...IN A NEW TOWN...
...DREW...
...AND VICKY...
...TOOK A STROLL IN THE COOL EVENING.

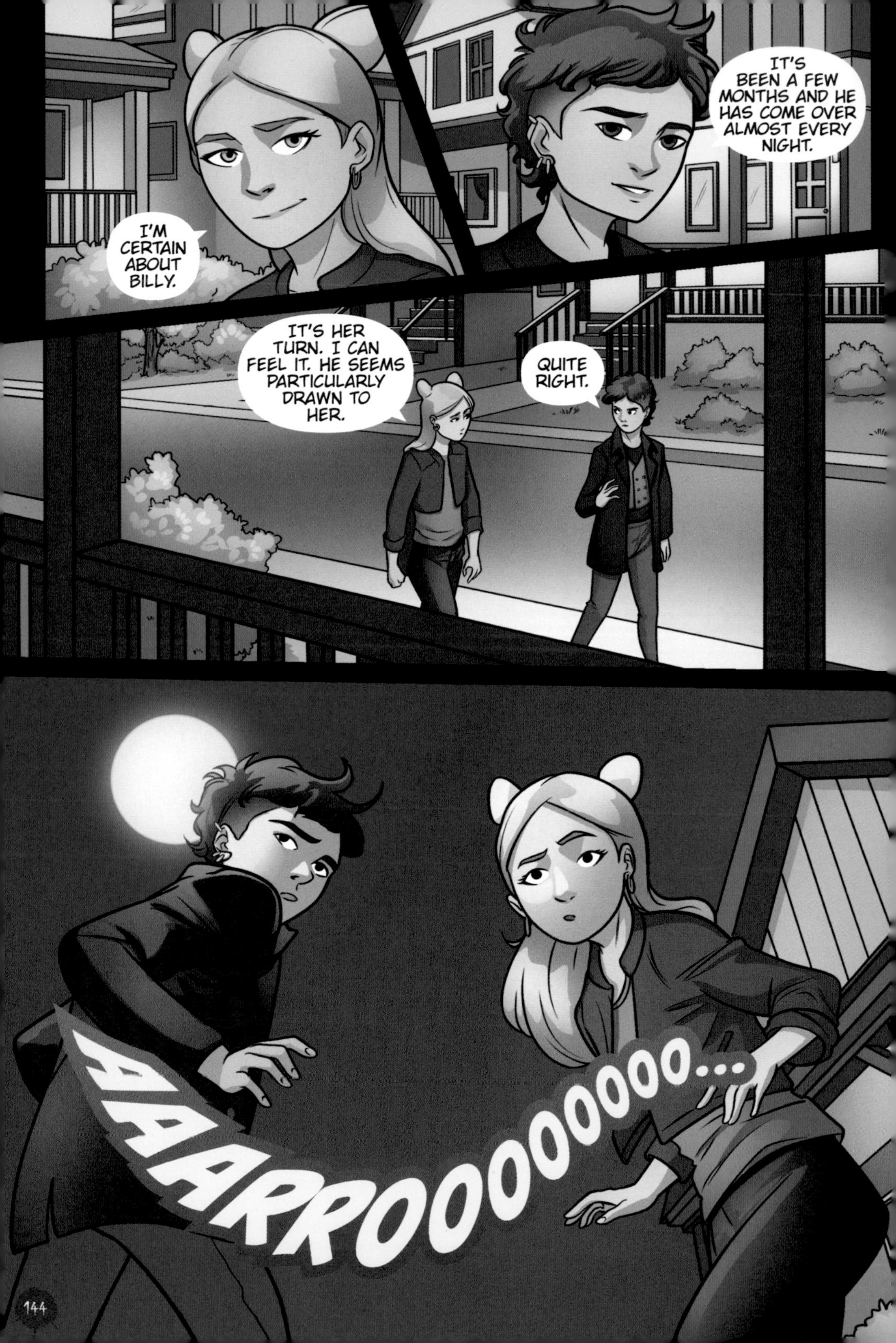
I'M CERTAIN ABOUT BILLY.
IT'S BEEN A FEW MONTHS AND HE HAS COME OVER ALMOST EVERY NIGHT.
IT'S HER TURN. I CAN FEEL IT. HE SEEMS PARTICULARLY DRAWN TO HER.
QUITE RIGHT.
AARROOOOOOOO...

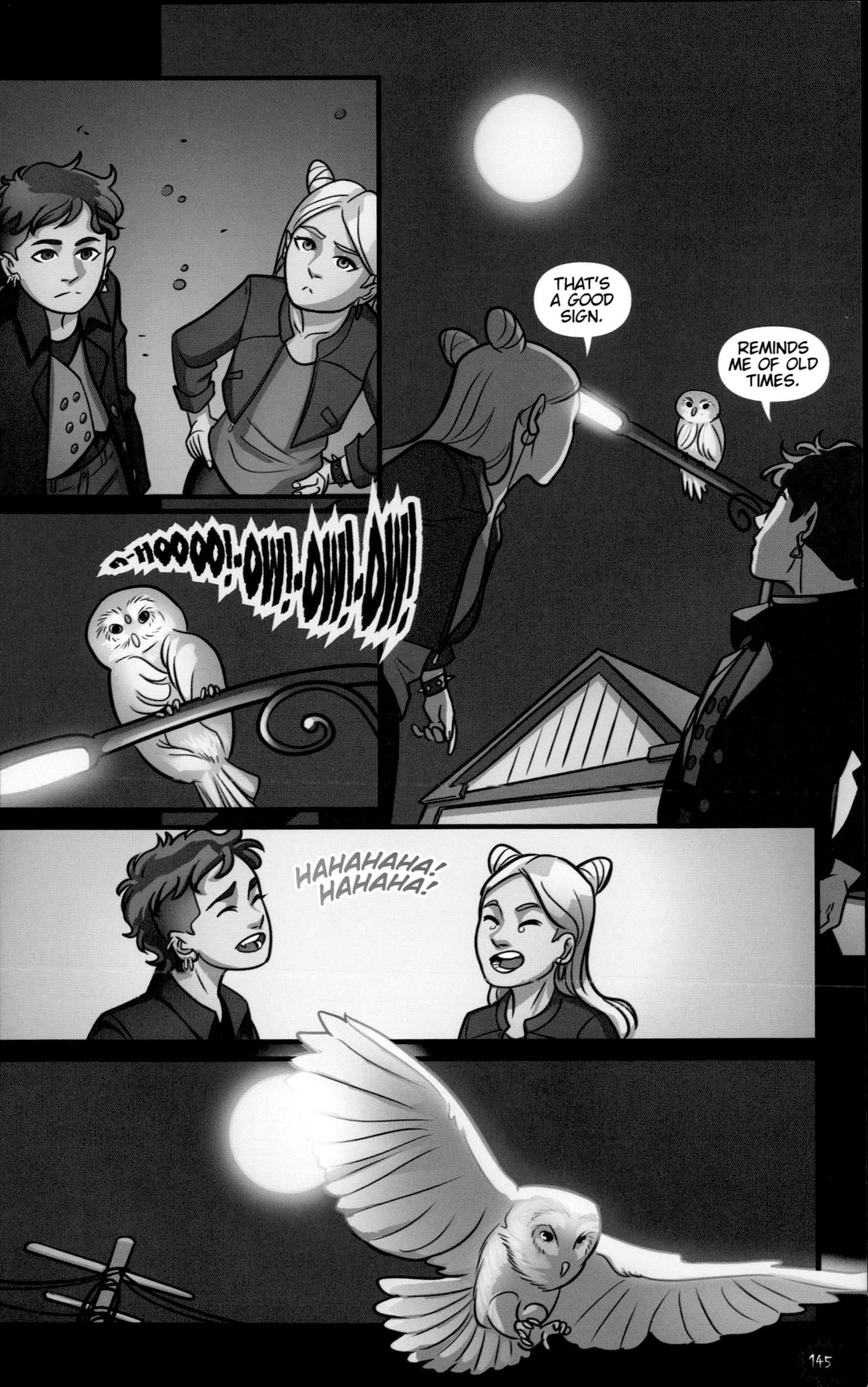
A-HOOOO!-OW!-OW!-OW!
THAT'S A GOOD SIGN.
REMINDS ME OF OLD TIMES.
HAHAHAHA! HAHAHA!

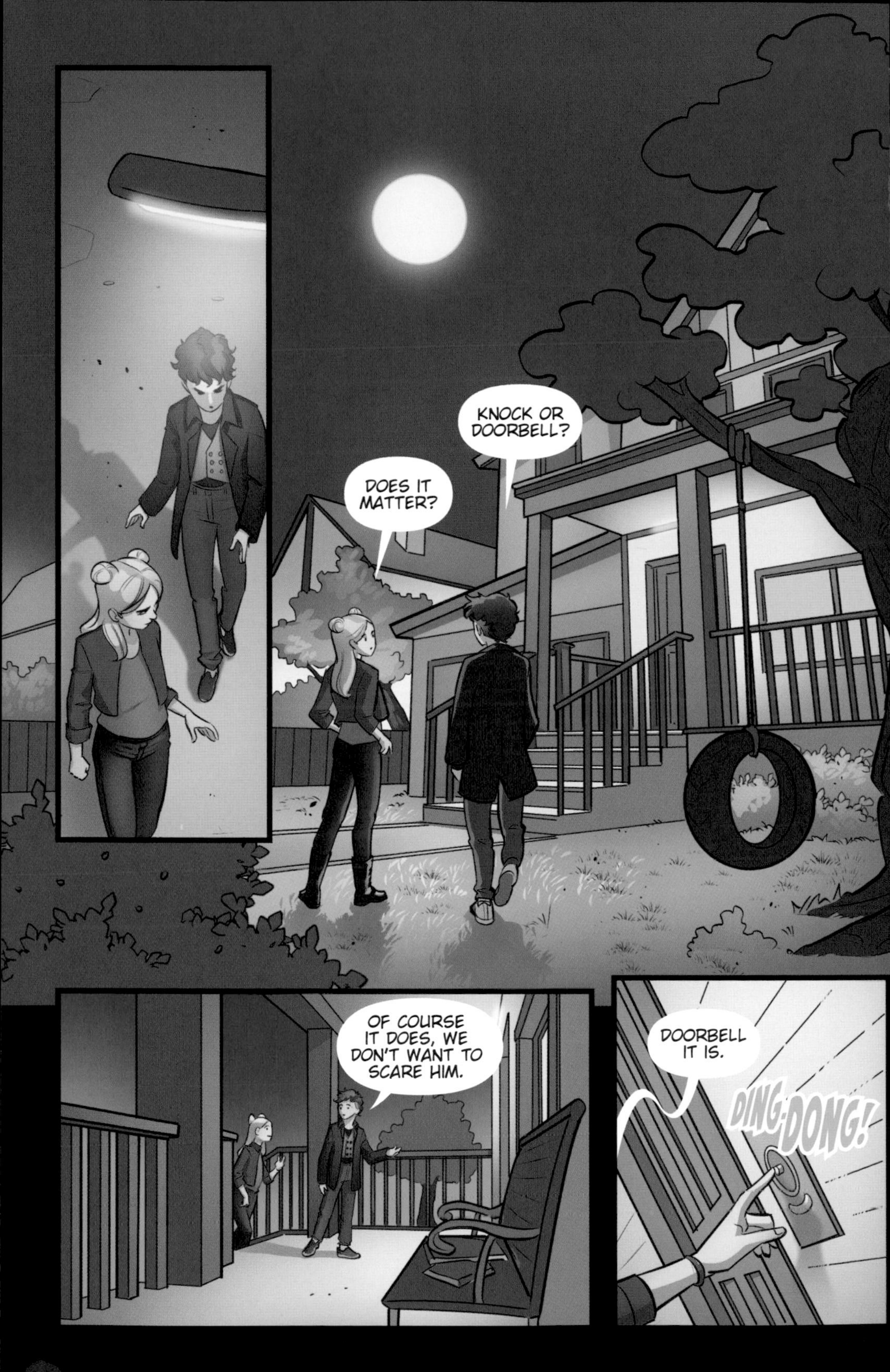
KNOCK OR DOORBELL?
DOES IT MATTER?
OF COURSE IT DOES, WE DON'T WANT TO SCARE HIM.
DOORBELL IT IS.
DING-DONG!

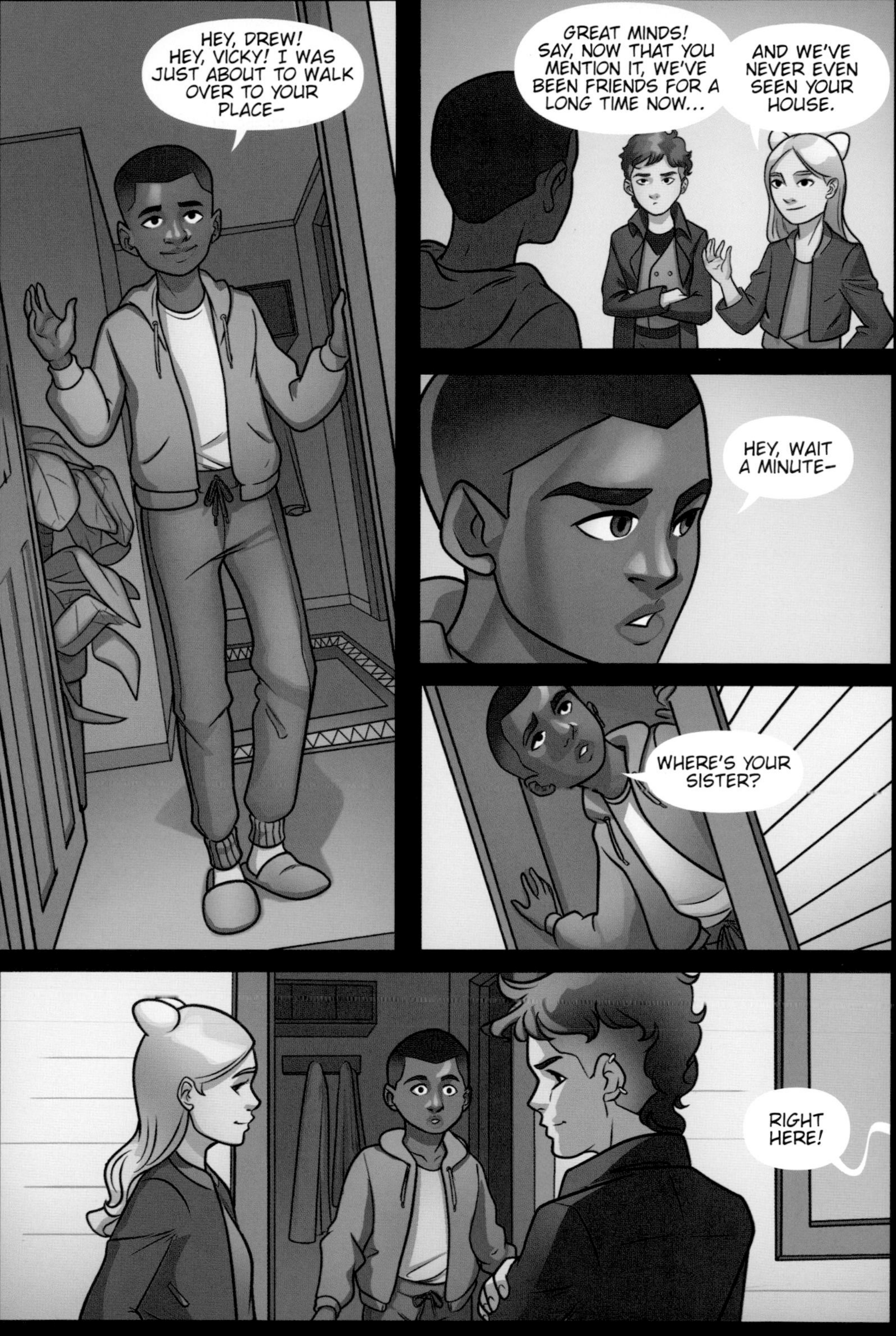
HEY, DREW! HEY, VICKY! I WAS JUST ABOUT TO WALK OVER TO YOUR PLACE-
GREAT MINDS! SAY, NOW THAT YOU MENTION IT, WE'VE BEEN FRIENDS FOR A LONG TIME NOW...
AND WE'VE NEVER EVEN SEEN YOUR HOUSE.
HEY, WAIT A MINUTE-
WHERE'S YOUR SISTER?
RIGHT HERE!

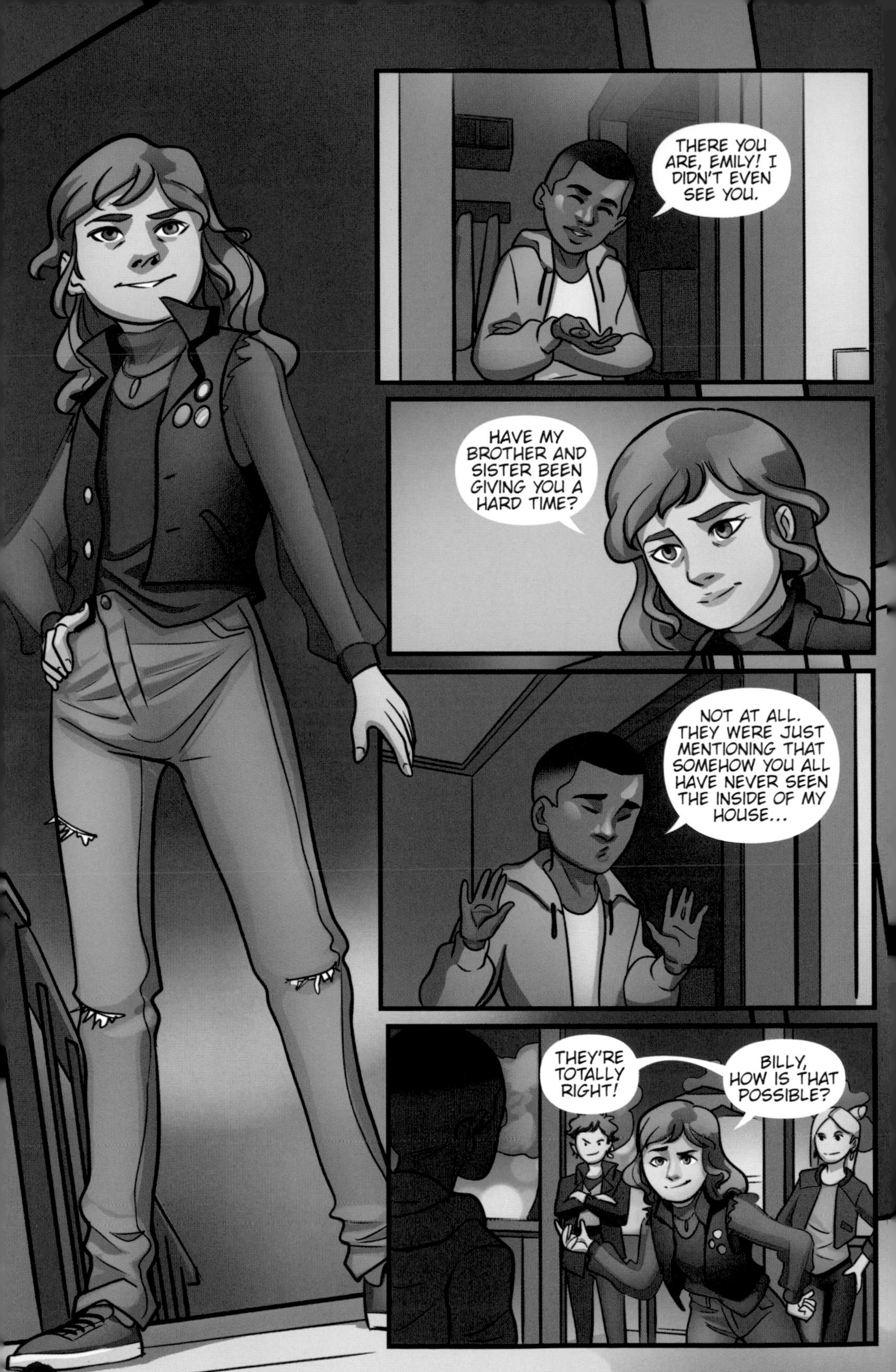

THERE YOU ARE, EMILY! I DIDN'T EVEN SEE YOU.
HAVE MY BROTHER AND SISTER BEEN GIVING YOU A HARD TIME?
NOT AT ALL. THEY WERE JUST MENTIONING THAT SOMEHOW YOU ALL HAVE NEVER SEEN THE INSIDE OF MY HOUSE...
BILLY, HOW IS THAT POSSIBLE?
THEY'RE TOTALLY RIGHT!

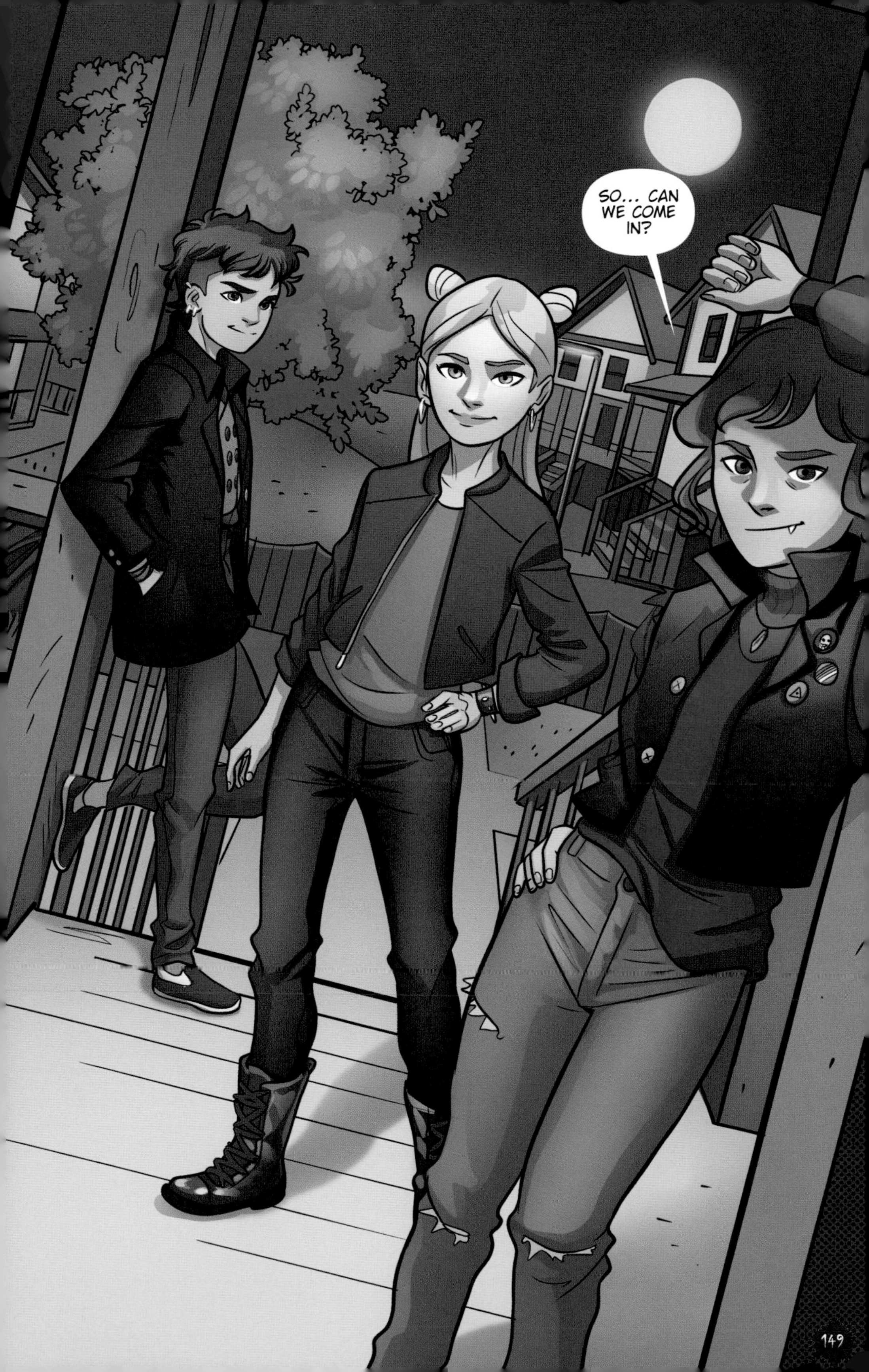
SO... CAN WE COME IN?

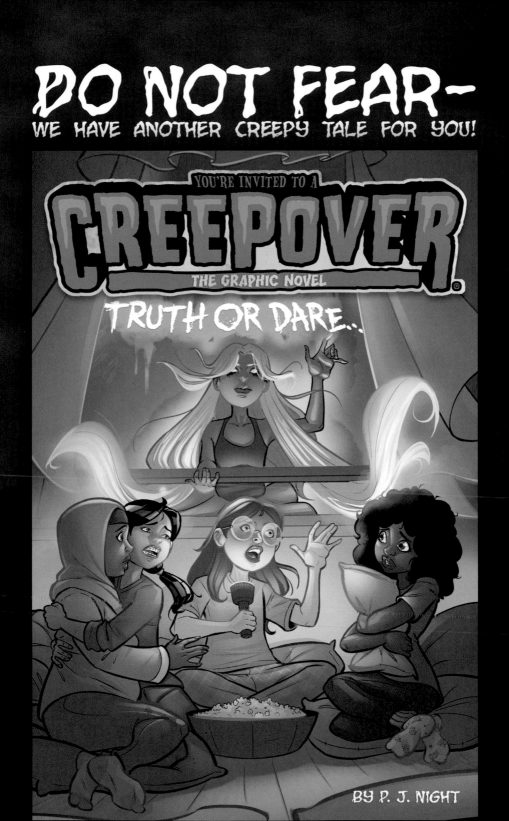

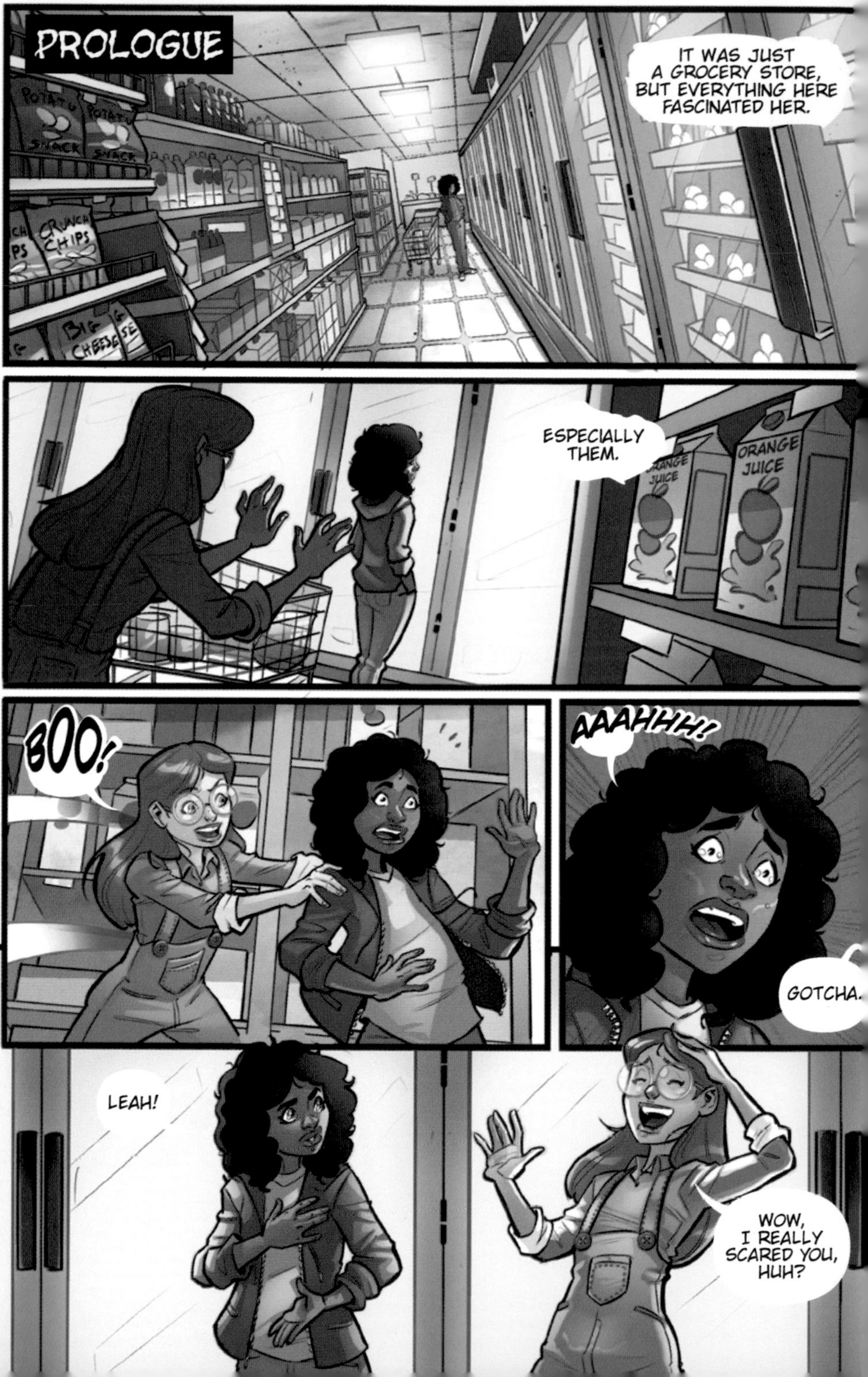
PROLOGUE
IT WAS JUST A GROCERY STORE, BUT EVERYTHING HERE FASCINATED HER.
POTATO SNACK
CRUNCH CHIPS
BIG CHEESE
ESPECIALLY THEM.
ORANGE JUICE
BOO!
AAAHHH!
GOTCHA.
LEAH!
WOW, I REALLY SCARED YOU, HUH?

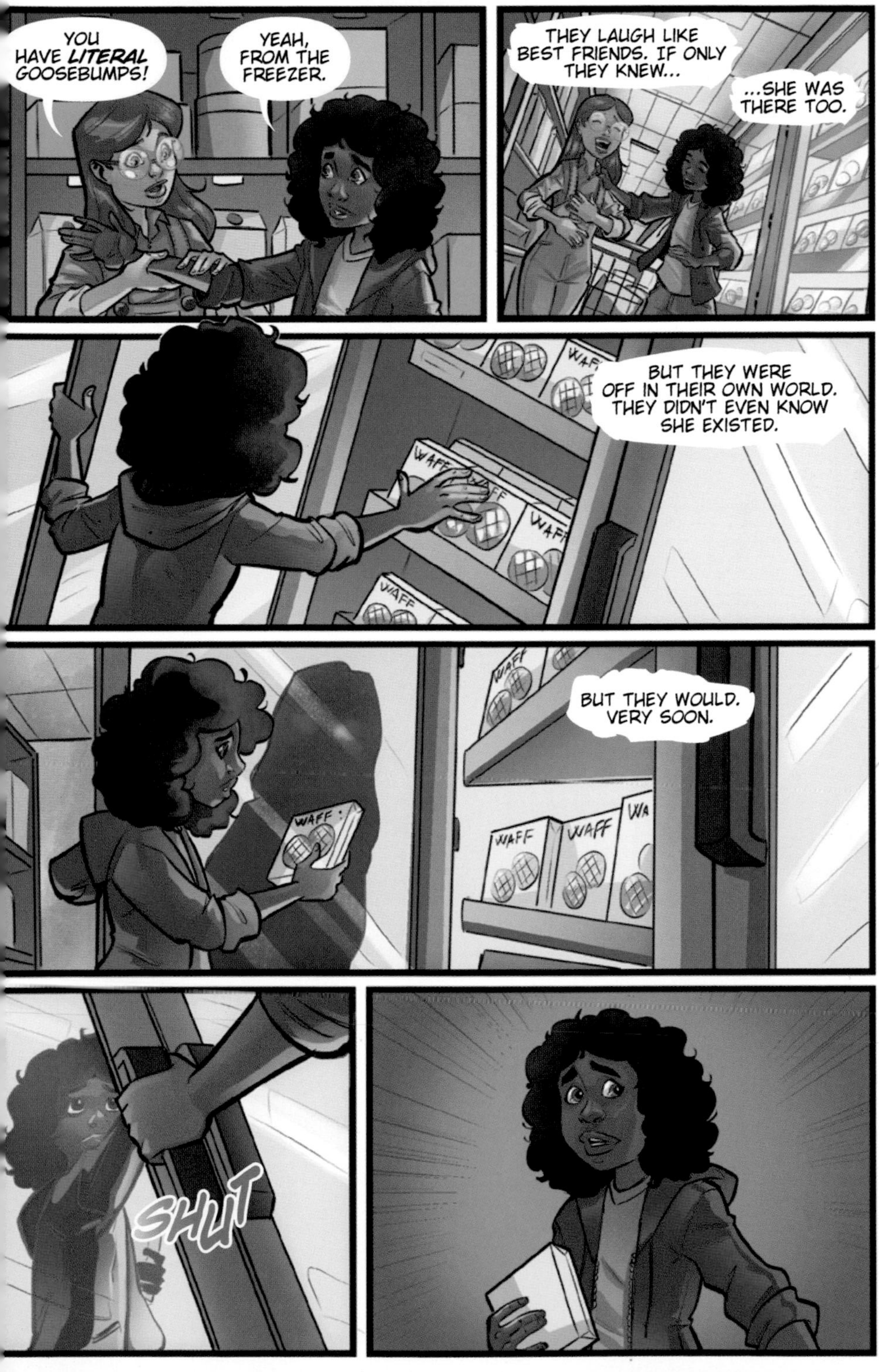
YOU HAVE *LITERAL* GOOSEBUMPS!
YEAH, FROM THE FREEZER.
THEY LAUGH LIKE BEST FRIENDS. IF ONLY THEY KNEW...
...SHE WAS THERE TOO.
BUT THEY WERE OFF IN THEIR OWN WORLD. THEY DIDN'T EVEN KNOW SHE EXISTED.
WAFF
BUT THEY WOULD. VERY SOON.
WAFF
SHUT

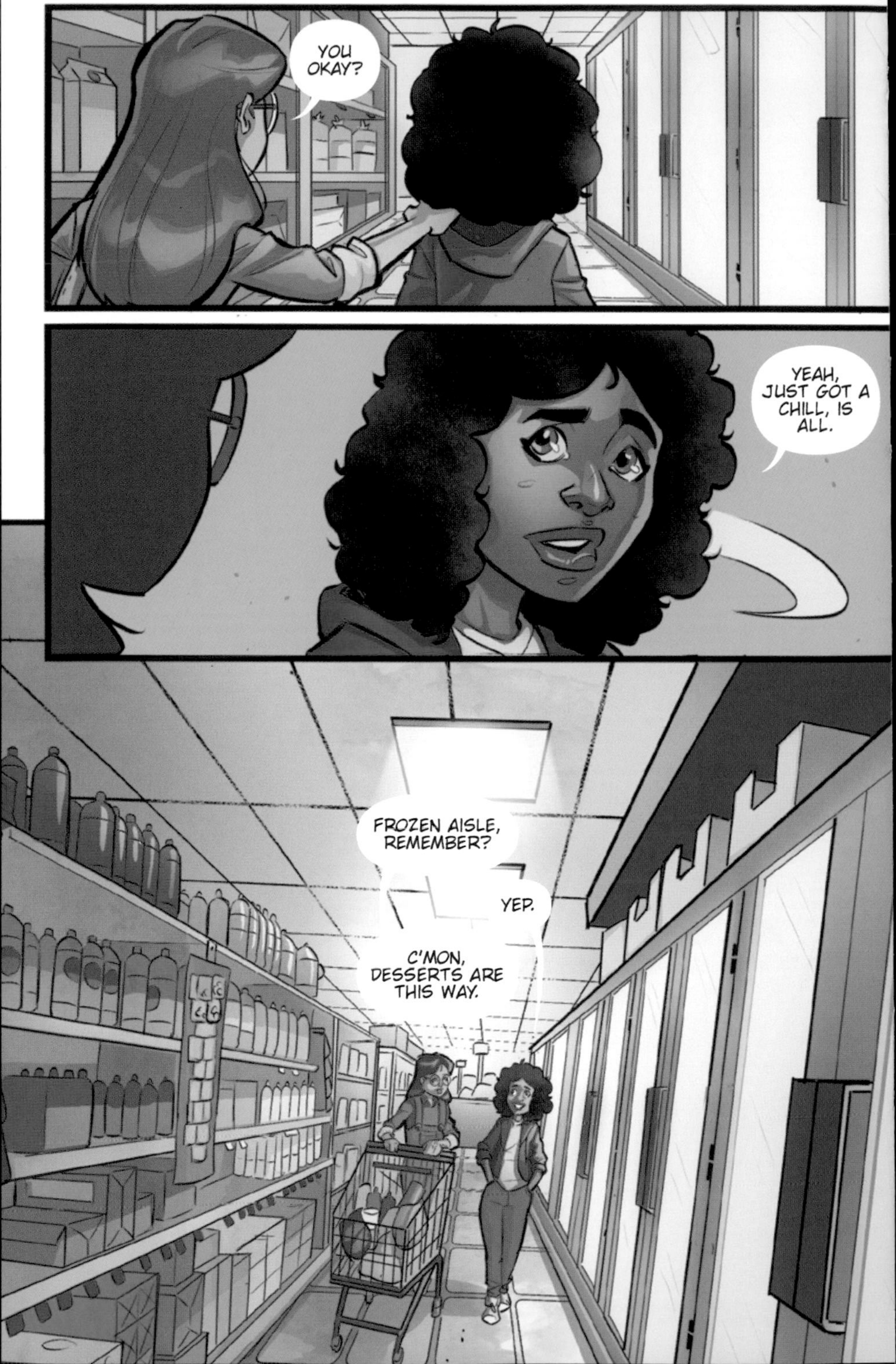
YOU OKAY?
YEAH, JUST GOT A CHILL, IS ALL.
FROZEN AISLE, REMEMBER?
YEP.
C'MON, DESSERTS ARE THIS WAY.

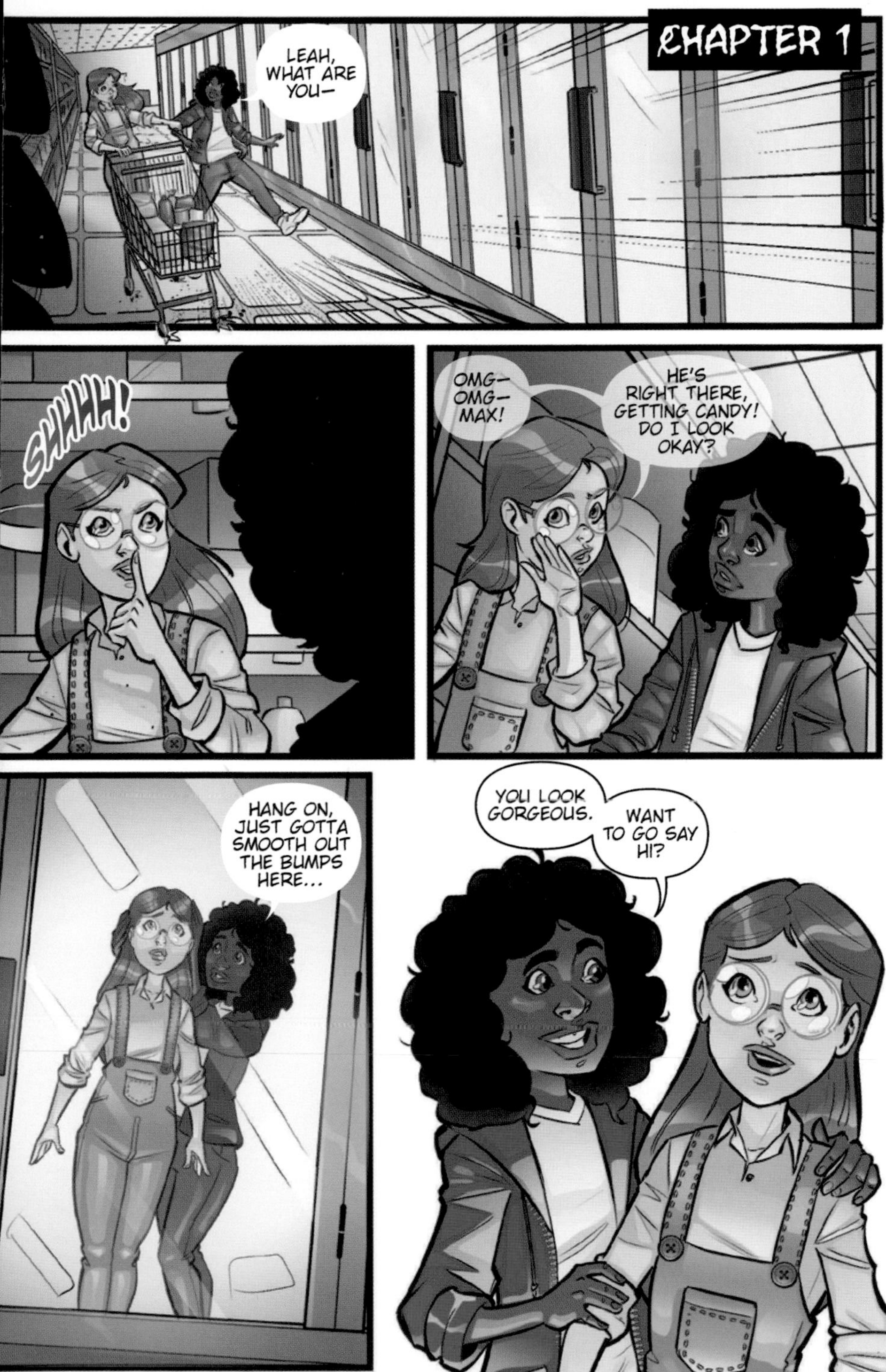
CHAPTER 1
LEAH, WHAT ARE YOU—
SHHHH!
OMG-OMG-MAX!
HE'S RIGHT THERE, GETTING CANDY! DO I LOOK OKAY?
HANG ON, JUST GOTTA SMOOTH OUT THE BUMPS HERE...
YOU LOOK GORGEOUS.
WANT TO GO SAY HI?

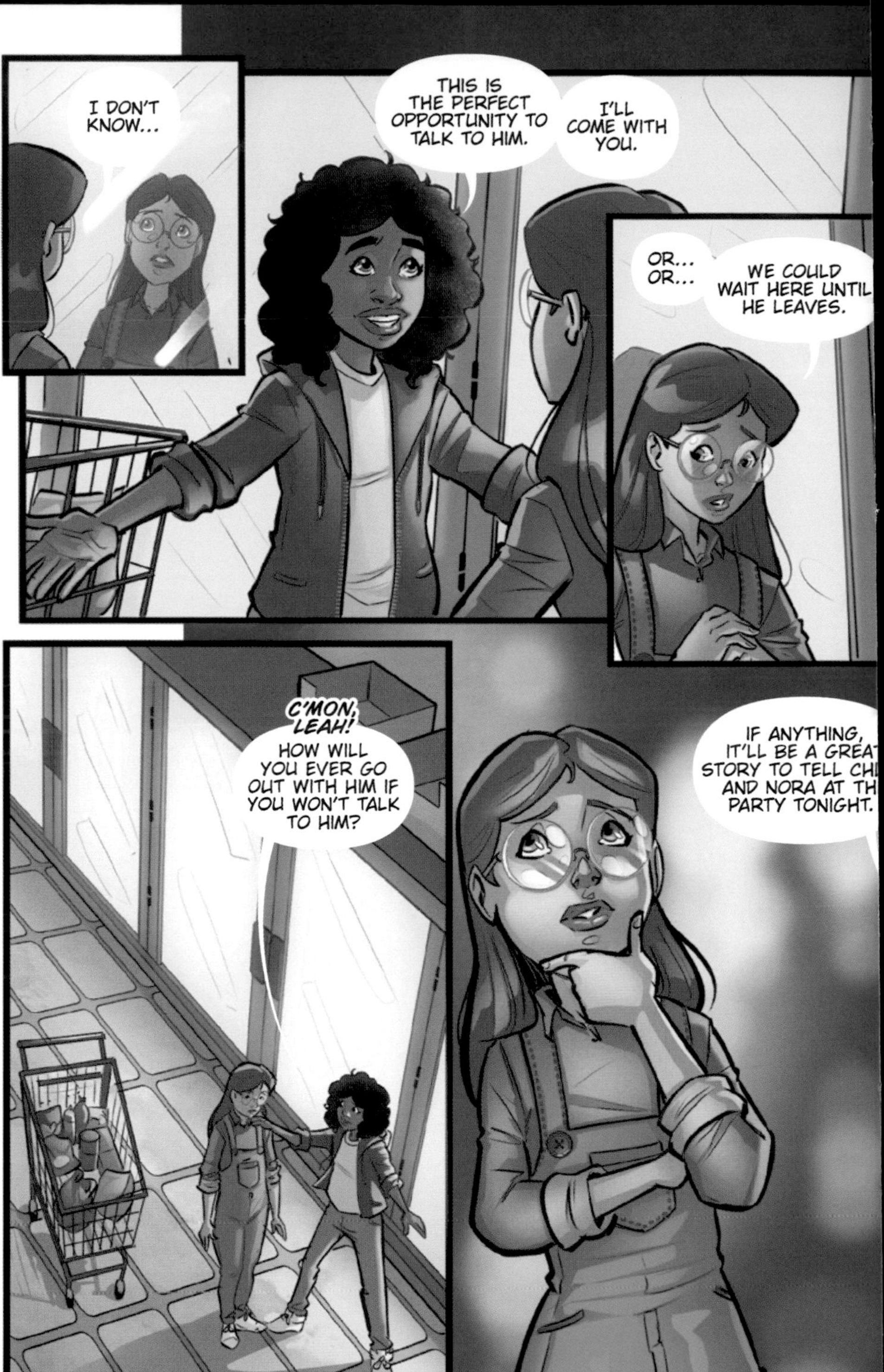

I DON'T KNOW...
THIS IS THE PERFECT OPPORTUNITY TO TALK TO HIM.
I'LL COME WITH YOU.
OR... OR...
WE COULD WAIT HERE UNTIL HE LEAVES.
C'MON, LEAH!
HOW WILL YOU EVER GO OUT WITH HIM IF YOU WON'T TALK TO HIM?
IF ANYTHING, IT'LL BE A GREAT STORY TO TELL CH AND NORA AT TH PARTY TONIGHT.

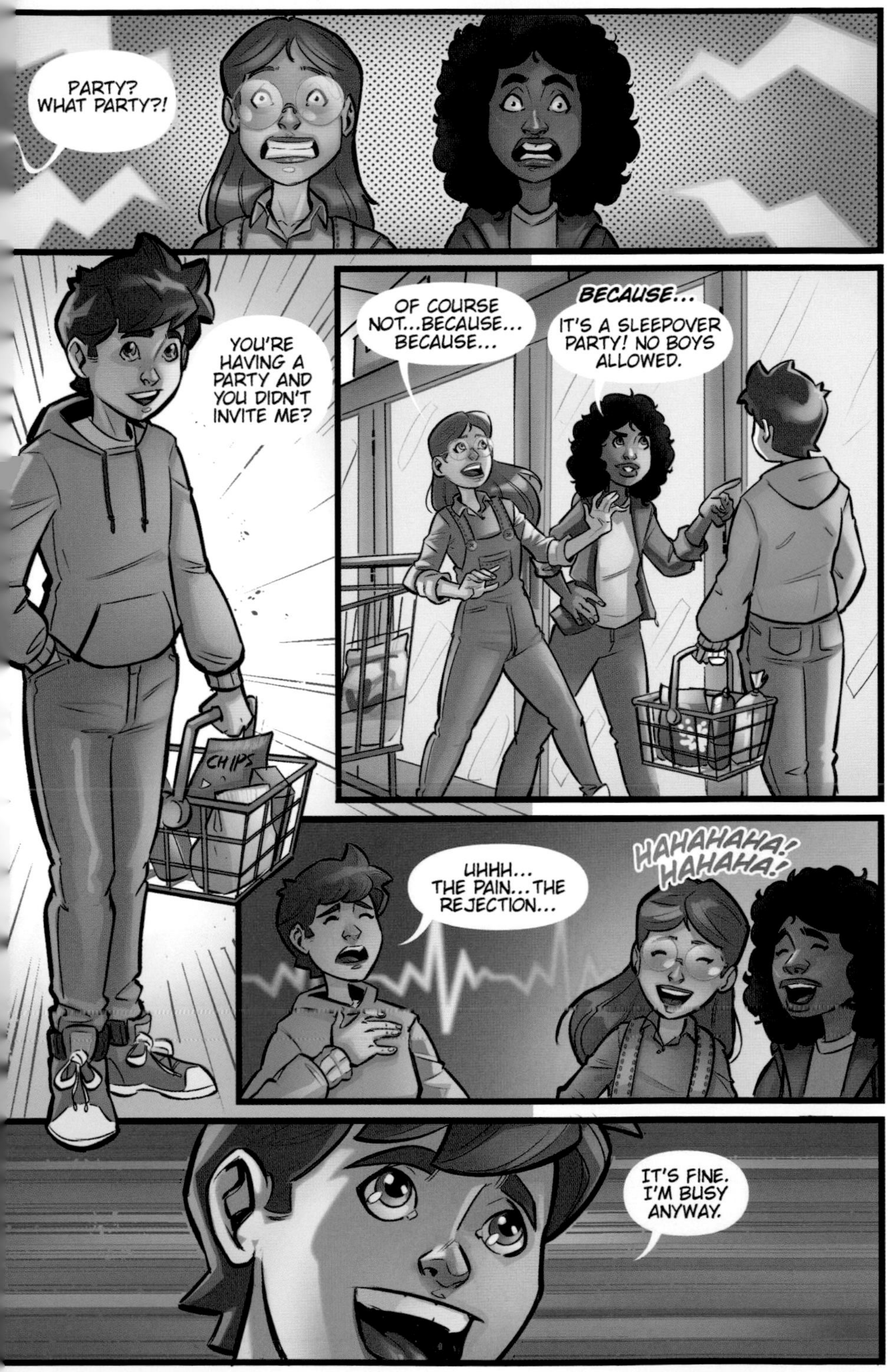

PARTY? WHAT PARTY?!
YOU'RE HAVING A PARTY AND YOU DIDN'T INVITE ME?
OF COURSE NOT...BECAUSE... BECAUSE...
BECAUSE...
IT'S A SLEEPOVER PARTY! NO BOYS ALLOWED.
CHIPS
UHHH... THE PAIN... THE REJECTION...
HAHAHAHA! HAHAHA!
IT'S FINE. I'M BUSY ANYWAY.

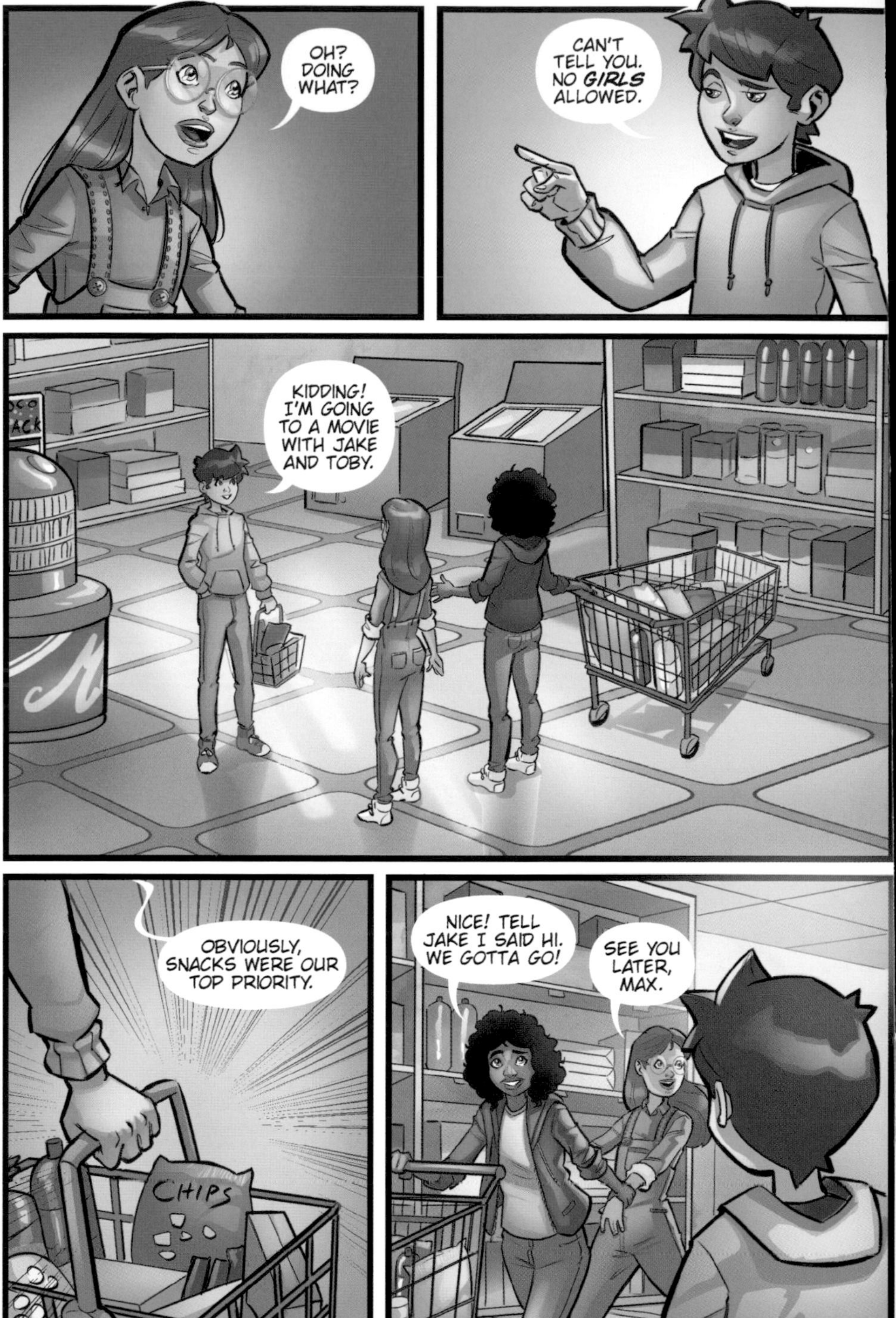
OH? DOING WHAT?
CAN'T TELL YOU. NO GIRLS ALLOWED.
KIDDING! I'M GOING TO A MOVIE WITH JAKE AND TOBY.
OBVIOUSLY, SNACKS WERE OUR TOP PRIORITY.
CHIPS
NICE! TELL JAKE I SAID HI. WE GOTTA GO!
SEE YOU LATER, MAX.

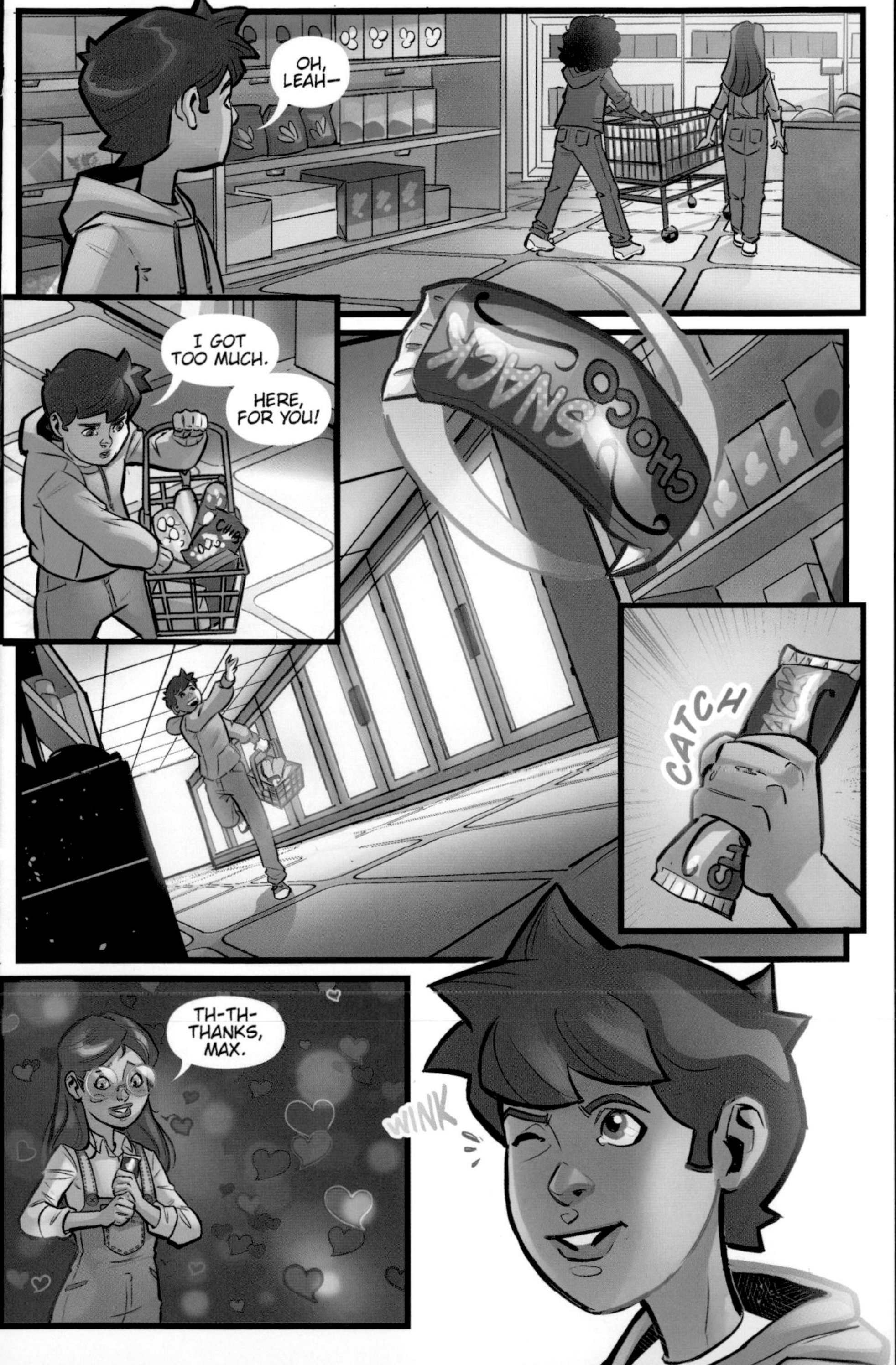
OH, LEAH—
I GOT TOO MUCH.
HERE, FOR YOU!
CHOCO SNACK
CATCH
TH-TH-THANKS, MAX.
WINK